GREATER LOVE

OTHER NOVELS BY ROBERT WHITLOW INCLUDE

GREATER LOVE

Book Three in the Tides of Truth series

ROBERT WHITLOW

THOMAS NELSON
Since 1798

NASHVILLE   DALLAS   MEXICO CITY   RIO DE JANEIRO

Published in Nashville, Tennessee, by Thomas Nelson. Thomas Nelson is a registered trademark of Thomas Nelson, Inc.

Thomas Nelson, Inc., titles may be purchased in bulk for educational, business, fund-raising, or sales promotional use. For information, please e-mail SpecialMarkets@ThomasNelson.com.

Scripture quotations are from the following sources: HOLY BIBLE: NEW INTERNATIONAL VERSION®. © 1973, 1978, 1984 by International Bible Society. Used by permission of Zondervan. All rights reserved; THE NEW KING JAMES VERSION. © 1982 by Thomas Nelson, Inc. Used by permission. All rights reserved; and the KING JAMES VERSION.

Publisher's note: This novel is a work of fiction. Names, characters, places, and incidents are either products of the author's imagination or used fictitiously. All characters are fictional, and any similarity to people, living or dead, is purely coincidental.

Library of Congress Cataloging-in-Publication Data

Whitlow, Robert, 1954-
  Greater love / Robert Whitlow.
      p. cm. — (Tides of truth series ; 3)
  ISBN 978-1-59554-450-6 (soft cover)
  I. Title.
  PS3573.H49837G74 2010
  813'.54—dc22

                            2009052635

Printed in the United States of America

10 11 12 13 14 RRD 6 5 4 3 2 1

To the unselfish among us. Your reward is sure.

Greater love has no one than this,
than to lay down one's life for his friends.

JOHN 15:13

Prologue

THE GIRL BOLTED INTO THE BLACKBERRY PATCH. SHE CRIED OUT in pain as the tiny briars ripped her skin. The two men chasing her thrashed about in the darkness. The girl stuffed her fist in her mouth, bit down on her knuckles, and slowly eased herself to the ground.

"Over yonder! I heard something!" one of the men called out.

The sound of the men came closer. The girl could see the beams of flashlights in the tops of the bushes. She was wearing a dark shirt and blue jeans. Tucked in her jeans was the smooth leather pouch she'd snatched from the edge of the table when the men dragged her stepmother's boyfriend into the night.

Her arms were tanned dark by the Georgia sun and streaked with red dirt. In the stillness tiny gnats found her face and began crawling across her cheeks and into her ears and nose. She didn't dare slap them away.

"Jessie, we know you're close by," the other man called out. "Ain't nobody going to hurt you. Come on out and show yourself, and we'll give you something nice."

"What are you talking about?" the first man hissed.

The cuts on Jessie's arms, hands, and face stung as sweat ran into the open wounds. She gritted her teeth then licked her lips. Her tongue brought several gnats back into her mouth. Growing up south of Macon, she'd eaten a bushel of gnats by the time she turned fifteen. In the distance, she heard the sound of thunder.

"She ain't coming out," the first man said to the second. "And now it's going to come a shower. That's why we should have brought the dogs. They'd love rompin' through this here thicket. Blackie would flush her out in no time."

"Well then, why don't you shut up and go back to the shed and get them on down here," the second man answered. "I'll stay close by in case she tries to make a run for it."

"Should I call Clay while I'm up at the house?"

"And tell him we brought his pouch into the house instead of leaving it locked up in the car? We had two jobs to do—teach Rod a lesson and deliver the pouch from the German guy in Atlanta. He ain't going to be happy with one out of two."

"I thought it would be better to keep it in sight in case Rod made a run for the car. He's got a set of keys. I didn't know the girl was there."

"And that's why we're in this mess. Now git. For all we know she may already be at the highway."

Jessie heard one of the men move away. The thunder rumbled closer. It wouldn't hurt her feelings if the men beat up Rod. Twice, the dark-haired man had hit her so hard it made her woozy. Her stepmother didn't say anything. Rod had bought her a new car and gave her twenties like they were ones.

Jessie wasn't afraid of the dogs, especially Blackie. They'd become friends since Rod brought them home. If the men brought the dogs to the thicket, Blackie would come straight to her, if for no other reason than to lick her face.

Jessie shared the men's fear of Clay. The way Rod acted when Clay came into the room and then talked about him after he left was proof enough for her. Rich people in fancy clothes could be scary, too.

There was a flash of lightning followed by gunshot thunder. The man who remained behind swore. Another flash of lightning hit a nearby pine tree. There was a loud crack as the tree split apart. Jessie screamed then clamped her hand over her mouth, sure she'd given away her location. Barely breathing, she crouched and waited for the man to come rushing toward her. But all she heard was the sound of a tree creaking and popping. The flashlight beam disappeared.

Jessie eased up from her hiding place. The damaged tree was clearly visible. Flickering flames marked the path the lightning took as it hungrily sought the ground. Another bolt of lightning lit up the thicket with daytime brightness. In the split second of illumination, Jessie saw a man lying at the foot of the tree, his arms splayed out and his legs in an awkward position. She didn't look twice.

She ran out of the thicket as fast as she could go. But not toward the highway. She'd read in a library book about a runaway girl who discovered the best way to travel without anyone knowing about it was along the railroad tracks. Unlike cars, trains don't have curious eyes.

As Jessie ran toward the train tracks, huge drops of rain began falling from the sky. She stopped for a second to rub the cool moisture across her arms and face, then kept running as fast as her brown legs could take her. She didn't know if dogs could pick up a human scent in the rain.

Jessie wasn't going to slow down and find out.

1

THROUGH THE WINDOW I COULD SEE A FEW BROWN LEAF STRAG- glers clinging to limbs of an oak tree. Powell Station was in the Appalachian foothills so snow wasn't uncommon in November, but it rarely fell until after the middle of the month. I rolled onto my side and pulled the quilt up to my chin. I was glad to be home, among my family, spending a few days in the daily routine of life.

I slipped out of bed so as not to wake the twins, Ellie and Emma. After retrieving the morning eggs, I joined Mama in the kitchen. Our diet was high in cholesterol, but there wasn't a carton of soft drinks on our property, and honey from hives behind the garden was our favorite sweetener.

Mama and I had worked together in the kitchen from the time I was old enough to be trusted at the stove until I left for college. When I returned home, familiar patterns returned without effort and we moved about efficiently without getting in each other's way. I loved meal preparation. There was a sense of fulfillment in fixing hot, delicious food for the people I loved. Daddy claimed my scrambled eggs were fluffier than cotton candy at the county fair.

Daddy and Bobby came inside and washed their hands at the garden sink beside the rear door.

"It's a glorious morning!" Daddy exclaimed to Mama. "Do you know why, Lu?"

Mama smiled. We all knew the answer.

"Because we're here together," Mama replied.

Daddy dried his hands and kissed me in the usual place on top of my head. He grabbed Ellie by the shoulders.

"Which one are you?" he asked, peering into her blue eyes.

"Daddy, you know!" she answered with a quick smile.

Daddy kissed her on the right cheek. Emma came up for a kiss on the left cheek. Daddy grabbed Mama and squeezed her waist.

The timer I used for the hard-boiled eggs went off. While I cooled the eggs enough to remove the shells, Ellie filled large bowls with steaming oatmeal. Emma set a cup of raisins and a jar of honey on the table, then put a cloth napkin at every place and correctly positioned on each a knife, fork, and spoon. I'd never been embarrassed by a lack of table manners. Mama's homeschool curriculum included a course in etiquette that we were expected to incorporate into everyday practice. We ate our meals at a long picnic table painted white. Mama and I sat across from each other at the end nearest the cooking area.

"Tammy Lynn, will you pray?" Daddy asked.

We held hands around the table. I reached across and took Mama's hand. It was slightly dry and coarse. Her fingers spoke of a lifetime of service to others.

"Thank you for this fresh food, my loving family, and this crisp, fall day. Bless them all. In Jesus' name, amen."

"Well done, Tammy Lynn," Daddy said. "Who said lawyers forget how to pray? That was downright poetic."

"I won't be a lawyer until I graduate from school and pass the bar exam next summer," I corrected.

"You'll do both," Mama said confidently as she stirred a few more raisins into her oatmeal. "And the Lord will direct your steps."

Ellie popped a large bite of hard-boiled egg into her mouth.

"Tammy Lynn woke me up this morning talking about moving to Savannah and getting married and having babies."

"That was her prediction for my future," I responded quickly.

"But you didn't disagree," Ellie answered, her voice muffled by egg.

"Don't talk with food in your mouth," Mama said.

I turned toward Daddy and Mama. "I have to tell Braddock, Appleby, and Carpenter by the first of December if I'm going to accept the job offer with them. If I turn them down, I could work with Julie Feldman and Maggie Smith in Savannah or come back to Powell Station and open my own office."

"I know what Zach wants you to do," Emma replied. "Take the job with Bradley, Applecart, and whatever so he can keep a close watch on you."

"That's not the way he looks at it."

"But it's the way he looks at you," Ellie replied. "I can still see the dreamy expression on his face when you were doctoring his hand after the catfish stung him."

"Has he given you any advice?" Mama asked, ignoring my sisters.

"He told me the advantages and disadvantages of coming to work for his firm or being part of a new practice like the one Julie and Maggie are setting up."

"Being around him every day would be a big, big advantage," Ellie said, taking a sip of orange juice.

"Last week Julie sent me pictures of the place Maggie rented in a new office park," I continued. "It looks nice. They have an office reserved for me if I want it."

"How can they afford that?" Daddy asked.

"Julie's father is loaning them a bunch of money. In return, Julie gets to be a partner from the start. She claims her daddy won't make them pay back the money."

"That's not right," Emma cut in. "The Bible says, 'The wicked borroweth and payeth not again.' Psalm 37:21."

"Tammy Lynn, you be the lawyer; your little sister can go to Congress." Daddy laughed.

AFTER BREAKFAST, ELLIE AND I RINSED THE BOWLS IN THE SINK. She leaned over and spoke in a soft voice.

"If you work at the law firm with Zach, you can find out if he's the one. I think he is, but I know it's up to Daddy, Mama, you, and God, of course."

"He's the first man I've courted," I answered, glancing over my shoulder to see if Mama was still in the kitchen. "And I can't be thinking about marriage all the time. Part of the reason to court a man is to learn how it feels to be around a male who isn't a member of the family."

"Doesn't the thought of him make chills run up and down your back?"

As if on cue, an involuntary shiver ran down my back.

"Not all the time," I answered, shrugging my shoulders.

Ellie continued. "And after you get used to his ponytail, it doesn't make him look girlie at all, especially when you see how broad his shoulders are."

"You shouldn't be paying attention to Zach Mays' shoulders."

"I'm not. It's a scientific observation."

MID-MORNING I FOUND MAMA SWEEPING THE FRONT PORCH. The autumn sun shining through the trees in the front yard cast mottled light against the well-worn wood.

"I'd like to see Mr. Callahan while I'm here and ask his advice."

Mama finished a stroke that sent several leaves swirling off the porch and into the cool air.

"That's a good idea. You can borrow the car."

It was about five miles to the retired attorney's large home on top of a gentle hilltop surrounded by lush pasture where his prize Angus cattle grazed. A jar of honey in my hand as a gift, I rang the doorbell. The white-haired lawyer opened it and inspected me with piercing dark eyes that contained both fire and compassion. It was easy to imagine Mr. Callahan giving a passionate appeal to a jury.

"Come inside," he said in a mellow voice.

I handed him the jar of honey. "This is for you and Mrs. Callahan."

"Thank you. I've been out of honey for a few weeks. Bobby brought a jar when he picked up a calf a few days after you and the young, healing prophet with the ponytail came by to see me."

"Zach wouldn't want to be called either a prophet or a healer. He's an admiralty lawyer."

"Didn't I get better after he prayed for me?"

"Yes, sir."

"Then it doesn't matter what he calls himself." Mr. Callahan held up the honey. "Let me prove my case. Your mama can make a pretty label to decorate the outside, but wouldn't you agree that it's what's inside this jar that counts?"

"Yes, sir."

"It's the same with people."

I followed Mr. Callahan through the living room to the kitchen, a spacious room that featured a decorative island and bank of windows that welcomed sunlight.

"My wife's in Chattanooga shopping with her sister," Mr. Callahan said, placing the honey on the corner of the island. "Your daddy told me Joe Carpenter offered you a permanent job, the first female clerk to receive an offer at Braddock, Appleby, and Carpenter since women got the vote."

"They've had a few woman attorneys over the years but never hired a female summer clerk."

"When do you start?"

"I'm not sure I'm going to accept."

"Why not?" he asked in surprise. "Do you have a better offer?"

"That's why I came to see you."

Mr. Callahan motioned to a small round table in the corner of the room. We sat, and I told him about the new firm Maggie Smith and Julie Feldman wanted me to join. His face remained impassive.

"Maggie's been with the district attorney's office for a few years and wants to go out on her own," I said. "Julie Feldman is the Jewish girl who also clerked at Braddock, Appleby, and Carpenter. She'll graduate from Emory in June. They want me to be their associate. It will be a small firm, but I believe they have a great future."

Mr. Carpenter rubbed his chin. "Wouldn't Ms. Feldman be an associate, too? She doesn't have any more experience than you do."

"Her father is a rich doctor. He's loaning the money to help them get started. In return, Julie gets an instant partnership."

"In nothing." Mr. Callahan snorted. "Braddock, Appleby, and Carpenter is the best firm in Savannah. It's okay to go out on your own after you learn your way around the courthouse. But two inexperienced lawyers and an assistant DA who's had her cases handed to her on a platter by detectives who did the hard work is a recipe for disaster."

I swallowed. I'd not expected Mr. Callahan to have such a strong opinion.

"You started your own practice in Powell Station. It worked out well for you."

"Don't forget. I worked three years for another lawyer in Cartersville before moving up here. I learned enough from him to keep from making any dumb mistakes that cost me my license or caused me to go broke. And I still had a few lean years before the decent cases started rolling in. Borrowing through a personally guaranteed credit line at the local bank just to survive isn't fun." Mr. Callahan leaned forward.

"How many of your classmates at the law school have multiple job offers?"

"I'm not sure. Except for the girls on my intramural basketball team, I don't talk to many people about their plans."

"How many of those young women have a decent job to go to after graduation?"

I quickly ran through the lineup of the seven girls. We'd played together for three years in a fall league at the University of Georgia.

"One is accepting a job with an insurance defense firm in Macon. Another is going to clerk for a superior court judge in Fulton County. The others are sending out résumés and trying to arrange interviews and so on." I paused. "If nothing develops they'll get desperate in a few months."

"Exactly." Mr. Callahan sat up straight and eyed me for a moment. "Are you looking for someone to tell you what to do?"

"I wouldn't mind it," I admitted sheepishly.

"Have you talked to your parents?"

"They know about the options, of course, but they haven't given me their opinion."

"Well, I don't want to create confusion with what they might say."

"No, it's okay. I'm already confused."

Mr. Callahan looked past my shoulder. "Tammy Lynn, do you know why you're struggling with this decision?"

I hesitated. "Because I want to do God's will?"

Mr. Callahan waved his right hand in a way that brushed aside my answer.

"That's important, but to get to that point it's necessary to be honest about yourself. I like pretending to be a cattleman, but sometimes I miss the chance to really grill a witness. Will you let me conduct a bit of a cross-examination to find out what's going on inside that pretty, intelligent head of yours?"

I managed a slight smile. "Go ahead. If it helps, it'll be worth it."

Mr. Callahan stood, pushed his glasses down his nose, and put his hands behind his back. "Ms. Taylor, isn't it true you've had a lot of success for a girl taught at home until high school?"

I sat up straighter in the chair.

"Yes, sir. Mama is the best teacher in the world. I'd read most of the books on the reading lists for my college literature classes before—"

Mr. Callahan held up his hand. "A simple yes is sufficient. You don't have to prove the value of your upbringing to me. I'm just laying the foundation for my question."

"Okay."

"And isn't it true that you've had athletic success, too?"

"Yes, sir."

"Didn't the girls' high school basketball team go to the state tournament your senior year?"

"Yes, sir."

"And weren't you named all-conference point guard?"

I blushed that Mr. Callahan remembered such a minute detail from my past. I nodded.

"And isn't it correct that you've done well in law school?"

"I'm not on the law review, but I'm in the top quarter of my class."

"A lot of successful attorneys weren't on the law review." Mr. Callahan grunted. "Including me. And now you've broken the gender barrier for summer clerks at an outstanding law firm in Savannah. I bet the partners didn't spend much time discussing the below-the-knee length of your dresses before deciding to offer you a job. Don't you think they focused on your analytical ability and personal character?"

"Are you asking me to speculate?"

Mr. Callahan pointed his finger at me. "Careful. A witness who toys with me usually regrets it."

I smiled. "I'm sure the partners at the firm cared more about my legal abilities than my conservative wardrobe."

"That's better." Mr. Callahan paused. "So, Ms. Taylor, after all your hard work in several areas of life, is there a possibility you're afraid of success at the next level?"

"No, sir. That's not it."

Mr. Callahan studied me for a moment. "When a witness doesn't give the expected answer, the attorney must try a different tact."

I waited. Mr. Callahan stepped closer.

"As a first-year associate attorney, you'll make an excellent salary at Braddock, Appleby, and Carpenter, probably two or three times what your daddy brings home in a year as a supervisor at the chicken plant. Are you worried the deceitfulness of wealth will draw you away from your love for God?"

I'd thought about that issue. "I won't know until the money is in my bank account. I'm praying for grace not to let it drag me down."

"And I doubt it will," Mr. Callahan replied, rubbing his chin. "What about Zach Mays? Do you believe God is drawing you together?"

I blushed a second time.

"I've not seen him since the end of the summer. He's busy at work, and I'm in the middle of the school term."

"If he'd wanted to visit you at school, would you have let him?"

I bit my lower lip. "Yes, sir. What does that have to do with the job?"

Mr. Callahan smiled. "That was a credibility question, just to let me know you're in a truth-telling mood."

"I always try to tell the truth. Or repent as soon as I don't."

"I'll hold you to that. Look, let's be real. Are you afraid working on a daily basis with the young healing prophet might ruin your relationship with him?"

Mr. Callahan's question produced a sudden ache of longing for

Zach Mays in my chest. My phone conversations with him had been light, not serious. We'd not voiced what we might feel in our hearts. As I'd told Ellie, I was just getting used to being around a man who wasn't a family member.

"No, sir," I answered slowly. "I want to be around him. But it's not necessary to work at the same firm for that to happen."

"Does Joe Carpenter's firm discourage two lawyers who work there from dating each other?"

"Ms. Patrick, the office manager, told me romance between summer clerks and lawyers wasn't allowed, but I don't know about lawyers. I don't think it would be a problem."

"Although it's awkward if a couple takes domestic squabbles to work in their briefcases."

I opened my mouth, then quickly shut it.

"There will be arguments," Mr. Callahan continued.

"I know. Even Mama and Daddy have their disagreements. She's taught me the biblical principles of conflict resolution and helped me understand the differences between men and women."

Mr. Callahan raised his eyebrows. "I thought it was the man's job to make all the adjustments."

"That's usually true," I answered with a straight face.

Mr. Callahan rubbed his palms together. "I know you've thought about this next question, but I need to ask it anyway. Are you worried the firm will assign you cases that violate your moral convictions?"

"That happened last summer," I answered, remembering the lawsuit the firm filed against Sister Rachel Dabney. "It all worked out in the end. But I can't count on that happening every time."

Mr. Callahan chuckled. "That doesn't sound like a woman who has the faith to move mountains. Here's what you could do. Tell the firm up front there are types of cases you want to avoid and get it settled before it comes up."

I tried to imagine delivering an ultimatum to Mr. Carpenter.

"I'm not sure Mr. Carpenter—"

"I wouldn't be afraid about confronting Joe Carpenter with an honest request. I've known him since law school. He loved your spunkiness and wants you to accept the job so badly he'll negotiate with you."

"How do you know that?"

Mr. Callahan sat down at the table. "He called and talked to me a few weeks ago. Wanted me to use my influence to convince you to come to work for him."

"He did?" I asked in shock.

"Yep, phoned me while I was on the tractor hauling a round bale of hay to the cattle in the south field. I told him I wasn't sure I'd see you before Christmas but would give my opinion if asked. During the summer, Joe saw what the rest of us already know about you."

I waited.

Mr. Callahan shook his head. "I'm not going to flatter you any more than I already have, but you're more likely to be forced into cases you don't want to handle at a start-up firm that needs every dollar it can collect in fees than a firm that can pick and choose its clients."

I sighed. "I don't have to guess what you think I should do."

"Right. I think Braddock, Appleby, and Carpenter is the way to go, at least until you learn the ropes. Law school may teach you to think like a lawyer, but it doesn't teach you how to practice law."

I shrugged. "Yes, the secretaries and paralegals at the firm knew more practical stuff than I did."

"And you don't have a clue whether either Smith or Feldman has the administrative abilities to run a law firm."

Julie was smart but not always organized. I didn't know about Maggie. My work history was limited to the processing line at the local chicken plant, a part-time job as a sitter for elderly women, and a three-month summer clerkship.

"Talk with your parents," Mr. Callahan concluded. "Their advice is more important than mine."

"But I respect your advice, and I wanted to know what you think. You've always helped me think through problems. Thanks for being honest with me."

"You deserve a straight answer. I'm confident that when the time comes, you'll know what to do. Once you make your decision, don't look back."

2

JESSIE SHUFFLED ALONGSIDE THE RAILROAD TRACKS. IT HAD stopped raining, but a midnight mist kept her from seeing far ahead. Her eyes fluttered shut as she tried to steal a few seconds' rest. Stumbling forward, she fell, skinning her left knee on a rough crosstie. The sharp pain woke her up.

There'd been no sound or sign of pursuit, but the grotesque image of the man lying at the foot of the tree was etched in her mind with photographic clarity. Every time she closed her eyes, the sight of the man's twisted body returned.

It wasn't the first time Jessie had seen a dead person. At age seven she found her father sprawled across the bed with his mouth hanging open and an empty bottle of pills on the floor. She dashed into the living room and found her stepmother passed out drunk on the couch in the living room. Jessie poured a glass of cold water on her stepmother's face, and fifteen minutes later an ambulance, sirens blaring, came to the house. It left slowly in silence with the body. There wasn't a funeral.

Jessie gingerly touched the sore place on her knee. Alone, she was more tired than afraid. The shifting shadows cast by tree limbs when the moon peered from behind the clouds didn't bother her. Jessie's

fears became real only when people were present. She found her greatest security in solitude, her favorite escape in the pages of a book.

After her father's death, Jessie and her stepmother spent a lot of
time in homeless shelters and more than a few nights huddled under
bridges. Jessie knew the worst enemy of the homeless was cold weather,
the unrelenting chill that made toes and fingers ache and dawn's
warmth seem light-years away. Tonight was warm and muggy. Jessie
licked her lips. She was thirsty. She'd not had anything to drink since
lapping dirty water from a rain puddle.

The tracks turned slightly left then crossed a broad ravine. Jessie
stopped and looked down a steep embankment. She couldn't see the
bottom, but it had to be deep. The tops of trees beside the tracks
barely reached the level of the rails. There wasn't a bridge, just tracks
laid on thick wooden pilings. She peered ahead, trying to determine
how long the span might be. Meeting an oncoming train with no
place to jump to the side would be a recipe for disaster.

Standing still, she listened, trying to pick up the sound of an
approaching train. Hearing nothing, she took a few cautious steps
forward. Then Jessie remembered a scene from a book set in the Old
West. In it, she'd learned that an Indian tracker would kneel down and
put his ear against the metal rails to hear the vibrations caused by an
approaching train. Lying on her stomach, Jessie rested her ear against
the cool steel. It gave off a low hum. She raised her head and strained
her eyes. The mist was getting thicker, not thinner. She listened again.
There was no mistaking the presence of a humming sound, but she
didn't know what it meant.

Returning to solid ground, Jessie decided to wait for a few minutes.
She found a large pine tree with a thick blanket of needles wrapped
like an apron around its base. The needles might be a nest of chiggers,
but she sat down anyway and leaned against the tree. In less than a
minute, she heard a rumbling sound in the distance. A train was coming. Not in front of her, but along the track she'd already walked.

Jessie watched the black cars zip past and breathed a sigh of relief. The flashing red light on the last car disappeared across the bridge. She pressed her hands against the slightly prickly pine needles that weren't much rougher than the ancient sofa someone gave her stepmother. An enveloping fog of fatigue convinced her she'd fled far enough for the night.

Lying down, Jessie took the pouch from the front of her jeans. Her stepmother had a leather jacket, but it felt like plastic compared to the supple pouch. Jessie rested her head on the pouch and closed her eyes.

MR. CALLAHAN SENT ME HOME WITH ENOUGH FRESH STEAKS FOR a feast. I handed Mama the heavy packet.

"Mix the marinade, and we'll eat steak for supper," she said. "This meat is too good to freeze."

Mama used a steak marinade that included olive oil, pepper, garlic, and several other spices. I mixed the ingredients in a bowl, then poured the liquid on top of the steaks and put them in the refrigerator to soak in the flavors.

"Did you have a good visit with Mr. Callahan?" she asked from the corner of the kitchen where she was scrubbing the floor.

"Yes. He appreciated the honey."

"Was Mrs. Callahan there?"

"No, she was with her sister in Chattanooga."

"Did you ask his advice about the job?" Mama stood and wiped her hands on her work apron.

"Yes."

"There's wisdom in a multitude of counselors," she answered evenly. "And there's no denying Oscar Callahan has played a big role in your becoming a lawyer."

I finished rinsing out the bowl used to mix the marinade.

"He thinks a multitude of counselors is the right move, which means I should accept the job at Braddock, Appleby, and Carpenter. Mr. Carpenter actually called him and asked him to use his influence to persuade me to work for the firm."

Mama and I sat at the table while I told her about my conversation with the retired lawyer.

"Being with Mr. Callahan made me wish he was still practicing law and could ask me to join him. It would be wonderful living at home, helping you when I was here, spending more time with the twins, going to church—"

"But that's not an option, is it?"

"Not really. I don't know anything about the two lawyers who bought Mr. Callahan's practice and doubt they need an associate so soon after getting started themselves."

"That doesn't sound much different than the situation with Julie Feldman and Maggie Smith."

"So, you and Daddy agree with Mr. Callahan," I responded quickly.

Mama rubbed her forehead. "Daddy and I have been praying about it. We'll talk after supper."

As much as I wanted to know Mama's thoughts, I knew our conversation would have to wait.

Later, while we fixed supper, my stomach growled in hunger. Mama cooked steaks in an old cast-iron skillet heated hot enough to make the oil sizzle. The finished product would be slightly crispy on the outside and running with tender juices on the inside. The steaks filled the kitchen with an aroma that seeped outside, causing the dogs to bark in anticipation of an after-dinner bone.

While Mama kept a careful eye on the steaks, I baked yeast rolls and fixed mashed potatoes. Gravy for the potatoes received extra zip from the skillet drippings. Ellie heated green beans on the stove and made sweet tea in a large pot of hot water. Emma set the table. With symphonic coordination, everything came out of oven and skillet for quick transfer to the table.

"Pray fast, Daddy," Ellie said when we sat down in our usual seats. "God knows we're thankful."

Daddy couldn't be rushed if he felt the nudge of the Spirit otherwise. But tonight, the Lord agreed with Ellie. In a few seconds the room was silent except for the passing of dishes and the sounds of forks and knives. Partway through the meal I stole a glance around the table while savoring a juicy bite of steak and took a mental snapshot of the scene to revisit while eating a chicken salad sandwich in my apartment at school.

"No room for dessert," Daddy said when he pushed away his plate.

"That's good, because we didn't fix any," Mama replied.

"I'm still hungry," Bobby protested.

Mama pointed to the bowl of mashed potatoes. "Eat those. They'll fill the hollow place in your legs."

"The twins and I will clean up," Daddy said when we were done. "Everyone else go into the front room. Bobby, do you feel like playing your guitar?"

My brother patted his stomach. "Yes, sir. I have an extra place to rest it for a couple of hours."

Mama and I went into the front room. My parents always sat in two comfortable chairs with a lamp in between. The rest of us grabbed places on the couch or used one of the straight-backed chairs that lined the wall. The room could hold up to twenty for a prayer meeting. When that happened, chairs weren't necessary because people spent most of the time kneeling on the floor.

Bobby brought his guitar downstairs and began to tune it. Mama closed her eyes. After finishing his tuning, Bobby began to pick individual notes. The fingers on his left hand moved smoothly up and down the guitar's neck. My brother had come a long way from strumming the same three chords over and over. Daddy and the twins joined us. The girls plopped down on the couch beside me without elbowing each other. We didn't own a TV, so spending time together as a family after a meal wasn't unusual. In addition to singing, we occasionally read a classic book out loud or played an educational game.

Bobby led us in a song popular in the youth group at church. Daddy had a fine baritone voice. Ellie and Emma could carry a tune. I didn't have a solo voice but could sing a natural harmony, which was nice in a small group. Mama's creative gifts were in her hands, not her voice. She hummed along.

By the second song, I felt myself touching the edges of worship. Bobby's skill had really improved. He played with his head turned slightly toward the fret board. By the time he started the fourth song, I felt like we were having church. Meeting with God in the simplicity of our home was a blessing I knew few households in America shared. I glanced at Mama. She was visibly affected.

Bobby played a long instrumental interlude that sustained the sense of the Lord's presence without words. I kept my eyes closed and let the glory in the room banish the worry lodged in the cracks and crevices of my soul. The greatness of God became real, and I felt an impartation of confidence that his love would influence the events to come. I silently thanked him, an act of faith before the future became sight.

The music stopped. We sat quietly. Even the twins seemed to bask in the goodness of the moment. Then Daddy spoke a blessing over our family that made me feel like the daughter of an Old Testament patriarch. Chills raced across skin. Daddy sealed his words with an emphatic "Amen."

"Thanks, Bobby," Mama said.

Bobby grinned. Even with his musical gift, he was still my younger brother whose skinned knees I'd cleaned and bandaged when he was a little boy.

"We need to talk to Tammy Lynn in private," Daddy added.

"Is she in trouble?" Ellie asked.

"No," Mama answered evenly. "Occupy yourselves upstairs. No eavesdropping."

Ellie looked at me and mouthed, *Zach*.

I shook my head. After everyone left the room, Daddy turned to me.

"How are you doing, Tammy Lynn?"

"Glad to be home."

"Worship puts things in perspective, doesn't it?" Mama said.

"Yes, ma'am. It calmed me down. I'd not realized how much I'd given in to worry."

Mama touched me gently on the shoulder. "Tell your daddy about the conversation with Oscar Callahan."

I gave a quick summary of the older lawyer's opinion, leaving out his comments about Zach, of course.

"Mr. Callahan has a lot of wisdom," Daddy said when I finished, "especially about the importance of being mentored by other lawyers after you graduate. But our greatest concern is that you avoid situations where you'd be under pressure to compromise your convictions."

"That's something I'm going to face wherever I work," I said. "Mr. Callahan thinks I can negotiate an understanding with Mr. Carpenter before accepting the job."

"Would you be willing to do that?" Mama asked.

"I've had to confront Mr. Carpenter a few times already, and he didn't fire me. Actually, I think it caused him to respect me. If I'm willing to stand up to him, he doesn't think I'll be intimidated by attorneys on the other side of a case. But it would be impossible to list every kind of situation that might create a problem."

"Do you have peace about working for the two women attorneys?" Mama asked.

"Not really."

"Then something else has to happen for your decision to become clear."

"I thought you and Daddy might tell me."

"We didn't dictate whether you should take the summer job with the law firm, and we aren't going to do so now." Mama paused and smiled. "Maybe I'm saving my strong opinions for your marriage plans."

"I wouldn't marry anyone unless you approved and gave your blessing," I answered quickly, then gave her a questioning look. "Has the Lord shown you anything about that? That's more important than where I should work."

"Nothing that should be mentioned now."

My stomach tightened. Daddy glanced at Mama and spoke.

"Let's don't get off track. Tammy Lynn, I believe your choice about a job won't be based on man's wisdom, but God's will."

"But I don't know what that is," I said, trying to fight off the frustration I'd so recently banished. "People who don't care about God's will have an easier time making up their mind about things than those who do. And I have to let Mr. Carpenter know by December 1."

Mama and Daddy exchanged a look. He spoke.

"We've prayed about it and believe you'll find the answer to your question in Savannah."

"In Savannah? I don't understand."

Daddy continued. "Acts 17:26 says that God hath determined the bounds of their habitation. When you're in the geographic place where you're supposed to live, you'll know it. We think you need to go to Savannah and ask the Lord what to do."

It was a depressing thought. I pictured myself sitting on a park bench in Savannah, staring up at the sky and waiting for the clouds to form words. Daddy came over and kissed me on top of my head.

"This is your path to discover. Our job is to pray for you."

"I liked it better when you told me what to do," I said with a sigh.

Mama smiled. "Please tell the twins that. They need to hear it."

3

JESSIE WOKE UP. IT TOOK HER A FEW SECONDS TO REMEMBER HOW she'd ended up sleeping on a bed of pine needles in the middle of nowhere. She rubbed her arms. They were laced with scratches from the briar patch but not covered in chigger bites. At least she'd found a bug-free spot to rest.

It was barely light. Jessie didn't know what time it was, but that didn't matter. The numbers on a clock wouldn't dictate the day. More basic concerns cried out for attention. She was thirsty and hungry. Standing up, she tucked the pouch into her jeans.

The train tracks ran across the ravine for at least a hundred yards. It would be a bad place to get caught in the open with a train either coming or going. She walked across the tracks to the other side of the ravine where she found a white plastic bag draped over a scraggly bush. Ripping open the bag with Christmas present excitement, she discovered treasure inside: three partially full plastic water bottles, half a container of skinny French fries as hard as the crossties that supported the steel rails, and a handful of crumbs from fast-food biscuits. She gulped down one of the waters, amazed that someone would waste such precious liquid, then left the other two bottles in the bag for later. The French fries were too hard to chew; however, the biscuit fragments were edible. There was a partially used packet of ketchup at the bottom of the bag. It wasn't strawberry jam, but it gave the stale bread flavor.

Reenergized by the simple meal, Jessie continued down the tracks. Over the next three hours, four trains passed by. South Georgia is pancake flat, and she could see the trains coming long before she heard the sound of the locomotives. All the trains were hauling pine tree logs. Each time a train got close, Jessie moved away from the tracks and crouched out of sight.

She'd read in a book about a man who'd tried to hop on a train for a free ride and ended up losing his leg. Jessie wasn't tempted to jump on one of the trains. It wouldn't have worked anyway. Without a city or town to slow them down, the trains shot past at top speed.

As she walked, Jessie scavenged along the tracks. To her, the littering by others was a virtue, not a vice. Within a few hours Jessie's plastic garbage bag contained two more water bottles and additional scraps of half-eaten fast food. She quickly learned to judge the freshness of discarded items. One bag with particular promise had been torn up by an animal. Jessie was afraid to eat the remaining scraps of country ham. She also found a full can of beer. She'd been given sips and gulps of beer by grown-ups since she was a little girl and could tolerate the taste. However, when she popped open the can, the brew smelled so foul she poured it out on the ground. She placed the can on the tracks to be smashed by the next train that came along.

As the sun reached its zenith, Jessie stepped away from the tracks into a pine thicket. It was a mature stand of trees. Many of the ruler-straight trees didn't sprout a limb until thirty or forty feet in the air. A rough dirt road ran parallel to the train tracks through the woods. Beside the road was a discarded wooden pallet. Jessie sat on the pallet and ate her remaining scraps of food. After taking a long drink of water, she took out the leather pouch. It was closed with a gold-colored snap.

When she'd snatched the pouch from the table, Jessie had hoped to find a few lower-denomination bills to hide in the secret place in the old wooden nightstand in her room. She didn't need a lot of money, just enough to give her some extra cash in case of an emergency. But when she retreated to her room and looked inside the pouch, she decided to return it. The discovery of her theft, and the uproar it caused, kept that from happening.

She emptied the contents of the pouch onto one of the wooden boards of the pallet. There were nine or ten square sheets of decorated paper written in a foreign language and an ordinary sheet of paper covered in an indecipherable gibberish of letters and numbers. Jessie held one of the sheets up to the sunlight. It was pretty. Red and blue highlights enhanced the predominant green ink. All the sheets seemed the same. She knew the colored pieces of paper had value; otherwise, the two men wouldn't have gone to the trouble to chase her into the thicket, but she couldn't read them to find out how much. To her, they were worthless.

Returning everything to the pouch, she lay on the pallet and stared at the tops of the trees. The combination of sun and food made her drowsy. She closed her eyes and dozed off.

She didn't wake up until it was too late.

EVERYBODY GATHERED ON THE FRONT PORCH WHEN IT WAS TIME for me to leave on Sunday afternoon. Mama had filled a grocery sack with food for Kyle. He was a freshman living in a dormitory. A taste of home might not remove his homesickness, but it could dull the edge.

A girl from Dalton, who was a graduate student in the history department, had agreed to pick me up at 2:30 p.m. She was as punctual as a chronological timeline and pulled into our driveway on schedule. It was always noisy when I arrived home and quiet when I left. Daddy carried my suitcase to the car then kissed me. Mama held me longer than usual.

"Let us know when you go to Savannah so we can pray," she whispered in my ear.

I nodded. Ellie hugged me and pressed a small present in my hand.

"Open it later," she said.

When Emma hugged me I could see that she was on the verge of tears. Bobby was friendly but nonchalant. Then I was gone.

I looked down at Ellie's present. It was no bigger than an earring box. I owned two pairs of simple earrings, but the use of jewelry by unmarried women in our church was discouraged. Karen, the girl giving me the ride, saw the little box.

"A present?"

"From one of my sisters."

"Are you going to open it?"

"No." I slipped it into the bag of goodies for Kyle. "I'll wait till later."

When we neared the University of Georgia campus in Athens, I called Kyle so he could meet me at my apartment. He had a key to the room in a converted motel where I lived.

Kyle carried everything into the apartment. He was as strong as one of the bulls he bought and sold when he was living at home. He began digging through the bag of food before I closed the door.

"What's this?" He held up the tiny box from Ellie.

"A gift from Ellie. I doubt it's edible."

I opened the little box. It contained a recent photo of Ellie with the words, "I love you," written on the back. I placed it in the corner of my computer screen. Kyle lined up everything from the food bag on the counter.

"The sun's gone down," he said. "What would you like to fix for supper?"

Our day of rest ended at sundown on Sunday. Kyle was a meat lover, so I fixed him an evening breakfast that included homemade sausage, fresh eggs from our hens, and biscuits made from ingredients in my sparsely stocked cupboard. While I worked, I told him all I could about life at home.

"I know the exact tree Bobby cut down," he said between bites of sausage biscuit when I told him about a dead tree that had to be removed. "I told Daddy this would be a good year to harvest it. I wish I could have been there to help."

"Did you listen to one of the sermons from Pastor Vick I loaned you?" I asked.

Kyle took another bite. "No."

"Why not?"

"It's not the same for me as being there."

The phone rang.

"Hi, Zach," I said. "Kyle and I are finishing a late supper. I just got back from Powell Station."

Kyle hurriedly shoved half a biscuit into his mouth and began packing up the food. He pointed at the peaches, applesauce, and green beans and left them on the counter.

"Should I call later?" Zach asked.

"No, he's on his way out. Bye, Kyle. I'll talk to you later in the week."

Kyle closed the door behind him.

"How's he adjusting to college life?" Zach asked.

"He's gotten knocked off center," I answered. "And I'm not sure how his faith is holding up. It's easy to live a righteous life in Powell Station surrounded by family and church folks. Moving away is a shock."

"Is he drinking, cussing, or smoking?"

"He wouldn't be able to look me in the eye if that was going on." I paused. "Was that supposed to be a joke?"

"If so, it was a bad one. I know you're concerned about your brother. Sorry, I shouldn't make light of it."

I put a jar of peaches on the narrow shelf reserved for fruit.

"What have you been doing?" I asked.

"Reading a book about the differences between men and women."

"Why?"

"So I can talk to you better. I haven't gotten to the chapter about not joking with a woman about a topic that is serious to her."

"Okay." I placed the applesauce next to the peaches. "What have you learned?"

"That women spend a lot of time thinking about family matters and like to express their thoughts and feelings in conversations with the significant men in their life."

"We do?" I smiled slightly.

"Yeah. Men are more interested in what's going to happen during the next five minutes. They rarely look in the rearview mirror of life, and they assume the family is running smoothly unless shown otherwise."

"Interesting. Is that why you called? To let me know you're studying the differences between men and women?"

"No, I wondered if your parents thought you should accept the job offer with the firm."

"I need a book that gives me the answer to that question." I told him about my conversation with Daddy and Mama in the front room of the house. I didn't mention Oscar Callahan's opinion. "I know it sounds strange, but they believe I'll get clearer direction if I come to Savannah and pray about it there. I'm not sure what to think."

"They're right. What time do you want me to pick you up?" Zach responded.

"What?"

"How are you going to get to Savannah if I don't come and get you? I can leave work early on Friday and be there by mid-afternoon. You could probably stay with Mrs. Fairmont."

The previous summer I'd lived with Margaret Fairmont, a wealthy widow who owned a beautiful home in the historic district.

"I could call her," I answered slowly. "Or maybe I should check with her daughter."

"If that doesn't work out, I'd be glad to pay for a hotel room."

"No," I answered quickly. "I'll check with Mrs. Fairmont and let you know."

"Okay. I hope I get to see you."

We ended the call. I glanced at the clock. It was after 9:00 p.m., which meant nothing to Mrs. Fairmont. The aristocratic old woman suffered from multi-infarct dementia, a condition characterized by ministrokes that was slowly eroding her mind. She might go to sleep after supper, wake up at 10:00 p.m. and go back to bed at 2:00 a.m., or completely reverse the schedule. I dialed her number. The phone rang five times.

"Hello," a vibrant Southern voice answered.

It was Christine Bartlett, Mrs. Fairmont's daughter.

"Mrs. Bartlett, it's Tami Taylor," I began. "I was wondering—"

"Why am I not surprised?" Mrs. Bartlett interrupted. "You must be psychic. Mother and I were talking about you not five minutes ago. She doesn't send out many Christmas cards anymore, but she is insisting that I add your name to her list this year. The problem is she doesn't have your address at school or at home. That's a huge oversight on her part. In the old days she would have written down all your contact information before you left town. What's the name of the place you're from in the mountains? Possum Station?"

"Powell Station."

"Of course, it wouldn't be something vulgar. Anyway, I have a pen in my hand ready for the information."

I gave her both addresses and my phone number.

"Excellent. Mother's had quite a few good days thrown into the mix since you left. Tonight is one of the best. We had a glass of wine after supper, and it didn't put her to sleep in ten minutes. Instead, she started talking about you. Did you ever sample the Bordeaux we ordered from New York? It was such a bargain at two hundred dollars a bottle that Ken and I bought six. Mother and I opened the last one this evening."

"No, ma'am. I don't drink."

"Or have a cell phone either, if I recall. None of my friends could believe a smart young woman like you preferred to stay in the dark ages of communication. But overall, you had a positive influence on Mother. She's been nicer to me, which has helped a lot since there's so much I have to give up in order to look after her. One of Gracie's nieces, a young woman I didn't even know existed, is spending four days a week at the house. She goes to school at night and uses the days to study. She's not you, but at least she's a warm body who's able to make sure Mother doesn't fall down the stairs and break her hip or trip over that rat of a dog that is always underfoot."

Gracie had been Mrs. Fairmont's housekeeper for years. Flip, a Chihuahua, was the love of Mrs. Fairmont's life. I could hear Flip barking in the background.

"It's Tami Taylor," Mrs. Bartlett called out. "Can't you keep that dog quiet while someone is on the phone?"

There was momentary silence, then the barking resumed.

"I'll ask her," Mrs. Bartlett continued as an aside, then spoke into the phone. "Mother wants to invite you for a visit. I know you're busy at school and probably don't have time to run down here for a week-end. I'm not sure there's still a bus that connects Athens and Savannah. Ken and I could rent a car for you like we did when you came for your interview to see if you and Mother were compatible. But this time it would have to be something simple. I never told you, but I couldn't believe he selected a convertible for someone who—"

"Would next weekend be convenient for a visit?" I asked quickly. "I can make my own arrangements for transportation."

"Next weekend?"

"Yes, ma'am."

"Ken and I are going to be out of town in West Palm Beach. You know, south Florida is so overrated, especially for people from Savannah, but these friends of ours insist on going down for a few days when the weather gets chilly. It's not like we live in Michigan or Ohio, trying to escape the snow and ice—"

"I'm sorry I won't get to see you," I interrupted, "but I could spend time with your mother."

"Uh, let me ask her."

Mrs. Bartlett put her hand over the receiver. I could hear a muffled voice. There was silence then more muffled talking.

"She'd love to have you," Mrs. Bartlett said.

I gave an estimated time of arrival on Friday.

"Mother might be asleep. Or awake. You never can tell about her schedule. When my father was alive they lived like normal people, but this multi-infarct thing has messed up more than Mother's mind. I've tried charts, reminder notes stuck all over the house, random phone calls to see what she's doing; nothing seems to work. She has enough mental capacity to be stubborn—"

"I still have my key in case I need to let myself in," I said. "Thanks for letting me come. I hope you and Mr. Bartlett have a nice time in Florida."

After an earful of Mrs. Bartlett, the silence of my apartment was sweet. I waited a few minutes then phoned Zach. His excitement made me feel slightly giddy.

THE WEEK PASSED QUICKLY. WHILE I PACKED FOR THE TRIP TO Savannah, I reminded myself that the main reason I was leaving town for the weekend wasn't to see Zach, but to figure out where I ought to work.

I was peeking out the window when Zach arrived in his small white car. I quickly checked my appearance in the bathroom mirror and commanded my heart to slow down. It hadn't pounded as fast at the end of my morning run. There was a knock on the door.

The young lawyer had light brown hair pulled into a tight ponytail that had mesmerized the twins. I'd gotten used to it. Tall, with blue eyes that could be kind one minute and penetrating the next, Zach leaned forward and gave me a quick hug that ended before I had a chance to decide whether it felt right or not.

"It's good to see you," he said, beaming.

I met the look in his eyes with an uncontrollable grin that spread across my face.

"You, too. Thanks for coming."

Zach peered over my shoulder into the apartment.

"Efficient," he said.

"That's why they call it an efficiency apartment. There's not much to see. I'm ready to go."

We both reached for my suitcase. Our hands touched. Zach's felt warm. I let him pick up the suitcase while I grabbed a jar of Mama's peaches as a gift for Mrs. Fairmont.

Zach and I had talked on the phone quite a bit but hadn't seen each other for two and half months. However, it took only a few minutes to make it seem like we'd been apart for only a couple of days. Driving southeast on two-lane highways, we passed through small Georgia towns with English names like Farmington, Madison, and Eatonton. Zach peppered me with questions about my family, not about school. As I talked about the twins, I stopped and turned sideways in my seat.

"Are you really this interested in my family or is this the book you mentioned talking?"

"If I want to know you better, I need to know more about them."

"Was that in the book?"

Zach smiled. "Yes and no. The book said women like to talk about family matters, but I'd already figured that out."

"Then what have you learned?"

"That I need to know more about your mother. A woman is influenced the most by her mother; a man patterns his behavior after his father."

"You've been around my mother; what did you think about her?"

"She has a lot of good qualities."

"Name one."

Zach tapped the steering wheel with his fingers. "Okay. Remember how much I praised your mother as a teacher?"

"Yes."

"She's passed that gift along to you. Whether advising a client or arguing a case to a jury, a lawyer is a teacher and has to explain new or unfamiliar concepts to people in a way they can understand."

"That sounds exciting."

"It depends on the concepts. If the practice of law ends up boring you, it's the wrong profession."

"I could always go back to the chicken plant. I can eviscerate a chicken moving down the line and clean it out as fast as anyone."

"I'm sure you're among the best with a sharp knife." Zach nodded. "But I see you carving up hostile witnesses, not dead birds. Don't worry. It took me over a year to settle on admiralty law. You'll find your niche in law practice."

"That's what one of my professors told me. He said to be patient in picking a specialty because I might end up doing it for the rest of my career."

"And it's just as important to work with people you like, coworkers who will challenge and encourage you."

"Who might that be?" I asked.

Zach pointed at his chest. "You're in the car with one. And my loyalty to the firm requires that I work hard to attract the best legal talent available. Believe me, when the talent is as attractive as you are, it's not an unpleasant assignment."

I wasn't used to playful flirting. But I liked it.

"What else stood out in your mind about my mother?" I asked.

"She has a strong commitment to her religious convictions and believes genuine Christian faith affects every day conduct. That's a good thing, if the convictions are right."

"Are her convictions right?"

"Mostly."

I stared out the window at the rural countryside that was becoming flatter as we neared the coast.

"There are differences between Mama and me," I said.

Zach glanced in my direction. "Tell me more."

"Mama's focus is on building and protecting the family. When I have a family of my own, I may be the same. But that's not where I am right now. This past summer in Savannah changed me. Representing Moses Jones, meeting Sister Dabney, working for Mr. Carpenter, and living with Mrs. Fairmont stretched me in ways I didn't know I could be stretched. And getting to know you was—" I stopped.

"The best thing that's happened to you in years," Zach said with a grin.

"A very good thing," I responded. "A lot better than being trapped every day in the library with Julie Feldman."

"Which is a snapshot of your future if you go to work for Maggie Smith and Julie."

"Julie and I wouldn't share an office."

"Do you think that's going to keep her quiet?"

"No."

Zach held his right hand out in front of him as if reading a billboard. "Put the three of you together and you have the plot for a TV show—conservative Christian attorney and liberal Jewish lawyer create all-girl law firm with a hard-nosed former DA and square off in a three-way ideological cage fight."

"You're determined to convince me that I should work for Braddock, Appleby, and Carpenter, aren't you?"

Zach nodded. "Yep. You're not the only one who's been praying about your job."

BUILT IN 1860, MRS. FAIRMONT'S HOUSE WAS A TWO-STORY, SQUARE, brick structure with tall narrow windows on the first level and broad front steps. On the side of the house was an attached screened porch. Two large live oaks were planted between the house and the sidewalk. An iron railing extended from the steps down the street on either side then turned toward the rear of the house. The original owner was killed at the battle of Cold Harbor during the Civil War and never got a chance to enjoy the house.

Zach parked alongside the curb. "Do you want to come in?" I asked.

"No, thanks. What are your plans for tomorrow?"

"I'm not sure."

"You could sit on the park bench where Tom Hanks sat when they filmed *Forrest Gump*."

"I never saw the movie."

Zach winced. "It probably wouldn't help you make up your mind. Can I call you?"

"Sure. How about three o'clock?"

Zach carried my suitcase to the front door. I could hear Flip barking in the foyer.

"Thanks again for coming to get me," I said as I looked for the key in my purse.

I felt Zach's right arm around my shoulders. After a slight squeeze he released me.

"Good night," he said. "It's great to have you back, even if it's only for the weekend."

"Thanks," I said, my head lowered. "Good night."

As Zach descended the steps to the street, I turned the key in the lock and pushed open the front door. Inside, Flip charged toward my right foot then stopped in his tracks. The next instant his body began shaking in excitement. I leaned over and scratched him in his favorite place behind his head.

"More than one of us is glad to see you," Mrs. Fairmont said, coming into the foyer.

The petite, elderly woman had dressed up. Diamond rings glittered on both hands. Her white hair was nicely coiffed. I wrapped my arms around her and squeezed so hard that I apologized when I released her.

"Did I hurt you?"

"No, dear."

"You look beautiful."

"Gracie helped me get ready when I told her you were coming. Where would you like to sit?" Mrs. Fairmont asked formally.

"The blue parlor is my favorite."

The house had mirror-image parlors separated by a foyer that faced the main stairway to the second floor. Mrs. Fairmont's bedroom was upstairs. To the right was the pale green parlor, to the left, one painted an ephemeral blue. Both rooms contained beautiful furniture and original paintings. An antique rug rested on the floor in the blue parlor. Mrs. Fairmont sat in a feminine side chair and I chose the end of a sofa near her. Flip jumped up onto the sofa and crawled into my lap.

"He remembers you." Mrs. Fairmont smiled. "I'd be jealous if I didn't know his little heart was big enough to love both of us."

I ran my fingers under the dog's collar.

"Have you forgotten your promise to take care of him if anything happens to me?" Mrs. Fairmont asked.

"No, ma'am," I answered, continuing to scratch Flip's neck.

"Good," the older woman said, nodding. "I talked it over with Sam Braddock. He agrees with you that it wouldn't be a good idea to change my will. He suggested I write a short note that he'd put in my file requesting you become Flip's guardian after I'm gone."

"You met with Mr. Braddock?"

"I called, and he came to see me. I know lawyers don't make house calls anymore, but he made an exception. He talked quite a bit about the young man from Charleston who came with you to the hospital after my stroke and read that beautiful psalm."

"Vince Colbert."

"Yes. Sam says he's going to bring him into the firm." Mrs. Fairmont lowered her voice. "You know, Sam's old enough to retire, but Eloise Braddock has expensive taste. If she bids on an item at an antique auction, she always gets it. There was a painting one time that would have fit perfectly in the green parlor . . ." Mrs. Fairmont's voice trailed off.

"Did Mr. Braddock say anything about me?"

Mrs. Fairmont gave me an odd look.

"Why would he talk about you? Did you ever go to their house?"

"No, ma'am. Joe Carpenter was my supervising attorney, but Mr. Braddock knows who I am. The firm offered me a job, too."

"Of course they did. Sam would be a fool not to see your potential. Then you and Vince can work together."

"Don't forget about Zach Mays."

"Who?"

"The young lawyer with the motorcycle and ponytail."

Flip opened his mouth in a wide yawn.

"Yes, yes. I think I remember him." Mrs. Fairmont rubbed her temples. "But make sure you remind me if I meet him again. Sam wouldn't let me set up a doggie trust. He didn't think it necessary. What if Flip gets sick and has a big veterinarian bill or has to have a surgery? Who'll pay for that? Christine thinks he's a nuisance."

"You'll outlive—," I started then stopped. The Chihuahua was eight years old and might live another ten years. Each day could be Mrs. Fairmont's last. "But whatever happens, I'll take care of him and always ask myself what you would want to do for him."

Mrs. Fairmont's eyes watered.

"You'll never know how much that means to me." She waved her hand at the room. "I'm surrounded by all this, but it doesn't mean a thing if no one loves you."

"That's true."

Mrs. Fairmont blinked her eyes and stared at me. "Did you know I love you?"

"Yes, ma'am."

I leaned over and placed my smooth right hand on her wrinkled, gnarled one.

"I told Gracie the same thing." Mrs. Fairmont touched her heart. "She's worked for me almost thirty years. It was about time I let her know how much I cared for her."

"I'm sure that meant a lot to her. She loves you, too."

"She cried like a baby and told me I was like a second mother to her." The elderly woman lowered her voice. "And I made arrangements with Sam to give something special to Gracie when I'm gone. He didn't try to talk me out of that one."

"But there's no substitute for words spoken now."

"That's right. You're young, but you've taught me a lot." Mrs. Fairmont dabbed her eyes with a tissue. "Do you remember helping me write out a prayer list?"

"Yes, ma'am."

"Some days I fall asleep before I get through it or forget why a name is on there. But it's made me believe there's a reason why I'm still here. I've been reading the Bible, too. Will you get it for me? It's in the den."

I left the parlor and went down a short hallway. The den was a combination study-library with wood-paneled walls, comfortable leather furniture, bookshelves, and a TV. Mrs. Fairmont spent a lot of time in the den, often asleep with the TV blaring and Flip curled up at her feet. Her Bible was on a narrow wooden stand beside her favorite chair. I returned to the parlor and handed it to her. It was a blessing seeing the book in her hands.

"I've heard this passage read for years at weddings," she said, putting her finger on a bookmark and opening the Bible.

I leaned forward. She was looking at 1 Corinthians 13.

"It talks about faith, hope, and love," she continued. "Have you read it recently?"

I'd memorized the chapter but simply nodded.

"My idea of love was too small," Mrs. Fairmont continued, then began reading in her soft coastal accent: "'Love is patient, love is kind. It does not envy, it does not boast, it is not proud. It is not rude, it is not self-seeking, it is not easily angered, it keeps no record of wrongs. Love does not delight in evil but rejoices with the truth. It always protects, always trusts, always hopes, always perseveres. Love never fails.'"

Mrs. Fairmont looked up from the page. "God's idea of love is greater than mine. When I tell you and Gracie that I love you, my love should include everything I read. Isn't that one of the most amazing things you've ever heard?"

To hear a woman in her mid-eighties lost in the wonder of newly discovered truth was amazing in itself.

"Yes, ma'am."

Mrs. Fairmont closed the Bible. "I've put 'Greater Love' on the top of my prayer list. I'm praying it for myself and everyone else I know. Do you think that means being so unselfish that you're willing to die for someone else?"

She yawned before I answered.

"When I get tired there's no use fighting it," she said. "If I don't get to bed in a few minutes, I won't trust myself to climb the stairs."

"I'll let Flip outside for you. Where should I sleep?"

"Gracie cleaned your room for you."

Flip obediently followed me to the veranda then pattered down a winding wrought-iron staircase to the formal garden. After sniffing around for a few minutes, he climbed the steps in short hops then ran upstairs to Mrs. Fairmont's room. I carried my suitcase downstairs.

Mrs. Fairmont's home was three stories in the rear. My bedroom was in a garden apartment that looked out into the garden where Flip had been minutes before. A dog bed surrounded by chew toys lay in the middle of the living area, evidence that Flip had been temporarily banished to the basement room during social events. I crossed the small living area into a bedroom with French double doors that opened onto a brick patio. Gracie had turned back the freshly laundered sheets and placed a small chocolate on my pillow. Moonlight shone in through the double doors.

Beside the bed was an intercom connected to Mrs. Fairmont's room. It had been installed by Mrs. Bartlett to make sure I could keep tabs on her mother. I pressed the button.

"Good night, Mrs. Fairmont. Everything downstairs is perfect. Thanks again for letting me stay with you."

I waited. In a few seconds there was a scratchy reply.

"Good night, Tami. I love you."

I smiled and pressed the Send button. "I love you, too."

4

JESSIE OPENED HER EYES TO THE SOUND OF STRANGE VOICES. SHE jerked her head up. The wooden pallet was surrounded by six brown-skinned men with straight black hair. One of them was holding a pine branch he'd used to poke her in the stomach. The men began to speak rapidly in a language Jessie took to be Spanish. Jessie started to jump up and run, but the man with the stick put a rough hand on her shoulder, pushed her back, and shook his head. The other men crowded closer around her, creating a thick-legged wall.

Past the men was a pickup covered with red dust from the dirt road. Jessie could barely make out a faded sign on the side of the truck that read Polk Brothers Lumber Co. Two chain saws were on the ground beside the truck bed. The men continued gesturing and talking. The one with the stick spoke directly to Jessie, who shook her head. A smaller man to her right stepped forward. He bowed his head slightly then smiled, revealing two rows of white teeth. The smile didn't look menacing.

"You from Hinesville?"

Jessie had heard of the town but shook her head.

"Bainbridge?"

Jessie shook her head. That was too close to where she'd been.

"Savannah?"

Jessie had been to Savannah once with her stepmother. They'd found a place to stay for a few days in a battered women's shelter. It had been one of the nicer refuges during a difficult time.

"Yes." Jessie nodded her head.

"Sí, sí." The man smiled and explained to the others in lengthy terms what he'd discovered.

The man with the stick pointed at Jessie and spoke rapidly. She started to get up, but the man held out his hand in clear indication she was not going to be allowed to walk away. The smaller man spoke.

"You go to Savannah."

Another man held out his hand and gave her the most beautiful bottle of clear, clean water Jessie had ever seen. She rapidly unscrewed the cap and took a long drink of the delicious liquid. Wiping her mouth, she took another drink while the six men watched in silence. Then the man with the stick spoke again. The others nodded in agreement. Apparently, they'd learned more about her by watching her drink.

"Hungry?" the smaller man asked, pointing to his stomach.

Jessie nodded.

The smaller man spoke to the others. The man who'd given her the water jogged over to the truck and returned with a can of beans and wieners and a plastic spoon. The smaller man pulled a knife from his pocket and used a can opener attachment to cut open the can. He handed it to Jessie. As she took her first bite, several of the men made the sign of the cross on their chests. She mimicked them, which caused another ripple of rapid-fire conversation.

The beans were slightly sweet and the miniature wieners spicy enough to tantalize every taste bud in Jessie's mouth. The fact that the meal was cold did nothing to lessen her pleasure. As she ate, Jessie began to relax. If the men intended to harm her, it would have already happened. The bottle of water and can of beans communicated what spoken language could not. She looked at the small man and pointed at herself then the truck.

"Take me to Savannah?" she asked.

"Sí, sí." The man smiled.

"Sí, sí," she responded.

I awoke early and put on my jogging outfit. I'd run regularly since playing basketball in high school. Physical exercise helped clear my mind as well as keep me in good shape.

Quietly leaving Mrs. Fairmont's house, I stretched and loosened up at the bottom of the front steps. It was surprisingly cool. During summer, the muggy coastal heat loosened its grip for only a few hours before dawn. A weather front had passed through in the night, though, leaving the air this morning mountain crisp. I rubbed my hands together before taking off toward the center of the historic district.

The pre–Revolutionary War area of the city had twenty-one squares. It had taken me weeks to learn my way through the labyrinth of interconnecting streets and alleys. Now I could run in any direction and randomly navigate to East Broad, across to Forsyth Park, and back to Mrs. Fairmont's house in time for a sprint around Chippewa Square. The flat coastland was an invitation to speed. There was little traffic early on Saturday morning, and I barely checked for cars before shooting across most intersections.

There was nothing like the feeling of wings on my feet as I entered the zone reserved for regular runners in which forward motion isn't associated with pain or oxygen deprivation. The light pat of my feet on the sidewalks was my only connection with earth, and gravity didn't seem to be my master. With my mind not distracted by the pain of exertion, it was one of my clearest times for thinking. Today, what became crystal clear was God's call that I come to Savannah. I knew that already, but the awareness of it while passing through the streets of the city strengthened my confidence even more.

When I finished in front of Mrs. Fairmont's home, the sun was up, but the streets remained largely deserted. I opened the front door quietly to see Flip waiting on me. After a quick pat, he scampered down the hallway and through the doggie door that led to a small side yard. I went into the kitchen and started a pot of decaf coffee. The pot was almost full when I heard footsteps in the hallway.

"Good morning!" I called out.

The response to my greeting was a loud gasp and the sound of something hitting the wall. I rushed out of the room and saw Mrs. Fairmont leaning against the wall near the foot of the stairs. She was wearing a robe. Her hair was messy and her slippers didn't match.

"Who's there?" she said.

"It's Tami Taylor," I answered in as calm a voice as I could manage. "I spent the night in the basement apartment."

Mrs. Fairmont rubbed her eyes. She was grasping something around her neck. I stepped closer. It was the lifeline device used to summon help if she was in distress.

"Where's Gracie?"

"It's Saturday. Gracie doesn't work on the weekends."

Flip, who was sitting on the floor near Mrs. Fairmont's right foot, ran over to me. I picked him up and he licked my chin. Lapses of memory weren't uncommon for the elderly woman, but this one seemed more serious than others.

"Tami?" Mrs. Fairmont repeated.

"Yes, ma'am. You don't need to push the button to call for help. I'm here."

"Flip likes you."

"Yes, ma'am. Do you have a headache?"

"Yes."

"Do you need to go to the doctor?"

"No." She shook her head vigorously.

I was willing to force a trip to the hospital but decided to watch her closely for a few minutes.

"I've fixed a pot of coffee," I said softly. "You can take your medication and drink a cup. Come into the kitchen and sit down."

Mrs. Fairmont shuffled into the room and sat in a narrow chair at a small table in the corner. Her medications were organized in a daily dispenser. I found the bottle of pain pills and shook one out.

"Take this first," I said, placing it on the table with a cup of water. "It's a pain pill. I'll fix your coffee just the way you like it, easy on the cream with an extra touch of sugar."

Mrs. Fairmont's fingers trembled slightly as she raised the pill and water to her lips. It was a sad scene, especially after our vibrant conversation the previous night. She swallowed the pill. I placed the cup of coffee in front of her. She put both hands around the cup and took a sip.

"That's good," she said with a sigh and closed her eyes. "I heard you downstairs and didn't know what was going on."

"I went out for a run," I answered, then carefully described my route in hope the mention of familiar places would help jump-start her memory. Mrs. Fairmont listened carefully.

"Is the Greenwald house on East Gaston Street still for sale?" she asked.

"Maybe. I saw several Realtor signs. Which house is it?"

Mrs. Fairmont described a wooden, Victorian-style home. "Mrs. Greenwald's aunt was a friend of my mother."

"I'm not sure I remember seeing it."

"I can't criticize you for that," the elderly woman said with a sigh. "My memory betrays me all the time."

Mrs. Fairmont's eyes looked less hazy. She sniffled and blew her nose on a tissue.

"Would you like breakfast?" I asked, placing her regular medicines in front of her. "I could fix an omelet."

"No, thank you. I'll take my medicine then sit in the den and drink this wonderful coffee you made."

I carried the coffee cup as she walked slowly to her favorite chair. Flip dutifully followed and curled up at her feet.

"Are you comfortable?" I asked, placing a small pillow behind her neck.

"Yes, don't let me hold you up. I know you must have big plans for the day."

"Not really. Is your headache going away?"

"What headache?"

I patted her lightly on the shoulder. "Rest while I go downstairs to shower and get dressed for the day."

When I returned forty-five minutes later, Mrs. Fairmont's eyes were closed. I quickly checked to make sure she was breathing. Every time I found the older woman sitting in the chair with her eyes shut, I had a moment's anxiety whether she was alive or dead. Almost imperceptibly, her chest was rising and falling. Her pain pills always made her drowsy.

I lay on a leather couch to read my Bible. Flip joined me, and I let him nestle between my arm and side. Several times during the morning, I took a break to walk around the house for a few minutes. I returned to the couch and picked up my Bible, but nothing I read contained the answer I needed for the job. The words *Braddock*, *Appleby*, *Smith*, and *Feldman* weren't in the Scriptures. The word *Carpenter* appeared a few times, but not in a context that fit my need. Around 11:00 a.m. Mrs. Fairmont stirred and opened her eyes. I offered up another quick prayer for her mental clarity. She rubbed her eyes and looked at me.

"How long have I been asleep?"

"Over three hours."

"It's nice having you in the house again. I rest better when I know you're here. Would you like to live here when you move to Savannah, at least until you find a place of your own?"

My heart leaped that she'd brought up the subject.

"I'd need to discuss it with Mrs. Bartlett."

"Posh," Mrs. Fairmont replied. "Christine doesn't own this house, not yet."

"Maybe we can talk to her together."

"We can talk, but as far as I'm concerned you can plan on moving in downstairs and stay as long as you like."

For lunch I convinced Mrs. Fairmont to share a salad with me. Getting her to eat was a challenge, so I put as much protein in it as I could.

"Could I borrow your car for a couple of hours?" I asked when we finished. "There's someone I want to visit on the other side of town."

"Of course, it needs to be driven."

I left Mrs. Fairmont watching a gourmet cooking show. When I returned, the TV might be tuned to a program hosted by a professional bass-fishing guide. I'd seen the same phenomenon with other older people—their interests widened rather than narrowed, even though the information gleaned would never be put to practical use and might be forgotten within fifteen minutes.

Mrs. Fairmont's car, a large sedan, had less than fifteen thousand miles on the odometer. She kept it in a detached garage. I'd memorized the address where I wanted to go. As I drew closer, my heart beat a little bit faster.

I turned into the parking lot of a one-story brick building with none of the flair of Braddock, Appleby, and Carpenter. The structure could as easily have been in Bangor or Lubbock as Savannah. At one end of the building a simple white sign with black letters announced SMITH LAW OFFICES. Julie's name wouldn't join hers until she passed the bar exam. The building also contained an insurance agency, a two-person CPA firm, and a company that built swimming pools.

There were several cars in the lot. I parked in front of Maggie's office, turned off the engine, and stared at the entrance. I closed my eyes and tried to imagine myself working at the office. I knew what it felt like to walk into the spacious reception area at Braddock, Appleby, and Carpenter. How would it feel to be part of a much smaller, less established, more risky environment? If the firm failed, or the other two women decided after six months I wasn't needed, where would I go? I would have burned my bridges with Zach's firm. As I pondered my decision, Mr. Callahan's wisdom seemed more compelling.

I decided to take a closer look at the office. If my fear increased, I would take it as a sign that working with Maggie and Julie probably wasn't a good idea. I got out of the car and walked to the front door. Putting my hand against the glass to cut down glare, I could see what looked like a reception area. Then, out of the corner of my eye, a figure came into the reception room, turned toward the door, and saw me.

It was Maggie Smith.

Before I could run, Maggie smiled and waved. I weakly waved back. The petite lawyer with short brown hair opened the door.

"Come in," Maggie said in the Southern twang she'd brought from Alabama to Savannah. "Julie and I were talking about you earlier today."

I stepped into an area with two chairs, a love seat, and a coffee table with several magazines strewn across it. Industrial-grade beige carpet covered the floor.

"I was in Savannah for the weekend and decided to see the outside of the office."

"Now you can see the inside, including your office if you decide to join us."

Maggie didn't seem uptight at all. In her early thirties, she had a girlish look that made her appear younger. She was wearing jeans and a loose-fitting sweater.

"You must be busy if you're working on Saturday," I said.

"Not really."

She led me down a short hallway. A door toward the end of the hallway opened, and Julie Feldman emerged. About the same height as Maggie, she had a fuller figure and dark hair.

"Tami!" she cried out.

She ran down the hall and almost knocked me over with a hug. She released me and patted me on the cheek.

"I told Maggie over lunch you were probably sitting in a cave somewhere fasting and praying about what God wanted you to do with the rest of your life. And here you are!"

"Savannah is a better place to pray than a cold cave."

"Totally." Julie nodded. "But you usually like to make everything so hard. How did you get to Savannah? Did you finally get a car?"

"No, Zach picked me up."

Julie tapped herself on the forehead. "Of course. Who needs a car? If Zach had been out of pocket, I bet Vinny would have flown down from Yale to squire you around. Are you staying with Mrs. Fairmont?"

"Yes."

"How is she doing?"

"About the same."

Julie turned to Maggie and began telling her about Mrs. Fairmont's stroke the previous summer.

"And when Tami and Vince Colbert went to the hospital, he quoted half the Bible to Mrs. Fairmont even though she was unconscious. And guess what, she got better by the next morning. I used to put my math book under my pillow when I was a kid, hoping to understand fractions, but unconscious osmosis never worked for me."

"It wasn't half the Bible; it was only a couple of psalms."

"That's a couple more than I know," Julie said. "And my people are the ones who wrote all of them!"

"I was about to show Tami around," Maggie said.

Maggie opened a door to the left.

"This is the clerical area."

It was a small room with two secretarial desks. One was in use, the other empty.

"Maggie and I are going to do a lot of our own word processing," Julie said. "I can type as fast as I talk."

"I doubt it," I answered.

"Don't be so catty. You've seen how quickly I can churn out a memo."

"Shannon Carver is doing triple duty as receptionist, secretary, and bookkeeper," Maggie said. "I met her when I was working in the DA's office."

"She wasn't a defendant in a case Maggie prosecuted," Julie added conspiratorially.

"But I met quite a few people in criminal court who surprised me," Maggie added. "They were ordinary folks who happened to be in the wrong place at the wrong time or made a random stupid mistake."

"That wouldn't happen to Tami," Julie said, pursing her lips. "She'd have to ask directions to get to a wrong place, and she left stupid mistakes behind when she turned thirteen."

Maggie laughed.

Behind the clerical area was Maggie's office, a plain room with a single window and view of the access road next to the building. It contained a wooden desk with computer, a bookcase containing legal treatises, and two side chairs facing the desk. If Julie's father was financing the office, not much of the money was being spent on fancy furniture. Of course, the wisest thing would be to make sure there was enough money in reserve to pay basic overhead costs until the firm began to have a cash flow.

"Come see my office," Julie called out.

Julie was standing in the next doorway on the same side of the hall. Across from Maggie's office I caught a glimpse of a windowless room with a wooden table surrounded by six chairs.

"That's the conference room," Maggie said. "That's where I meet with clients, just like they do at the Braddock firm."

When Maggie was in law school she'd worked as a summer clerk at Braddock, Appleby, and Carpenter, but, as with Julie, she didn't receive a permanent job offer and ended up as an assistant in the district attorney's office.

When I got my first glance at Julie's office, I knew where some of her father's money had ended up. It was identical in size to Maggie's office with the same view through a single window, but that's where the similarity ended. It looked professionally decorated. A stylish wooden desk was surrounded by matching furniture. Paintings hung on the walls. Two richly colored rugs hid much of the plain carpet underneath. A floor lamp and two desk lamps gave the room a warm glow.

"These are original paintings." Julie pointed to a vibrant coastal landscape created with sweeping brushstrokes. "I brought the last piece down with me from Atlanta this morning. You're the first to see it on the wall."

"And you've not passed the bar yet," I blurted out.

"Neither have you," Julie shot back. "I've had fun decorating the office so it will be ready when I do. What do you think I should have done? Put in a table like the one we shared in the library last summer?"

"No, no, you have the right to do what you want."

I glanced at Maggie.

"Julie will probably meet with clients in her office instead of the conference room," she said evenly. "I think it's very tastefully done."

I wondered what Maggie really thought. After all, she was the senior partner in the firm, the person who would initially generate most of the business for both of them. Something didn't seem right about Maggie's spartan work environment compared to Julie's lavish one.

"This is for an associate attorney," Maggie said, opening a door on the same side of the hall as the conference room.

"Which means you," Julie added, tapping me on the shoulder.

It was a windowless interior space, smaller than the secretarial area. A copy machine rested against one wall.

"The copy machine is temporary," Maggie said. "Once the shelves are installed in the workroom at the end of the hall, it will go in there."

"I told Maggie you wouldn't want the distraction of a window," Julie said. "You can focus on one thing at a time, just like a man. Not me. I may be working on a research memo with most of my brain, but in the rear corner of my mind I'm deciding whether I want to go out for drinks tonight at a place on the river or settle for a few glasses of wine at my apartment."

"This is the best we have to offer," Maggie said, resting her hand against the wall. "I shared my first office with an investigator who dipped snuff and spit into a cup he kept in the bottom drawer of his desk."

"They allowed that?" I asked.

Maggie shrugged. "Smoking was prohibited, but Al Houghton was quick to point out that even when he used spicy dip he didn't set his mouth on fire. He was the best investigator we had. Fortunately, he spent most of his time out of the office working cases. I just stayed away from that drawer."

"Don't act so shocked," Julie said. "I'm sure you've been around people like that all your life."

"Not in my family."

"There's no need to worry. Maggie and I are going to make this a nonsmoking, nondipping, non-tobacco-chewing office."

"That's one thing we'll have in common with Braddock, Appleby, and Carpenter," Maggie said with a tight smile. "Let's sit in the conference room for a minute."

The room was bare except for the table, chairs, and a painting on one wall. Maggie flipped on the light. There was a speakerphone in the middle of the table. Maggie sat at one end of the table with Julie and me on opposite sides.

"This is exciting," Julie said. "Our first firm meeting."

"I haven't turned down the offer from Mr. Carpenter," I said.

"But I hope you will," Julie said. "You're going to be an awesome lawyer, and I want to work with you."

I waited for a wisecrack to undo the compliment, but none came.

"Are you in Savannah to talk to Mr. Carpenter?" Maggie asked.

"Not specifically; I came here to pray about the decision. That's what I was doing in the parking lot before I came to the door."

"I knew it—," Julie began, but Maggie cut her off with a look.

"That's personal, and I respect your privacy," Maggie said. "But since you're here, did you have any questions? I tried to cover all the practical stuff in the e-mail I sent."

A week after I returned to school, I received a formal job offer from Maggie and Julie. Like the proposal from Braddock, Appleby, and Carpenter, it was contingent on my passage of the bar exam. Beyond that, there was little similarity: the amount of money involved was significantly less, there was no profit sharing plan, and the health insurance coverage wasn't as comprehensive.

"It was clear."

Maggie spoke. "I know we can't compete with the initial salary and benefits, but here you'll have an opportunity to develop your own business. If you don't want to build your own practice, you should probably take the job at Braddock, Appleby, and Carpenter. They can give you plenty of work. Not everyone has the temperament to be independent."

"Tami is the most independent person I've met in my life," Julie scoffed. "She's so independent it borders on the bizarre."

"And I never have to guess what you're thinking," I responded.

"That's why we're the perfect storm." Julie patted me on the arm.

"Is that a good thing?" Maggie asked.

"It's a bad comparison." Julie scrunched up her nose. "I should have said perfect team. Anyway, Tami and I are the dynamic duo. That's what other lawyers in town will be calling us after we beat them up in court."

"You shouldn't brag until you've done something," Maggie said. "Even then, it's not a good idea. The facts of the case, not the skill of the lawyer, usually dictate the result."

Julie pointed at her chest. "That may be the politically correct thing to say, but the bar hasn't met me."

Being around Julie gave me the answer I needed. I'd developed a tolerance for her abrasiveness during the summer when I had no option but to endure it. But now I had a choice. Working with her and Maggie would submit me to unrelenting verbal torture with no end in sight. This wasn't God's will. I checked my watch.

"I've got to go," I said. "I'm expecting a call."

"Zach?" Julie asked.

I nodded.

"Is he taking you for a ride on his motorcycle?"

"No, it's too cold for that."

As I moved toward the door, Julie launched into a recap of my summer motorcycle adventures.

"Tami is the only woman in America who always wears a dress when she rides a motorcycle."

"I rode in a sidecar."

Julie put her finger to her lips. "Don't say that. It ruins the story."

Maggie held the front door of the office open for me. "Thanks for stopping by."

"Tell Zach I said hi," Julie chimed in. "Give that cute ponytail of his a tug from me."

Maggie stepped outside with me. "I'm glad you're praying about your decision. I should do more of that myself."

As I drove out of the parking lot, I felt sorry for Maggie Smith. If she'd prayed about setting up a practice with Julie, she might not be sitting in a bare-bones office with a legal diva moving in down the hall.

5

"Let's go to Tybee Island," Zach suggested when I called.

"Okay."

"I'll be there in fifteen minutes."

Zach and I had gone to the beach several times during the summer, but I'd never put my toe in the water. I owned a one-piece bathing suit; however, I never wore it when men were present. Our church organized swim trips during the summer. Girls and boys were kept strictly segregated.

Zach's car rumbled over the cobblestones as we left Mrs. Fairmont's house. I glanced out the window as we came to a stop at an intersection. I felt a lot of relief that I'd made up my mind about the job. I wanted to tell Zach, but it didn't feel right. Not yet.

Crossing the bridge to Tybee Island, we had a nice view of a coastal waterway that meandered through the landward side of a large marsh. The tops of the marsh grass rippled slightly in the breeze. A few white egrets swooped low over the water. The tide was going out, exposing mussel beds at the edges of the watery channels. Expensive homes lined the edge of the marsh on both the island and the mainland.

Zach parked in front of a rambling store that sold beach items. It had warmed up during the day, and I left my jacket in the car. Zach was wearing a long-sleeved shirt and jeans.

"Let's walk on the sand," he said.

We stepped onto the beach south of the pavilion that had been busy during the summer. It was largely deserted today. Zach kicked off his shoes and stuck his socks in his pocket. I slipped off my shoes and held them in my hand. The sand above the tide line was cool and dry. Pieces of shattered shells lay strewn about.

"Why aren't there any whole shells?" I asked.

"They're beaten up beyond the surf. Early in the morning, it's possible to find a few nice ones when the tide comes in. Let's see what the water feels like."

Zach rolled his jeans up above his knees and turned toward the ocean. He had the well-developed calf muscles of a former soccer player.

There was a breeze blowing off the water. I'd not brought a hat and my hair splayed out behind me like an untamed bridal train. I followed in Zach's steps. My footprints fit easily within his. He reached the water and kept going until he was knee-deep. I stopped at the edge. The next wave came farther up the beach and washed over my feet. The water was cold.

"This is as far as I go," I said, stepping back.

"You should feel the Pacific," Zach said as he jumped higher to avoid a wave. "This is like bathwater."

Zach waded out of the water with a huge smile on his face. "When are you going to visit California with me?" he asked. "During Christmas break would be perfect. My parents would love to meet you, and my sister will be home from Africa."

"What?" My mouth dropped open

"Do you want me to repeat it slowly?" Zach answered with a smile.

"No, I heard you. I mean, I'm not saying no, it's just the idea that I would go to California."

"It's a four-hour plane ride. I'd like to buy the tickets as soon as possible so I can look for a good discount."

"I've never flown in a plane."

"It's a bus with wings," Zach said with a straight face. "My mother was excited when I mentioned it to her. I guess she's been worrying I'd never find someone I like enough to bring home." He paused. "Truth is I hadn't, until now."

Although I was standing still, I felt slightly breathless.

"I'd need to ask my parents."

"Sure, that's why I brought it up. But please do it soon. If I'm going to get any kind of deal on plane tickets, I need to book the flight as soon as possible."

My mind was spinning at the thought of traveling across the country. We didn't talk as we continued walking toward the south end of the island where Tybee Creek emptied into the Atlantic. We were completely alone when we reached the tip of the island.

"Would you be able to swim across?" Zach pointed to the shore of Little Tybee Island.

"Maybe, but I'm a much better runner than swimmer."

"Last summer, Julie said you claimed to be able to walk on water."

"She told you that?"

"Yeah, but she said it with a smile on her face."

I dug my toes into the sand at my feet.

"I saw Julie and Maggie this afternoon."

Zach turned toward me. "You went by their office?"

"Yes. I didn't know they would be there."

"What's it like?"

I told him about it and concluded by saying, "The spot they have for me isn't nearly as nice as the office the firm has available for me down the hall from you. It doesn't even have a window."

I dug my toes a little deeper into the sand, but as soon as I popped them up, the sand gave way.

"Did seeing them and their office help you make up your mind?" Zach asked after a few moments of silence.

"Yes. Working for Maggie and Julie would be a lot like building a house directly on this sand." I paused. "And we both know what the Bible says about that." The wind shifted and I brushed my hair away from my face. "It was a big relief. I didn't say anything to Maggie. I'll send her an e-mail later in the week."

"Do you want to go by the office and see if Mr. Carpenter is there? It would be great to tell him in person."

It was a much easier decision than whether to fly to California.

"Yes," I said. "It would be nice to talk to him in person. But if he's not there, I can call him later this week."

We retraced our steps. I held my hands behind my back while we walked. Zach was intent on finding an unbroken seashell larger than a fingernail.

"Here's a decent one," he called out from where he stood ankle-deep in the surf.

He brought the shell over and placed it in my hand. It was a nice semicircle with ridges that mimicked the waves. Underneath, it was smooth with a beautiful purple color along the edge.

"It's pretty. What kind is it?"

"A clam. They have tougher shells than most, except for oysters, of course."

"Mama never taught us about seashells."

"You have a few things left to learn in life," Zach answered with a smile. "That part of your education will be one of the jobs the firm won't have to pay me for."

We returned to his car.

"Should we go by Mrs. Fairmount's house so I can change into nicer clothes?" I asked as I brushed the sand from my feet before getting into the car.

"No, you look fine. If Mr. Carpenter is at the office, he'll be wearing casual clothes."

A combination of excitement, anticipation, and nervousness built inside me as Zach drove us back to Savannah. I silently rehearsed my speech, particularly the part about making clear that I wouldn't be forced to work on cases that violated my conscience and convictions.

"What chance is there he'll be there?" I asked at one point.

"I'm not sure. He's not required to get my approval of his work schedule."

I punched Zach in the arm.

"Hey, that hurt. Did you get that left jab from your mother?"

"No, that comes from having two brothers." I paused. "And the need to get rid of a little bit of anxiety."

We reached the office. A prominent white sign in front of a two-story structure announced Braddock, Appleby, and Carpenter— Attorneys at Law. The main entrance was guarded by a set of small stone lions. Everything about the place spoke of prosperity and attention to detail. I'd been afraid the first time I entered the building. That fear was born of the unknown. The nervousness I felt today came from the momentousness of the decision. I quickly scanned the cars in the parking lot.

"Mr. Carpenter's car isn't here," I said with a sigh of relief.

"Yes, it is," Zach replied, turning into the parking lot and pulling next to a shiny black Mercedes. "He bought a new one."

I flipped down the car visor and inspected my hair in the tiny mirror.

"I look like I stuck my head in a clothes dryer."

"Tami, you look great. Don't be vain. It's a sin."

I raised my fist to punch him again, but Zach held up his hand.

"And don't give in to anger. Sorry. I was uptight when I met with Mr. Appleby to accept the job. I'll be good if I can take you out to dinner to celebrate after you talk to Mr. Carpenter."

"Okay."

We walked past the lions and through the front door into a spacious lobby with a two-story ceiling. The floors were covered in dark wood, and a curving staircase led to the second floor. Oriental rugs and ornate furniture were arranged throughout the area. It oozed prosperity.

"I'll find him and let him know you're here," Zach said.

"If he's too busy, it's okay. I can—"

Zach held up his hand. "Just let me check."

He left me in the lobby. There was a much broader selection of magazines available than at Maggie and Julie's office. The firm included publications that might interest clients who actually had money to pay for a lawyer. I paced back and forth. After a couple of minutes, Zach returned. Mr. Carpenter was beside him. The tall lawyer with gray hair and well-trimmed goatee was wearing a golf shirt and khaki slacks.

"Tami!" he exclaimed. "What a pleasant surprise."

He quickly came over to me and shook my hand.

"Good to see you, Mr. Carpenter."

"I hope you're having a pleasant weekend in Savannah," he replied. "This place gets in your blood and draws you back."

"Yes, sir. Zach was kind enough to pick me up in Athens and bring me. I'm staying with Margaret Fairmont."

"How's she doing?" Mr. Carpenter asked, then continued without waiting for an answer by saying, "Come to my office so we can chat."

I looked at Zach, who pointed up the staircase toward his office on the second floor.

"I'll be upstairs," he said. "Come see me when you finish."

"I won't keep her from you too long," Mr. Carpenter replied smoothly.

The principal partners in the firm had offices on the first floor. Mr. Carpenter led me down a hall covered in a thick carpet and through his private reception area, then held open the door to his office. The litigator liked boats. The walls were covered with pictures of yachts.

The one in the picture that hung over his credenza belonged to him. Mr. Carpenter sat behind a large desk with a leather inlaid top and motioned for me to sit across from him.

"How's your family?"

"Fine," I responded, not remembering a time Mr. Carpenter had previously asked about my family. "I saw them last weekend. I also went by to see Oscar Callahan."

"Oscar's a fine lawyer." Mr. Carpenter nodded. "I always thought his talent was wasted up in the mountains, but he liked to play the gentleman farmer role. To each his own."

"Yes, sir. You like Savannah; he loves the mountains."

Mr. Carpenter put his fingers together in front of his face. "But the important question is whether you like Savannah, isn't it?"

"Oh, yes, sir. I like Savannah. And I want to come to work here."

It wasn't the way I had intended to give my acceptance of the job, but the words were out of my mouth before I could edit them.

"Splendid." Mr. Carpenter clapped his hands together so sharply that it made me jump. "You and Vince Colbert make the best pair of young lawyers who've joined the firm in years, maybe ever."

"Thank you. It's very kind of you to say that."

"And I'm sure you'll prove me right." Mr. Carpenter glanced down at a legal pad on his desk. "Well, I don't want to interrupt too much of your weekend fun. Ms. Patrick will be in touch with you about your schedule upon graduation. Of course, we'll allow ample time for you to prepare for the bar exam and won't expect you to start until after the test."

Mr. Carpenter stood. I remained seated.

"Is there anything else?" he asked.

"Uh, I want to make sure that I work on cases that I think are just, the kind that I can put my heart into without compromising my ethical beliefs."

GREATER LOVE 65

Mr. Carpenter stared down at me with a slightly puzzled expression.

"No lawyer who's worked here has ever been reprimanded or sanctioned by the state bar for an ethics violation. If an ethical issue comes up, we'll go to the rules and find the answer. I might even ask you to develop extra expertise in that area so you can be the firm's de facto ethics expert." Mr. Carpenter paused. "Yes, that would be a very helpful niche. We all get rusty over time about some of the nuances of the rules and opinions."

"Yes, sir, but I was thinking more broadly than that—"

Mr. Carpenter dismissed my comment with a wave of his hand. "Don't jump ahead to hypothetical problems. The practical issues that come up in real cases will provide enough stimulation."

Mr. Carpenter looked at his watch. "I'm so glad you could stop by and give me this good news in person. The reason I came to the office today was to participate in a conference call that's scheduled in a few minutes, and I have to get ready. We'll have plenty of time to talk ethics once you're here on a permanent basis. See you in a few months. You're going to be a great addition to our litigation team."

"Yes, sir."

Mr. Carpenter went to the door and held it open for me. There was nothing else I could do now but leave. I backed out of the office. He shut the door behind me.

I returned to the lobby and trudged up the stairs and down the hall to Zach's office. He was on an Internet sports site.

"That was quick," he said when he saw me standing in the doorway.

"Mr. Carpenter had to prepare for a conference call."

"How did he take the news?"

"Oh, he's glad I'm going to be part of the litigation team. And he may turn me into the firm's ethics expert."

"Ethic's expert?"

"You know, the lawyer who knows all the ins and outs of the disciplinary rules and advisory opinions. If you have an ethics problem, send Tami a memo, and she'll tell you what to do."

Zach pulled his ponytail. "How did that happen?"

"When I was trying to get his commitment not to ask me to work on a case if I believed it violated my ethical convictions."

"And he knew what you meant."

I nodded. "Anyway, I accepted the job. I guess I'll have to work out any problems as they come up."

"That's the way it is in law practice. You can't anticipate every scenario. And there's still reason to celebrate." Zach stood up. "Do you want to go to that French restaurant on Greene Street?"

"Sure. Vince took me there one time. It's very nice."

We had a wonderful meal. The unhurried pace helped me calm down. And Zach made no attempt to hide his excitement that I'd decided to work at the firm. He talked about the future with as much animation as I'd ever seen in him.

"You'll have a generous budget to decorate your office," he said as we finished the main course. "It makes sense considering how much time you'll be expected to be there."

I told him about the contrast between Maggie's and Julie's offices.

"That's a recipe for resentment," he said.

The waiter arrived and we ordered dessert. After the meal he drove me the few blocks to Mrs. Fairmont's house.

"Do you think you'll live here when you come back?" he asked as he pulled alongside the curb.

"Mrs. Fairmont brought it up last night. I'd love to start out here."

"It makes sense." Zach turned off the car's motor. "Are you going to Sister Dabney's church in the morning?"

"Yes. Do you want to go with me?"

"No, thanks. I'm helping with the middle school kids' class at my church in the morning."

"That sounds more intimidating than Sister Dabney."

"It's not too bad."

"Thanks again for being with me today," I said. "What time do you want to leave for Athens?"

"I want you to stay here."

It was such a sweet comment that I didn't know what to say. I looked across at Zach. He put his hand on mine. I didn't pull away.

"Good night," he said.

"Good night."

Inside, I found Mrs. Fairmont dozing in her chair in the den with a college football game on TV. I touched her on the shoulder. She opened her eyes.

"Did you have a nice time with Vince?" she asked, blinking her eyes.

"I was with Zach. We drove to Tybee Island and walked on the beach. Then I went by the office and accepted the job at Braddock, Appleby, and Carpenter."

"That's nice. But it's too cool to go to the ocean."

"The sun warmed up nicely, and we walked all the way to the south tip of the island. We had the beach to ourselves. Later, we ate dinner at the French restaurant on Greene Street."

Mrs. Fairmont stared at me for a second. "Tami, you look like a woman in love."

I wished for a mirror so I could know what that looked like. I felt myself blush. I decided to change the subject.

"Would you like a cup of hot tea before going to bed?" I asked.

THE FOLLOWING MORNING, MRS. BARTLETT SURPRISED ME BY CALL-ing the house shortly after Mrs. Fairmont came downstairs.

"Make sure Mother is ready by ten thirty," she said. "Ken and I will be by to pick her up."

"Ready for what?"

"Didn't she tell you? Ever since this summer she's been insisting we go to Sunday morning services. Half the time I'm not sure she stays awake through the sermon, but she seems to enjoy the choir. It's a hassle to fit into my schedule, but she's nagged me about it so much that it's easier to go along than try to get out of it. Something came up, and our friends had to cancel our planned trip to West Palm Beach this weekend, but she knows there won't be any church for her next Sunday unless she can get someone else to take her. I have a trip planned to do some early Christmas shopping in Atlanta. A close friend and I have booked a couple of nights at a new hotel and spa in Buckhead. They've got a staff of Swedish masseuses"—Mrs. Bartlett paused—"is that how you say the plural of masseuse?"

"I'm not sure."

"Will you be joining us?"

"No, ma'am," I said in shock. "I've got to go back to school."

"You're leaving this morning? I thought you'd spend most of the day in Savannah. Mother would like having you with her in the pew."

I realized my mistake and laughed.

"I'm going to a church I attended a few times when I was here last summer."

"The one with the woman minister located in the poorer section of town?"

I was surprised Mrs. Bartlett remembered Sister Dabney and the Southside Church.

"Yes, ma'am."

"Are you driving Mother's car?"

"Yes, if it's okay with you."

"All right, but make sure you lock it. It may be Sunday morning, but I don't trust that neighborhood. Did you know they've had to hire private security guards to watch the parking lot at Mother's church? And it's not in the middle of a ghetto. Thieves have figured out that cars at churches will be unattended for at least an hour."

"Or longer, if the service doesn't end at noon."

"That would be a nightmare. At least Reverend Harwell knows how to tell time. He ends the service on the dot. Where is Mother now? Has she come downstairs?"

"Yes, ma'am. She's drinking a cup of coffee in the den."

"Don't let her dillydally or fall asleep in her chair. I want her dressed and ready to go when we get there."

Mrs. Bartlett ended the call. I went into the den. Mrs. Fairmont was sipping her coffee and watching a religious show on TV.

"Mrs. Bartlett says she's going to take you to church this morning."

"She has it backward," the older woman answered, turning down the volume. "I'm the one who's been taking Christine and Ken. He's started listening to the sermons. Christine fidgets worse than she did when she was a little girl. I started back, thanks to you and the young man who came with you to the hospital to pray for me—"

"Vince."

"That's right. If you get a third boyfriend, I'm really going to get confused."

"Vince isn't a boyfriend. It's Zach and I that are courting."

Mrs. Fairmont smiled. "Isn't it amazing how terms come back in fashion? I never would have guessed that one would recycle. Hemlines go up and down, only now when they go up I'm not sure they know when to stop. I guess it's the same with words. Your clothes have a classic look."

My wardrobe had been called old-fashioned, dowdy, dull, and a lot of even less-complimentary terms. *Classic* was a new one.

"Thank you. It's about modesty and neatness."

"Two other words some people want taken out of the dictionary. What time is Christine going to be here?"

"She wants you ready by ten thirty. I'll have to leave before that to make it to Sister Dabney's church."

"Who?"

"The lady with the rocking chairs on her porch."

"Oh, yes." Mrs. Fairmont nodded her head. "Those chairs reminded me of the ones in front of my aunt Abigail's house in Vernonburg. Maybe we can all go to her church one Sunday."

"Mrs. Bartlett would find that more unique than a trip to a Swedish spa." I laughed.

I put on a loose-fitting dress. A light swipe of lipstick added a hint of color to my lips. Sister Dabney wore her hair in a bun, but her congregation was a polyglot group of poor people. I brushed out my hair and let it cascade down my back. Mrs. Fairmont was dressed and ready before I left.

"Have a good time," she said when I left her in the den.

Sister Dabney's church was a long, white, single-story building with a crooked wooden cross in front and a hand-painted sign that read: Southside Church—R. Dabney, Overseer. Next to the church was Sister Dabney's home, a small brick house with low shrubs in front. There were about twenty cars in the parking lot. Some of the people who attended the church walked to the service.

Inside, bare bulbs illuminated cement-block walls painted a pale yellow. Rows of simple wooden pews stretched from the rear to the front platform. A thin gray carpet covered the floor. The music service had already started. A skinny woman was playing the piano, and the sound of enthusiastic voices reverberated off the block walls. The sanctuary could hold more than two hundred people, but only about eighty or ninety were present. Every color of skin was represented.

On the platform stood a rickety podium with a purple rocker behind it. Sister Dabney, an obese woman with gray hair wrapped in a bun and wearing a dark blue dress, was sitting in the rocker with her eyes closed. She wasn't singing but held her right hand high in the air. I slipped into one of the rear pews and opened a hymnbook. The song was familiar, and I quickly found it. Sister Dabney's hand shook and several of the people in the congregation cried out as the power touched them. I felt nothing.

The pianist began another song I recognized as the church anthem, an exuberant melody similar to some of the older songs we sang at my home church in Powell Station. My grandmother would have enjoyed it. The message of the lyrics was simple—the sinner's desperate need and the Savior's sufficient grace. Sister Dabney stood and began to shuffle around the platform. I'd not seen this before and wasn't prepared for the congregation's reaction. Most of the people rushed to the aisle and began dancing toward the front. Those able to do so jumped in the air. Even the older members bobbed and weaved. I didn't move an inch. We had lively worship at my church, but dancing, of any kind, was off-limits. I was glad Zach hadn't been able to come.

The dancing lasted for several uncomfortable minutes until the pianist played a more worshipful song. Sister Dabney sat down and continued rocking. The congregation returned to their seats. After the music stopped, the people transitioned into the prayer service without any prompting from the front. Everyone prayed out loud at once. This, too, was different from Sunday morning meetings at my home church; however, I'd been to informal prayer services where a similar pattern was followed. I joined in, thanking God for his recent direction for the future and praying that he would bless the unknown twists and turns of the path ahead. Then, as if on cue, the room grew quiet. My heart beat faster.

"Does anybody want to hear the word of the Lord?" Sister Dabney called out in an accent forged in the Appalachians.

A smattering of "Yes, Lord," responses could be heard across the room.

Virtually the entire congregation streamed back to the front of the room. As I joined the group, I wondered what was happening at Mrs. Fairmont's church. It was probably about time to pass the offering plates.

When I reached the front Sister Dabney saw me. A slight smile creased the corners of her mouth. I smiled back, relieved that I didn't have to worry about public exposure of any secret sin or open rebellion. Sister Dabney directed her attention to another area of the room and spoke to a woman about to be evicted from her apartment. The woman had never been to the church. After praying for her, Sister Dabney ordered the woman to stand in front of the platform and receive an offering directly from the congregation. People came forward and pressed small amounts of money in the woman's hand while she wept in gratitude. I grabbed most of the bills from my purse and without counting them, gave the money to her.

Sister Dabney then pointed to a young man who'd remained sitting in a pew. In a loud voice she started naming the sins in his life.

"Stop!" the man cried out as he scrambled out and made his way to the altar.

A male member of the congregation knelt down and prayed with him. The young man's back shook as he sobbed.

"Tami!"

Startled, my head jerked up. Sister Dabney was staring at me, her eyes flashing.

"See me after the meeting," she said, then turned her attention to someone else.

"Yes, ma'am," I managed in a weak voice.

I stumbled back to my seat. The rest of the service was a blur. I seriously considered simply leaving the building, but a mixture of curiosity and holy fear kept me glued to the pew. With Sister Dabney, it wouldn't be enough to politely listen. The preacher's words demanded a response. Accept or reject. Admit or deny. To corral my racing thoughts, I tried to pay attention to the sermon. Sister Dabney was preaching on the parable of the mustard seed from Matthew 13.

"The kingdom of heaven may start out small in your spirit," she said, holding her fingers together, "but once it takes root in your heart, God's will becomes big! Grow where God plants you! Reach out to those in need. Freely you've received, freely give. Who dares reject his purpose? Who shrinks back to destruction? Who treats salvation as cheaply purchased?"

A few people shouted, "Amen."

"Don't say that unless you mean it!" she thundered.

The room was completely silent. I was taking shallow breaths. Sister Dabney took something from the pulpit and held it up.

"This is a packet of mustard seeds," she said.

Tearing open the envelope, she reached in it and then held up her hand.

"Can anyone see this seed?"

No one responded.

"So it is with you. The people of this world will not see the seed of God planted in your heart, but they won't be able to deny the fruit when the plant grows to maturity. Cultivate that seed, and it will become a shelter and source of help for many."

As the service ended my nervousness increased. Several people went forward to request prayer. I watched and waited. Sister Dabney didn't seem to be in a hurry. When the last person turned away, I expected her to summon me forward. Instead, she walked slowly toward me.

"Come over to the house," she said.

During the service Sister Dabney was so animated that it was odd seeing the difficulty she had walking. When we left through the building, she didn't stop to lock the door.

"We have nothing worth stealing," she said, answering my unspoken question. "And if someone did, the Lord would chase them down. Everything in the church has been marked as heaven's property."

"The same as the land," I said.

"You have a good memory."

We made the short walk across slightly uneven ground. Sister Dabney didn't seem upset with me and my anxiety lessened.

"Does your family raise chickens?" she asked.

"Yes, ma'am."

"Once a chicken hatches can it go back into the egg?"

"No, ma'am."

I waited for the theological implications of her observation, but she didn't add anything else. We reached the house. A blue rocker rested on the porch. It was the one Mrs. Fairmont sat in when we'd visited Sister Dabney.

"Bring that rocker inside."

Sister Dabney held the front door open while I carried the wooden rocker inside. The living room was rectangular with an old red rug on the floor, a yellow rocker in one corner, and a red one in the other. Unlike Mrs. Fairmont's home, it wasn't suitable to appear in a home-decorating magazine.

"Put it beside that other one," she said, pointing to an open spot to the left of the yellow rocker. "Then sit in the yellow one."

"Why are the rockers different colors?"

"All you need to know about is the one you're sitting in. God is about to shine light into your darkness."

I glanced at the yellow arms of the rocker. Sister Dabney sat in the blue rocker and closed her eyes. My nervousness returned. I was sitting in a strange house with a stranger woman. Because Sister Dabney might be able to read my thoughts I frantically tried to think about something I wouldn't mind her seeing. I quickly settled on reading the Bible in my apartment at school.

"A word for you has been building in my spirit since we met last summer." Sister Dabney opened her eyes. "But you wanted me to wait before telling you."

"Yes, that's what I told you the day of your deposition at the law office."

"Which was your day to speak to me. Now, it's my turn."

"Yes, ma'am."

"Do you know about the threefold cord?"

"From Ecclesiastes?"

Sister Dabney nodded. "A threefold cord is not quickly broken. Do you believe that?"

"Yes."

"It's a powerful verse about marriage. A man, a woman, and Jesus come together in beautiful unity." Sister Dabney paused.

Now I knew where she was heading. I liked Zach a lot but wasn't sure if we should get married. Vince, or perhaps a man I'd not yet met, lingered in the realm of possibility for a life mate. That was my darkness. God could certainly use an intermediary like Sister Dabney to reveal his will, but on an issue like marriage, I wanted to receive revelation directly. I steeled myself to hear what was about to be spoken.

"The verse has other meanings," she continued. "God is joining you with two other women to accomplish his purposes. Together, the three of you will be much stronger than you would be individually. You will create a threefold cord that will not be quickly broken. Does this make sense to you?"

I nodded weakly. Sister Dabney closed her eyes for a few seconds and rocked before opening them to continue.

"The life of faith requires risk. Without risk there is little chance of reward. Do not allow yourself to be caged in a place that seems safe. You have the heart of a lioness. A female lion knows how to take care of cubs. That's all for now."

I wasn't sure what she meant by the lioness and her cubs, but the rest of the message left no room for interpretation.

"If what you're saying is true, I'm in trouble," I began.

"If it's true!" Sister Dabney's voice burst forth in preaching volume. "Do you think I speak lightly?"

"No, ma'am," I managed.

She pointed her finger at me. "Beware of going your own way! God wants to lead you. Will you follow?"

6

JESSIE SAT IN THE BED OF THE PICKUP TRUCK WITH HER SCARRED and dirty legs dangling over the end of the tailgate. The men had moved the truck several times since finding her. At each stop, they scattered into the pine thicket with chain saws and cut smaller trees that were sapping nutrients from the clay soil.

Having eaten real food and drunk fresh water, Jessie was content. The men left her alone while they worked, and she could have run away. But she saw no reason to strike off on her own through the woods. By now the railroad tracks were far away, and she would quickly get lost in the woods, especially since she didn't know the way to go in the first place. The men hadn't shown any interest in the leather pouch stuck in the front of her jeans.

The sound of the chain saws in the distance resembled a thousand angry bees. When Jessie and her stepmother lived in a mobile home near Valdosta, there had been a hornet's nest in a tree in the backyard. Jessie enjoyed watching the fierce insects come and go from their gray paper house.

One day a man came by to buy bootleg whiskey from the man living with Jessie's stepmother. After taking a few gulps of white lightning, the man got a shotgun from his truck and fired a shell that ripped a gaping hole in the nest. The hornets swarmed out in an angry army and swooped to the ground. Jessie was stung twice in the right leg as she ran back to the mobile home. The man who shot the nest and her stepmother's boyfriend weren't as fast on their feet. They were stung a bunch of times. Before the sun set, the men's eyes were swollen shut. They looked funny, but Jessie was afraid to laugh at them.

Watching the friendly interaction of the men on the crew made Jessie wish she could speak Spanish. None of the jokes or teasing seemed directed at her. The men treated her with casual kindness. Every time the man in charge returned to the truck he offered her water to drink. Another man gave her half an apple to eat.

The sun began to sink in the sky. The men returned to the truck and stowed the equipment in a metal storage box. The boss man offered to let Jessie sit in the cab, but she shook her head and pointed to the back of the truck. She climbed in and sat next to the man who'd given her the beans and wieners. The truck bounced as it went faster over the dirt roads. One particular jolt sent those sitting in the truck bed airborne for a split second. The men laughed like kids on a ride at the fair. The dirt road ended, and the truck turned left onto a two-lane asphalt road. The man next to Jessie closed his eyes, and in a few minutes his head bobbed against his chest. A man across from him pointed and smiled. Jessie closed her eyes, too, but only to savor the rush of the wind against her cheeks.

Miles passed. Jessie thought about her stepmother, who would be more afraid about Jessie's disappearance than worried. Three times in the past year and a half, a black woman from the Department of Family and Children Services had come to the house. Jessie over-heard the woman threaten to take Jessie away and place her in foster care. Each time, her stepmother promised to do better. Because Jessie lived in the house, her stepmother received money every month from the government. Jessie wasn't sure how much she got, but there was often a party when the check arrived.

It was dusk when the truck reached the outskirts of Savannah. Nothing looked familiar to Jessie. The men stopped at a convenience store. Jessie went inside to use the restroom. When she came out, the leader of the men was standing beside the truck.

"Sú casa?" he asked.

Jessie had no idea what he meant. The man made a sign as if sleeping and pointed down the street. Jessie glanced up and saw a street sign that read Oglethorpe Avenue.

"Sí, sí," she said.

Getting back in the truck, they turned onto Oglethorpe Avenue. When they reached the bus station, Jessie tapped on the window glass. The driver stopped the truck, and she hopped over the edge onto the sidewalk. The boss said something to her in Spanish. She smiled and nodded. The driver started forward, but the boss, with a puzzled look on his face, signaled for him to wait.

Jessie turned and ran away into the gathering dark.

MRS. FAIRMONT HUGGED ME, THEN HELD MY RIGHT HAND IN A bony grip when it came time for me to leave. Flip circled our feet. Zach took my suitcase to the car. I'd spent two hours in personal agony following my encounter with Sister Dabney but hid it from Mrs. Fairmont.

"Call me when you get back to school," Mrs. Fairmont said. Peering around my shoulder, she added, "Is he a good driver? I suppose anyone who can ride a motorcycle can drive a car."

"Yes, ma'am."

"And do I have your address so I can send you a Christmas card? I haven't sent cards in years, but this has been such a special year for me, I want to let my friends know about it."

"Mrs. Bartlett told me about that. I wrote both my addresses in the book you keep by the phone."

Zach returned to the foyer. I leaned over and kissed Mrs. Fairmont on the cheek.

"I have to go now. I love you."

"I love you," she replied, giving my hand a final squeeze.

I leaned over and patted Flip on the head.

"I love you, too," I said to the little dog.

I followed Zach out of the house.

"Do you love me?" he asked when we reached the sidewalk.

"What?"

"It seems those words are rolling off your lips fairly easily at the moment. It seems like a good time to ask."

"Of course I love you," I answered, glad for a lighter moment. "The Bible commands us to love our enemies, our neighbors, everybody."

Zach held the door open for me. "That's not exactly what I had in mind."

Not sure when or if I should tell Zach what Sister Dabney had said to me, I stalled by asking him questions about his church until we'd cleared the outskirts of Savannah.

"How was your time with the middle schoolers?"

"Not bad. At one point, three of the boys listened to me for at least ninety seconds before they continued poking one another in the ribs."

After pumping all the information I could from him about the Sunday school class, I asked him about the sermon.

"Enough about my day," Zach said after giving me a detailed outline of the minister's message. "Charlie's a good speaker, but he can't compare to Sister Dabney when it comes to oratorical fireworks. What did she talk about?"

I took a long time to describe everything that happened, leaving out the part where she ordered me to stay and see her after the service.

"I should go back to the church sometime," Zach said when I finished.

"Why? I thought you didn't like it."

"I don't doubt Sister Dabney is doing some good. It just comes wrapped in such a bizarre package. I'd like to give some money to the woman who needed rent money."

"Mail a check to the church with a note attached."

He nodded. "I'll do that. Did you have any one-on-one time with Sister Dabney?"

I sighed. "Do I have to answer that question?"

Zach glanced at me. "Absolutely."

"Why is it impossible for me to have secrets from you?"

My question brought a self-satisfied smile to his face. "It's covered in the book about men and women. All a man has to do is ask enough questions, shut up, and a woman will reveal her innermost thoughts."

"You were asking me questions like that before you read the book."

"And now I'm more dangerous. What did she say to you?"

I'd written it all down as soon as I got back to Mrs. Fairmont's house. Taking out my notes, I read them to him without looking up to see his reaction. When I finished, I could see from the side that his face was serious, his jaw set.

"What do you think?" I asked, then braced for his reaction.

"What do *you* think?" he responded.

"It's crystal clear. I've made a terrible mistake. I shouldn't have accepted the job at the firm because I'm supposed to work with Maggie and Julie. What else could it mean?"

Zach shook his head. "Dabney could be referring to two other women, possibly people you haven't met yet."

"That's speculation."

"Who's speculating the most?"

I bit my lip. "I don't want to make you mad. I'm trying to obey God the best I can."

Zach flipped on the car's blinker and changed lanes to pass a slow-moving truck.

"Think about it. You've already told Mr. Carpenter that you accepted the job. How is that going to look to him if you renege on your commitment? Talk about ethical issues."

"That's not fair."

"But it's the truth. Christians are supposed to keep their promises."

"I know it won't look good. But I haven't signed any paperwork—"

"That sounds like a lawyer!" Zach exploded.

I lowered my head. "All I can do is tell him I made a mistake and apologize."

Zach was silent for a moment.

"Did you call your parents and tell them about this yet?" he asked in a calmer tone of voice.

"No."

Zach pulled his ponytail. "What Sister Dabney told you may not have anything to do with work. It could relate to some type of ministry. Didn't she say it had to do with God's purposes?"

"I want my legal work to be part of God's purposes."

"Is that what Julie Feldman and Maggie Smith want?"

"No," I admitted.

"I know you respect Dabney's insight, but you can't make a major decision like this based on something she said to you." His voice got louder again. "God gave you a brain and a Bible. Use them!"

I felt my face turn red.

"And he sends people into our lives to help us find the way," I said, my voice trembling. "Sister Dabney is one of those people. I just know that I have to seriously consider what she told me even if it's tough."

Zach's grip on the steering wheel tightened.

"What about me?" he asked.

"You're also a person God has sent into my life to help me find my way." I paused as tears came into my eyes. "And I care very much about you and your opinion."

Zach shot a glance in my direction. I saw his hands relax on the steering wheel.

"It's no secret that I believe the best place for you to be is at Braddock, Appleby, and Carpenter. There are tons of practical reasons and at least a few very important personal ones. I want to see you every day so we can get to know each other better." He paused. "And Julie won't be there to harass you."

I wiped my eyes. "I'm just confused. I thought everything would be clear after coming to Savannah, but in some ways it's worse than ever."

"Talk to your parents," Zach replied. "I know they'll have a big influence on your decision. But don't forget about me."

We didn't talk a lot more on the return trip. My cool, analytical mind was a jumbled mess. Zach parked in front of my apartment.

"Thanks for the ride," I said. "I'm sorry you have to turn around and drive back."

"I was glad to do it. Are you going to talk to your parents about flying out to California with me for the holidays?"

"You still want me to come?"

"Yes. I'm not mad at you. I just disagree with what you're considering. I have feelings about your decision because I care."

"And I'm glad you do."

Zach carried my suitcase to the door. When he put it down I reached to pick it up and our hands touched. The brief contact caused an inner ache. Inside my apartment, I plopped down in a chair then immediately got up so I could pull back the curtain a few inches and watch Zach leave the parking lot. As soon as his car was gone, I returned to the chair and stared across the room as a tornado of emotions swirled around inside me.

AFTER UNPACKING AND SPENDING SOME TIME PRAYING, I CALLED Daddy and Mama to tell them about my trip.

"What's wrong?" Mama asked after I'd spoken only a few sentences.

I immediately started to cry. The next few moments became a jerky attempt, interrupted by sobs, at explaining what had happened and what I'd done.

At one point, Daddy interrupted. "Do you want me to come to Athens and bring you home? If you do, I'll be on the road in fifteen minutes."

Daddy's offer made me cry harder.

"Give her a minute, Walter," Mama said. "She's getting rid of the tension bottled up inside."

"Yes, ma'am," I managed. "I'll be better in a minute."

Finally, I was able to take a few deep breaths and begin again with a more organized, chronological account of the weekend.

When I told them that I'd accepted the job with Braddock, Appleby, and Carpenter, Mama interrupted.

"How did the Lord direct you to accept the job? Did I miss that part?"

"I'm not sure he did. It was more a reaction to the negative aspects of the job with Maggie and Julie and the positive things about the firm that Mr. Callahan mentioned. Of course, the chance to spend more time with Zach also influenced me. But the real problems came when I went to church on Sunday."

I didn't mention much about the service but went directly to my conversation with Sister Dabney at her house.

"I hate the thought of breaking my word to Mr. Carpenter," I said, "but I believe I have to consider what Sister Dabney told me."

"Does Zach know about this?" Daddy asked.

"Everything. He's upset that I'm considering what Sister Dabney told me."

"And his vision is clouded by his feelings for you," Mama added.

"Not just his. Mine is, too," I said. "It hurts like crazy to know he's upset with me."

Neither Daddy nor Mama spoke for a few moments.

"Let's all pray about it and talk again on Wednesday," Mama said.

It seemed like a long time to hang in limbo.

"Okay," I sighed. "I'm trying to act grown up, but right now I wish I was one of the twins."

"It's going to be fine," Daddy said, with an air of confidence in his voice that came through the phone receiver.

I SPENT THE NEXT FEW DAYS ON SPIRITUAL PINS AND NEEDLES, constantly alert for ways God might choose to speak to me. I memorized the passage in Ecclesiastes about the threefold cord and prayed that every way it applied to my life would be fulfilled. I spent time in intercession, not just for myself, but for everyone else who might be affected by my decision. I listened to Christian songs on the radio. I even read billboards, not wanting to miss a random opportunity for God to speak through the world around me.

The breakthrough came Wednesday morning.

As I was reading another passage in Ecclesiastes, I came across the first line of a verse in chapter 5 that said, "Do not be rash with your mouth." I immediately stopped. That's what I'd done. I'd been rash with my mouth in accepting the job at Braddock, Appleby, and Carpenter. It was as simple as that. And being rash was sin. Sin required repentance. In this case, repentance meant telling Mr. Carpenter I'd made a mistake—even if he didn't understand, and even if it upset Zach.

But did that mean I should accept the job with Maggie and Julie?

As I asked the question, I was surprised by a sudden surge of compassion for the two women that welled up with irresistible force in my heart. And in that moment I knew my decision wasn't based on salary or benefits or security or firm prestige or whether I'd be asked to work on a case I didn't believe in. The Lord loves people, and he wanted me to work with Maggie and Julie because he loved them. My main job wasn't to be a lawyer, but to be a human expression of God's love they could see on a daily basis. I laughed out loud. The two greatest commandments truly are to love God and to love others.

Then the thought of Zach squelched my joy.

I prayed and waited for my heart to respond in a way that would help me know what to think and how to feel. Nothing came. I waited some more without a response. Finally, I closed my Bible with a prayer that God would show me at the right time where and how Zach fit into the future. That night I called home again.

"I agree," Mama replied after I nervously explained what I thought. "The situation with the two women has the mark of the Lord's destiny upon it. I'm not sure what that means, but you'll have opportunities there that won't exist if you work for the other firm. God put us here to touch other people's lives, and I'm thankful you've seen how that applies to this situation."

"Daddy, do you agree?" I asked.

"I won't disagree," he said slowly. "I'm less confident than you and your mama about this, but I don't have a reason from the Lord to tell you to go in another direction. I know you're in a tight spot and have to make a decision."

"It's going to be tough talking to Zach and Mr. Carpenter," I said. "I dread both, maybe Zach more." I paused. "Oh, I forgot to tell you that he invited me to fly out to California with him over Christmas break to meet his parents. It may help if I can tell him you've given me permission to go. He needs to get the tickets as soon as possible."

"Just a minute," Mama said.

I could hear muffled conversation as one of them placed a hand over the receiver.

"You can pray about it and let me know later," I said.

"That's not necessary," Mama replied. "We believe it's too soon for that step. A trip to California at this point would put too much pressure on the emotional and physical parts of the relationship before there's a spiritual foundation to support it."

"But I'm going to hurt Zach's feelings when I turn down the job. I don't want to discourage him or drive him away."

"If you tell him why you've changed your mind, do you believe that will happen?" Mama asked.

"I don't know."

"We knew this request was coming and already discussed it. We like Zach, but we want to help you guard your heart so things between you can progress at God's pace."

Guarding my heart was a phrase I knew well. It was a linchpin of all I'd been taught.

"His ideas and beliefs are different from yours," Mama continued, "and it's going to take time to find out if those differences can be compatible or not."

Mama was right, and it stung. I thought for a second.

"Daddy, are you still there?"

"Yes."

"Do you still think it's okay for me to be excited about Zach?"

"Yes, but I also agree with your mama. And if Zach is the kind of man I think he is, he'll understand."

When I hung up the phone, I hoped that Daddy, too, was right.

THE FOLLOWING DAY WHEN I RETURNED FROM CLASS, I KNEW I had three phone calls to make. I quickly decided Zach wouldn't be first. He was going to get an extra dose of bad news—about the job and the trip to California. I debated whether to call Maggie Smith and accept the job or contact Mr. Carpenter first and tell him I'd made a mistake. It made sense to call Maggie and make sure there hadn't been a last-minute change in plans after she and Julie met with me in Savannah. Calling Maggie first would avoid one disaster scenario. If I backed out of the job at Braddock, Appleby, and Carpenter and then found out there was no longer a job available with Maggie and Julie, I would look like a double idiot. I took a deep breath and dialed Maggie's number at her new office. An unfamiliar voice answered.

"Smith Law Offices."

"Is this Shannon?" I asked.

"Yes, may I ask who's calling?"

"Tami Taylor. I'd like to speak to Maggie."

"Just a minute."

While I was on hold, I wondered what, if anything, Shannon had been told about me.

"Congratulations," Maggie said as soon as she came on the line.

"What?"

"I heard late yesterday afternoon that you'd accepted the job with Joe Carpenter. I have to admit that if I'd been in your shoes I'd have done the same thing. Most people coming out of law school would jump at the chance to join a firm like Braddock, Appleby, and Carpenter. Opportunities to work with a small firm like ours are ten times easier to land than a position at a prestigious, established firm. Not only will you make more money, you'll receive the best training available. There's no way to put a price tag on that. Maybe five or six years down the road it will make sense for us to join forces. By that point, you'll have clients of your own you can bring along with you.

And just because you're working someplace else doesn't mean we can't—"

"I've changed my mind," I cut in. "I'm interested in accepting your job offer."

"You what?"

"I want to discuss working with you and Julie after I graduate and pass the bar exam."

"Did I get wrong information? I heard it from a paralegal I know very well. She received a memo about it."

I winced that the news had already been broadcast so widely.

"No, I met with Mr. Carpenter on Saturday and accepted the offer, but I've changed my mind."

"Does he know?"

"Not yet. I thought I should call you first and make sure you still want me."

"This is a shock," Maggie said. "But Julie warned me that you were unpredictable."

"I'm sure I wouldn't agree with everything Julie told you about me, but if by unpredictable she meant I don't always follow the path in life most people take, she would be right. Is the offer with your firm still open?"

"Yeah, sure. But I'd like to know why you changed your mind."

"I believe God wants the three of us to work together."

"Okay, but I have no idea what that means."

"I believe working with you and Julie will give me a better chance to make the practice of law a ministry, not just a business."

Maggie didn't immediately answer. "If you want to preach to your clients, I won't stop you. However, if you want to talk to my clients about God, you'll need to clear it with me first."

"That's fine, but there's more to it than that. I hope to get involved in cases that God wants me to handle."

Maggie coughed and muffled the receiver. "That's something I've never considered, but you'll discover that the people in almost every case are a mix of good and bad. Bring in your fair share of business, and you won't find me limiting the type of work you do."

"What if I don't want to work on a particular case for moral reasons?" I persisted.

"If it involves an ethical violation, I wouldn't want either of us to continue—"

I wasn't going to repeat my mistake with Mr. Carpenter.

"No, I mean a violation of my personal code of conduct."

"We'd have to discuss that on a case-by-case basis. I wouldn't be interested in making you work on a case just because I'm your boss. The negatives of that management style outweigh the positives."

It was a fair, acceptable answer. I liked Maggie Smith. Unlike Julie, she treated me with respect and seemed willing to discuss things important to me without resorting to sarcasm.

"Okay, if you promise to give me a right to explain my position."

"Of course. That's one of the strengths of a law firm. Lawyers in a group can discuss whether to accept a case, then debate the best course of action to help the client. That keeps everyone out of trouble. Personally, I've not found the practice of law to be a moral minefield. People come to attorneys because they have legal problems and need help solving them. I spend more time worrying about giving the right advice than looking in the mirror at myself."

"Put the mirror in my office."

Maggie laughed. "And everyone will think you're vain. Hey, now that I'm over my shock, I'm glad you've changed your mind. I'll send you an employment contract based on the terms in the e-mail. Look it over and get back to me. Are you going to call Julie?"

I hesitated. "Do you want me to?"

"No, I'd like the pleasure of telling her she's wrong. She bet me a dinner at a seafood place on the river that you would accept the job at Braddock, Appleby, and Carpenter. My only regret is that she won't get a chance to think she won before I tell her she didn't."

I hung up the phone and stared at the direct number for Mr. Carpenter's office. Now there was no reason to put off breaking the news of my decision to the senior litigation partner. I dialed his number.

7

JESSIE HID BEHIND A LARGE LIVE OAK TREE UNTIL THE LIGHTS OF the pickup truck slowly disappeared down the street. She went into the women's restroom inside the bus station. Placing the leather pouch on a metal ledge above the sink, she cleaned up as best she could. The warm, soapy water felt good on her face, arms, feet, and ankles. She scrubbed her closely cropped brown hair and then put some soap suds on her finger and rubbed it across her teeth before spitting out the bitter-tasting foam. By the time she finished, Jessie was standing in a spreading puddle of water. It took eight cycles of the blow-dryer to dry her hair and body. Partway through the process a woman came into the restroom and washed her hands in a sink as far from Jessie as possible. When Jessie finished, her clothes were still grimy, but the visible portions of her skin were clean. She returned the pouch to her jeans.

Jessie spent the night in the bus station. It wasn't a long-term solution for a place to stay, but for a single night she felt confident she could pass herself off as a teenager waiting to catch a bus or a person hanging around until someone she knew arrived. She didn't stay in the same seat but moved from place to place to avoid being labeled as a vagrant. Several times she got up from her seat when a bus pulled into the station and stood on the curb as if expecting a family member or friend to get off. Fortunately, that didn't happen.

Around midnight she dozed off. When she awoke a couple of hours later, Jessie walked around for a few minutes carrying a half-full cup of coffee she'd found beneath an empty seat. Twenty-four hours earlier she would have thankfully savored every drop of the coffee. Now, she had the luxury of a water fountain with an inexhaustible supply of fresh water, and the coffee cup merely became a prop in her show. Another bus arrived. After everyone got off, Jessie caught a few more hours of sleep. When the sun rose, she was still tired, but not being cold or afraid counted for a lot. An early morning bus from Brunswick pulled into the station, and Jessie left the building with a small group of passengers who'd been on board.

It was a beautiful morning, clear with a cool crispness in the air. Jessie glanced down the street to make sure the men in the pickup weren't coming by the bus station area to look for her on their way to another day's work. There was no sign of the truck. Jessie was hungry. The trash cans on each street corner probably contained food, but she hoped for something better. Wandering toward the river, she came to a bakery shop with a display of free samples on the counter. Rich fragrances drifted out to the sidewalk. No one was behind the cash register. Jessie slipped through the door and in a flash grabbed two indiscriminate handfuls of food from the plate. When she turned the doorknob she dropped precious crumbs in her haste to get away. Running a few feet down the sidewalk, she ducked into an alley and immediately stuffed a combination of vanilla-cream pastry, pumpkin bread, and blueberry muffin into her mouth. It was an odd combination but tasted heavenly. After the first bite, she slowed down and enjoyed each morsel. The sugar in the pastries sent energy coursing through her body.

When she finished, Jessie darted out of the alley and ran all the way to the river. She stopped not far from the old Cotton Exchange where she sat on a bench and enjoyed the early morning sun as it welcomed her to her first day on her own in Savannah.

Finding a pen that contained three different colors of ink on the ground, Jessie took out the sheet of paper with the gibberish on it from the pouch and, on the clean side, designed an intricate tattoo. When she finished she laid the piece of paper across her right thigh.

It fit perfectly.

I DIDN'T IMMEDIATELY CALL MR. CARPENTER. AFTER TALKING TO Maggie, I took a thirty-minute break to pray, compose myself, and tweak the notes I'd prepared for the conversation.

The direct line to Mr. Carpenter's office rang to his secretary, an aloof woman with considerable clerical skill. To her, summer clerks were a nuisance barely tolerated. I recognized her slightly nasal voice.

"This is Tami Taylor. May I speak to Mr. Carpenter?"

"Hi, Tami, how is school going?" the woman asked with a friend-liness that caught me off guard. "We look forward to seeing you after graduation."

"Uh, thanks. Is Mr. Carpenter available?"

"Let me check."

While I waited on hold, I reviewed my notes. My plan was to be as precise as possible. I'd communicate my appreciation for the job offer, tell Mr. Carpenter I'd made a mistake accepting it, apologize, and ask for his forgiveness. If Mr. Carpenter asked any follow-up questions, I'd simply reiterate that I'd given the offer a lot of serious consideration and prayer. I was halfway through the review of my notes when Mr. Carpenter's smooth Southern drawl, which oozed aristocratic educa-tion, came onto the line.

"Tami, your name was mentioned in conversation yesterday. You remember Jason Paulding, the developer who sued that crazy woman preacher?"

"Yes, sir. I wanted to call and—"

"Did Zach tell you what happened to him?"

"No, sir."

"Yesterday the U.S. Attorney's Office in Atlanta granted Paulding immunity from prosecution in return for his cooperation and testimony in a sting operation originating in Miami. We weren't handling the criminal matter, but the lawyer I referred him to called me to let me know what happened. It all started with the money trail you uncovered when you were working on the civil case."

"I didn't really uncover—"

"Who would have imagined that Paulding would end up helping the government prosecute Venezuelans illegally hiding oil profits in the U.S.? Your instincts about him were right on. You suspected all along more was going on than what he told us. That's an ability that can't be taught and usually comes with more life experience than you have. I credit your upbringing with giving you a much better than average ability to judge people. But enough about old business. Have you been in touch with Gerry Patrick to work out the details for your start date? I sent her a memo that you'd accepted our offer."

"She's not contacted me, but the reason I called today was to turn down the job." I glanced in frustration at my notes. I was totally off script. "It's, uh, not that I don't appreciate the confidence you showed in offering me a position, but I've prayed about it, and I shouldn't have told you that I wanted to come work for the firm. It's my mistake, and I owe you an apology. I hope you'll find it in your heart to forgive me."

There was a brief pause.

"I must say this is a shock to me," Mr. Carpenter replied in a carefully measured tone of voice. "I saw nothing but a bright future for you here at the firm. The partners and I discussed at our lunch meeting today the need to allow you appropriate leeway to accommodate your religious sensibilities."

"You did?" It was my turn to be shocked. "All we talked about on Saturday was legal ethics."

"I could tell it was a concern to you. And I also had the benefit of a helpful conversation with Oscar Callahan on Monday. He gave me good advice. Does he know about this?"

"No, sir."

"He'll be disappointed. Is this your final decision?"

"Yes, sir."

"Best of luck to you."

I slowly hung up the phone. The relief I'd expected to feel at delivering the news to Mr. Carpenter seemed as far away as the hills of Powell Station. I glanced at the clock. I had a lot of studying to do before the next day's classes. Talking to Zach Mays could wait another day.

THE FOLLOWING MORNING, I WENT BACK TO MY APARTMENT after my first class to call Zach. I recognized the voice of the receptionist, a middle-aged woman who could give better directions than a GPS to anyplace in Savannah. She put me on hold for a couple of seconds.

"This is Zach Mays. Thanks so much for calling."

"Zach? It's Tami."

"Uh-oh, I picked up the wrong line. Let me put you on hold while I take care of something important."

Before I could speak, I was listening to the music on the firm's phone system. It was a loop of light classical designed to soothe the frayed nerves of anxious clients. It didn't work for me. My nerves were fraying more by the second. Fifteen minutes passed. Normally, I would have hung up and called back, but I waited five more minutes. That passed, and I extended it five more.

"Are you still there?" Zach asked.

"Should I have hung up?"

"Probably. I had to take a call from a solicitor in London who's working with us on a contract for a British shipping company. The exchange rate is fluctuating so much it's difficult to set a schedule that isn't messed up by changes in currency valuations. We had to figure out the precise language for a provision that allows for the ups and downs in a way that should work over the long term."

The line was silent for a moment.

"But you didn't call about exchange rates, did you?" Zach asked.

"No."

I told him about my conversation with Mr. Carpenter.

"Did you mention Sister Dabney?" Zach asked when I paused.

"No, he would have thought I was crazy."

"Yeah."

"Along with you?"

"I didn't say that," Zach answered. "We went over all this in the car."

"But is it over?"

"My opinion that you're making a mistake hasn't changed, but I have to accept your decision and deal with it."

I suddenly felt like a temperamental woman.

"I'm sorry," I said.

"Did you talk to Maggie?"

"Yes, and she's sent an employment contract."

"Do you want me to review it?"

I thought about the starting salary and pitiful benefit package. I was too embarrassed to let Zach see it.

"No thanks; it's nothing fancy." I paused. "And I talked to my parents about the trip to California. They don't think it's a good idea. I would have liked to go but need to honor their wishes."

I hoped my voice sounded sincere.

"That's okay. I'd had second thoughts about it, too. If it's supposed to happen there'll be another chance in the future."

"Sure."

"Hey, I'm due for a meeting in the downstairs conference room with Mr. Appleby and a new client. I'll talk to you soon."

"Okay."

The call ended without a hint of a shiver down my spine or a single goose bump.

ZACH CALLED ME ONCE WHILE HE WAS IN CALIFORNIA FOR THE holidays. I was at home in Powell Station, and after we had a brief conversation, he talked to each member of my family. Ellie changed her voice to make it sound huskier. The result left Emma laughing and Mama rolling her eyes. I wasn't in a laughing mood.

"Are you upset with us for not letting you go to California?" Mama asked after the call ended and we were alone in the front room.

"Not really," I answered, giving her a hug. "When it comes to men, I'm not sure that I'm much further along than Ellie."

I RETURNED TO SCHOOL IN JANUARY. AFTER THE SECOND DAY OF classes, I came home to find a note attached to my door.

I'm in town for the evening. Could I take you to dinner? Please call.
    Vince

He'd written his phone number on the bottom. I took the note inside and laid it on my computer desk. After pacing back and forth a few times, I picked up the note and stared at it again. Vince wrote in an easy-to-read print style that matched his organized personality.

He must have gotten my address in Athens from information I'd made available at Braddock, Appleby, and Carpenter. There could be no explanation for his being in town except to see me. That thought made me uneasy. I'd not received permission from Daddy and Mama to court Vince, and it would be completely inconsistent with the courting process to spend time with two men. My phone rang, causing me to jump.

"Hello?" I answered tentatively.

"Tami, it's Vince. I'm in town for a few hours. Are you free for dinner?"

"Hey," I answered, staring again at the slip of paper.

"I left a note on the door of your apartment but then thought I'd better call, since you might be staying at the law school to study."

"I just got back to my apartment and found the note. How did you get my cell phone number?"

"Your father."

"My father?"

"Yeah, I called information for Powell Station. I remembered that your father worked as a supervisor at a chicken plant and tracked him down. He told me that you finally got a cell phone."

"Did he say anything else?"

"No, but the way he talked reminded me a little bit of you."

I'd heard that comparison before.

"I know it's short notice," Vince continued, "but my connecting flight from Atlanta to Hartford was canceled, and I won't be going back to school until morning."

"You drove to Athens from the Atlanta airport to see me?"

"I rented a car. Look, if it's not a good night, I'll understand."

I was torn between good manners and confusion over how to relate to Vince Colbert. I suddenly remembered a prior commitment.

"My intramural basketball team has its first practice tonight."

It sounded like a ridiculous excuse as soon as the words escaped my mouth.

"I could watch and then we could grab something simple to eat," he responded evenly.

"No," I answered quickly. "I can miss the practice."

The idea of Vince watching me run up and down and sweat on the basketball court would be neither good manners nor appropriate interaction with a man.

"Could you come around six?" I added. "I guess you know where I live."

"Okay, six it is. Pick someplace casual where you like to hang out with your friends."

"Okay."

Later, as I brushed out my hair after shampooing it, I took comfort in knowing there was no chance of running into Zach in Athens.

At 6:00 p.m. there was a knock on the door. I opened it. Vince took a step back and smiled. He was about the same height as Zach, but more lanky. He had dark eyes and wavy brown hair. No ponytail sprouted from the back of his head. In his right hand, which had been scarred in a high school chemistry accident, Vince held a sleek, lightweight laptop. The computer was his constant companion.

"You brought your computer?"

"Nice to see you, too," he answered.

"Sorry." I laughed.

"I have some pictures I want to show you."

It was cool outside. Vince helped me put on a long coat.

"Where to?" he asked as we walked across the parking lot.

I named a chain restaurant. Vince shook his head.

"Isn't there someplace local?"

"What do you mean?"

"Something more Southern. There's not much of that available near the Yale campus."

"There's a restaurant that's famous for catfish, but I haven't tried it."

"You will tonight."

The restaurant, named for the man who founded it, was located a few miles from the campus.

"Have you been in Savannah recently?" I asked as we left the parking lot.

"Yes. I drove down from Charleston for a couple of days after Christmas to finish a few projects Mr. Braddock sent me."

"Was Zach at the office?"

"No, he was still in California." Vince glanced at me. "But I'm sure you know that."

"Not the exact dates."

"I heard you made a trip to Savannah, too."

"Yes. I turned down the job."

"I know. Mr. Carpenter wanted me to explain it to him."

"What did you say?"

"That I was sure you'd prayed about it and believed it was the right choice. He just shook his head and walked away. Faith inside the walls of the church is familiar. Making it a part of day-to-day life is from a different universe, especially for a man like him."

"Did he know I'm going to work with Julie and Maggie Smith?"

"He didn't mention it. Is that what you decided to do?"

"Yes."

We stopped at a traffic light.

"How did you know it was the right choice?"

Vince rarely asked idle questions, and I didn't give him a watered-down version. The only thing I left out was the strain the decision placed on my relationship with Zach. We were seated and sipping water at the restaurant by the time I completed my story.

"How much of this did you tell Mr. Carpenter?"

"None."

Vince sipped his water. "It's a good thing you didn't accept the job at Braddock, Appleby, and Carpenter. You wouldn't fit in the firm culture."

"And you will?" I asked, raising my eyebrows.

Vince smiled. "We're not all called to the same mission field."

Food was served buffet-style. The catfish were fried bone-in and served with a broad assortment of vegetables. For those who didn't like fish there was crisp fried chicken. Vince piled a generous portion of collard greens onto his plate next to a heaping mound of squash casserole.

"Hungry?" I asked when we returned to our table.

"For the right kind of food. Collard greens aren't considered a delicacy in some parts of the country."

When he blessed the food, Vince quoted a few verses from Psalm 40 about the wonderful things God has planned for those who do his will. Whether for legal principles or Scripture, Vince had a very sticky memory.

Catfish caught fresh in Putnam's Pond and cooked by Mama was the best on earth, but the restaurant did a respectable job. The sweet white meat separated easily from the bones and didn't taste greasy. Vince loved it. He left nothing but the skeleton on his plate. His tendency to focus intently on one thing at a time carried over to eating. He paid more attention to the food on his plate than to me. Knowing this about him kept me from feeling ignored. After polishing off the food selected on a second trip to the buffet, he looked up and sighed.

"This was what I needed."

"Are you going to eat any dessert?"

"Where is it?"

I pointed to a table on the opposite end of the room. Without a word, Vince got up. I followed him. Further conversation would have to wait until he finished a good-sized helping of both banana pudding and peach cobbler. I avoided the banana pudding, not because I didn't like it, but because a woman in our church made such glorious banana pudding that I never ate it anyplace else.

"Are you driving back to Atlanta tonight?" I asked.

"Yes, I'm staying at a hotel near the airport."

Vince cleared our table himself, placing the dirty plates and silverware on a large round tray used for that purpose by the restaurant staff. Then he placed his laptop on the table and moved his chair so we could both see the screen.

"What are you going to show me?" I asked as the computer booted up.

"It's better to show than tell."

He clicked on an icon for photographs. Black faces filled the screen.

"Where is this?"

"Rwanda."

"You went to Rwanda?"

"Directly from school at the end of the semester. I was there for ten days working on this project before flying into Charleston to see my family for Christmas and then going to Savannah. It's been a busy vacation."

"What kind of project?"

Another photograph appeared. A smiling black woman was standing next to a smiling black man in front of a simple house. The woman had her arm around a teenage boy.

"That's a beautiful family," I said.

"They're not a family. The man is a Hutu; the woman and her son are Tutsi. They've known each other since childhood and lived in the same village. During the genocide in 1994, the man was in a group that killed the woman's husband and two daughters."

I put my hand over my mouth in shock.

"But—"

"It was a process. Most would say an unbelievable process. But some people are willing to forgive. This woman is one of them."

He clicked an arrow and a picture of two men with grotesque

scars on their faces appeared. They had their arms around each other's shoulders.

"These men tried to kill each other with machetes. Now, they're deacons in the same church."

Vince showed me several more photos, each different yet with a common message.

"I was in the country as part of a justice survey sponsored by Yale. But when my translator found out I was a Christian, he took me on side trips to meet these people."

I stared at the photo on the screen—three women and a man who helped kill their husbands.

"This man served these women for several months before a breakthrough came. He worked a laboring job then walked to their village to help them. At first they didn't want him around, but eventually his repentance won them over." Vince pointed to one of the women, a regal-looking, middle-aged lady with a colorful scarf on her head. "This is Candice. She told me she had to forgive the killer because God had forgiven her sins. When she forgave, the joy came back into her life."

I looked at Vince as he talked. There was a different light in his eyes.

"The forgiveness in the hearts of these people was greater than anything I've ever seen. They're living in a place of love and grace I didn't know existed."

"I can tell," I responded. "I'm glad you went on the trip."

"Me, too. And I wanted you to hear about it. That's why I drove here to see you when my flight was canceled."

"Why me?"

"You're the only person I can talk to like this."

"Thanks," I said, suddenly feeling awkward.

Vince didn't seem to notice. He turned off his laptop and closed the top.

VINCE WALKED ME TO THE DOOR OF MY APARTMENT. WHEN I unlocked the door quickly to go inside, he rested his hand against the door frame to stop me. I felt nervous.

"Maybe I'll see you at the bar exam," he said.

His comment took me by surprise. The last thing on my mind at the moment was the bar exam given in July to the law students who'd recently graduated.

"Uh, there'll be a lot of people there."

"Yes. I enjoyed dinner."

"Me, too."

"I'll e-mail those photos to you."

"That would be nice."

Inside, I plopped down on my bed and stared up at the ceiling. The bar exam would be easy compared to finding the correct answers to questions of my heart.

8

"DO YOU THINK THERE WILL BE A QUESTION ABOUT THIRD-PARTY beneficiaries?" Julie asked as we stood in line at the entrance to the testing facility in Atlanta.

"Yes," I answered. "But you'll spot that immediately. It's the ones with hidden issues that worry me."

"I thought you weren't supposed to worry. It's a sin."

"It is, but I'm sure David got nervous before he fought Goliath."

"A touch of nerves gets the blood flowing to the brain," Julie said as the line inched forward. "Keep talking. I like it when your fighting side comes out. It psyches me up."

I was more scared than I let on. My palms were sweating so badly the registration confirmation in my right hand was getting slightly damp. If David's hands had been this moist, the sling would have slipped through his fingers and wrapped itself around Goliath's ankle. I scanned the crowd of several hundred candidates. It was a somber group. Many would pass the two-day test. All wanted to avoid being among those who didn't.

"Did you talk to Zach this week?" Julie asked.

"No."

"How about this month?"

"No, I've been studying."

"Is he still mad at you for taking the job with Maggie and me?"

"He's disappointed."

Julie shook her head. "What does it feel like to be you? You're like a movie star. The whole world wants a piece of you."

"I don't know what you're talking about."

"I saw Vinny the other day," Julie continued. "After telling me that he'd scored over ninety percent on five multistate practice tests, he asked a bunch of questions about you."

"He did not."

"Well, he told me about the practice tests, but I could tell he was thinking about you the whole time."

"I hate it when you lie to me."

We entered a large convention room. Almost every candidate carried a laptop. In my hand was a new one Daddy and Mama had given me as a graduation present. I'd never received such an extravagant gift.

"Do you want to sit together?" Julie asked.

I hesitated. Even if Julie didn't say a word, her presence would be a distraction. And the chances of her keeping completely quiet were nil. I didn't want a proctor to issue a warning, or worse.

"Me either," she continued before I said anything. "I'll see you at the break."

I gratefully watched Julie blend into the crowd, then settled into a seat at a small table and plugged in my computer. Including college, I'd spent seven years preparing for this moment. I bowed my head and offered a silent prayer for wisdom, insight, and the ability to remember what I'd learned. I'd prayed before taking bunches of tests, but this was a big hurdle. I dived into the first section of the exam.

I worked steadily, relieved that most of the questions raised familiar points of law. But the bar exam wasn't primarily a memory test. Every question required analysis of the problem before application of the correct principles. My brain felt like a computer as I rapidly shuffled data and concepts. One thing I could say with confidence about law school—it taught me how to think.

I finished the first section a couple of minutes before time was called and then joined the mob going to the restroom. I ran into Julie as I exited.

"How's it going?" she asked.

"Okay, how about you?"

"It's a piece of cake. Did you see Vinny?"

"No."

"He's down front. I saw him get up a couple of times during the test."

I wandered to the front of the room. Clusters of people were gathered together discussing specific questions. I avoided group debriefing sessions in law school and skirted the groups. Nothing created more anxiety than hearing someone mention an issue I'd missed. I tried to spot Vince's laptop on one of the tables, but they all looked alike.

"Tami!"

I turned around. It was Vince. He looked pale and haggard.

"What's wrong?" I asked with concern.

"I'm sick," he said, rubbing his chin. "Didn't sleep much last night. Spent most of my time in the bathroom at the hotel. I ought to be in bed now."

"I'm sorry. Is there a way to postpone—"

"I'm not sure. I thought I would bounce back. Now I'm committed to the test."

Vince looked pitiful. He needed to be tucked into bed sipping a sports drink to keep hydrated.

"Would you like me to get you a bottle of water?" I asked.

Vince pointed at a desk. There were three bottles of water underneath it.

"I have water. I just can't keep it in me."

"Is there anything else I can do for you?"

"Would you pray for me?"

"Sure."

"I mean right now. I feel horrible."

Without waiting for an answer, Vince bowed his head and closed his eyes. I glanced around. A couple of people were watching us. Some of them had probably asked God for help within the past few hours. I closed my eyes.

"Lord, I ask you to touch Vince and heal him. Drive this sickness from his body and give him the strength to finish the test and pass it. Amen."

When I opened my eyes there were at least a dozen people staring at us. Vince lifted his head.

"How do you feel?" I asked.

"Weak, but I think I can try another sip or two of water."

The chief administrator of the exam instructed us to return to our seats. As soon as we were settled I looked toward the area of the room where I'd been with Vince. I couldn't see him, but as the proctors handed out the next battery of questions, I didn't pray for myself. I directed my prayers toward another part of the room.

At the end of the day, I found Vince. He still looked pale.

"How are you?" I asked.

"Not a hundred percent, but after you prayed for me I could think more about the questions on the page than the condition of my stomach."

"Is there anything I can do for you before tomorrow?"

"No, I'm going back to the hotel to crash."

"You need to have more than just water."

"I will. Room service can handle anything I might want."

I'd never used room service at a hotel.

"Are you sure? I'd be glad to go to a store and bring something to you."

"You've already been too close to me. I don't want you to pick up this bug. It's probably a nasty virus."

Julie came rushing up.

"Hey, Vinny," she said. "Did you answer the questions with half your brain tied behind your back?"

Vince looked at me. "More like half my stomach."

"That's me. I'm starving." Julie turned toward me. "There's an Italian place you've got to try. I ate there a bunch when I was at Emory. Pasta is great brain food, and you enjoy dishes with a kick to them, don't you?"

"If they're done right."

"Then let's go. I'll treat and deduct it from your first paycheck. Vinny, you're welcome to join us. Just because we won't be working at the same firm doesn't mean we can't be friends. However, I've got to warn you that one of the things Tami is looking forward to is dragging Joe Carpenter back and forth across the courtroom and then telling Zach about it over a romantic dinner."

"You should tie up three-fourths of your imagination and put it behind your back," I said.

"I'll pass on dinner," Vince said, giving me a wan smile. "I'm more in the mood for a pack of saltine crackers. Anything more might kick my stomach out of my body." He looked at me. "I'll see you tomorrow."

As Julie and I walked out of the building I told her about Vince's illness.

"That's too bad," she said with a concerned look. "I hope we don't get it."

A COUPLE WEEKS LATER IN SAVANNAH, DADDY LINGERED IN MY new apartment at Mrs. Fairmont's. The last box had been unloaded from the pickup. I'd left home many times to go to school, but this time was different. From now on my loyalties to place would be divided.

"Do you want me to help you unpack?" Daddy asked.

"There isn't anything heavy. It would be better if I put my clothes in the right spot."

"Yeah, I don't try to rearrange your mama's closet."

I smiled. Every item in Mama's closet knew its place. Daddy looked at his watch.

"I'd better get going. The chickens will be coming down the line in the morning, and I have to be there to greet them."

Daddy didn't move toward the door. Instead, he pointed to a box of books.

"Do you want me to put that in your bedroom?"

"No, I'm going to buy a bookcase for this room."

"Don't settle for pressboard covered with vinyl. Find a used one made from wood."

"There are lots of secondhand furniture shops in Savannah that sell nice things that aren't antiques. I can find a solid maple or cherry bookcase with a nick or two for a good price."

"Right," he said, still not moving toward the door.

"I'll come home," I said in answer to his unspoken thoughts.

"Of course you will."

"And with me living in Savannah, there won't be any excuse for the family not to come for a vacation. Don't forget Zach's offer to move out and let you stay in his townhome for a few days."

I heard Flip pattering down the wooden steps to the basement. In a few seconds the Chihuahua bounded into the room and sniffed Daddy's ankles for the tenth time since we'd arrived. Flip didn't protest when Daddy scooped him up and began to scratch the back of the little dog's neck.

"Maybe I should get your mama a little dog like this," Daddy said as Flip closed his eyes in pleasure. "Not now, but when the twins leave home."

"That won't happen for five more years."

"It seems like five days since you were their age."

Tears suddenly welled up in my eyes.

"That's my fault. I'm sorry," Daddy said when he saw my reaction.

I rubbed my eyes. "It would have happened as soon as you left. I'd rather you see them so you'll know how much I'll miss you."

Daddy put Flip on the floor and wrapped his arms around me. The unselfish purity of his affection was the best example of God's love I knew this side of heaven. If every girl and boy could be so blessed, the world would be a much better place. I buried my head in his shoulder. He held me for at least a minute before letting me go.

"Call as much as you want," he said.

"I will." I touched my heart. "But we'll always be connected in here. You and Mama are the best parents in the world. If I ever have children, I hope they love and respect me as much as I do you."

I'd never seen Daddy cry except in church, but two tears suddenly gushed from his eyes and ran down his cheeks. He wiped them away, reached out, and put his right hand on my head.

"The Lord bless you, Tammy Lynn."

I closed my eyes to receive his words and anything that followed. He didn't speak anything else but kissed me in the usual place on top of my head.

AFTER DADDY LEFT I JOINED MRS. FAIRMONT IN THE DEN. THE TV was tuned to a sports show about turkey hunting. The host of the program was demonstrating different types of turkey calls, some produced by holding a device to the mouth, others by scraping something across a box. The host issued a call that generated interest from a large tom turkey. I'd seen wild turkeys within yelling distance of the house on Beaver Ruin Road. When a group was startled and suddenly took flight it created a tremendous racket.

I sat on the couch to Mrs. Fairmont's right, my teeth pressed firmly against my lower lip to keep it from trembling. I knew it would be hard saying good-bye to Daddy. The call of the hills where I'd grown up would always be at the edge of my hearing.

"I told Christine you were going to use my car until you can buy one of your own," Mrs. Fairmont said.

I forced myself to leave thoughts of home.

"Is that okay with her?"

"She wants you to check with my insurance company to find out what would happen if you have a wreck."

"As a consensual user residing in the household, the policy would cover me so long as I operated the car within the scope of my permitted use," I stated, then stopped. "That sounds like a lawyer answer, doesn't it?"

Mrs. Fairmont smiled. "It's nice having someone as smart as you living in the house. Sam Braddock won't have to make any more house calls."

"You should keep Mr. Braddock as your lawyer. He's forgotten more about the law than I'll ever know. If you give me the name of your agent, I'll call tomorrow to check on it and reassure Mrs. Bartlett."

"When are you going to start calling her Christine?"

"Not until you start calling me Ms. Taylor," I answered with a slight smile. "Habits of respect are hard to break."

"Your parents have done a fine job raising you." Mrs. Fairmont's eyes twinkled. "And I'm going to keep you in line."

"I hope you do."

The front door opened and Flip raced toward the foyer. I followed. It was Mrs. Bartlett. I grabbed Flip away from her feet. The little dog never bit her, but Mrs. Bartlett lived in constant fear that he would.

"Did he tear into you when you entered the house?" she asked.

"He made sure I was friendly."

"If he had more than three brain cells in that microscopic skull of his, he'd learn how to treat me."

"I think his brain is fairly large for such a small animal."

"Who knows." Mrs. Bartlett sniffed. "Speaking of brains, I talked to Mother a few hours ago, and she sounded fine."

"Yes, it's a good day."

Mrs. Bartlett lowered her voice. "Those are getting rarer. Gracie's niece got a scholarship offer to college and is leaving town next week. If you hadn't been moving in with her, we would have placed Mother at Surfside. They've opened a new wing for the memory-impaired."

Surfside was an upscale nursing home where Mrs. Fairmount had recuperated for a few weeks the previous summer following a stroke.

"And before we discuss anything else," Mrs. Bartlett continued, "I want you to promise that you won't fight me if it becomes necessary to move Mother. I know we didn't agree about what should have been done last year, but I trust you've matured enough to realize tough decisions like this have to be made."

Mrs. Bartlett had an amazing knack for misrepresenting my intentions and offending me in a very short space of time.

"That's a decision the family should make," I said, trying to keep my voice level. "I've always taken that position with the elderly women I've worked for. Two of the ladies I took care of while I was in college ended up in nursing facilities. I helped with the transition and visited them after they were situated."

"Your references confirmed your cooperation. But it never hurts to get things out in the open so there won't be a misunderstanding later. When do you start work for the law firm?"

"In the morning. But I didn't accept the job with Braddock, Appleby, and Carpenter. I'm working with Maggie Smith, a former assistant DA, and Julie Feldman, a woman who clerked with me last summer."

Mrs. Bartlett gave me a startled look. "Doesn't the fellow you date work for Sam Braddock? You know, the young man from Charleston."

"Vince Colbert works there, but I'm courting Zach Mays, an associate at the firm who specializes in admiralty law."

"Courting? What quaint terminology. Perfect for a lawyer. Well, Mother is certainly confused about all that. She thought you were dating the young man from Charleston. I won't stick my nose into your personal business. Just make sure you don't cross the line into our family business."

"Yes, ma'am. And I'll make sure the insurance coverage on the car covers me while I'm driving. Do you know the name of the agent?"

"It's in the glove box. Make sure it always has a full tank of gas."

I wasn't sure how to keep a gas tank perpetually full but believed I could satisfy the intent of her demand.

"Yes, ma'am."

"Christine!" Mrs. Fairmont called out from the den. "Is that you?"

"Yes, Mother! There were some things I had to discuss with Tami."

"If it has to do with Surfside, you can forget it. The only way I'm leaving this house is in a hearse with flowers!"

Mrs. Bartlett pressed her lips together for a moment then leaned over and spoke to me in a softer voice.

"You're right. She is having one of her better days."

9

JESSIE MOVED LAZILY FROM PLACE TO PLACE ALONG THE RIVER walk. With no place to go, she wasn't in a hurry. She looked at the displays of merchandise in shop windows but didn't go inside any of the stores. Even with a clean face, arms, and hair, she couldn't pass for a legitimate customer and didn't want to attract unwanted attention. She sat on a bench and watched ships come and go in the channel.

By mid-morning other homeless people began to congregate in the area. Jessie avoided them. She knew street people were usually suspicious of others. For some, that made them reclusive. Others could be grumpy. A few might be weirdly dangerous. Jessie didn't want to get close enough to find out.

The rich breakfast snatched from the bakery didn't beat back her hunger very long. By twelve o'clock Jessie's stomach demanded attention. A return to the bakery would be too risky. Dumpsters at the rear of buildings could be a source of food, but there were too many people in the area to allow her to privately dive into a trash container. She vainly scanned the ground for coins. She moved away when a policeman walked by.

The lunchtime business crowd started coming to the small restaurants that dotted the area. Jessie watched with envy as well-dressed men and women entered the eateries. She sat on a curb near the entrance of an Italian restaurant. Rich fragrances tormented her attention.

"Are you new to Savannah?" a voice beside her asked.

Jessie turned her head and saw an obese older woman dressed in a faded yellow dress and wearing a floppy hat. The woman looked homeless, but on second glance Jessie wasn't sure. Jessie wasn't interested in a conversation.

"Some questions don't have to be answered," the woman continued.

Jessie got up to move away. Ignoring the older woman was the best response. Jessie stepped closer to the restaurants. A man and woman exited and approached her. The woman was carrying a take-out box with the name of the restaurant on the side and a clear plastic top. Jessie could see a thick piece of lasagna inside. She had a sudden urge to grab the box and take off running. She took a furtive step toward the woman.

"Stop!" a voice called out.

The man and woman stopped and looked past Jessie at the older woman who was still standing beside the bench where Jessie had been sitting. Jessie spun around and glared. With fire in her eyes, the old woman took a step toward her and pointed her finger at Jessie's chest.

"The devil wants you, but I told him he can't have you! You belong to the Lord!"

The man and woman with the food quickly walked away. Other people gave Jessie and the old woman a wide berth.

"Leave me alone," Jessie spat out.

"I can't," the woman answered, coming closer.

The old woman walked with a slight limp. It would be easy to run away. Jessie told her legs to move, but they didn't obey. She looked down at her feet.

"Are you hungry?" the woman asked, lowering her voice.

"Leave me alone."

"Are you hungry?" the woman repeated.

Jessie's stomach growled so loudly she suspected the woman could hear it.

"Yeah," she admitted.

"There are many kinds of food in this world. Do you know the difference between good and bad?"

"Sometimes I have to eat what I can get," Jessie answered defensively, then noticed the woman was carrying a big black pocketbook. "Give me five dollars. That way I can get a good dinner."

As soon as she said it, Jessie wished she'd asked for more money. The woman obviously considered herself a preacher. That sort of person was supposed to help people like Jessie.

"If I give you five dollars, will you buy better food than what you found walking down the train tracks?" the woman asked, her blue eyes twinkling.

Jessie's mouth dropped open.

I CHECKED MYSELF IN THE MIRROR, AND I THOUGHT ABOUT MY first day at public school. As a homeschooler, I didn't start until the ninth grade. The first day Mama allowed me to wear my most stylish blue dress. But I had no illusions about what lay ahead. Other girls from the church attended the local high school. Stories of ostracism and teasing by other students were common. We reminded ourselves that our modest clothes and long hair were badges of honor, but it was still nice supporting one another.

When I made the varsity basketball team, my classmates rarely harassed me about my clothes and beliefs. There were exceptions, but I learned that success was a ticket to respect. More important, I discovered success could be achieved without violating my convictions. I hoped the same opportunity awaited me in the practice of law.

Mrs. Fairmont wasn't awake and the house was quiet. Gracie was scheduled to clean the house, so I added extra coffee and water to the pot and pushed the button. With the coffeemaker dripping, I wrote Gracie a note of greeting and put it in a place where only she would find it. I left a second note for Mrs. Fairmont with the address and phone number for the new firm. I'd walked to work when I clerked for Braddock, Appleby, and Carpenter, but those early morning strolls through the historic district were no longer an option.

When I backed Mrs. Fairmont's car from the garage and turned into the cobblestone street, my cell phone rang. I fumbled through my purse and answered just before it went to voice mail.

"Hello."

"Welcome to Savannah," Zach said. "Are you still at Mrs. Fairmont's house?"

"No, I'm on my way to the office. She's letting me borrow her car for a few weeks."

"I wish you were walking toward Montgomery Street. I'm sitting in my office looking out the window in the direction you came from this summer."

"Did you used to spy on me?"

"Only a few times."

"Have you checked your e-mail this morning?"

"No, I don't have any access at Mrs. Fairmont's house."

"You should get online as soon as you get to the office. Vince received the bar results yesterday afternoon."

My stomach flipped sideways then wrapped in a knot.

"Did he pass?"

"Of course. Who would have any doubt about that?"

I remembered how pale and sick Vince looked the first day of the test.

"The list of everyone who passed was posted early this morning," Zach continued. "I'm looking at it right now."

I took a deep breath. "Let me have it."

"Don't be silly. You passed. So did Julie."

I let out a huge sigh of relief and raised one hand in the air while keeping the other on the steering wheel.

"Thank you, Lord!" I exclaimed.

"Yeah, I remember how I felt. Was it okay for me to tell you instead of letting you find out on your own?"

"I'd rather get the news instantly instead of enduring the agony of opening the e-mail."

"Good. We should celebrate. Maybe the four of us could get together for dinner tonight."

"Four?"

"Vince, Julie, you, and me. I'll talk to Vince. You check with Julie and call me later."

"Where would you want to go?"

"Vince and I will discuss it. I'll pick up the tab."

"Okay," I answered slowly. "We'll talk this afternoon."

After we hung up, I checked the time. Daddy would be on his way to work, but I called Mama and shared the good news with her. She took it calmly, but when she told the twins I could hear their screams.

"They're happy for you," Mama said. "I am, too. Do you want me to hold off telling your daddy?"

I thought for a moment. Expecting the twins to keep a secret was unrealistic.

"No. Let him know. I'll phone tonight and give you a report about my first day on the job."

I PULLED INTO THE PARKING LOT WITH A SENSE OF SATISFACTION. As soon as I was sworn in by one of the local superior court judges I would, in one way at least, be as much a lawyer as Oscar Callahan or Joe Carpenter.

The sign in front of the building still read Smith Law Offices. Now that Julie had passed the bar exam, it would be changed to Smith and Feldman. Whether my name joined theirs wasn't a question that would be answered for a while. Sister Dabney's prophecy about the three of us forming a cord of three strands might hold the promise of a partnership.

It wasn't quite eight o'clock, and no one else had arrived. I got out of the car, then stopped to laugh at myself. I might be smart enough to pass the bar exam, but I'd not arranged with Maggie to get a key to the office. There was nothing to do but wait. I walked slowly around the outside of the building, praying that God would bless all that I might do there. I was on my third circuit when another car pulled into the parking lot. A woman I didn't recognize got out and gave me a puzzled look. She was in her mid-thirties with short hair dyed blonde.

"Tami?" she asked.

"Yes."

"I'm Shannon Carver."

"I drove to the office then realized I didn't have a key," I said.

"No problem. A key is in a packet of stuff I have for you inside."

We walked to the door.

"Maggie says you're working as receptionist, secretary, and book-keeper," I said. "That's a lot of jobs to keep straight."

"Is that what she says? Maybe I should ask for a raise."

I glanced sideways and saw she wasn't smiling.

"Will you always get here before eight?" Shannon continued as she unlocked the door.

"Sometimes earlier. I'm a morning person."

"Ugh. I'm not, but I have to get up at the crack of dawn to get my kids ready for school and day care. It's a thirty-minute drive from the day-care facility to school, then another fifteen minutes to the office."

Shannon wasn't wearing a wedding ring. A single mother juggling responsibilities with children could be a more difficult task than performing the three jobs assigned to her at the office.

Inside the office there were now pictures on the walls of the reception area and a nice area rug on top of the bland carpet. Brass lamps rested on shiny end tables. An attractive sofa and three side chairs surrounded a coffee table.

"It looks better," I said.

"Yeah, it's coming along. Opening a new law office is brutal."

Shannon's office was behind the reception area. There was an opening in the wall so she would see when someone entered. Her desk was piled high with papers and files. At least Maggie appeared busy. A picture frame contained photos of two little boys taken at the beach.

"Are those your sons?" I asked.

"Yeah."

"They're cute."

"Not when they fight or refuse to eat their cereal. This morning combined a fight with a refusal to eat cereal, and the younger one ended up with a bowl of milk on top of his head. He had to take a second shower."

Ellie and Emma occasionally disagreed, but I couldn't imagine one of them dumping a bowl of milk on the other's head, even when they were younger. That level of anarchy was unthinkable in our household.

"Sorry you've had such a rough morning."

"It's typical. Here's your stuff." She handed me an envelope. "Let me know if you have any questions."

Shannon sat down and turned on her computer. I stayed by her desk.

"Any idea when Maggie or Julie will be here?"

"If you wait until I boot up I can check Maggie's calendar. Julie comes in when she pleases. It depends how late she stays out the night before."

If Julie already knew the results of the bar exam, it would have been reason for a late-night celebration and morning hangover.

"Maggie had several cases on a hearing calendar first thing," Shannon said after a few moments. "She may have gone directly to the courthouse."

"What kind of hearings?"

"DUI cases. Ever since Maggie ran an ad in the paper, the calls have been pouring in."

"She advertises for DUI cases?"

"Yeah."

Shannon took a folded newspaper out of the stack on her desk. She opened it and handed it to me. In the bottom corner was an advertisement featuring the line "DUI??? Former Assistant DA Now Ready to Work for You."

"She prosecuted hundreds of them and knows the ins and outs of the system, which cops do a good job and those who are sloppy. It makes sense that she would flip to the defense side."

The phone rang.

"That's probably another one," Shannon said, picking up the phone. "Smith Law Offices." She listened for a few seconds. "Breathalyzer or blood test?" She was quiet again. "Okay. Who was the arresting officer and when's your court date?"

I made my way down the short hallway, the thrill of passing the bar exam slightly squelched by the reality that a law license could be used to represent people irresponsible enough to drink and drive and jeopardize the lives of innocent people.

I passed Maggie's office on the left. It, too, had been spruced up. The conference room on the right had two more pictures on the walls but was basically unchanged. It contained a simple table surrounded by six chairs and bore no resemblance to the splendid meeting room at Braddock, Appleby, and Carpenter with its shiny wooden table, thick carpet, and original oil paintings on the walls.

My office was next. When I'd visited before, it had been an empty room except for a copy machine. The copy machine was gone, and in its place was a simple wooden desk with a secretarial chair behind it. A desktop computer and printer sat on a side table. The walls were bare. There weren't any chairs in front of the desk. No bookcases, no credenza, no window to let in natural light. I entered slowly and sat down. I put the packet of materials on a used desk that had several obvious scratches. If God was going to help me build a law practice, we would begin at the most basic level.

I turned on the computer and encountered an immediate problem. Access was password-protected. I started to go ask Shannon, then decided I should check my packet first. Inside was a copy of the employment agreement I'd signed, information about the firm's health insurance policy, a holiday schedule, and the codes I would need to operate the copy machine, postage meter, and my computer. I entered the access information into the computer. As soon as I was online, I checked my personal e-mail and saw the heading regarding the results of the bar exam. Even though I knew what it contained, there was still an anxious moment as I clicked it open and read the congratulatory message. I printed out a copy and used it to cover up the worst scratch on the desk. I moved my phone a few inches to cover up another one. It took a few more minutes to set up my computer. As I finished, the phone on my desk buzzed. I jumped, the abrupt sound loud in the small room.

"Tami, can you hear me?" Shannon asked.

I picked up the receiver.

"Yes."

"I think you have a client here to see you."

"I don't have any clients."

"Were you expecting someone to come by the office?"

"Nobody knows I would be here."

Shannon lowered her voice. "Should I tell them you're not in?"

Getting Shannon to lie about my whereabouts was not how I
wanted to start my career.

"No, I'll come out."

Puzzled, I left my office and stepped into the hallway.

I ENTERED THE WAITING ROOM. IT WAS SISTER DABNEY. DRESSED
in a baggy brown dress with her gray hair unkempt and a frown on her
face, she was inspecting the reading material on the coffee table. It was
littered with gossip magazines, probably placed there for female
divorce clients. I tensed for a sharp rebuke that would give Shannon
something else to think about besides her sons fighting at the breakfast table.

"This is the place of women?" Sister Dabney asked.

"Yes."

Shannon was staring, not pretending to work.

"Is she one of the lawyers?" Sister Dabney pointed her finger in
the direction of the opening in the wall.

"No, that's Shannon Carver. She's the secretary, receptionist, and
bookkeeper." I motioned to the woman preacher. "This is Ramona
Dabney. I met her last summer. She has a church on Gillespie Street
and helps a lot of poor people."

The woman preacher fixed her gaze on Shannon, who quickly
lowered her head. My heart pounded as I waited for a public exposé
of Shannon's sins. Trying to explain to Maggie why her office worker
quit within an hour of my arrival would be a challenge. Sister Dabney
stood in front of the opening in the wall.

"Would you take him back?" Sister Dabney asked.

"Who?" Shannon responded with a puzzled look.

"Your husband."

Shannon's face went pale.

"Do you know Peter?"

"A new wind is blowing across his life. The changes are real. And the boys need him."

Shannon looked at me with desperation in her eyes. "Tami, this woman has no right to talk to me about my personal life!"

"Is anybody in your life telling you the truth?" Sister Dabney continued.

I stepped forward and lightly touched Sister Dabney on the arm.

"Could we go back to the conference room?"

Sister Dabney pushed a piece of stray hair away from her face. I led her down the short hall into the conference room, then closed the door after her. I stuck my head in Shannon's office. She was dabbing a tissue to her eyes.

"Are you okay?"

She spun around. "I don't want to talk to that woman again! When she gets ready to leave, tell me so I can hide."

"All right."

I returned to the conference room. Sister Dabney had placed her large black pocketbook on the table. I sat across the table from her. I realized that I'd forgotten to bring a legal pad to take notes but didn't want to leave her alone to get one.

"Why are you here?" I asked, trying to keep my voice from shaking.

"Why are you here?" she responded evenly.

"This is where I'm going to work unless I get fired because you scared the receptionist to death."

"Repentance leads to life. The wages of sin is death. The choice is hers."

I took a deep breath. "That approach to people doesn't always work."

Sister Dabney leaned forward. "My way of plain speaking is better than standing by silently while someone's life is ruined. When the Lord gives me revelation, I have to speak it or pray it."

"Why didn't you just pray it?"

"Because I know the difference. We can't judge the effect of a word at the time it's given. It's like a seed that needs time to grow and mature. Then its fruit can be judged."

Sister Dabney was speaking calmly, and it was hard to disagree with her reasoning. However, the emotional impact of her methods was hard to accept.

"Well, you've spoken to Shannon. Is that why you're here?"

Sister Dabney leaned back in her chair and seemed to relax. "No, I came to see you. I spoke into this situation for you and want you to get started with a firm foundation."

"Rebuking Shannon made it shaky, not firm."

Sister Dabney's eyes flashed with fire.

"I'm sorry," I added hastily. "I'm used to being different myself and having people react negatively to me. It's just that you're more different than I am."

The fire faded from the older woman's eyes.

"That's true. And you're not supposed to copy me. But there will come a time when you will know what the Lord wants you to do before it happens, and you'll need to be ready to cooperate with the gift."

I believed in foreknowledge. Mama knew she was having twins long before the doctor confirmed there were two babies in her womb.

"Is that how you knew I'd arrived in Savannah?"

"No, I looked up Mrs. Fairmont's phone number and called before I left the house."

I cracked a smile. At least the woman preacher needed to use a phone book.

"You can also be called to a situation without advance warning," Sister Dabney continued. "The main thing is to walk in God's way."

"Yes, ma'am."

"And it's important that the firstfruits of your work as a lawyer be offered to God."

Sister Dabney stared at me for a few seconds without speaking. I suddenly had an idea why she'd come to see me and decided to test my new insight.

"If you want me to help you, I'm sure I could do it without charging anything. I mean, I'd have to talk to the other lawyers in the firm, but when I explain—"

"No, the Lord was my lawyer when the other law firm sued me last summer," she said, interrupting me. "I'm going to stick with him."

"Okay," I said, slightly embarrassed. "Maybe I can help someone who goes to your church."

Sister Dabney paused. "We'll see. The work of the kingdom is based on a sacrifice that costs you something. Don't forget."

"I won't."

I excused myself from the conference room to warn Shannon that Sister Dabney was coming out. The secretary was staring at photos on her computer monitor. I caught a glimpse of her sons and a man I assumed was her husband before she quickly closed the screen.

"She's going to leave now," I said.

"Then I'm heading to the break room," Shannon said briskly. "I hope you don't have any other clients like that woman. Strange people have come in here, but she is the most bizarre—" Shannon didn't finish the sentence.

I escorted Sister Dabney to the door. Before leaving, she turned to me.

"Are you coming to the church on Sunday?"

I hesitated. I didn't want to commit to Southside Church without praying about other options.

"There's a reason you're supposed to be there," Sister Dabney continued.

"Should I come alone?"

"No, the purpose of the meeting is to share the good news with as many people as possible."

"Okay. I'll be there."

I watched Sister Dabney walk slowly across the parking lot. As she reached her vehicle, I saw Julie speed into the parking lot. She hopped out of her car and watched intently as Sister Dabney got in hers. A few seconds later Julie burst through the door.

"Was that who I think it was?"

"Probably."

"What was she doing here?"

"She came by to see me."

"And ruin my day," Shannon added through the opening in the wall.

"I thought you were in the break room," I said.

"I peeked and heard you tell her good-bye."

"Did Sister Dabney let out one of her bloodcurdling yells?" Julie asked. "Remember when she did that during her deposition in the Paulding case?"

"Yes," I said wearily. "I was there and told you about it. Otherwise, you might not know about it. She didn't do any yelling this morning."

"But she told me I should get back together with Peter," Shannon said. "Without any idea what he did to me."

"She asked you if you would take him back," I corrected. "Maybe he's changed."

"Do you know what Peter did?" Julie asked me.

"No."

Julie turned to Shannon. "Tami means well, but remember what I told you the other day. She comes from an extremely religious background, maybe even a cult. If you approach her ideas from a sociological point of view, it can even be interesting to listen to her. Just don't take her opinions too seriously. That's how we survived working in the same room together last summer. I didn't agree with her; she didn't agree with me. But Tami's beliefs won't keep her from being a good lawyer.

She's got this schizophrenic ability to separate her legal reasoning from her attachment to the Bible."

"That's not true—," I protested.

Julie cut me off with a wave of her hand. "Not now. The good news is that we passed the bar exam. Congratulations!"

Julie leaned forward and gave me a big hug.

"Let's go back to my office and catch up," she said. "Shannon, please tell anyone who calls that Tami and I are in a conference."

"What if it's Maggie?" the secretary asked.

"Put her through. She'll want to know Tami arrived in a blaze of controversy."

Julie's office was identical in size to Maggie's but exquisitely decorated. I sat in a comfortable leather chair.

"I'm so excited you're here," Julie said, closing the door. "Don't let Shannon's negative attitude get under your skin. I can understand why Peter bolted from the marriage. What did Dabney say to her?"

I repeated the message.

"I don't disagree with her," Julie said thoughtfully. "My big question would be whether Shannon has changed. She needs a new wind, whatever that means, to blow across her life. And those boys of hers need a spanking. She brought them to the office for a couple of hours one day last week before taking them to the doctor for a checkup. I was ready to rip off a tree limb and break it on the backside of the older one."

"You believe in spanking?"

"Not beating, of course. But a kid needs to experience enough pain to communicate the need for a change in behavior or attitude. Shannon's boys need to know there are limits."

I told her about the cereal incident.

"Exactly what I'm talking about. I bet you never did that to one of your ten brothers and sisters."

"There are five of us."

"Whatever. Maggie hired Shannon because she felt sorry for her and saddled us with the rehabilitation project. I mean, she can do the job; it's just the personal drama that goes along with it."

"You didn't help make that decision?"

"Don't start trying to create division between Maggie and me. We've got to be unified to make this work."

"I know. I just wondered—"

Julie cut me off with a wave of her hand. "And don't take everything I say literally, like you do the Bible. Maggie and I talked in advance about hiring Shannon, and I came over from Atlanta to sit in on the interview. Shannon worked as a temp for the district attorney's office, and Maggie saw she had the skills to be a one-woman support staff. That's what we need, even if we have to put up with the fallout from Shannon's personal life. None of that caught us by surprise. We assumed the risk, and except when her little hoodlums are on the premises, it's working out fine."

"Will I be giving her work to do?"

"Sure. She's lightning fast with dictation and knows the accounting software like a programmer. Every two months the books are reviewed by an outside accountant to make sure she's not stealing from us."

Not being able to trust someone who worked for me was a new thought to me. I suddenly felt naive.

"What have you been doing at the office since you moved down here?"

"Helping Maggie. There's not nearly as much research to do as we had at Braddock, Appleby, and Carpenter, but some cases have to be fine-tuned, and I've streamlined her process. You're going to like Maggie. She's more like you than I am."

"That would be easy. We're not anything alike."

Julie smiled. "Nice try at sarcasm, but you're way too indirect and gentle." Julie held up a brown arm. "And I've spent a lot of time at the beach working on my tan."

"Are you still seeing Joel?"

"No, he moved to Seattle about six months ago and got a job working for a movie production company. It was a fun relationship, but both of us were ready to move on."

"That's another way we're different. I couldn't be so casual about romance."

Julie held up her right index finger. "At least I was only seeing one man at a time. You've held this love triangle together with Zach and Vinny longer than one on a TV soap opera. Does Vinny still have the short end? If he doesn't have a chance of success, shouldn't you cut him loose so he can try in vain to find happiness with another woman?"

"In vain?"

"Compared to you."

The phone buzzed, and Julie picked it up.

"Okay, put her through."

She set the phone on speaker. It was Maggie.

"How many did you win?" Julie asked, pretending to turn a steering wheel with a drunken look on her face.

"Two out of six were dismissed on motion. The others are set for trial, but I should be able to get a plea agreement on all of them. The clients are mostly kids. No repeat offenders."

"Not yet. Did Shannon tell you Tami is here?"

"Yes. Where is she?"

"Sitting here waiting on me to put her to work. We're on speaker."

"Hey, Tami," Maggie said. "Congratulations on passing the bar. Julie called me with the news last night."

"Thanks."

"I talked to the presiding superior court judge. The general swearing-in will be scheduled later this week. Would you and Julie want to be part of that or do it privately in chambers?"

"My parents want to come so the big ceremony would be best for me," Julie said.

I hadn't thought about it. Graduation from law school had been my time to celebrate with my family. Asking them to drive five hours to watch me raise my hand and repeat a simple oath to uphold the Constitution and obey the court didn't seem necessary.

"It doesn't matter to me," I said.

"Tami can't wait to file suit against one of Joe Carpenter's clients," Julie said. "I'm sure he was hiding in his office and felt the ground shake beneath his feet when she arrived in town."

"We'll do both of you at once," Maggie said. "And Joe Carpenter isn't hiding in his office. He was in court this morning."

"Mr. Carpenter doesn't handle DUI cases," I said.

"I know, but this wasn't a DUI-only calendar. He had a hearing on a motion for reduction of bond. It caught my attention because of the amount. He asked the judge to reduce the bond from $1 million to $250,000. The judge lowered it $500,000. Mr. Carpenter and his client seemed pleased."

"What was the charge against the defendant?" Julie asked.

"It was a conspiracy charge, probably some kind of white-collar crime."

"Was the defendant's name Paulding?" I asked, wondering if the developer had gotten into more trouble.

"No, it was Hacker, Hackney, something like that. Whatever his name, he has enough money or unencumbered property to post a large bond. Hey, I'm getting in my car. I'll be at the office in about fifteen minutes."

"I'll make sure Tami is busy by the time you get here," Julie said. "I hope it's okay that I gave her permission to address us by our first names."

I heard Maggie laugh. "I don't want anyone calling me Ms. Smith until I'm sixty."

"You didn't mention Sister Dabney stopping by," I said when the call ended.

"That's too good a story to waste on a phone call. The Dabney debacle, as I'm going to call it, will be the subject of a long lunch that will end with your first disciplinary write-up. I predict within one year your personnel file will be at least an inch thick."

I returned to my office and then remembered I'd forgotten to mention Zach's invitation for dinner. Instead of going back to Julie's office, I sent her an interoffice e-mail:

Zach wants to take Vince, you, and me to dinner this evening to celebrate our passing the bar exam. Okay?

Within a minute after I sent the message, I received a reply:

Sure. Wouldn't miss the chance to see you drink champagne. And if this is a sneaky scheme to set me up with Vinny, I'll play along, but I'm not going to steal him away from you. He's still my favorite in the Tami Sweepstakes.

I called Zach. He'd talked to Vince, who liked the idea of a celebratory meal.

"Vince and I will pick you up at Mrs. Fairmont's house at six thirty," Zach said. "Tell Julie to meet us at the restaurant about six forty-five."

"You're coming together?"

"Yeah, we'll be at the office until then. There's no need to drive an extra car."

After we hung up I confirmed with Julie, who replied immediately.

This is going to be soooo much fun.

I hoped she was right.

10

I heard Maggie's voice in the hallway followed by a knock on my door.

"Come in," I said.

The former assistant DA was dressed for court in a dark blue suit and black shoes. She had a smile on her face.

"Still believe God wants you to work here?"

Coming from her, the question sounded different than if Julie had asked it.

"Yes."

"Good. Meet Julie and me in the conference room in five minutes so we can get organized."

"Don't make us wait," Julie said, sticking her head in the door a couple of minutes later.

I grabbed a legal pad and followed her into the conference room. Maggie was sitting at one end of the table with a laptop in front of her and three stacks of files beside her right hand. She glanced up when we entered.

"Do you own a laptop?" she asked me.

"Yes."

"Can you use it a few days for work away from the office until we buy you another one?"

"Yes, I'll bring it with me tomorrow."

"I told you Tami is a team player," Julie said.

Julie flipped open an ultralight computer.

"It will be easier if we exchange typed memos," Maggie said. "I'm sure that's what you did at Braddock, Appleby, and Carpenter."

"All day, every day," Julie replied.

"I spent a lot of time earlier this week reviewing my caseload," Maggie continued. "Julie has been helping with all the divorce cases, and once she's sworn in all that business will flow through her. She's met most of the clients who've hired us thus far, and I think we can make a smooth transition with the rest."

"We've taken a few high-end cases," Julie added. "Assets of several million that are worth fighting over, along with the kid issues, of course."

"How do you get the clients?" I asked.

The concept that someone would actually phone a law office was still a bit of a mystery to me.

"Mostly women I met when I was working at the DA's office," Maggie said.

"How?" I asked.

"People who served on juries and liked what they saw. Witnesses I interviewed for cases. Things like that. When their marriages crashed they looked me up. I guess they figured if I could prosecute criminals, I could go after their husbands."

"And we're also representing a handful of men," Julie said brightly. "That will be a fun change of pace."

"I'm not that interested—," I said.

"Your only involvement in the domestic area will be to focus on the financial records," Maggie interrupted. "Julie says you have a knack for that sort of thing."

I gave Julie a puzzled look.

"Don't pretend you're dumb. You were a whiz at secured transactions and the complex business issues Bob Kettleson gave you last summer."

"We're all learning," Maggie said. "I'll continue to handle the criminal cases since that's my comfort zone. And we'll be opportunistic about bigger cases, which will be either hourly work or on a contingency. However, the key to long-term success as a lawyer is finding a niche and developing a high level of expertise in that area."

I'd heard the same basic line from Oscar Callahan. Maggie put her hand on a stack of files.

"Tami, until you find your niche, I'm turning the miscellaneous files over to you. As you work on different types of cases, you'll have a chance to see what interests you."

"And I promised Maggie you wouldn't commit legal malpractice while learning," Julie said. "Don't let me down."

"But you'll supervise me?" I asked Maggie.

"As much as I can, but a lot of these files represent work that came in because of an existing client. I would have turned away this extra business as outside our areas of interest and expertise except I knew you were coming and needed something to do."

Maggie slid the files over to me. I quickly read down the labels and saw everything from a bailment action against a country club to a zoning request before the city of Savannah. Without a senior lawyer to lean on, I felt overwhelmed.

"I'll check your billing," Maggie said. "It wouldn't be right to charge a client for every minute of the time you spend figuring out what to do. But don't worry; I'll keep a separate file of your actual hours so Julie won't be able to accuse you of slacking off."

Julie narrowed her eyes. "I'll still accuse you, but I may not be able to make it stick."

"And other research projects will surface," Maggie said to me. "Do you have any interest in doing appellate work?"

"I like writing briefs, but Julie is a better writer than I am. Her memos last summer were great."

"Not good enough to get me a job offer."

"That's not the reason—"

"Did Mr. Carpenter tell you why they offered you a job and not me?" Julie shot back.

"No."

"Zach didn't give you a clue?"

"He's an associate."

Julie pouted. I fidgeted in my seat. Maggie broke the awkward tension.

"Whatever happened in the past, the three of us are in this together now. We're the first all-female firm in the history of Savannah. People inside and outside the legal community are watching us. Some want us to succeed; others would be glad if we failed. But if we work hard and do a good job for our clients, there's no reason why we can't prosper and have a good time doing it. I'm looking forward to the future."

Julie's face brightened. "Good speech, Coach. We ought to put our hands together and yell 'Team!'"

I returned to my office with the thick stack of files and Maggie's final instructions ringing in my ears that my first priority was to make sure we weren't about to miss a time deadline or statute of limitations. Fear produced a burst of adrenaline. A couple of hours later I turned down Julie's invitation to go to lunch because I was in the middle of researching the deadlines and notice requirements in the materialman's lien case. It was an area of the law in which particularity of language developed hundreds of years ago in England still held sway in the United States.

"Do you want me to bring you something?" Julie asked.

"Uh, any kind of salad would be great."

I reached for my purse.

"No money necessary; today is on me," Julie responded. "When you get a paycheck you can buy me a drink."

"Of iced tea."

"With a shot of hard lemonade. See you in a bit."

I was creating the forms for the lien when Julie returned and placed a clear plastic container of food on my desk.

"It's mixed greens with oriental chicken and a sesame dressing," she said.

I lifted the lid. It looked and smelled good.

"Thanks. I'm almost ready to file the lien for a concrete company that didn't get paid for paving the parking lot at a new convenience store."

"Oh, that's my client," Julie said.

"Yours?"

"I met the owner's son at a bar. When he asked for my phone number, I gave him the one here at the office. When he realized this was a law office, he asked if I could help him out. He's in the business with his father. I asked a few questions, and we ended up talking about the claim so long that he forgot to ask me out."

"Would you have said yes?"

"No, but it would have been a painless rejection. I can stick a knife in a man's heart and pull it out, causing only a minor, momentary discomfort."

"I wouldn't mind representing a concrete company," I said. "Maybe I can meet with the son and his father."

"Sure. Set it up and leave me out of it. The son had cement under his fingernails. I'm sure the father is as bad, or worse."

After Julie left, I munched my salad, surprised at how excited I was about marketing my legal services. I guess it had to do with building something that could be concrete to me—a law practice.

BY THE TIME I MADE SURE WE WEREN'T IN IMMINENT DANGER OF committing legal malpractice, it was late afternoon. I was tired, but it was a good kind of fatigue. Julie poked her head in my door.

"Shannon's gone. You can come out now."

"What?"

"I know you didn't want to face her again today. Don't worry. By tomorrow her kids will have driven out any memory of your connection to Dabney."

"I doubt it. People don't forget Sister Dabney."

"True," Julie admitted. "But maybe Shannon won't hold it against you. Hey, you'd better go home now if you want to change clothes before dinner and plaster on your makeup the way Zach likes it."

"What are you going to wear?" I asked.

"Nothing that will embarrass you or distract the men," Julie said, straightening her shirt. "This is your tea party. Zach set it up because he wants you to see that he's a better candidate for your hand in marriage than Vinny."

"Whatever." I laughed.

"So, don't worry," Julie continued. "I only express my honest opinion when we're having girl talk. Guys have to be kept in the dark. They can't handle the truth."

AT MRS. FAIRMONT'S HOUSE I GAVE THE ELDERLY WOMAN A QUICK summary of my first day on the job while I heated up supper. Tonight, she didn't remember meeting Sister Dabney. When her memory of the present day dulled, Mrs. Fairmont could more easily remember names and faces from the distant past than recent contacts. When I gave her the goods news about passing the bar exam, she gave me a satisfied nod.

"I'm glad you didn't stop at a bar on the way home," she said. "Christine should listen to you. She drives after having a couple of drinks. Someday she'll be sorry if the police stop her."

After eating supper, Mrs. Fairmont returned to the den to watch TV. I had time to clean the kitchen then change into a nicer dress before Zach and Vince arrived. I stood in the foyer and watched the street. Zach pulled up in his white car. As soon as he stopped, Vince got out. I didn't wait for him to ring the doorbell.

"If I'm not back before you go to bed, have a good night's sleep!" I called out to Mrs. Fairmont.

Flip barked at the sound of my voice, and I couldn't make out the older woman's response.

Vince held the car door open for me. He looked tanned and rested. After I got in, he sat behind me. I turned slightly sideways in my seat so I could see both men. It had been a long time since I'd been with both of them at the same time. They were both wearing dark pants and white shirts with conservative ties.

"Congratulations," Vince said. "Are you ready to celebrate?"

"Yes."

"How was your first day at the office?" Zach asked as he pulled away from the curb.

"I survived. What did you two do today?"

It was odd listening to the two men describe their activities at the firm, knowing that I wasn't going to be part of their working world.

"Maggie saw Mr. Carpenter in court at a criminal motion calendar this morning," I said when there was a pause in the conversation.

"What was his client's name?" Vince asked.

"Hacker, Hackney, or something close to that."

Zach and Vince exchanged a look. Neither spoke.

"Do you know who it is?" I asked.

"Not much beyond a name," Zach said. "Mr. Carpenter sent out a firm-wide e-mail early in the week to make sure we didn't have a conflict of interest with several individuals and a few companies. One of the people listed was named Hackney. Mr. Carpenter is going to pull in several lawyers to help him in the cases."

"What kind of cases?"

"Some business matters and a big criminal case. One of the women in the word-processing department made a comment to me, but I'm not sure she really knew anything."

"What did she say?" I asked.

"I can't tell you," Zach replied.

"If you'd taken the job with the firm, you'd probably be in the middle of it," Vince added with a cough. "Mr. Carpenter wanted me to do some research, but Mr. Braddock nixed the idea."

I would have to get used to being an outsider when it came to Braddock, Appleby, and Carpenter. We arrived at the restaurant, a local steak place. I didn't see Julie's car in the parking lot.

"Not a lot of tourists come here," Zach said as we got out of the car. "They want seafood, not steak."

We waited inside for Julie, who arrived, somewhat breathless, a couple of minutes later. She'd not kept her wardrobe promise. Her neckline plunged a few inches past modest. I felt sorry for Zach and Vince.

"Hope you haven't been waiting long," she said, flashing her best smile. "Let the party begin."

The host took us to a table for four. Julie and I sat across from each other with Zach on my right and Vince on my left. We'd barely opened our menus before Julie launched into the story about Sister Dabney's appearance at the office. Unlike Mrs. Fairmont, Julie's memory was razor-sharp, and she told the story with such detail that I had to remind myself she'd not been there.

With Julie dominating the conversation I devoted my attention to the menu. When the waiter approached to take our order, I glanced up and saw that Zach was looking at me, not the menu, not Julie's neckline. I rewarded him with my best smile.

"Order whatever you want," he said to the three of us. "You only have a day like this once in life."

I ordered the filet mignon. When the food arrived, Julie slowed down the conversation long enough to cut into her steak.

"Tami was really out to impress Maggie," she said between bites. "She worked right through lunch even though we don't pay overtime to salaried employees."

"I didn't want to commit malpractice my first day on the job," I replied, then told Zach and Vince about the stack of files I'd been assigned.

"That's a good idea," Zach said. "Try a bunch of different things and decide what you like to do."

"Today, she's into concrete," Julie said. "Tomorrow, it may be condemnation actions. There's nothing more thrilling than arguing the value of a piece of dirt."

"If the state is involved in taking the property, you'll be dealing with Ned Danforth at our firm," Zach said. "He represents the state. Another law firm handles the county."

"It's a state case," I replied.

"I'd like to condemn Ned and bury him beneath a thick piece of asphalt," Julie said, sticking her knife in her steak for emphasis.

"Why are you mad at Ned?" Vince asked.

Julie put the back of her hand to her forehead. "The mention of his name makes me want to faint." She turned to me. "Has the statute of limitations run out on my claim against the firm for harassment? Get me a memo on that first thing in the morning."

Ned had bothered Julie on a sailboat outing the previous summer. She put him in his place in about five seconds, but it shook her up.

"If Ned did something wrong—," Vince began.

"No, forget about it," Julie said, removing the knife from her steak. "If Tami has to file a condemnation suit, I'd rather have Ned on the other side than someone smart. If he gets fired, the firm might assign those cases to one of you. That would be a fight to the death."

Zach and Vince looked at each other, then at me, and shrugged. The waiter returned, and Julie refused a refill of red wine.

"I'm cutting back," she said.

"Really?" I asked.

"Don't get your hopes up. I'm driving home and don't want to see the judge on a DUI ticket before I'm sworn in as a lawyer."

As the meal progressed, I couldn't sense any tension between Zach and Vince about me. Contrary to the story line of the few romance novels Mama allowed in the house, the two men didn't seem bent on destroying each other in order to win me. The conversation turned to baseball.

"My father has season tickets in Atlanta," Julie said. "I used to go when I was a little girl. He has great seats behind first base, but all I cared about was the hot dogs."

"Wow," both men said simultaneously.

Julie shook her head and turned to me. "Did you hear that? It's so hard for men to have an original thought. The program running a man's brain is like those early computers that read holes punched in cards."

While we waited for the check, Julie phoned her father about the tickets. She listened for a moment and then gave Zach and Vince a thumbs-up sign.

"Thanks, Dad. Is it okay if I give Zach your e-mail address so you can make the arrangements directly with him?"

She listened for a moment. "Yes, he's the admiralty lawyer with the cute ponytail. You know, the one I thought should wear a sailor suit to work."

Zach rolled his eyes.

"You'll meet all of them at the swearing-in ceremony. See you then."

We topped off the meal with a single serving of a rich dessert that we shared in the middle of the table. It contained four different kinds of chocolate.

During the ride home from the restaurant, Zach and Vince started talking about baseball, and I felt like a spectator.

"Do you think we should try to find two more tickets so you and Julie could go?" Zach asked me.

"It wouldn't be four in a row," Vince said before I answered. "Who'd sit together?"

I braced for an argument about who would sit with me.

"I guess the guys and girls would have to separate once the game started," Zach said.

Startled, I imagined myself next to Julie while she crammed hot dogs slathered in mustard into her mouth and washed them down with warm beer.

"I'm not that interested," I responded. "And if Julie wanted to go she'd have told her father. He could probably get tickets from some of the people he sits next to on a regular basis."

"Of course," Vince said, "Why didn't I think about that? Season ticket holders get to know one another. It turns the games into a social event."

"You and Zach have a good time. Buy Julie a cheap souvenir. She'll love it."

Vince hopped out and opened the car door for me. As I walked up the steps to Mrs. Fairmont's front door, I wondered what the two men would discuss after dropping me off. They seemed to have reached some kind of unspoken truce when it came to me. If so, I sure wish I could find out the terms of agreement.

A COUPLE NIGHTS BEFORE THE SWEARING-IN CEREMONY, MRS. Fairmont and I were sitting in the blue parlor after supper.

"The swearing-in ceremony for new lawyers is Thursday morning at ten o'clock," I said, yawning.

"What time is your family going to get here?" she asked.

"They're not coming."

"If your family can't come, then I will," Mrs. Fairmont replied, sitting up straighter in her chair. "Someone should be there to support you and witness such an historic moment."

"That's nice, but it's just a formality, not the signing of the Declaration of Independence."

"I couldn't make it to Philadelphia for that, so I'll let this be my substitute," she said with a twinkle in her blue eyes. "Don't argue with me, or I'll call Christine and tell her you're being mean to me."

"You wouldn't do that."

"I'm trying to turn over a new leaf in life, but if you press me I could revert to my old, manipulative ways."

I laughed. It was worth a pretend argument to enjoy a few moments with Mrs. Fairmont so clearly in touch with her full faculties.

"Yes, ma'am. Don't revert. That would be scary. Just promise that if you don't feel well, you won't insist on going. I don't want to be worrying about you when I should be focusing on raising my right hand and not my left hand to take the oath."

Mrs. Fairmont scratched Flip's head. "There's a dress in the back of my closet that would be the perfect thing to wear. I hope I can still fit into it."

Keeping weight on Mrs. Fairmont, not watching calories, was the challenge at this stage of her life.

THURSDAY MORNING I HEARD THE QUICK PATTER OF FLIP'S FEET on the wooden stairs, followed by the much slower click of Mrs. Fairmont's shoes coming slowly behind him. I went into the foyer. The elderly lady saw me and gave a quick wave before clutching the railing to take another step.

"I can't believe I used to wear these shoes all the time," she said. "I feel like I'm walking on stilts."

Low heels were strapped around her ankles. She was wearing a light blue dress that shimmered. A diamond and sapphire necklace was draped around her neck. More diamonds glittered on her fingers.

"Then don't wear them," I said. "Your white shoes with the silver buckles would go with that outfit."

"Child, those shoes are so scuffed up I wouldn't wear them to the grocery store. I called Sam Braddock yesterday, and he told me the swearing-in ceremony was almost a formal affair."

"You talked to Mr. Braddock?"

"He's my lawyer, at least until tomorrow, and I'll switch to you."

"My first piece of legal advice is that you stick with Mr. Braddock."

Mrs. Fairmont reached the bottom of the stairs and let out a sigh of relief.

"You look beautiful," I said. "What do you think about my outfit?"

I'd selected a yellow dress that was the second-fanciest item in my humble wardrobe. Mrs. Fairmont pressed her lips together in a tight smile for a moment before answering.

"A beautiful girl like you makes the outfit, not the other way around. And you're lovely on the inside, which is very rare."

I stepped forward and gave her a big hug. The night before, she'd not been feeling well, and I'd wondered if she'd be able to attend the ceremony. But a night's rest and a few prayers made a difference. She seemed very alert.

"Not too hard," she said, patting me on the back. "It took me over an hour to build this facade, and it needs to last until we come home."

Mrs. Fairmont talked the whole way to the courthouse. She knew the history of many of the houses we passed and remembered people and events from decades ago. I'd heard some of her stories several times, but instead of reminding her, I used my previous knowledge to ask questions I knew she enjoyed answering. When I parked the car, Mrs. Fairmont lowered the sun visor and checked herself in the mirror on the other side.

"There's no statute of limitations on a woman's concern about the appearance of her hair," I said.

Mrs. Fairmont carefully smoothed a stray strand in place. "You never know who might be here. There might be a man I find interesting."

I laughed, and we got out of the car. Thankfully, we didn't have to walk very far in the morning heat. Mrs. Fairmont took small steps. I matched her pace. One of the younger lawyers from Braddock, Appleby, and Carpenter passed us on the sidewalk without acknowledging my presence. I knew I might receive a cool reception from members of the firm.

We rode the elevator to the upstairs courtroom where the swearing-in ceremony would be held. A few people I didn't know were gathering. Julie, Vince, and Zach hadn't arrived. I led Mrs. Fairmont to a seat on the front row so her view wouldn't be blocked.

"Do you want to introduce me as your great-grandmother?" Mrs. Fairmont whispered.

"You're not that old, and it wouldn't be true."

"You're right. No one could look at your long legs and believe we're from the same family tree."

"I'm honored to have you here. It's sweet that you wanted to come."

"Margaret?" An older woman across the room waved in our direction. "Is that you?"

Mrs. Fairmont squinted slightly, then smiled. "It's Harriet Wilson. I haven't seen her in ages."

Mrs. Wilson, who was about ten years younger than Mrs. Fairmont, came over. After Mrs. Fairmont introduced me to her, the two women sat down and began chatting. The back door of the courtroom opened, and the lawyers from Braddock, Appleby, and Carpenter entered in royal procession, with Mr. Braddock and Vince in front. Zach saw me and smiled.

Maggie and Julie came in behind the group from the firm. I immediately spotted Julie's mother, a fifty-year-old version of her daughter. Julie's father was a short, balding man in a dark suit. Maggie and Julie saw me and joined us. I was glad Mrs. Fairmont wanted to come. It made me feel less alone and like a hillbilly outsider. The diamonds on her fingers were at least as large as the ones shown off by Julie's mother.

Judge Cannon, the senior superior court judge, strode into the room as the clerk of court called out, "All rise!"

Six people, three women and three men, were going to be sworn in. In addition to Julie, Vince, and me, there was a young man who would be joining the public defender's office, a woman who would be taking over Maggie's place at the district attorney's office, and a young man joining another small law firm. Mr. Braddock came to the front with Vince and introduced him.

"Your Honor, it is my privilege to introduce Vince Colbert, who will be working with me in the transactional and estate-planning area of the firm. He is a summa cum laude graduate of Vanderbilt University and a magna cum laude graduate of Yale Law School, where he served on the staff of the *Yale Law Journal*."

Everyone clapped. Vince's academic and legal pedigree was impressive. Seeing him standing beside Mr. Braddock, I had no doubt Vince's future would be one of unqualified success. Maggie stood and motioned to me. I joined her at the front of the room.

"Your Honor, it is my privilege to introduce Tami Taylor, who will be working in our firm. She graduated from Berry College and the University of Georgia School of Law."

The applause was more muted except for Julie, who let out a whoop that caused the judge to glance in her direction. I returned to my seat beside Mrs. Fairmont, who patted me on the hand. Julie, who was on the other side of me, leaned over and whispered, "I should have brought an air horn."

"I'm supposed to be the redneck."

Julie's mother beamed when her daughter was introduced. Seeing her joy made me miss Daddy and Mama, but they wouldn't have felt comfortable in the room. Next up was the young woman who was going to work in the district attorney's office. She was related to Harriet Wilson.

"That's Harriet's great-niece by the second daughter her sister had with her first husband."

"Good," I answered, not commenting on the information, but rather Mrs. Fairmont's ability to remember and communicate it.

After everyone was introduced, the judge instructed all the admittees to rise for the administration of the oath. Standing next to her, I was especially aware of how much taller I was than Julie. After we finished the oath, Judge Cannon said a few words of congratulation to us and our families. As he finished his remarks, he motioned to the court administrator standing near the jury box.

"Except for Mr. Baldwin, who will be joining the public defender's office, and Ms. Crittenden, who will be prosecuting Mr. Baldwin's clients, give your name and contact information to Ms. Coutts so you can be placed on the appointed list. Pro bono work should be part of every lawyer's caseload. For the first three years of your practice in this circuit, it won't be an option. Court is adjourned."

"What kind of appointed cases?" I asked Julie as we waited our turn to see the court administrator.

"I guess criminal cases like the ones we did last summer."

Julie had easily taken care of her case. The Moses Jones case assigned to me had been a huge responsibility. We reached the court administrator, and I repeated my question.

"Whatever the judges want to give you," she replied. "It could be anything, criminal, juvenile, even general civil."

"I guess that's what it means to be an officer of the court," Julie said. "We're the privates; the judges are the generals."

"That's correct," Judge Cannon said.

We turned around and found the senior judge's dark eyes boring holes through us.

"Ms. Feldman and Ms. Taylor, correct?" the judge asked.

"Yes, sir," I answered.

"Yes, Your Honor." Julie nodded. "I didn't mean any disrespect."

"Of course not," the judge answered without smiling. "I'll be on the watch for something special that will challenge you and make you feel less like a private."

"I'm ready to serve," Julie said.

"I'll make sure of that," the judge replied. "I look forward to seeing both of you in my courtroom."

The judge left. Julie and I watched until he was a safe distance away.

"I didn't like the sound of that," Julie said. "What's he going to do when he gets us in his courtroom? Hold us in contempt for not wearing a color-coordinated outfit? We've not been sworn in five minutes, and we're on the outs with the presiding superior court judge."

"He was talking to you, not me."

"Don't be so preachy," Julie replied. "You're the one who went judge-shopping last summer to get what you wanted for your client. Don't kid yourself. He's not forgotten about it."

I glanced across the courtroom and saw Mrs. Fairmont was talking to Sam Braddock. She motioned me to come over. The senior partner of the firm had a smile on his face.

"Congratulations, Ms. Taylor," he said, extending his hand. "I'm confident you'll be a fine attorney, and I want to thank you for being such a tremendous help to Margaret."

"And Flip," Mrs. Fairmont added.

Mr. Braddock cleared his throat. "Right, did she mention our discussion about Flip's future a few months ago?"

"Yes, sir."

"Are you agreeable?"

"Yes."

Mr. Braddock leaned forward. "It's generally better for matters like that to be handled in an informal way. Margaret told me you'd be open to the idea, but I wanted to make sure myself."

"I love Flip," I said, deliberately using strong words of affection to reassure Mrs. Fairmont.

"See, I told you," she said with satisfaction to Mr. Braddock. "That settles it. I don't want Christine to bully either one of you."

"Together, we can hold our own," Mr. Braddock replied with a gentle smile to me.

Mr. Braddock moved away, leaving me relieved at the cordial conversation with the senior partner of the firm. Mrs. Fairmont yawned.

"It's time to take you home," I said.

"No, you should stay for the party."

"There's not going to be a party."

"Sam said there was going to be one."

"That's for his firm."

Mrs. Fairmont rubbed her temples. "Maybe you're right about leaving. My head is starting to hurt."

"You need to be relaxing in your den chair."

We made our way to the center aisle where Zach and Vince met us. We congratulated each other. Zach leaned over and gave me a quick hug. Then, to my surprise, Vince did the same.

"Mrs. Fairmont is tired and not feeling well," I said quickly. "I need to take her home."

"We'll talk later," Zach said.

I ushered Mrs. Fairmont down the aisle. At the rear door, we encountered Mr. Carpenter, who was returning to the courtroom. He bowed his head slightly to Mrs. Fairmont.

"Good to see you, Margaret," he said.

She gave him a puzzled look.

"And you, too, Mr. Carpenter," I spoke for her. "Vince is going to be a great asset to the firm."

"I'm glad you approve," he replied in a condescending tone.

I didn't slow down to try to explain my comment but gently guided Mrs. Fairmont out of the courtroom. Within forty-five minutes she had changed into comfortable clothes and was napping in her chair with Flip content at her feet.

I BEGAN TO FEEL MORE AND MORE CONFIDENT AT THE OFFICE with each passing day. Problems that seemed overwhelmingly obscure and complex at first reading became solvable when broken down into smaller parts.

One afternoon, Shannon buzzed me in my office. Since Sister Dabney's visit to the office, the secretary receptionist had treated me with casual indifference.

"Zach Mays on line two," she said.

"Busy?" he asked when I answered.

"Yes. And you?"

"Not too bad. Hey, I want to go for a motorcycle ride this evening after supper. It would be a thousand times better if you'd come with me. I promise to get you home before dark."

"Isn't it supposed to rain?"

"No, I checked the weather before I called and it's moving north of here. Say yes, and I'll buy you an ice cream. It won't be as good as the homemade stuff we ate with your family, but I know a local place where it's edible."

I loved ice cream. "Will I have to eat it riding in the sidecar?"

"No, but it might go well with a sunset."

An ice cream and a sunset might thaw out the chill my job choice had caused in our relationship.

"An ice cream and sunset sounds wonderful."

When I hung up the phone, Julie stuck her head in my open door.

"Did I hear you say ice cream and sunset?" she asked.

"Yes."

"With Zach?"

I nodded. Julie grinned.

"Sharing a cone with a man while the sun sinks below the waves is about as romantic as it gets. Get orange sherbet. It'll go perfectly with the sunset."

"I like chocolate, and I've never shared an ice-cream cone with a man."

"There's always a first time. And with you—that's an everyday occurrence. Go with the sherbet. Chocolate is way too messy. Save that for the day when you take your four children under the age of five out for a treat."

11

Since arriving in Savannah, Jessie had stayed in three different places. The past week, she'd been sleeping on a discarded mattress hidden in some dense bushes a couple of blocks from Sister Dabney's church. It was an isolated spot, and no one bothered her. Next to the mattress was a small metal box she found near a furniture store. Inside the box, she kept the leather pouch and a few bits of stolen food.

Sister Dabney's house was the only place Jessie had found to get a home-cooked meal. However, the preacher's world had many strange rules. One dealt with the blue rocker on Sister Dabney's front porch. The rocker was off-limits to Jessie. It wasn't a big deal. Jessie didn't mind sitting on the steps, as long as she had an apple or a banana in her hand.

One evening while Sister Dabney was rocking back and forth, Jessie sat on the front steps eating an apple. Sister Dabney suddenly called out, "Jessie!" so loudly that the girl jumped. "Get up here and sit in this rocker!"

Jessie gave Sister Dabney a puzzled look.

"Why should I do that?"

"Because it's your destiny in God!"

Jessie obediently came over to the rocker.

"Get rid of that apple core," Sister Dabney ordered. "This chair is for seeing, not eating."

Jessie took a last nibble, tossed the core onto the grassy weeds that covered the front yard, then sat down. Dabney gave the chair a shove.

"I'll have to help you at first, but later you'll be able to rock on your own."

"I can do it," Jessie replied, grabbing the arms of the chair and pushing off with her feet.

"You just think you can."

Jessie rarely argued with Sister Dabney. It only made her more confused. The older woman kept her hand on the back of the chair, moving it back and forth. Jessie let her feet dangle without touching the porch.

"Close your eyes," Sister Dabney said.

"I'm not sleepy."

"I don't want you to go to sleep, at least not yet. You have to be able to see while you're awake before you can see while you're asleep."

"Okay, but I can see a lot better if my eyes are open," Jessie replied in a matter-of-fact tone of voice.

"I can do that, but most folks can't, including you. Start seeing by closing your eyes. It grows from there."

"But—"

"Close your eyes!"

Jessie squeezed her eyes shut for a few seconds, then popped them open.

"Keep them shut!"

She closed them again. The chair rocked rhythmically back and forth.

"What do you see?" Sister Dabney asked in a softer tone of voice.

"Nothing. You believe in God. That's why he gave us eyelids. So we can give our eyes a rest."

Sister Dabney didn't respond. She continued to rock the chair. Jessie rested her head against the back of the chair and tried to relax. An evening breeze brushed across her cheeks. If this went on much longer, Jessie might be able to take a short nap.

Suddenly, her head jerked forward.

"Don't let it get away!" Sister Dabney said. "Stay with it."

Jessie grabbed the arms of the chair so hard her knuckles turned white. The scene raced across her vision and then faded. She took a deep breath.

"Can I open my eyes?" she asked in a subdued voice.

"Yes."

Jessie opened her eyes. Darkness gathered about the house. Sister Dabney reached over and turned on the bare yellow lightbulb.

"What did you see?"

Jessie hesitated.

"Tell me," Sister Dabney said. "There's a reason behind the rocker. Don't try to hide it from me."

"I saw you lying on the ground with your eyes closed," Jessie answered soberly. "Were you sleeping? Are you going to be okay?"

Sister Dabney stared hard at her. Whenever she did that, Jessie felt uncomfortable, as if the woman preacher was looking inside her skin.

"Can I spend the night with you?" Jessie continued. "I don't want to go back to my aunt's house."

"If she says it's okay," Sister Dabney replied.

"Uh, it won't be a problem. She left for Jacksonville this morning and isn't coming back until tomorrow. All I have to do is make sure the cat gets fed. I did that before I came over here."

Sister Dabney shook her head.

"The devil is the father of lies. Remember what I told you down by the river. He wants you, but he's not going to get you! Get in the house." Sister Dabney shooed her with her hands toward the front door. "You can sleep on the couch in the living room, after you take a hot shower and I wash your clothes. While you get clean on the outside, think about getting clean on the inside."

LATE-SUMMER AFTERNOONS IN SAVANNAH COULD BE STIFLING HOT and humid, but today an offshore breeze swept away all hint of swelter. I felt the refreshing wind on my face when I left the office and walked across the parking lot to the car. I paused to take in a deep breath. Even a half mile inland I could sense the purifying presence of salt in the air.

I fixed a fresh salad with baked chicken for supper, and Mrs. Fairmont and I ate on the veranda. The circulating fan over the wrought-iron table supplemented the pleasant breeze. While we ate, we watched Flip play in the courtyard below. I told Mrs. Fairmont about the invitation from Zach.

"You have to take advantage of evenings like this," Mrs. Fairmont said. "When I was a girl, we'd go to the ocean islands for picnics. After supper, we'd eat ice cream, just like you're going to do. Most ice cream was homemade. My father would buy block ice on the way, and one of the house servants would turn the crank while we ate."

"Did everyone get to eat ice cream?"

"Yes, this was a couple of years after the end of the Civil War."

"I didn't mean—"

"No, prejudice was real. Fortunately, my father and mother were more enlightened than most. Everyone in our household was treated with kindness and respect."

Mrs. Fairmont spent the rest of the meal reminiscing about her childhood outings to the beach. At times like this it took only a few questions from me to bring out the stories. The way she described ice cream made with fresh strawberries threatened my allegiance to chocolate. She paused and looked away as an unspoken memory played across her mind.

"Those were happy days," she said with a sigh.

"You've treated me with kindness and respect," I said.

Mrs. Fairmont smiled. "You're not a household servant."

"I want to be."

"I know. And my father would have enjoyed you a lot."

Before I could ask why, the doorbell rang. I went to the foyer and opened the door to Zach. Alongside the curb was the motorcycle with sidecar attached. Since I always wore a dress or skirt, the sidecar was the only way I could travel by motorcycle.

"Mrs. Fairmont is on the veranda. Do you want to talk to her while I go downstairs for a minute?"

"Okay."

I went to my apartment to collect a few items to throw in a beach bag. When I returned to the veranda, it appeared Mrs. Fairmont had taken up the story where I'd left off.

"Your father sounds like a remarkable man," Zach said.

Mrs. Fairmont nodded. "He was very well read. I wish I'd gotten more of his intelligence to pass along to Christine. But we all make choices about what to do with the gifts and talents we have. I think Tami is getting the most out of her abilities. Don't you?"

"Please don't make Zach critique me," I said, picking up on the conversation as I rejoined them on the veranda. "He's already too quick to point out what's wrong with me."

"I am?" he asked.

"And I need it," I added quickly.

Mrs. Fairmont stared at us for a moment. "I think eating ice cream is a good idea for both of you."

"I won't be late," I said.

"Enjoy yourselves."

Zach and I left the house. I stopped to lock the front door behind me.

"Am I that mean?" Zach asked as we walked down the steps.

"No, it came out wrong. Mrs. Fairmont was telling me how kind her family was to their employees."

"You're not my employee. You work for Maggie Smith and Julie."

"I know. That's not the point." I stepped around the motorcycle. The helmet I used was sitting in the sidecar. "Let's take Mrs. Fairmont's advice and concentrate on ice cream."

There was a microphone in each helmet, but we didn't talk as we rumbled across the cobblestone streets of the historic area. We turned onto a paved road.

"Are we going to Tybee Island?" I spoke into the microphone.

"Is that okay?"

"Yes."

The silence resumed, but it wasn't quiet in my head. I replayed Zach's comments. As soon as we crossed the bridge onto the island, Zach pulled into a beach shop that advertised "Homemade Ice Cream."

"I doubt it's really homemade," he said as we took off our helmets.

"I'm sure it will be great," I responded, trying to sound cheerful.

We entered a store that offered the typical collection of beach toys and novelties. Large inflatable animals hung from the ceiling; racks of suntan lotion were at the front of the store. The ice-cream display cooler was beside the cash register. The cashier was a teenage girl with multiple piercings and a bored expression on her face. A man was buying a pack of cigarettes. She handed him his change but made no eye contact with us as he turned away.

"We'd like some ice cream," Zach said.

The girl sighed and walked over to the cooler. There were six varieties that included chocolate and orange sherbet. While Zach peered into the white tubs, the girl twirled one of several posts inserted into the side of her nose. I tried to remember if she'd washed her hands after handling the previous customer's change.

"What would you like?" Zach asked me.

My desire for ice cream was at an all-time low.

"Uh, orange sherbet, please, in a cup," I said, deciding it was the best way to avoid the girl having direct contact with a cone that would touch my lips.

"One dip or two?" the girl asked in a tired voice.

"One."

The girl ran her fingers through her hair, picked up a metal scoop, dug out the sherbet, and plopped it into a cup.

"Spoons and napkins are down there." She pointed toward the other end of the cooler.

Thankful that I could select my own spoon, I inspected three spoons and picked the one that looked the whitest. Zach ordered a single scoop of vanilla in a cone. I watched with revulsion as he casually accepted the cone from the girl's hand. Her fingernails were painted dark purple, making it impossible to tell if they were clean or dirty. Zach reached for his wallet and handed her a twenty-dollar bill. She placed the bill in the cash register and counted out Zach's change on the counter. He stared at it for a moment and then pushed it toward her.

"Keep it," he said.

The girl stared at Zach for a few seconds. Tears pooled in her eyes. She sniffled and reached for a tissue beneath the counter. She blew her nose, which had to be hard to do with all the metal paraphernalia impeding air flow. She couldn't have been more than eighteen. Suddenly, I saw her in a different light. She was a person, not a collection of artificial holes, metal posts, and garish colors.

"Thanks, but I can't keep it." She wiped her eyes and pointed at a surveillance camera. "My boss wouldn't believe me if I told him you wanted me to have the money."

Zach took out his wallet again and handed her one of his business cards.

"Tell him to call me if he has any questions."

The girl stared at the card for a moment.

"You're a lawyer?"

"Yes." Zach motioned to me. "She is, too. And you can become whatever God wants you to be."

The girl stared at him for a moment and then turned away. Outside, Zach took a big lick of his ice cream.

"Do you think I helped her?" he asked.

"At least you tried."

Zach sat on the motorcycle seat. "I ignore people all the time. But there was something about her that made me stop and ask if there was something I could do or say that might help her."

"You're a good man. All I could see was how messed up she was."

Zach turned on the motorcycle.

"Eat a bite, then we'll go just around the corner to finish."

A few hundred feet from the store, Zach took a side road. The pavement ended and gave way to sand. I recognized the area. We'd been here before. Zach turned down a driveway with no house at the end of it and stopped the motorcycle. We walked into a clearing where the charred foundation of a house remained.

The house had been destroyed by a fire and never rebuilt. A rickety pier with many missing boards extended out into the water of Tybee Creek. In the distance I could see cars crossing over the bridge to the island. The store where we'd gotten ice cream wasn't visible. There was a gazebo near the edge of the water. Only a few flecks of white paint remained, and the wood was covered by untamed vines. We sat on the steps of the gazebo with a few inches of separation between us. Julie's prediction of a romantic sunset accentuated by orange sherbet wasn't coming true. My sherbet was rapidly turning into orange goo, and the sun hovered like a yellow ball in the sky. Zach's ice cream was now safely beneath the lip of the cone. I didn't mention the likely presence of germs from the girl's dirty hands. God would eradicate germs on Zach's behalf.

"I'm sorry for what I said at Mrs. Fairmont's house," I said.

"You've encouraged me a lot during the past year, even when I was less deserving than the girl at the ice-cream shop."

"But I've hurt your feelings, especially about the job situation."

I stretched my legs out in front of me. "A woman's feelings are more complex to navigate than the marsh on a moonless night. You'll go crazy trying to sort them out. I know you gave me an honest opinion about the job. I'm the one who hurt you." I glanced over and met his eyes. "And I didn't take the job with Maggie and Julie because I don't want to be around you."

"Who do you want to be around?"

"I don't know what you mean."

Zach swallowed the last bite of his ice-cream cone and pulled a piece of vine from the post beside him. "The first time we came here I said you're the type of girl who deserves the truth, the whole truth, and nothing but the truth. Do you remember that?"

"Yes."

"Does that work both ways?"

"Yes."

It was Zach's turn to look me in the eyes. "Is there another issue between us besides our disagreement about the job? And I'm not thinking about Sister Dabney's influence on you."

As soon as Zach spoke, I knew what he meant. My mouth went dry.

"Vince?"

Zach nodded. "He's been interested in you since your first week in Savannah. I thought you made up your mind between the two of us when you took me to visit your parents, but now I'm not so sure."

"Why?"

"Because I feel you pushing me away. I thought the reason behind the courtship approach was to encourage two people to focus on each other, not play the field."

"I'm not playing the field."

"But you've thought about it."

"People have thoughts," I answered defensively. "But that doesn't mean they're going to act on them. Vince came to see me in Athens in January, and we went to dinner and talked about his trip to Rwanda. That's it. Since then, we've not seen each other except at the bar exam and here in Savannah when you've been there, too."

I didn't know how to deal with Zach's new insecurity.

"Have you talked to anyone about this?" he asked.

"What?"

"You, me, Vince."

I swallowed. "Yes. It's come up with Mrs. Fairmont and Julie. Mrs. Fairmont's comments are mostly a by-product of her confusion. Julie's been dishing out soap-opera logic, not Godly counsel."

"But not with your parents?"

"Maybe a little bit. I'm not sure."

Zach looked skeptical.

"Look," I responded more sharply. "This isn't a deposition transcript in which I can check everything that I've said over the past year. Have you talked to Vince? That's the most important question."

"Vince is a friend, a good friend."

"And?" I asked after waiting a few moments.

"We've talked, and we're waiting on you. You're going to have to decide. It's as simple as that."

The idea of the two men sitting around analyzing my feelings over a cup of coffee suddenly made me furious. I felt my jaw set.

"I'm sure you've had some fascinating conversations. Are you giving me a deadline?"

"No. This isn't a brief to the court of appeals. But it's a lot more important to me. To us."

I stood and brushed away a few stray pieces of marsh grass from my skirt.

"I'd like to go home. It's already darker out here than I thought."

We rode back to Mrs. Fairmont's house in total silence. Zach could be maddening. And he'd enlisted Vince in the latest effort to irritate me. When we stopped in front of Mrs. Fairmont's house, I resisted the urge to rip off the helmet, jump out of the sidecar, and run to the door. Instead, I deliberately, if not gracefully, got out of the sidecar and handed Zach the helmet. He still straddled the motorcycle with the engine running.

"Will you take off your helmet?" I asked.

He flipped up the face shield. I started to speak but couldn't figure out what to say.

"Bye," I said.

"After you calm down, we'll talk," he replied.

It was such a condescending response that I was thankful when he immediately lowered the face shield and pulled away from the curb. I trudged up the walk to the front door and went inside. All the lights were off, an indication that Mrs. Fairmont and Flip were upstairs. I went downstairs to my apartment and flopped down on the bed. When my mind stopped racing, I couldn't deny that I'd secretly considered whether I'd be more compatible in the long run with Vince than Zach. And if marrying the wrong person was the greatest mistake a person could make in life, destroying the chance to marry the right one had to be a close second. Combining the two sins would be a deadly potion from which there could be no recovery.

As I lay on the bed in frustration a third, less toxic option for my future floated to the surface. I grabbed my Bible and turned to 1 Corinthians chapter 7. If a male-female relationship could be this stressful and traumatic, it made the prospect of a celibate life as recommended by the apostle Paul more attractive. Along that path my primary concern wouldn't be what someone else thought about me, but how I could love God and others with my whole heart, mind, soul, and strength.

After I put on my pajamas, I drank a glass of water, turned on my laptop, and prepared to write down some of my thoughts. Remembering Mrs. Fairmont's prayer journal, I typed "Greater Love" at the top of the page.

To my surprise, Julie's car was in the parking lot at work when I arrived the following morning. I used my shiny new key to let myself in and went immediately to her office. Her door was closed. I knocked lightly.

"Come in!" she said.

I cautiously peered inside. "Are you okay?"

Julie was dressed up in a dark suit with papers spread across the desk in front of her.

"Better than okay," she announced cheerily. "I knew there had to be a case on point, and I just found it. Were you praying for me without knowing how much I needed it?"

"No."

Julie stuck out her lower lip. "I thought you prayed for me every morning before you ate your cereal."

"Most days, I do."

"Relying on myself, without divine assistance," Julie continued, "I discovered a 1955 Court of Appeals decision that nails the other side to the wall in the hearing I have this morning." Julie began pulling together the papers on her desk. "Now, I have time to drink a third cup of coffee and enjoy it."

"Congratulations," I said. "I guess I'd better get busy."

"Hold on, Ms. Associate Attorney. First of all, your new laptop arrived. It's sitting on your desk, so you can stop using your personal computer. And, I expect a detailed report about the midnight motorcycle ride and sloppily shared ice-cream cone. I hope you took my advice and got the sherbet."

"Yes, I did."

"And?" Julie asked, slipping her papers into a file. "That's not enough. One scoop or two?"

"I really don't want to talk about it."

Julie stopped and stared at me. Tears that had not been a part of the previous night's agenda threatened to burst forth. I desperately held them at bay and backed away from the door.

"Don't hold out on me," Julie said.

I fled across the hall to my office and closed the door. For the first time, I noticed the knob didn't have a lock. The door opened, bumping into me.

"Sorry," Julie said. "But you have to talk to me. It will drive me crazy if I don't know what's wrong. I won't be able to focus during my hearing, and my client may lose his liquor license."

"Liquor license?"

"It's an oddball case Maggie decided not to hand off to you. But don't use that as an excuse to change the subject. What happened with Zach? That ponytail of his may be wavy and soft, but underneath that skull he's a tough guy."

"I can't joke about this." I sniffled.

"Okay. No teasing allowed. Please talk to me."

I hesitated.

"You know I care about you," she continued, her face serious. "You're so innocent and inexperienced that I want to help. What happened?"

"Zach brought up Vince."

"Uh-oh."

"They've talked about me, us, them, and decided I have to choose."

Julie sat down in the single chair across from my desk.

"Did you try to deny it?"

"What? That I've thought about Vince and me?"

She nodded. I shrugged.

"It caught me off guard. Because I'm courting Zach, I've tried not to think about Vince that way. It's Zach's fault for bringing it up."

"Of course, it's always the man's fault." Julie paused. "But it's always the woman's job to fix it."

"I have the answer," I replied.

"Really?"

"Yes, celibacy."

"Excuse me," Julie answered, her eyes wide. "Could you spell that?"

"You know what I mean. There's nothing wrong with singleness. In fact, the Bible recommends it."

"The Bible also says not to eat shellfish. That hasn't stopped you from eating an entire shrimp cocktail appetizer by yourself."

"We're not talking about dietary laws. This has to do with devotion to the Lord without the distractions of a spouse."

"You'd become a nun?"

"No. It's just a thought I had last night after Zach brought me back to the house. It's something I ought to consider. I don't expect you to understand."

"And I'm not sure I want to. Here's what I think." Julie leaned forward and spoke rapidly. "I've joked with you about Vinny following you around with puppydog eyes, but I've always thought Zach was a more intriguing match for you. Not that you should necessarily marry Zach, but he stretches and challenges you. Vince would be supportive and kind, but I think you need your pot stirred, not put on the back burner with a lid on it."

"Huh?"

"That came out fast, but you get the point. They are two very different guys, but each is awesome in his own way. Most girls would give up a no-limit shopping spree in New York for a choice like yours." Julie looked at her watch. "Look, I've got to get on the road to Brunswick County for my hearing. When I get back later today, I want you to tell me you're over this celibacy nonsense and ready to get back in the game. Isn't that what they call repentance?"

"Not exactly."

"Then call it whatever you need to."

MID-MORNING, SHANNON BUZZED ME. I PRESSED THE INTERCOM button.

"Ms. Coutts, the court administrator, is on line one."

I picked up the phone. "This is Tami Taylor."

"Ms. Taylor, do you know a woman named Ramona Dabney?"

"Yes, ma'am."

"That's what she told Judge Cannon. He'd like to see you in his chambers in thirty minutes."

"What's this about?"

"The judge will discuss it with you. Can you be here?"

I had nothing on my morning calendar except research and figuring out whether I ever wanted to get married.

"Yes, ma'am, I can come."

"Good. I'll let him know he can expect you in half an hour."

I slowly lowered the phone to its base. Sister Dabney could get into trouble in innumerable ways. A bit of advance warning about the type of problem the woman preacher had created could be a big help when meeting with the judge. I picked up the phone and entered the number for Sister Dabney's house. No answer. I tried the church. Nothing, not even an answering machine message. My heart sank at the most obvious possibility. I called the jail.

"Has a woman named Rachel Ramona Dabney been arrested or cited for a criminal violation in the past few days?" I asked, trying to sound professional.

"Just a minute, please."

While on hold, I had to admit that I knew this day would come.

It would have been better after I had a few years', not a few weeks', experience as a lawyer. But Sister Dabney waited for no one's permission to act. As I waited, I only hoped there might be a First Amendment religious freedom argument to justify her conduct. It would take both the Constitution and the Bible to counter whatever she'd done. Finally, the woman came back on the line.

"No, we have no record of an arrest for anyone named Dabney within the past six months."

"Are you sure?"

"Positive."

Stymied, I hung up the phone and resigned myself to having to wait until entering Judge Cannon's chambers to discover the legal quagmire the woman preacher had fallen into.

I ARRIVED AT THE COURTHOUSE WITH NOTHING BUT AN EMPTY folder. As the senior member of the bench, Judge Cannon's chambers were on the second floor in a corner office conveniently close to the main courtroom. In the waiting area I encountered a woman with gray hair sitting at a secretarial desk leafing through a file. There was no sign of Sister Dabney. I walked up to the woman's desk.

"I'm Tami Taylor. Judge Cannon wanted to see me about a—"

"Go in." The woman motioned toward a large door beside her desk. "He just got off the phone. Don't wait for him to answer."

I knocked softly on the door then entered. Judge Cannon was sitting behind a large desk. Law books lined one wall, a sign the judge still performed some of his legal research the old-fashioned way. The white-haired judge looked up with a scowl on his face. Up close, his white eyebrows were bushy enough to be hedge trimmers. He made a loud sniffing noise and cleared his throat.

"Ms. Taylor, have a seat."

I sat in a wooden chair in front of his desk and crossed my feet at my ankles. The judge reached for a thin file on the corner of his desk.

"Tell me what you know about Rachel Ramona Dabney."

It was a broad question.

"Do you know who I'm talking about?" the judge growled when I didn't immediately answer. "She claims to know you."

"Yes, sir. I met her last summer when I was clerking for Braddock, Appleby, and Carpenter. She was the defendant in a defamation case Mr. Carpenter filed for a client named Jason Paulding."

The judge nodded. "The man who is cooperating with the federal authorities in Miami?"

"Yes, sir. You heard a motion for summary judgment. Partway through the hearing Mr. Carpenter dismissed—"

"That's it. I remember," the judge said, interrupting me. "I knew I'd seen this woman before but couldn't place her. A lot of people have passed through my courtroom during the past thirty years. I can't be expected to remember all of them."

"Yes, sir."

The judge glanced down at the open folder on his desk.

"Do you know a young woman named Jessie Whitewater?"

"No, sir."

"You're about to," the judge grunted. "I'm appointing you to represent Ms. Whitewater, who may or may not be a juvenile. She claims to be eighteen, but the intake worker at the Department of Family and Children Services thinks she looks fourteen or fifteen. DFACS considers her a runaway and wants me to treat her as a minor until proven otherwise. She was picked up by the police on a burglary charge after breaking a window at a store on Maxwell Street and stealing a bag of donuts."

"Bacon's Bargains?"

The judge adjusted his reading glasses, flipped over a sheet of paper, and gave me a puzzled look.

"Yes. That's not the best part of town. Have you been there?"

"I interviewed a couple of witnesses at the store while investigating the case involving Sister Dabney."

"Sister Dabney?"

"That's what everyone calls her. She's a woman preacher with a little church on Gillespie Street who helps a lot of poor people. It doesn't surprise me that she's taken an interest in a runaway."

"Dabney thinks highly of you, too, even though you were involved in a lawsuit against her." The judge took off his glasses. "It happens all the time. Someone is sued by a law firm and likes the other side's lawyer better than her own."

"She didn't have a lawyer."

Judge Cannon twisted his mouth. I couldn't tell if it was a smile or a sneer.

"That's right. She claimed representation by the Almighty. It worked out well for her if Joe Carpenter dismissed the motion. You can't argue with results."

"No, sir."

The judge tapped the file with his hand. "Here's the status of the Whitewater case. At an arraignment calendar this morning, Dabney demanded I appoint you to represent this girl. I don't like being told what to do, but someone has to represent the defendant and you're on the list. Whitewater has been charged as an adult based on what she told the detective investigating the case, but if she's a minor this case should end up in juvenile court. Either way, you're going to represent her."

"Yes, sir." I paused. "How do you suggest I find out how old she is?"

"Not by sitting here in my office." The judge pointed toward the door. "There's an order on Ms. Fletchall's desk appointing you to the case. Pick it up on your way out."

"Yes, sir. Thank you."

"No thanks necessary."

Apparently, sometimes the wheels of justice in Chatham County could spin at racecar speed.

"Here's the order appointing you to the case," the judge's secretary said as soon as I reached the edge of her desk. "File your bill with me. The judge reviews them before submitting to the county for payment. Don't be shocked if he cuts it."

"I'm going to get paid?"

"Yes, there's a fee schedule for appointed criminal cases."

She opened a drawer of her desk and handed me a sheet of paper with numbers on it. All the rates were less than the hourly rate Maggie charged for my time, but the fee for handling a felony in superior court was almost twice what was paid for a juvenile court case. I furrowed my brow.

"If there's a possibility a case could stay in superior court instead of juvenile court it creates a conflict of interest for a lawyer—"

"Do you want me to interrupt the judge and tell him you have a question about the fee schedule?"

"No, ma'am."

ON MY WAY BACK TO THE OFFICE, I HOPED MAGGIE WOULD BE there to point me in the right direction. When her car wasn't there, I debated my next move. I could go to the jail and interview my new client or I could try to track down Sister Dabney and find out what she knew. I decided it was better to begin with the person I knew, not the one I didn't. I left the parking lot and turned in the direction of Gillespie Street.

12

I PARKED MRS. FAIRMONT'S BIG CAR IN THE GRAVEL DRIVEWAY OF Sister Dabney's house. When I got out, I instantly regretted that I'd worn shoes with heels. After climbing the steps, I went to the front door and knocked. There was no answer. I knocked again and waited. I glanced toward the street and saw a disheveled man pushing a shopping cart filled with his earthly possessions on the sidewalk. He stopped when he saw me look in his direction. I quickly gauged the distance to the car, trying to calculate whether I could kick off my shoes and outrun him barefoot to the driver's-side door.

"You looking for the preacher woman?" he called out.

The fact that he knew Sister Dabney calmed my rapidly beating heart.

"Yes."

"Me, too. Have you done checked the church?"

"No."

"She don't leave it locked. Ain't nobody gonna take nothing 'cause it would be cursed if'n they did."

I could see the front door of the church from the porch, but the thought of entering the building to look for Sister Dabney while the homeless man was around wasn't an option.

It would have been better after I had a few years', not a few weeks', experience as a lawyer. But Sister Dabney waited for no one's permission to act. As I waited, I only hoped there might be a First Amendment religious freedom argument to justify her conduct. It would take both the Constitution and the Bible to counter whatever she'd done. Finally, the woman came back on the line.

"No, we have no record of an arrest for anyone named Dabney within the past six months."

"Are you sure?"

"Positive."

Stymied, I hung up the phone and resigned myself to having to wait until entering Judge Cannon's chambers to discover the legal quagmire the woman preacher had fallen into.

I ARRIVED AT THE COURTHOUSE WITH NOTHING BUT AN EMPTY folder. As the senior member of the bench, Judge Cannon's chambers were on the second floor in a corner office conveniently close to the main courtroom. In the waiting area I encountered a woman with gray hair sitting at a secretarial desk leafing through a file. There was no sign of Sister Dabney. I walked up to the woman's desk.

"I'm Tami Taylor. Judge Cannon wanted to see me about a—"

"Go in." The woman motioned toward a large door beside her desk. "He just got off the phone. Don't wait for him to answer."

I knocked softly on the door then entered. Judge Cannon was sitting behind a large desk. Law books lined one wall, a sign the judge still performed some of his legal research the old-fashioned way. The white-haired judge looked up with a scowl on his face. Up close, his white eyebrows were bushy enough to be hedge trimmers. He made a loud sniffing noise and cleared his throat.

"Ms. Taylor, have a seat."

I sat in a wooden chair in front of his desk and crossed my feet want you to tell me you're over this celibacy nonsense and ready to get back in the game. Isn't that what they call repentance?"

"Not exactly."

"Then call it whatever you need to."

MID-MORNING, SHANNON BUZZED ME. I PRESSED THE INTERCOM button.

"Ms. Coutts, the court administrator, is on line one."

I picked up the phone. "This is Tami Taylor."

"Ms. Taylor, do you know a woman named Ramona Dabney?"

"Yes, ma'am."

"That's what she told Judge Cannon. He'd like to see you in his chambers in thirty minutes."

"What's this about?"

"The judge will discuss it with you. Can you be here?"

I had nothing on my morning calendar except research and figuring out whether I ever wanted to get married.

"Yes, ma'am, I can come."

"Good. I'll let him know he can expect you in half an hour."

I slowly lowered the phone to its base. Sister Dabney could get into trouble in innumerable ways. A bit of advance warning about the type of problem the woman preacher had created could be a big help when meeting with the judge. I picked up the phone and entered the number for Sister Dabney's house. No answer. I tried the church. Nothing, not even an answering machine message. My heart sank at the most obvious possibility. I called the jail.

"Has a woman named Rachel Ramona Dabney been arrested or cited for a criminal violation in the past few days?" I asked, trying to sound professional.

"Just a minute, please."

While on hold, I had to admit that I knew this day would come.

"Is it locked?" she asked.

"No."

"I don't like being in closed-up places," she said, running her hand through her hair. "It makes me jumpy on the inside."

"I'm sure I'd feel the same way."

Jessie's eyes narrowed as she seemed to inspect me for the first time.

"Are you here to get me out?"

"Not today, but maybe soon. I was appointed to represent you by Judge Cannon about an hour ago, so I haven't had time to do anything yet. I'll look into filing a motion for bond as soon as possible."

"They usually set the amount of a bond for a person getting arrested in cases like this within twenty-four hours."

"How do you know that?" I asked in surprise.

"A woman in my cell block told me, so I asked one of the guards. She looked it up and said my bond was ten thousand dollars." Jessie's eyes narrowed again. "Are you sure you're a lawyer?"

"Yes, but I don't have much experience in criminal cases. I'm here because Sister Dabney knows me and asked the judge to assign the case to me."

Jessie rolled her eyes.

"How do you know Sister Dabney?" I asked.

"I eat over at her house sometimes. I don't want to hear about God and the devil from you. I get enough of that from Sister Dabney."

"Do you go to the church?"

"Yeah, it's part of the deal if I want Sunday dinner. What does that have to do with getting me out of here?"

"Nothing, I'm asking background questions. When's your birthday?"

"December 22."

"What year?"

Jessie hesitated before giving me a year.

"The deputy already copied my driver's license."

"I have to check for anything that attorneys aren't allowed to have in the presence of a prisoner," the woman replied patiently.

I sheepishly handed my purse to her. She placed it on a small metal table and proceeded to take out my cell phone, a pen, and a metal nail file.

"I'll have to hang on to this until you leave," she said, holding up the nail file.

"Of course. I wasn't planning on coming to the jail."

The officer gave me an odd look. I blushed.

"Don't let the prisoner use your cell phone."

"Okay."

"Wait here while I get her."

I sat down and fidgeted. I had a pen but no legal pad. All I had in my folder was the order from Judge Cannon and the attorney fee schedule. I'd never considered myself claustrophobic, but sitting in the windowless interview room, I understood why someone could become anxious when confined in a tight space like this. The door to the interview room opened.

"Here she is. I had to pull her out of the mess hall."

In the instant I saw Jessie Whitewater, I knew the answer to Judge Cannon's question about her age. The slightly built young woman with short brown hair, brown eyes, and deeply tanned skin wasn't eighteen years old. She wasn't even as tall as the twins, but there was a hard maturity about her face that made me believe she was slightly older, maybe fifteen or sixteen.

"I'm Tami Taylor, the lawyer appointed to represent you by Judge Cannon. Are you Jessie Whitewater?"

"Yeah."

"Have a seat."

The young woman looked over her shoulder at the door before she sat down.

"No," I answered in exasperation. "But I've got to go."

"It'll be all right," the man said with a wave of his hand as his head sank below the back of the pew. "I ain't got nothing worth toting off."

I BACKED SO FAST DOWN SISTER DABNEY'S DRIVEWAY THAT I CAME close to hitting the shopping cart. It was past noon, but I wasn't hungry so I turned in the direction of the jail.

The lobby of the Chatham County Correctional Center smelled as clean as a hospital. I gave the order from Judge Cannon appointing me to represent Jessie Whitewater to a female deputy in the lobby area of the jail. The deputy typed in the name and watched her monitor for a couple of seconds.

"I'll have someone bring her up to the interview rooms."

"Where do I go?"

The deputy examined me more closely. "Can I see some identification?"

"I'm a new lawyer," I explained as I fumbled through my purse for my driver's license. "I've only handled one other criminal case, and my client was a man. I've never been to the female side of the jail."

"It's much nicer."

I looked up to see if the deputy was joking but couldn't tell. I handed her my driver's license, which she inspected closely and then copied. My picture would now be part of the jail archives.

"Go through that door." The deputy pointed. "A guard will meet you on the other side."

I opened the heavy door. At the far end of the hallway a large black woman motioned for me to come forward.

"This way," the correctional officer said.

I followed her into a shorter hallway with two doors on either side. Each door had a number. The officer opened door number two.

"May I see your purse?" the deputy asked.

"I'll go and have me a look-see and let you know," he called out when I hesitated. "You wait yonder."

I wasn't sure exactly where "yonder" might be to the man but decided it should be beside the door of the car. As I stepped off the porch, the man stuck a rock beneath one of the back wheels of his cart.

"Watch my stuff," he said as he started up the slight incline toward the church. "There are thieves and criminals all over this place."

Committed to guard duty, I stayed by the car and watched as the man entered the long, narrow building. When he didn't immediately come out, I assumed he'd found Sister Dabney inside. As the minutes passed, I checked my watch. The man was probably so focused on his own problems that he forgot to tell Sister Dabney I needed to talk to her, too. I knew I should probably go over to the church, but lingering apprehension about the homeless man, coupled with my responsibility to guard his shopping cart, kept me beside the car. Ten minutes passed, then fifteen.

No one who walked by on the sidewalk showed any interest in stealing the homeless man's shopping cart. Sure that the man must have finished talking to Sister Dabney, I abandoned my post.

The front door of the church was cracked open. I put my ear next to the opening to listen for a conversation inside. I heard nothing. With one last glance at the shopping cart, I cautiously opened the door and went inside. The purple rocker was motionless on the platform. The old piano rested against the far wall. There was no sign of the homeless man or Sister Dabney. Fear welled up inside me that the man might have done something to her. At that moment I heard a muffled noise coming from one of the pews and cried out in alarm.

"Huh-uh," a man's voice said.

Before I could run, the homeless man raised his head above the back of one of the rear pews. He looked at me with blurry eyes.

"Sister ain't here so I lay down for a little rest. Did anybody mess with my stuff?"

"That would make you seventeen," I said, quickly doing the math. "You won't be eighteen until your next birthday."

"No, it was a year before that."

"Why do you want to be eighteen?"

"Because that's how old I am."

"How long have you lived in Savannah?"

"I'm visiting my aunt. I got here a few weeks ago."

"What's your aunt's name and where does she live?"

"Sue Ellen. I can't remember the name of the street. It's not far from the church."

"What's her last name?"

"Whitewater. Same as me."

"If I look her up in the phone book will her number be listed?"

"No, all she has is a cell phone."

"What's her cell number?"

"I don't think she's been paying the bill. She gets letters from them all the time. It's disconnected."

So far, I doubted the truth of everything the young woman had said.

"If you get me out of here, I can take you to her house," Jessie continued.

"What's her address?"

"You already asked me that. It's not far from the church."

"Does your aunt know you're in jail?"

"No, she's been in Jacksonville for a few days. I also need to get out so I can feed her cat. He's going to starve or tear up the house. There will be a mess to clean up."

"Where are your parents?"

"My father is dead. I don't know where my mother is. She left when I was a baby." Jessie raised her voice. "Why are you asking me a bunch of stuff that doesn't have anything to do with getting me out of here?"

"If I'm going to represent you, I need background information.

The social worker who talked to you believes you're a runaway. Why would she say that to the judge?"

"Because she's crazy, just like you and Sister Dabney. I'm ready to go back to my cell. You made me miss dessert."

"How far did you go in school?" I asked, ignoring her outburst. "Can you read and write?"

"Yes, I can read and write. I've read lots of books."

"What kind of books?"

"Anything I think is interesting."

"Do you ever read stories about lawyers, their clients, cases, things like that?"

"Yeah, but I don't remember the names of books very well."

"In the books you read about lawyers and their clients, did you learn about the confidentiality rules for communication between an attorney and a client? Do you know what that means?"

"Yes, you can't repeat what I tell without my permission."

"Exactly, which means you can tell me the truth without worrying about the consequences."

Jessie didn't respond. I pointed at the folder on the table.

"Right now, you're being charged as an adult with burglary. If you're found guilty you could go to prison. If you're not really eighteen, then your case would likely be sent to juvenile court where the punishment would be a lot less severe."

Jessie shrugged. "There's a girl in the next cell block who's only seventeen. She's not going to juvenile court."

"What did she do?"

"Nothing. She's not guilty."

"What's the charge against her?"

"That she stabbed another girl in the leg with a knife. But she says it was her boyfriend who did it. He convinced her to tell the police that she did it because she would be charged as a kid, but they're going to make her go to adult court anyway."

"Aggravated assault is a violent crime against a person. The police claim you broke a window and stole a bag of donuts. I don't think the district attorney's office would try to keep your case in superior court if it turns out you're a minor."

Jessie studied me for a moment. "I thought you didn't know much about criminal law."

"This is basic stuff every lawyer knows. Did you break into the store and take the donuts?"

"Yeah, but they weren't very good. The policeman who took them from me said the expiration date had passed. That ought to be a crime."

"How did the police catch you?"

"Someone saw me inside the store and called them. I shouldn't have turned on the lights. I was in the woods behind the store when the police got there. I tried to run, but there was another car waiting for me when I came out of the woods."

"Did you admit you'd broken into the store?"

"Yeah, I couldn't lie about it because I cut my arm on the glass when I broke the window."

Jessie held up her right arm that had the remains of an ugly gash near her elbow.

"Was that the first time you'd stolen something?"

"No, just the first time I'd been caught."

Surprised, I paused.

"But you can't tell the police that, can you?" she continued. "It's confidential."

"Right," I said, regaining my focus. "How many other thefts or break-ins have you committed?"

Jessie shook her head. "Maybe ten or twelve. I didn't count. It depended on whether I had anything to eat or not."

"Didn't your aunt give you food?"

Jessie narrowed her eyes. "You don't know what it's like to be poor, do you?"

"No, and I'm sorry you didn't have enough to eat. Did these other break-ins take place since you came to Savannah?"

"Yeah, but I'd never broken a window or anything like that. Mostly, I took something that was out in the open."

"Always food?"

Jessie thought for a moment. "I grabbed some clothes that were on the sidewalk in front of a store."

"That's shoplifting. Did you ever go inside someone's house and take something?"

"Yeah, if the door was unlocked."

I winced. Each incident of illegal entry into a home would be a felony burglary.

"Did anyone ever see you?"

"I don't think so. I mean, I never saw anyone when I was inside a house."

"What would you steal?"

"Food, food, food!" Jessie's voice got progressively louder. "I'd grab what I could and run out! Is this some lawyer trick? Asking me the same thing over and over, hoping I'll give a different answer?"

"I'm just trying to see what you're up against. Right now, there's only one burglary charge against you. If more charges are filed that means your bond could go higher, the punishment more severe." I glanced down at the order from Judge Cannon. "Did the officer who arrested you read your Miranda rights before he questioned you?"

"Yeah, just like they do on TV."

"Did the police ask you about other break-ins or thefts?"

"Yeah, but I didn't tell them anything except admit to the donut deal. I figured if they solved that crime they might not try to connect me with anything else."

It wasn't a bad strategy, but the possibility of multiple felonies raised the stakes considerably. Jessie studied me for a moment.

"How would you prove how old I am?" she asked. "I've already told everyone I'm eighteen."

"You have a birth certificate. Where were you born?"

"I don't know."

"You don't know?"

"I'm not even sure what state it was. It might have been Alabama. My daddy used to say he found me under a rock."

"What's his name and where could I find him?"

"Ben Whitewater, and he died when I was a little girl. If you can't remember stuff, why aren't you taking notes?"

"I don't have a legal pad. I wasn't planning on coming to the jail to talk to you until later. Who did you live with after your father died?"

"My stepmother, mostly."

"What's her name?"

Jessie started to answer then stopped. "I'm not going to tell you."

"Were you staying with her before you ran away?"

Jessie shook her head. I was close to getting valuable information she didn't want to give up.

"Where did you go to school? It would have records showing how old you are. I could contact the school officials without letting your stepmother know about it."

"I wasn't going to school. I graduated last year, right before I turned eighteen."

"How could that be true if your birthday is December 22?"

"Uh, I got out in the middle of the year because I'd gone to summer school."

I sighed. Jessie Whitewater was able to think on her feet better than some of my law school classmates.

"Okay, remember what I said about juvenile court," I said, closing my file. "It will be a lot easier on you later in life if you don't have a criminal record. Juvenile court proceedings are sealed to the public, and no one would ever know you got into trouble. If there are more felony charges filed against you as an adult, it will get a lot more complicated."

I waited. I could see Jessie trying to decide whether to say anything else.

"If you stop being my lawyer, would the things I told you still be confidential?" she asked.

"Absolutely. Why?"

"I just wanted to make sure."

I watched as Jessie Whitewater followed the guard through the door. The most important information I'd obtained was that the young woman harbored a great fear—one so terrifying that remaining hidden was her highest priority.

WHEN I ARRIVED BACK AT THE OFFICE, MAGGIE AND JULIE HAD returned and were in Shannon's office. The secretary had a tissue in her hand. When she saw me, she turned her head away.

"Tami, you won't believe what—," Julie started.

"In my office," Maggie interrupted, motioning to Julie and me.

Mystified, I followed the other two women. Maggie closed the door. Julie and I stood in the open space in front of Maggie's desk.

"Your minister friend made another visit," Maggie said. "What you saw out there was the fallout."

I licked my lips.

"She wanted to see you," Julie added. "Claims you came by her house a couple of hours ago. I checked the open files and didn't find her name. Are you secretly representing her?"

"No, it has to do with a case Judge Cannon assigned me this morning. Sister Dabney asked him to give it to me, and I wanted to find out what she knew before beginning my investigation. She wasn't home so I went to the jail and talked to the client first."

"You can fill us in on that later," Maggie said. "Whatever Dabney's reason for coming here, she used it as another opportunity to intimidate Shannon."

"What did she say to her?"

Julie spoke. "That if she doesn't give her husband a second chance, he'll marry someone else, and Shannon will regret it for the rest of her life. It may be true, but I can't believe she had the nerve to say that to her."

"Truth or not, tell Dabney to stop coming to the office," Maggie said to me. "I'm not blaming you for her conduct, but if you want to meet with her, it will have to be someplace else. I'm not going to allow Shannon to be harassed by a client. We banned several people a year from coming to the district attorney's office. I didn't expect it to be a problem for us, but since it is, I'm taking action."

"I agree," Julie added with a wink in my direction. "It's bad enough having Tami trying to cram her brand of religion down my throat. I can't imagine how hard it would be to swallow a dose from Reverend Dabney."

"Enough," Maggie said, obviously not in a joking mood. "Tami, will you take care of it?"

"Yes."

"Good." Maggie motioned for me to sit down. "Now tell me about the case Judge Cannon gave you."

Julie left, and I told Maggie about the meeting with the judge and the interview with Jessie at the jail.

"I spent six months handling juvenile court cases when I first started working at the DA's office," Maggie said when I finished. "The client would get a slap on the wrist with a few months' probation. It makes no sense to keep the case in superior court, especially if there are other charges floating around out there."

"What should I do next?"

"File the standard motions in the superior court case and talk to

Dabney. You have two reasons to meet with her. Do you know who has the file at the DA's office?"

"No."

"Find out. If it's Tim Corwin, I can definitely help you out."

I returned to my office, thankful that I had Maggie as a resource in the Whitewater case. To that extent, Sister Dabney's word that I would benefit from working with two women was true. However, Maggie's decision banning Sister Dabney from the office was also understandable, even if I personally believed Shannon should heed the woman preacher's warning. Toward the end of the day Julie knocked on my door frame.

"Well?" she asked.

"If it's about Zach and Vince, I haven't had time to think about it. It's been a busy day."

"I thought about it," she replied, "all the way back to Savannah from my hearing in Brunswick. If you don't pick Zach, he's going to marry someone else and you're going to regret it for the rest of your life."

My mouth dropped slightly open. Julie smiled and nodded her head.

"I wanted to see what it felt like to be Reverend Dabney. It's quite a power trip. How did it feel on your end?"

"Scary."

"Remember that when you talk to her. However, I really did think a lot about you, Zach, and Vinny. Maybe it's not the best time for you to ramp up a romantic relationship with either one of them." Julie held up two fingers. "In the past month you've left your home in Powell Station and moved to Savannah to start a new job. That's a lot of new territory, especially for someone like you."

"But what if Zach did meet someone else—"

"I'd take a bet at 1,000 to 1 on that," Julie interrupted. "If he wants a girl like you, it's going to take him years to find another one. Zach's standards are your best safety net."

"But I've got to say something to him. This morning you told me I needed to go to Zach and repent."

"Repent of that singleness nonsense. Anyone can look at you and see motherhood written across your forehead."

"Huh?"

"Hear me out. I know about these things. In relationships women want feedback. Men benefit from space. The more you think about Zach, the more stressed you'll get. The more he thinks about you, the more he'll miss you. Vinny is a little bit fuzzier to me. He's not shown his hand, but the same holds true for him. For a man, absence makes the heart grow fonder. Trust me. I'm right about this."

Julie left me confused. When I walked to Shannon's office and handed her the information needed to open the Jessie Whitewater file, I assured her that I would talk to Sister Dabney.

"Will that stop her?" Shannon asked.

"I'm not sure," I admitted. "But in the past she's recognized the point when a person doesn't want her input and backed away."

"In those situations was she right?"

"Do you really want to know?" I asked.

Shannon paused. "No, I guess I don't."

THE FOLLOWING MORNING I TRIED AGAIN, WITHOUT SUCCESS, TO contact Sister Dabney, then worked on some other matters. A couple of hours later, Shannon buzzed me.

"Judge Cannon on line one."

I rushed to Shannon's desk, retrieved the Whitewater file, and made it back to my chair in a matter of seconds.

"Yes, sir," I said, somewhat breathlessly.

"Your defendant doesn't write like a high school sophomore," the judge said. "Did you help her compose this letter she sent me?"

"What letter?"

"I received a letter this morning in a packet from the jail. Ms. Whitewater demands I appoint someone else to represent her."

"Did she give a reason?" I asked in surprise. "I met with her the first time yesterday afternoon."

"It's similar to a pro se habeas corpus motion alleging ineffective assistance of counsel," the judge grunted. "Usually, the defendant waits until the lawyer loses the case to claim incompetence. Whitewater can't wait to get rid of you—claims you're biased against her because of religious reasons and can't competently represent her. Can you help me understand what she's talking about?"

"I'd be guessing."

"Go ahead."

I took a deep breath. "It's probably related to Sister Dabney, who, as you've observed, is a woman with strong religious convictions. Ms. Whitewater may see me as an extension of that effort."

"A little religion is good for anyone."

"Yes, sir. More is even better."

"Unless it compromises the integrity of your duty as a lawyer to your client," the judge replied. "Would your religious beliefs prevent you from providing competent representation to this client?"

I hesitated. Saying yes would be an easy way to get out of the case. I held a quick internal debate.

"No, sir, unless she asks me to do something unethical."

"The rules of professional responsibility will guide you in that event. Ms. Smith has experience in criminal law cases. Consult with her; that's one of the benefits of a firm."

"I already have."

"Good. One other thing, the defendant claims she has an uncle who is a retired lawyer in Birmingham. Did she mention that to you?"

"No, we talked about an aunt in Savannah, but she said she couldn't remember where she lives. The defendant has an active imagination, which makes me wonder—"

"Counselor, don't breach the attorney-client privilege."

"Yes, sir." I swallowed.

"Ms. Fletchall checked the active roster of attorneys with the Alabama State Bar and couldn't find him. Of course, if he's inactive it would be harder to track him down. The defendant insists I contact him about the case, but I'm going to leave that up to you."

"Yes, sir. How are you going to answer her letter?"

"I'll treat it as a motion to remove you as her attorney, issue a one-sentence order denying the request, and send it over to the jail. Tell your client she'd better cooperate with you if she wants the benefit of a lawyer in her case."

I flipped over to a page of notes I'd made after meeting with Jessie.

"Your Honor, since I have you on the phone, there are a couple of things I didn't get to bring up in chambers yesterday—"

"Follow proper channels, Ms. Taylor. I don't like ex parte communication with attorneys on active files, but the defendant's letter raised an unusual issue."

"Yes, sir."

I hung up the phone. Judge Cannon's idea of teaching a young lawyer to swim was simple—throw her in the water and watch her flail about without a word of guidance from the shore.

13

Julie came into my office shortly before noon.

"Do you want to grab lunch?" she asked.

"Only if we can go to Gillespie Street. I'm still trying to locate Sister Dabney."

"I didn't sign up for that field trip. And I have a good reason you should reconsider. I'm on my way to pick up Vinny and thought you would want to be included."

"You invited Vince to lunch?"

"No, he called me. I can pretend he enjoys my company, but he always uses these times to pump me for information about you."

"What would he want to know?"

Julie rolled her eyes. "I'm sure he knows about your conversation with Zach, and Vinny wants to know whether or not he's in the running for the Tammy Lynn Taylor Sweepstakes."

"You think Zach told him about that?"

"Zach said he and Vinny are best buddies, didn't he? Dumping the decision into your lap is their way of avoiding having to settle the matter in a fistfight."

"But Vince called you. He didn't invite me to lunch."

"Trust Dr. Julie. If I show up with you hiding behind me, Vinny isn't going to run screaming out of the restaurant. I think you need to get a current vibe from Zach's competition while I'm there to chaperone."

I hesitated.

"You can get with Dabney later," Julie continued. "She'll know when you're coming and be sitting on her front porch in that green rocking chair."

"It's blue. I don't think she has a green one. The one at the church is purple and there is a yellow one and a red one in her living room."

"Which is weirder than I thought." Julie checked her watch. "Are you coming to lunch or not? The only way you can defend your maiden honor is in person. If you're not there, I'm prepared to tell Vinny anything I want."

"Okay." I leaned over and picked up my purse. "Judge Cannon should have appointed you to represent the young woman accused of burglary. You both have overactive imaginations."

"Burglary? What did she break into?"

"Bacon's Bargains and stole a bag of donuts. Remember when you abandoned me there because you were afraid to get out of the car?"

"Oh, yeah," Julie answered, making her eyes big. "I would have wanted to break out of there, not break in."

On the way to lunch, Julie mapped out an entire conversation with Vince.

"You can't predict what people are going to say," I protested. "It doesn't work with witnesses; it won't work with Vince."

"How did you get to be such an authority on witness psychology? Have you been secretly taking depositions?"

"No."

"Then leave Vinny up to me. The purpose of lunch is to put you in close proximity to him and find out if he makes your blood boil with passion."

"No one has ever made my blood boil with passion."

"Then I'll settle for a slight tingle in the uppermost layer of skin."

I thought of the few times I'd felt tingly around Zach. Julie, who was driving, glanced sideways.

"That's familiar territory, isn't it?"

"Not familiar, but I've been there."

Julie took both hands off the steering wheel and clapped.

"At last, scientific evidence that you're not a department store mannequin."

WE DROVE TO THE RIVER DISTRICT TO MEET VINCE AT A DELI THAT was one of his favorite lunch spots. It was a short walk to the restaurant across uneven cobblestones that had originally served as ballast for sailing ships coming to the new world. I felt more and more nervous as we drew closer. Vince was waiting for us inside the front door of the deli.

"I brought along a street person who hasn't eaten a good Reuben sandwich in weeks," Julie said as soon as we entered. "I hope it's okay with you."

"That's fine," Vince replied a bit awkwardly.

We ordered our sandwiches and drinks at a counter where the meats were displayed then joined him. Julie sat down first and maneuvered her chair so that I would have to be closer to Vince.

"How's life at the old law firm?" Julie asked.

Vince, who was wearing a nice blue suit, white shirt, and yellow tie, furrowed his brow slightly.

"It's different being an associate than a summer clerk. I worked hard for Mr. Braddock last summer, but now that I'm responsible for billable hours, the demands have gone way up. He doesn't ask me if I have time to work on the project; he gives it to me and expects me to figure out a way to get it done."

"It's been the same for Tami at our place," Julie replied seriously. "I only allow her to use my first name when we're in a social setting like this, but at the office she has to call me Ms. Feldman and bill at least nine hours a day."

Vince looked at me and smiled. "I know you're doing great."

"Not completely," Julie added.

"What do you mean?" Vince asked.

Before I could kick Julie under the table, she blurted out, "Judge Cannon appointed Tami to represent a defendant in a criminal case based on the recommendation of that crazy woman preacher we sued last summer."

"Dabney?"

"The one and only," Julie replied. "The only way I could keep Tami from skipping lunch to talk to Dabney about this new case was to tell her you would be here. It was touch-and-go, but you won out in the end."

Vince picked up his sandwich to take a bite.

"I'm not competing with anyone."

Julie cut her eyes toward me. I pretended that I'd found the perfect potato chip and closely inspected it before putting it in my mouth.

"When are we going to have another night out with the boys?" Julie asked, breaking the silence.

"Not for at least a week. Zach's going to Washington, D.C., with Mr. Appleby. I'm on my way to Atlanta later today for a dinner meeting with an estate client."

"By yourself?" Julie asked.

"Yes. The client is a wealthy individual the firm has represented for years. He has children our age, and they're going to be at the dinner. Mr. Braddock hopes the firm will continue to represent the family in the future and wants me to develop rapport with the next generation."

"Wow," Julie said with big eyes. "Tami and I are trying to convince the poorer cousins of the present generation to give our firm a try."

"I saw Maggie's ad in the paper," Vince said. "How is that working?"

Julie leaned in. "Tacky, isn't it? She didn't ask my advice, which ticked me off, but the cases have been rolling in. People pay when they're in danger of losing their driving privileges. It's hard to believe, but every defendant charged with DUI only admits to drinking two beers. Some of them must have been barrel-size mugs."

"Who's handling the cases?" Vince asked.

"Mostly Maggie. I'm learning the ropes, but it's not in Tami's contract. She'd rather be run ragged researching the areas of the law we don't know anything about."

Julie kept the conversation on the practice of law. As I watched Vince's face, I began to wonder what, if anything, Zach had told him about the discussion at the gazebo. Toward the end of the meal, Julie went to the restroom.

"How are you really doing?" Vince asked as soon as Julie was away from the table.

"In what way?"

"At work."

"Oh, there are a lot of adjustments to make, but Maggie is a good boss. And Julie, well, she's Julie. I knew what I was getting into when I agreed to work with her. She jokes around a lot, which—" I stopped, not wanting to criticize Julie behind her back.

"Is a by-product of her insecurity."

It wasn't the way I would have finished the sentence, but Vince was probably right.

"We all have areas of vulnerability and different ways to protect ourselves," he continued.

I glanced across the room to make sure Julie was still out of sight.

"Did Zach tell you about our conversation the other night on Tybee Island?"

"Yes," Vince replied, looking me in the eyes. "I'm not trying to cause a problem, but I have to be honest with you, Zach, and myself."

My insides turned over.

"And it's up to me to decide?" I asked. "How am I supposed to do that?"

"I'm not that smart. But for now, you're committed to spending time with Zach. If that doesn't lead where you believe it should, I'm waiting."

Julie returned and plopped down in her chair. "Were you able to carry on a conversation without me being here? I ran into a girl in the restroom I met at a bar a couple of weeks ago. We're going to get together for dinner later in the week. She works for the head of the convention bureau and has access to all kinds of free stuff. Can you think of anything you'd like to see or go to?"

Both Vince and I gave her a blank stare. Julie rolled her eyes.

"It's hard for either one of you to imagine having a good time. I'll choose and make it a surprise."

After we finished eating, Julie and I walked with Vince to his car.

"Have fun in Atlanta," Julie said. "If one of the young heiresses is cute, don't forget to get her phone number as well as her Social Security number and bank account information."

Vince got in his car and waved as he drove away from the curb.

"Well?" Julie asked as we continued down the sidewalk.

"What?"

"Did you get the tingles? I didn't peek under the table to make sure, but it looked like Vince slid his leg next to yours and bumped you several times. It reminded me of a fish checking out the bait before it strikes."

"The only leg touching me belonged to the table. You had me squeezed in so tight there wasn't any place for me to put my legs."

"You could be wrong. Vince is muscular, kind of lean and sinewy. His leg is as hard as a tree."

"When did you touch his leg?"

"Bunches of times, but he never touched back."

We got in Julie's car.

"You haven't answered the important question," Julie said. "What kind of vibe did you pick up from Vinny?"

"He's interested in me."

"Duh."

"But I didn't get a hint of the tingles. However, that's not all it's cracked up to be. It only lasts a few seconds."

Julie sniffed. "If you're going to hunker down in self-righteous, self-controlled, Tammy Lynn mode, there isn't much I can do for you."

"Then give up."

"Oh, no. I'm going to hang around to see how hard and long you fight before either Zach or Vinny reels you in and mounts you as a trophy on his wall."

"That's a lame analogy."

Julie shrugged and smiled. "At least we agree on something."

UPON RETURNING TO THE OFFICE, I CALLED SISTER DABNEY. BY this point I'd memorized both her home and the church numbers. On the fifth ring, she answered.

"Judge Cannon appointed me to represent Jessie Whitewater," I said. "I'd like to come by and ask you a few questions about her."

"Are you sure you're ready to meet with me?" Sister Dabney asked.

"Yes. I've talked with the judge and interviewed Jessie at the jail."

"That's not what I mean. It may be too soon." The woman paused. "But you're going to have to make up your mind eventually."

"I've accepted the case, although I didn't really have a choice."

"Of course you didn't have a choice."

I shook my head in bewilderment.

"Do you want to come over now?" she continued.

"Yes, ma'am. I guess so."

"I'll be here."

WHEN THE HOUSE CAME INTO VIEW, I COULD SEE SISTER DABNEY sitting on the front porch in the blue rocker. As I walked up the steps she took a drink from an oversized plastic convenience-store cup.

"Let's go inside," she said. "It's hot and getting hotter."

The living room was only slightly cooler than the front porch. I could hear a window-unit air conditioner laboring in another room I took to be a bedroom. Sister Dabney sat in a red rocker and motioned for me to sit in the yellow one.

"Is the Lord about to show me something?" I asked, remembering the last time I'd been in the yellow rocker.

"He's saying a lot more than most folks are hearing and less than some are claiming," Sister Dabney replied.

It took a second to wrap my mind around the statement, but when I did, I nodded in agreement.

"Are you ready for Jessie?" Sister Dabney asked.

"I'm ready to represent her."

"No, you're not listening to me," Sister Dabney spoke in a louder voice. "Are you ready for Jessie?"

I stopped rocking. "I don't know how to answer that unless you explain what you're really asking me."

"Is Jessie going to get out of jail?"

"Only if she can post bond. Right now, it's set at ten thousand dollars, but I doubt she has the ability to pay anything. Most bondsmen charge a fee of ten percent."

"I can cover her bond. This house is worth a lot more than that, and the bank doesn't have a claim against a square foot of it."

"You'd post her bond?" I asked in surprise. "If Jessie gets out and runs away, you'll have to pay the money or lose your home."

"That's right. I also know that if she gets out and has no place to stay except here or on the street, Jessie is going to leave town, and we'll lose our chance to snatch her from the fire." Sister Dabney pointed her finger at me. "But if she gets out and stays with you and Mrs. Fairmont, the Lord says she won't run. It's part of his plan."

My mouth dropped open. "Mrs. Fairmont would never allow—"

"How do you know that if you don't ask her?"

"And you have to consider her daughter. Mrs. Bartlett had a hard time agreeing to let me live with her mother. If I mention the possibility of a defendant in a criminal case moving into the house, it may be the end of my staying there."

"Do you really believe that?"

I hesitated. "No, Mrs. Fairmont wouldn't let that happen."

"She still rules her house."

"Yes, ma'am."

"The Lord is asking both of us to take a risk, to sacrifice something. Do you remember what I told you about risk?"

"It's related to faith."

"And about you as a lioness?"

"That I shouldn't be afraid."

"What else?"

I thought for a moment. My eyes grew big.

"That she has cubs. Are you saying I should treat this young woman as my child?"

Sister Dabney laughed. I didn't think it was funny.

"Your decision only affects you," I continued. "Letting Jessie stay with Mrs. Fairmont isn't my choice to make."

"Which means your job is to ask her permission and trust God for the answer."

I sighed. Sister Dabney stared at me for a few seconds and then spoke in a more tender voice.

"Tami, the Christian life consists of one sacrifice after another.

When you view those situations as opportunities, not problems, you'll understand what it means to take up your cross and follow the Lord. The ability to really help people is God's gift to those willing to lay down their lives for others."

"Okay," I responded slowly. "I'll talk to Mrs. Fairmont, but you've got to pray for me."

"I already have."

"Is she going to agree to do it?"

"Sometimes the Lord takes delight in hiding things as much as he does in revealing them."

I rocked back and forth in the chair a few times as I tried to imagine myself talking to Mrs. Fairmont. Sister Dabney interrupted my thoughts.

"And your search for love will only succeed when you're more interested in giving than receiving. There's a greater love that romance doesn't know."

I felt the blood rush from my face.

"What did you say?"

"You heard me. The Lord is jealous. He won't share the deepest devotion of your heart with any man."

"Are you saying I'm never going to get married because it's not the kind of love God has for—"

Sister Dabney cut me off. "I said what I said. And it's true whether you like it or not. Be careful that your selfish desires don't knock you off course."

My stomach clenched in a knot. "I need to go. I'll let you know what I decide about Jessie."

When I reached the car, I turned on the air conditioner full blast. In my mind I returned to the night in my apartment when I read 1 Corinthians 7. The apostle had no qualms recommending singleness for those who could accept it. And logic couldn't deny that undistracted dedication to the Lord was easier without the competing presence of a spouse. Now, Sister Dabney held up an even more austere future—one marked by the sacrificial life of Jesus *and* the celibate life of Paul.

WHEN I PULLED INTO THE OFFICE PARKING LOT, I REALIZED I'D NOT said a word to Sister Dabney about Shannon. I could have returned to Gillespie Street, but, lioness or not, I didn't have the strength to do so. After walking quickly through the reception area to avoid Shannon, I put my head in my hands and rested my elbows on my desk.

Toward the end of the day, I'd calmed down enough to at least make a stab at evaluating Jessie's case. Tackling my own future would have to wait. Taking out a fresh legal pad, I decided to write down my options. I wrote my new client's name at the top of the page.

One approach would be to allow Sister Dabney to post a property bond and talk to Mrs. Fairmont about Jessie moving in with us. I put large question marks at both ends of that statement. Beside one of them I wrote "Christine Bartlett." Beside the other I wrote "Breakdown of Attorney-Client Relationship." Even as a brand-new lawyer, I knew a certain detachment was best between attorney and client. Living in the same household would make that impossible.

Second, I could simply represent Jessie to the best of my ability. That could be done whether Jessie was in jail or released on bond. In fact, it might be easier to help her if she remained confined and unable to get into more trouble or run away from a criminal charge I had a reasonable chance of taking care of. It was an avenue that made sense as the best legal solution, although it might leave Jessie sitting in jail.

Third, I could file a motion to lower Jessie's bond and make an effort to contact Jessie's aunt, uncle, or some other relative. A family member could post bond and Jessie would be released into the care and custody of the people God ordained to take care of her in the first place. If she ran away, it would be their responsibility, not mine.

Fourth, if Jessie was eighteen or older, she was an adult responsible for herself. If released from jail on bond, it would be appropriate for her to seek refuge in a local facility that served homeless women. I could provide money for her needs either directly or to the shelter. I brightened at the idea, which would allow me to be unselfish yet maintain the kind of distance needed for a healthy attorney-client relationship.

Seeing options on paper made me feel better. Trying to get my arms around the whole problem was overwhelming; separating it into parts made it manageable. I then spent forty-five minutes trying unsuccessfully to locate Jessie's lawyer uncle in Alabama.

When I left the office for the day, I carried the legal pad with me in case I had any other ideas later in the evening.

I was thankful for Flip's unpretentious greeting in the foyer. He pattered down the stairs from the second floor and skipped into the foyer. The little dog held me to no greater standard of conduct than my willingness to scratch the favorite place behind his right ear for a few seconds.

"Mrs. Fairmount! I'm home!"

There was no answer. Seeing that Flip had been upstairs prior to my arrival, I called up the stairwell.

"Mrs. Fairmont! It's Tami!"

Again no answer. I checked in the kitchen and then the den, but the TV was lifeless. It wasn't the first time I'd arrived to a quiet house, but it always made me nervous.

"Let's go upstairs," I said to Flip, who had been following me from room to room.

The little dog scampered up the stairs in front of me and disappeared into Mrs. Fairmont's bedroom. I followed and peeked through the open door. The elderly woman was propped up in bed, still dressed in her nightgown with a book on the floor where it appeared to have fallen out of her hand. I put my purse and the legal pad on the dresser near the door and hurried over to her. I couldn't see her chest rising and falling and gently touched her on the shoulder.

"Mrs. Fairmont. Wake up."

She suddenly snorted so loudly that I jumped. Flip barked. Her eyes fluttered open. She blinked several times and gave me a puzzled look.

"Did I oversleep?" she asked groggily. "Is it morning?"

"No, ma'am. It's six o'clock in the evening. I just got home from work."

"Have I been in bed all day?" she asked.

"I don't know," I answered, glancing around the room and looking for signs of activity. "This wasn't one of Gracie's days to work. Are you hungry?"

Mrs. Fairmont rubbed her eyes. "I'm thirsty."

"Do you want me to bring something to you?"

"No," she said, swinging her legs slowly over the side of the bed. "I should have gotten dressed hours ago."

"There's no use going to that trouble now. It will be time to go back to sleep in a few hours."

"Nonsense. I'm not going to eat supper in my nightgown. See what's in the refrigerator, and I'll be down in a few minutes."

"Are you sure?"

"Of course. I'm sorry I wasn't properly dressed."

Getting dressed every day was part of Mrs. Fairmont's strategy for maintaining an independent lifestyle.

"What would you like to eat?" I asked.

"Something light. Maybe a salad."

I returned to the kitchen and put together a fresh spinach salad with cherry tomatoes, then added roasted chicken for protein. I heard Mrs. Fairmont's footsteps in the hallway.

"I've fixed a nice salad. Do you want to eat in here or the dining room?" I asked when she reached the door.

"Who is Jessie Whitewater?"

I glanced up. Mrs. Fairmont, wearing a slightly wrinkled dress, was standing in the doorway with my legal pad in her hand.

"Oh, I didn't mean for you to see that," I said, stepping forward.

Mrs. Fairmont gave the pad to me. "It was on top of my dresser."

"I know."

"Why is Christine's name written on there? Is she having some kind of legal trouble?"

"No, ma'am."

"Then what does she have to do with Jessie Whitewater? I don't remember Christine mentioning anyone by that name, although it would be easy for me to forget."

"Mrs. Bartlett doesn't know Jessie Whitewater."

"Then why are their names beside each other?"

I sighed. Mrs. Fairmont was being as persistent as Julie.

"We'll talk about it over supper."

We ate in the dining room. Mrs. Fairmont liked the table set with silverware and cloth napkins, even when it was only the two of us. Once, I'd gently suggested using paper napkins, but she'd turned up her nose and replied it was cheaper and more civilized to use cloth ones. We settled into our usual places with Flip beneath Mrs. Fairmont's chair. I prayed a blessing then began to eat. Mrs. Fairmont seemed to enjoy the salad and began telling me about the book she'd been reading when she fell asleep. She stabbed a small piece of chicken with her fork and held it over the floor. Flip stood on his hind legs and caught it in the air when she slipped it off her fork.

"One day, when Christine is here, I'm going to let him eat a morsel directly from my fork, then continue as if nothing out of the ordinary had happened."

Mrs. Fairmont held out her hand and let Flip lick the ends of her fingers.

"I'm listening," she said to me.

"Ma'am?"

"I'm waiting for you to tell me about Christine and Jessie Whitewater."

I swallowed a bite and then took a sip of water.

"She's a young woman Judge Cannon appointed me to represent."

Mrs. Fairmont listened attentively as I told her about receiving the call from the judge and going to the courthouse. I tried to walk the line between public information and confidential communication. The most important piece of data I knew I couldn't relate had to do with Jessie's other thefts and break-ins.

"She stole a bag of donuts?" Mrs. Fairmont asked when I told her the nature of the charge.

"Yes, ma'am."

"Aren't there public facilities where homeless people can get a meal?"

"Yes, ma'am. And she'd been eating regularly at Sister Dabney's house. It wasn't a case of starvation."

"The woman with the rocking chairs?"

"Yes, ma'am."

"We talked for quite a while, then after I left she sent a letter to the judge asking for a different lawyer."

"Why?"

"Maybe she didn't like my connection with Sister Dabney or was afraid to put her freedom in the hands of an inexperienced lawyer."

"You'll work as hard as anybody."

"Yes, ma'am," I answered, grateful for the compliment. "But she doesn't know that. Anyway, the judge refused to take me off the case."

Mrs. Fairmont nodded. "Cliff Cannon was stubborn when he was a little boy."

"You knew Judge Cannon when he was a child?"

"Oh, yes. His mother and aunt were friends with my mother, and they'd bring him over to the house. I was in high school, and my mother would ask me to watch him while they drank tea in the parlor of our house at Beaulieu. He'd stamp that foot of his and refuse to obey me. The only way to get him to cooperate would be to give him something sweet to eat."

I tried to wrap my mind around Judge Cannon as a little boy who could be bribed with sugar.

"He was the kind of boy who would have stolen a sugar donut if a batch was left unwatched on a plate," Mrs. Fairmont continued. "Would that be burglary?"

"Not if he had permission to be in the house, but it would still be theft. Anyway, I don't think reminding him about his love for sugar donuts is a good idea."

"How do you think Christine can help?" Mrs. Fairmont asked. "I saw a question mark by her name so I guessed you wanted to ask her something."

I put my napkin beside my plate. "Actually, the first question is for you. Sister Dabney is willing to post a property bond so Jessie can get out of jail, but she wants her to live with us while the case is pending in court. Otherwise, Sister Dabney believes Jessie will run away."

"Live here?" Mrs. Fairmont asked, blinking her eyes.

"I know, it's a crazy idea," I replied, speaking more rapidly, "especially when I consider bringing it up with Mrs. Bartlett. That's why I wrote all the other information on the legal pad. It was a way for me to get my options on paper and sort them out. I only listed Jessie living here because it was the first possibility mentioned. Legally, the best thing to do would be to leave Jessie in jail while I—"

"Have you prayed about it?" Mrs. Fairmont interrupted.

I stopped. It was my turn to blink my eyes.

"Kind of."

"Isn't that what both of us should do?"

"Yes, but if a stranger came into the house, there's no way to guarantee she wouldn't steal something a lot more valuable than a bag of donuts and leave."

"Will you get my Bible from the den and bring it to me?" Mrs. Fairmont asked.

"Yes, ma'am."

Mrs. Fairmont kept the Bible on a small table beside her favorite chair. When I picked it up, I saw there were bits of paper protruding from the pages. I returned to the dining room and handed it to her. She pushed her salad bowl aside and laid the book on the table.

"Where are those verses I was reading the other day? You'd probably know exactly what they say."

"What's the general idea?"

Mrs. Fairmont didn't answer but began opening the pages at the places she'd marked.

"No, it's not here," she said, then moved her wrinkled finger to another spot.

"Can you give me a hint?"

"It's about sheep and goats, only Jesus isn't talking about being kind to animals."

"Matthew chapter 25," I replied, leaning over and flipping the pages to the correct spot.

Sure enough, Mrs. Fairmont had marked the place with a slip of yellow paper. The elderly woman spoke.

"Jesus says if we take a stranger into our home and feed him, then the Lord will reward us. When I read that, I thought about the kindness my parents showed to poor people and realized that except for sending a check every so often to a charity, I haven't been that way."

I stared, slightly openmouthed, at Mrs. Fairmont. Her eyes returned to the page.

"He even talks about visiting people in prison. That's what you did."

"No." I held up my hand. "It wasn't exactly a voluntary visit. Judge Cannon ordered me to represent this young woman. But are you sure this passage applies to Jessie Whitewater?"

"Can you give me a reason it doesn't?" Mrs. Fairmont leaned forward and touched my arm. "I don't know nearly as much about faith and the Bible as you do, but there is something inside me that says I should try to help this girl."

"What will you say to Mrs. Bartlett?"

Mrs. Fairmont sat up straight in her chair. "The truth. You came home and found me, still in my pajamas, unconscious in bed. I hadn't fallen and hurt myself, but I finally had to admit it would be wise to have someone with me during the day while you're at work. Miss Whitewater is willing to look after me for room and board, which is a lot cheaper than the sitting services Christine contracted after you went back to school. This way there won't be any frivolous squandering of my estate."

"Okay." I laughed. "But I think you should meet Jessie before making up your mind about letting her stay here. I'm going to file a motion to reduce the amount of the bond. Jessie will be brought over from the jail to the courthouse for the hearing, and you can talk to her then."

Mrs. Fairmont smiled. "This is exciting."

"If it happens, I hope you feel good about it in a few weeks."

14

USED TO RUNNING WILD AND UNSUPERVISED, JESSIE HAD TROUBLE adjusting to being locked up. Boredom bred from inactivity can push anyone toward insanity, and by the third day Jessie had started begging the guards to assign her any odd jobs they would give her. The slightly built girl who'd stolen a bag of donuts didn't fit the profile for a security risk, and within a week she was working in the kitchen an hour before mealtime and staying an hour later to help clean up. In between, she spent a few hours in the library, a small room with an odd collection of donated books. Her job was to dust and organize the volumes according to author. When she finished she was given permission to read. Books had always been a welcome escape for Jessie, even though her stepmother said reading was a waste of time. Jessie also stayed in the library to avoid the crowded TV room. The prisoners' preference of soap operas and sordid reality shows didn't interest her anyway.

Jessie didn't know if her stepmother had reported her disappearance to the police or not. If so, there was a risk one of the guards would see a picture and identify her. If she hadn't, then Jessie could begin a new life without having to look over her shoulder. Jessie's dilemma was not knowing. Until she knew her stepmother's decision or enough time had passed that her trail down the railroad tracks to Savannah grew too cold to follow, a slip of the tongue or random encounter with a person who recognized her might send her back into a place worse than the jail.

Jessie's best idea since running away had been to change her last name. She really liked the one she'd chosen. Whitewater had a clean, crisp sound, much prettier than Beanfield, which had caused Jessie a lot of problems in school. The new name came to her while she was admiring the white spray and foamy wake caused by a beautiful yacht sailing up the river toward the harbor. The only boat she'd ever been on was an aluminum johnboat her cousin Barry borrowed from a neighbor when Jessie lived in Alabama. They'd paddled out a few yards from the shore of a small pond and fished using worms they'd found under a rotting log.

She kept the name Jessie because it had been given to her by her real mother, and she was used to responding to it. Most women changed their last name when they got married, so, even though she had no current interest in boys, Jessie figured changing her last name would eventually happen anyway. Also, she'd read in a magazine that movie stars often went by different names. Jessie didn't know if she'd ever be famous, but Whitewater was a better name for fame than Beanfield.

Jessie was proud of the letter she'd written to the judge asking for a new lawyer. Luckily, she'd been reading a book about a murder case in which the defendant requested and received permission from a judge to have a different lawyer. It would have helped if Jessie could have copied exactly what the defendant in the book wrote, but she remembered enough to make her point.

The tall, young lawyer didn't fool Jessie. Like Sister Dabney, she was more interested in getting Jessie to be religious than helping her out in a way that really mattered. It was always the same with church people. They'd come by the house and ask if they could take Jessie to a meeting. Her stepmother often said yes, especially if she wanted to get her out of the house for a few hours. Jessie would end up squirming in her seat while a man told her she needed to repent so she could go to heaven. Jessie thought about walking down the church aisle a couple of times, but even her nicest clothes weren't much to look at. After the church meeting was over, whoever brought her would act disappointed because Jessie didn't go down to the front for the altar call.

Jessie had attended several Sunday services at Sister Dabney's church. She had to admit that the meetings on Gillespie Street were different from any others she'd gone to; however, she spent most of the time thinking about the dinner to follow. One Sunday morning she took the paper from the leather pouch with her tattoo design on it along with one of the certificates. When she should have been singing a song, she created a second tattoo design that incorporated some of the curlicues from the certificate. It wasn't as pretty as the flower tattoo, but she decided it would look okay on her shoulder.

Jessie was carefully stacking clean plastic plates that still steamed from the dishwasher when one of the guards came into the kitchen.

"Whitewater!" she called out.

Jessie held up a steamy hand. "Over here."

"You have a letter from the courthouse."

Jessie quickly wiped her hands on her apron and took the letter from the guard. She looked at the envelope. It had her new name typed neatly on the front with "c/o Chatham County Correctional Center" underneath. Because she worked so many hours in the kitchen, Jessie's fingernails had never been cleaner. She slid her index finger beneath the flap and carefully peeled it back. Inside was a single sheet of paper. It, too, had her new name at the top along with a case number and the words "Chatham County Superior Court." Beneath the heading, she read:

ORDER

    The Court having considered Defendant's Motion for Change in Counsel, said Motion is hereby, DENIED.

    Clifton Cannon

    Superior Court Judge

With a sigh, Jessie returned the sheet to the envelope and put it in her pocket. As soon as she could return to the library, she would read more of the book to find out what to do next.

THE FOLLOWING MORNING I RECEIVED A FAX COPY OF JUDGE Cannon's order denying Jessie's request that I be taken off her case. At the bottom of the page was a notation that indicated a copy had been delivered to the jail.

I finished researching the standards applicable to reduction of a defendant's bond and prepared a simple motion that cited a couple of the more important appellate court decisions. One of my uncertainties as a new lawyer involved whether or not to point out the obvious. Everything was new to me, but Judge Cannon might consider a reference to well-established legal principles as condescending. Maggie stuck her head in my door and I asked her about the cases.

"Should I include them in the motion?" I asked. "I don't want to offend Judge Cannon."

"Leave them in. It will make the motion look like a form that's used over and over. Of course, guessing whether or not Judge Cannon will be offended is a lot tougher than predicting the weather. When I was in the DA's office, he gave prosecutors a hard time and put defense lawyers through purgatory. The best way to earn his respect is to anticipate what he'll consider important in a case and bring it out before he asks."

"That sounds impossible."

"Focus on survival first; respect can wait."

I drove to the courthouse to file my motion. Seeing the official date and time stamp on the top sheet of the motion made me feel like a real lawyer. The court administrator provided a date later in the week for the hearing, and I stopped by the district attorney's office to hand-deliver the motion and notice of hearing. I placed it on the receptionist's desk. She took it from me without a word and quickly typed something on her computer.

"Ms. Crittenden is available. I'll tell her you're here."

"Uh, I didn't really think I'd be able to see her—"

"Have a seat."

It would have been awkward to walk out, so I sat down in a plastic chair. The DA's office was devoid of frills. In less than a minute, a young woman I recognized from the swearing-in ceremony came into the room. She was slightly overweight with medium-length brown hair, a broad nose, and thick glasses. Ms. Crittenden didn't fit the stereotype of an aggressive prosecutor. Instead, she reminded me of my high school English teacher who loved James Joyce. For me, reading Joyce was like drinking from a fire hydrant; I could absorb it only in small doses.

"I remember you from the other day at the swearing-in ceremony," the prosecutor said, extending her hand. "Jan Crittenden."

"Tami Taylor. I stopped by to deliver a motion to reduce the bond in the Jessie Whitewater case. I didn't mean to interrupt you."

"No problem. We can talk in one of the conference rooms."

Not sure what there was to talk about at this early stage of the case, I followed Crittenden down a hallway and into a rectangular room not unlike the simple conference room at Smith and Feldman. She didn't have a file folder.

"Have you met your client?" Crittenden asked.

"Yes, I interviewed her the same day Judge Cannon appointed me to represent her."

"How old do you think she is?"

"That's one of the things the judge wants me to find out." I answered. "If she's not really eighteen, would you be willing to send the case to juvenile court?"

"Absolutely. It wasn't a violent crime. Burglary is serious, but more so when it has the marks of theft for purposes of profit. Your client stole a donut."

I liked the straightforward way Crittenden talked.

"What do you suggest?"

"We have to know her true age and name to do a background check that would uncover any trouble she's been in before. If there's nothing serious in her past, I'd recommend to the juvenile court judge that she be placed on probation for six to twelve months. I've been assigned a lot of juvenile cases, and Judge Gott is easy to work with. If the case is sent to him, we can get a hearing fairly quickly."

"You're not sure about her name?"

"Of course not. She didn't have any identification, claimed she'd lost her driver's license and Social Security card. Her fingerprints aren't in the system, which is a positive sign that she's not been previously arrested for a felony. We checked her name against school data for Georgia, South Carolina, Alabama, and Florida and didn't come up with a match. I think she's a runaway who doesn't want to go back to where she came from."

"I agree." I nodded.

"If the case is processed in juvenile court, your client will either be sent home if we can find it, or, if that's not an option, placed with an approved foster family."

"Okay, that makes sense."

"When is the bond hearing?"

"Day after tomorrow on the morning calendar."

"If your client gets out of jail, will she get into trouble?"

"I don't know, but it will help if she has enough to eat."

"You can't guarantee her conduct. At any rate, I won't oppose the motion and will leave it up to the judge."

"From what I've heard, he does what he wants to."

Crittenden gave a slight smile. "He reminds me of my high school track coach who never had a problem finding something to criticize. At least Judge Cannon doesn't scream."

"You ran track?"

"No." Crittenden smiled. "Discus and shot put."

I'd not considered that Crittenden's bulk might be muscle.

"I played basketball."

"Where?"

I gave her the name of my high school.

"Up in the mountains." Crittenden nodded. "I attended a private school here in Savannah. My aunt told me you were living with Mrs. Fairmont. She has a lovely home."

"You know her?"

"Not personally, but I'm familiar with the house. It was on the house-and-garden tour a few years ago. I went with my mom and aunt."

So, Crittenden was a female weight lifter who enjoyed pretty houses. The assistant district attorney stood up.

"If your client tells you anything about her past, let me know and I'll use our resources to find out what we can. There's no reason why we can't cooperate on a case like this one."

"Thanks."

"But don't expect the same attitude toward one of your firm's DUI clients," Crittenden said, her voice hardening. "Especially the repeat offenders."

"That's Maggie's area."

I left the DA's office hopeful that a positive resolution of Jessie's case was around the corner.

Upon returning to the office, I phoned Sister Dabney. I gave her the date and time of the motion to reduce Jessie's bond.

"Mrs. Fairmont will be there to meet Jessie. I'll let you know what she decides."

"I'll be there."

"It's not necessary," I responded quickly. "There isn't an opportunity to post bond in the courtroom. That has to be handled later through the sheriff's department."

"I'll be there."

"Okay." I sighed. "Do you want to testify? It's not necessary, but if you insist—"

"Only if I'm supposed to," she interrupted.

"Okay." I started to hang up the phone. "Are you still there?"

"Yes."

"Please don't come to the office and talk to Shannon. You and I can meet at your house or the church."

"I've wiped the dust of her sin from my feet," Sister Dabney replied in a matter-of-fact voice. "It's up to her to nurture the seed of faith. I planted the word; she has to water it."

The call ended. I stared at my blank computer screen for a few moments. While in law school, I'd often imagined what it would be like to practice law. During those times, I assumed the serious challenges to my convictions would come from those with a worldly perspective. I never considered that difficult tests would come from people of faith. The door to my office opened and Julie came in.

"You've been locked up in your office like a nun in a convent." She stopped and put her hand over her mouth. "I want to take that back. It wasn't meant to encourage your insane flirtation with celibacy."

"I've been busy working, not meditating."

I brought her up to date on Jessie's case. As soon as I mentioned Jan Crittenden, Julie turned up her nose.

"She's more self-righteous than you are. I asked her for a continuance in one of Maggie's DUI cases because our only witness was unavailable for a couple of weeks. She turned me down without a reason. I had to file a motion with Judge Howell, who granted it on the spot. It was a waste of time and money to have to go through that for something so simple."

"She wants to work with me."

"Because you're kindred spirits." Julie sniffed.

"Maybe she doesn't like drunks operating motor vehicles."

"Alleged drunks. Not everyone who's charged with DUI is guilty." Julie paused. "Have you talked to Zach? That's what I'm really interested in."

"He's still in Washington with Mr. Appleby."

"Oh, yeah. And as much as I hate to say it, I don't think Vinny is going to be waiting for you at the altar. After our lunch the other day, I tried to visualize it, but my mind refused to form the picture. Is that how God tells you stuff? Kind of like flipping to a TV channel? However, I can easily tune in Zach wearing a white tuxedo and looking down the aisle as you prepare to walk in with your daddy. I even got your dress. I've never seen anything like it. It came all the way up your neck to your chin." Julie motioned with her hands around her throat. "Your face was behind a thick veil, making it hard for Zach to know he was getting the right girl."

"Like Rachel and Leah," I interjected.

"Rachel and Leah?"

"Sisters in the Bible. Their father fooled Jacob, the groom, by bringing Leah to the wedding instead of her sister Rachel. When Jacob found out who was behind the veil, he was upset."

"I'd guess so. It would be a great lawsuit. The worst case of bait and switch ever."

"But he got to marry Rachel, too."

"And years of counseling couldn't straighten out that mess.

Anyway, the only flesh showing in my version of your wedding dress was enough of your hand so Zach could slip on the wedding ring. What do you think?"

"That you still have an overactive imagination. And who knows? Marriage may not be in my future."

"I wish you'd stop that talk. I told you not to pay attention to what I said a minute ago. It's not funny."

"Funny or not, it's something I have to consider."

Julie rolled her eyes. "Tami, I'd say you've been out in the sun too long except you don't believe in getting a tan. Look, there are girls who've sworn off marriage because they want to conquer the working world, but you're not in the same zip code as those women."

"It's something I'm praying about, but it probably doesn't make any sense to you."

"Yeah." Julie threw up her hands. "Just promise you won't say anything stupid to Zach or Vince while you grope your way out of your current delusion. If you mess this up, you're going to need as much counseling as Rachel and Leah."

THAT NIGHT I CALLED HOME. MY LIFE IN SAVANNAH HAD BEEN such a storm of activity that, for a few minutes, I hoped to find a safe harbor. Mama answered the phone. Daddy was at a men's prayer meeting at the church. I told her about my conversation with Zach and subsequent reading of 1 Corinthians 7, then waited a bit anxiously for her response.

"I had the same thoughts before I met your father," she said. "I was serving the Lord and seeing him work in people's lives. Love can be found in sacrificially giving yourself on behalf of other people. I wasn't looking for a husband."

This was news to me. I'd always assumed she and Daddy were praying for a spouse and saw the other as the answer to prayer. And, the similarity between Mama's words and what I'd heard from Sister Dabney stunned me.

"What changed?" I asked.

"It takes a special grace to be single," Mama replied. "And it takes a special grace to be married. My ability to remain single ended when I met your daddy. Then, I had to call out for a different kind of help. Not that he's a hard man to get along with. But every marriage has its struggles. If you don't sense the grace needed for your relationship with Zach, the best thing to do is stop it. As for Vince, we'd need to meet him before giving permission for you to court him."

"That's not what I'm asking. Vince is a good man, but I don't want to bring him home. Not yet."

"That's fine. I'm glad you told me what's going on. It makes me proud of you."

"Why?"

"Because you're not forcing yourself beyond the place God has for you. I can't argue with what the Bible says about these things, and you have my full support if you believe you're supposed to stay single."

"What about Daddy?"

"He's the romantic," Mama answered in a voice I knew came with a smile. "But he's practical enough to know the foundation has to be strong for a house to last. If a man and woman don't have confidence the Lord is the cornerstone of the relationship, the marriage is going to be shaky from the beginning."

"That's how I feel now—shaky."

"There's your answer."

I glanced at the clock in Mrs. Fairmont's kitchen. It was late for Mama to be on the phone.

"This has helped me a lot. Please don't say anything to the twins. They're totally on the romantic side of things."

"Which is one reason why they're not ready to interact with boys."

"Thanks, Mama. I love you."

After listening to Mama, Sister Dabney's challenge to unselfish living as the way to greater love seemed less like a rebuke and more like an opportunity.

15

THE FOLLOWING DAY, JULIE RETURNED TO MY OFFICE SHORTLY before noon.

"Listen, Maggie and I are going to grab a quick bite to eat. Want to join us?"

I hesitated.

"Come on," Julie pressed. "It's going to be the closest thing we've had to a firm meeting since we started thirty days ago."

I hadn't realized it had been a month since I first sat down in this chair and turned on my computer.

"I know," Julie responded, reading my expression. "It seems like a year to me. One month down, four hundred and seventy-nine months to go."

"Four hundred and seventy-nine?"

"Assuming we practice law for forty years. Now that you're going to devote yourself totally to your work, you need to be planning for the long term."

"That's not what I meant yesterday."

"It's what will happen."

Maggie joined Julie at the door. "Unless you're too busy, I'd like you to go with us to lunch."

"I'd like that," I answered.

"You make me deliver a three-minute oral argument in favor of going to lunch without getting a commitment," Julie protested, "and Maggie persuades you in one sentence."

"She's good," I responded, reaching for my purse.

Maggie drove us to a local diner that served home-style meals.

"I eat salads all the time for supper," she said as we pulled into the restaurant's crowded parking lot. "Every so often, I need something that reminds me of home."

"That's why I eat barbecue," Julie chipped in.

Maggie and I both stared at her.

"Did your mother fix barbecue when you were growing up?" Maggie asked.

"No, but once I lied to my strict kosher cousins and told them I ate some. I got in big trouble for that one."

"These days, I'm filling in for Julie's cousins," I said to Maggie as we got out of the car.

"Not exactly. You've got more fight in you than they ever did."

Maggie led us through the door to a back table in a quieter corner of the restaurant.

"How are the chicken livers?" I asked Maggie as I scanned the menu. "When Julie comes to Powell Station for a visit, I'm going to ask my mama to fix them."

"Now who's doing the harassing?" Julie pointed at me.

"The chicken livers at this place aren't that good," Maggie responded. "I recommend the meat loaf and fried squash. Beyond that, you're on your own."

After we ordered, Maggie turned to me.

"How would you grade your first month at the firm?"

"You're the one to grade me."

"I'd give you an A," Maggie replied. "Julie and I agree."

"I guess so," Julie added. "Of course, I saw how hard you worked last summer, so I wasn't at all surprised when Maggie showed me how many hours you've billed and the volume of work you've put out."

"It's the volume that's impressed me the most," Maggie said. "Clients don't mind paying if they think they're getting their money's worth. When you provide results and answers quickly at a reasonable rate, they appreciate it."

"Thanks. I'm doing my best, but I still feel lost at times."

"Everyone does. And that brings up my main suggestion for you," Maggie said. "You almost never ask me questions about a project. My door is open unless I'm on a phone call and don't want to be interrupted. Occasionally, you give me too much information. I'm not asking you to write a law review article."

"Tami wasn't on law review," Julie said.

"Neither were you," Maggie replied evenly.

"Maggie was a notes editor for the law review at Georgia," Julie whispered across the table.

"And it didn't get me a job offer at Braddock, Appleby, and Carpenter. That honor went to Tami."

"Mr. Carpenter didn't want me to interrupt him with questions," I said. "But that may have been part of my evaluation as a summer clerk. He probably wanted to see how we could perform without close supervision."

"You don't need close supervision, just guidance that will make you even more efficient."

"Thanks." I turned to Julie. "You're my boss, too. What critique do you have for me?"

"That will take more than an hour lunch. Here comes our food."

The waitress set our plates on the table before us. Maggie was right. The food reminded me of home, especially the carrots that were slightly sweetened with brown sugar and butter, just like Mama prepared them.

"Did you talk to Ms. Dabney and tell her not to come to the office?" Maggie asked after we'd eaten a few bites.

"Yes, it's taken care of. She's finished what she thought she should do."

"What do you mean?" Maggie asked.

I explained what Sister Dabney told me.

"She's right, you know," Julie chimed in. "Shannon is making a mistake. I met her husband. You could see in his eyes that he still cared for her."

"Which is none of our business," Maggie replied. "Shannon hasn't asked any of us for advice about her personal life. How many times she gets married and divorced isn't our concern unless it interferes with her work."

"Is that right?" Julie asked me.

"Maybe."

"Don't be a wimp."

"I'm not, but there's more wrong with the world than any one person can fix. If I think I'm supposed to help someone, then I'll get involved, even if it's risky. That's what may happen with Jessie Whitewater."

"Your appointed case?" Maggie asked.

"Yes."

"How would you get involved beyond representing her?"

I took a deep breath. "If she makes bond, she may live with Mrs. Fairmont and me."

"What?" Julie exploded. "Drop her in the middle of all those antiques and diamonds? Mrs. Fairmont wears enough rocks on her fingers to finance a trip around the world. It wouldn't be safe to have someone you don't know around her. I can't believe you're considering this!"

"Mrs. Fairmont wants to meet Jessie at the motion hearing, then decide."

"She's not mentally competent to make that judgment," Julie answered before looking at Maggie. "Does this sound as crazy to you as it does to me?"

Maggie nodded. "It's rarely a good idea to become personally involved with a client, especially at the level you're suggesting. Doesn't Mrs. Fairmont suffer from a form of dementia?"

"Multi-infarct dementia as a result of ministrokes. But most of the time she's fine. She's been lucid when we've discussed this."

"And what will happen when she isn't lucid and a stranger takes a hundred-year-old silver tea set out of the house and sells it to a pawnshop for twenty-five dollars?" Julie asked.

"That's a possibility anytime you help someone," I answered with more confidence than I felt. "We take a chance that our clients won't pay us."

"Please," Julie responded. "That's not even close."

"What time is the bond hearing?" Maggie asked.

"Tomorrow morning at nine o'clock. It's a general motion calendar, so I don't know when it will be heard."

Maggie checked her phone. "I can stay until ten, then I have to leave for an appointment. Even if the motion isn't heard while I'm there, I want to talk to Mrs. Fairmont. The firm isn't directly responsible for what you're considering, but I don't feel comfortable letting you make the decision on your own."

"Sister Dabney will be there, too," I added, deciding it was better to avoid another surprise. "She's going to post a property bond so Jessie can be released."

Julie pressed her lips tightly together for a moment before she spoke. "I should have known she was behind this. That woman is going to ruin your life if you let her."

"You thought she was right about Shannon," I replied defensively.

"Maybe, but she thinks she's right about everything and everyone! That's dangerous."

The tension created at the table stayed with us during the return trip to the office. There was no conversation in the car, and we immediately went to our offices and shut the doors. I suspected Maggie and Julie would have a private conversation later about the issue. It didn't take much imagination to guess what Julie would say. Maggie's reaction was less predictable.

That evening during supper I reminded Mrs. Fairmont of the hearing in the morning.

"What's the child's name?"

"I think it's Jessie Whitewater, but I'm not one hundred percent sure. And she's not a child. She may be eighteen."

"Where is her family?"

"That's unknown, too. Both the assistant district attorney and I suspect she may be running away from a bad situation, which would explain why she won't help in locating them."

"There are a lot of teenage runaways. I watched a TV show about it this afternoon. Usually, they don't take off on their own but travel with another person, often someone older."

I'd not considered Jessie might have a companion hiding out there.

"I don't think that happened here."

"Good. I talked to Christine."

I put down my fork. "What did she say?"

"It was a first conversation, so I didn't get very specific. All I mentioned was that you were interviewing a young woman who might be willing to stay with me for room and board in return for keeping an eye on me."

"Did you say I interviewed her at the jail?"

"No, but she complimented you for taking the initiative to find someone to help when you're at work. Of course, she wants to interview anyone before they come to stay."

"When and where would that happen?"

"Here, after I make my decision."

"But if you've already made your decision, and Mrs. Bartlett doesn't agree—"

Mrs. Fairmont dismissed my words with a wave of her hand. "By the time I finish with Christine, she'll go home and tell Ken it was really her idea in the first place."

"Maybe, but Jessie isn't polished and sophisticated."

"Like you?" Mrs. Fairmont asked with a twinkle in her eyes.

I stared at her for a second and then burst out laughing.

EARLY THE NEXT MORNING, I DROVE TO THE JAIL. A FEMALE GUARD escorted me to one of the interview rooms. A few minutes later Jessie came in wearing a white apron on top of her orange jumpsuit. She was slightly skinnier than I'd remembered.

"Why are you wearing that?" I asked, pointing to the apron.

"I work in the kitchen. I was scrambling eggs when the guard came to get me."

"Did you get a copy of Judge Cannon's order refusing to remove me from the case?"

"Yeah, but I'm going to appeal it to the United States Supreme Court."

"What?"

"Appeal it to the United States Supreme Court. It's in Washington, D.C."

"I know where it is, but you can't appeal an order like that to the Supreme Court."

Jessie's face looked resolute. "Watch me."

I stifled a smile. "Okay. But until the Supreme Court reverses Judge Cannon's order and takes me off your case, I'm still representing you. Would you like to sleep in a soft bed in a quiet place?"

"What?"

I repeated the offer. Jessie gave me a puzzled look.

"Are you trying to send me to a mental hospital?"

"Have you ever been to one in the past?"

"No."

"Are you sure?"

"I think I would remember if I'd ever been in a place like that. And I've never been locked up before either. Why did you say something about a soft bed, then start talking to me about other stuff?"

"I'll get to the point. A nice elderly woman may be willing to let you stay with her if you can make bond and get out of here. Would you be interested in that?"

"Who is she?"

"Mrs. Margaret Fairmont. I have an apartment in her basement."

Surprise flashed across Jessie's face. "You want me to live with you?"

"Both of us. Sister Dabney is willing to post a property bond to get you out if you agree to stay with Mrs. Fairmont and me while I work on your case."

"Post a property bond? What does that mean?"

"She would put up her house in return for the police releasing you from jail while your case is pending. If you run away, she would have to pay the bond or lose her home."

And in an instant Jessie Whitewater changed from a hardened young woman into a girl. Her eyes watered and she rubbed them with the back of her hand.

"Why would she do that?" she asked with a sniffle.

"Because she cares what happens to you. I've filed a motion to reduce your bond so it will be less of a risk for her. But the only way Sister Dabney agreed to do this is if you agree to stay with Mrs. Fairmont. The judge is going to hear the motion later this morning. You'll be brought over to the courthouse from the jail. Mrs. Fairmont will be there, so she can meet you and decide for sure if she's willing to help."

"And I'd stay at the house where you live?"

"Yes."

"Would I have to go to church?"

"Not unless you wanted to. Sister Dabney would be glad to see you, but it wasn't a requirement for the bond."

I could see Jessie trying to process what she was hearing.

"This is real," I said. "You're not dreaming, although you might think you are when you see the house. It's a beautiful old home in the historic area of the city."

"Where would I sleep?"

"Probably on a bed in my apartment."

"And I would eat there?"

"Yes, all the good food you want. Mrs. Fairmont's health isn't that great. She's had several strokes. You'd be expected to check on her during the day and call me or 911 if she has a serious problem."

Jessie nodded. "My cousin Barry's grandfather had a stroke. He couldn't move his right arm when he came home from the hospital. I used to open jars for him."

"Where did he live?"

"Not far from my stepmother and me after we moved to—" Jessie stopped. "I wish you would stop trying to trick me."

"I'm not trying to trick you; I'm trying to help you. Getting out on bond doesn't mean the burglary case against you is going to be dropped. The best way to take care of that is to get the case transferred to juvenile court, but my hands are tied until you give me enough information to prove you're a minor."

Jessie shook her head. "I can't."

"What could be so bad about where you came from that you'd risk going to prison as an adult convicted of a felony? Remember, everything you tell me is confidential."

"Everything?"

"Yes, not even the judge can make me tell him."

Jessie looked puzzled. "If everything I tell you is secret, how could you get my case sent to juvenile court? My age would have to come out in the open."

Finally, Jessie had admitted she wasn't eighteen.

"Juvenile court proceedings are closed to the public; the judge would hear the evidence in private. The only people who would have to know would be the judge, the assistant district attorney, and a caseworker."

"And if I'm not eighteen, the police would try to find my stepmother and tell her where I am, wouldn't they?"

"Yes."

"And send me to live with her?"

"I don't know. If the situation is bad enough, you could be removed from the home."

"And sent to foster care?"

"Maybe. There are a lot of good foster parents. A family in my hometown took in several kids over the years. Many of those children came back when they grew up to thank them."

Jessie shook her head. "No. I've talked to a woman who works back in the kitchen with me. She told me that even if I broke the window at the store and took some food, the judge won't send me to prison. The worst thing that will happen is prohibition."

"You mean probation."

"Yeah."

"She may be right unless you're charged with multiple thefts and burglaries. In that case, a prison sentence is much more likely. And with even one felony conviction on your record, it would make it harder to find a job, buy a car, rent an apartment, lots of things."

I could tell from the look on Jessie's face that she had no interest in thinking about any of those things. She was living in the moment.

And her main concern was maintaining her anonymity. Her lips were tightly shut.

"Okay," I said. "Do you want to talk to Mrs. Fairmont?"

"Yeah."

I started to coach Jessie in what to say but hesitated. I didn't want to manipulate the situation. Mrs. Fairmont needed to appreciate what she was getting into.

"I'll see you in court in a couple of hours," I said.

Jessie got up to leave the room. I came to the door and watched her walk toward the cell block. She stopped and turned around. Her face had a more mature sadness.

"Thanks for helping me."

I SPENT AN HOUR AT THE OFFICE, CONFIRMED THE TIME OF THE hearing with Maggie, then drove home to pick up Mrs. Fairmont. I walked into a quiet house. I checked my watch. If Mrs. Fairmont wasn't ready, there wouldn't be time for her to get dressed. She wasn't in the den or either parlor. I called upstairs.

"Mrs. Fairmont! It's Tami. Are you ready to go?"

At the sound of my voice, Flip raced down the steps. I met him a few steps from the bottom.

"I'm looking for something!" Mrs. Fairmont replied.

I took the steps two at a time. The elderly woman was in her bedroom, wearing an attractive green dress with a colorful scarf. She'd already put on her shoes.

"I have a necklace that goes with this outfit," she said, rummaging through the bottom drawer of one of her three jewelry boxes.

I'd never helped Mrs. Fairmont find a piece of jewelry and considered the boxes off-limits. Seeing them on top of her dresser made me nervous.

"It has a few emeralds that set off the diamonds nicely."

"Should you wear something that fancy to the courthouse? I think the scarf is pretty enough."

"It would be for you. I need more help than a scrap of cloth."

She pulled out a drawer in one of the other jewelry boxes.

"Here it is!" She held up a narrow necklace in front of the mirror. The precious stones glistened.

"It's beautiful," I admitted.

"Please help me with the clasp. I don't want it to fall off."

I fastened it securely around Mrs. Fairmont's neck. She adjusted it with her right hand.

"This used to be snug. Now it hangs down. I'm shriveling up like a prune."

"A sweet prune."

She smiled at me in the reflection in the mirror. "I hope so. I can count on you for compliments. If your young woman comes to live with us, I'll put the expensive pieces in the safe-deposit box at the bank. There's no use providing unnecessary temptation."

"Yes, ma'am," I quickly agreed. "And there might be other items that should be taken from the house."

"We'll see. The silver tea set in the blue parlor is a museum piece, but to an untrained eye it just looks old." She smiled. "Like me."

WE ARRIVED EARLY AT THE COURTHOUSE SO MRS. FAIRMONT wouldn't be rushed. A handful of people were seated in the spectator section in the courtroom. Neither Sister Dabney nor Maggie had arrived. I led Mrs. Fairmont to the same row where she'd sat for the swearing-in ceremony.

"Please, sit here. I want to introduce you to Jessie and let you talk before the case is called. I don't think Judge Cannon will have any questions for you, but it may come up where Jessie will stay if her bond is reduced."

People began to drift into the room. I'd attended a few of these motion calendars the previous summer. What struck me then and now were the faces of the men and women. The public read crime statistics. But there were no numbers in the courtroom, only people with unique problems and feelings. Most were probably family and friends of defendants who were being brought over from the jail. For them, the calendar call was a chance to see a loved one, even if only briefly from a distance.

Jan Crittenden and two other employees of the district attorney's office arrived with a thick stack of files. Jan came over to Mrs. Fairmont and greeted both of us.

"Here to watch?" she asked the elderly lady.

"You could say that. Give my regards to your aunt when you see her."

"Yes, ma'am." Jan turned to me. "Any new information?"

"Not yet. I'm still working on it."

"Okay. I'm sticking with what I told you the other day. I won't put up any evidence or argue against reduction in the bond. It's up to the judge."

"Thanks."

Jan left. The back door of the courtroom opened and Sister Dabney entered. Her face was red, her hair plastered to her head with sweat. When I saw her my stomach tightened. She must have walked several blocks in the morning heat. She slipped into one of the back rows. I sighed in relief.

"Sister Dabney is here," I said in a low voice to Mrs. Fairmont when I sat down.

The elderly woman turned her head.

"Where is she?" she asked. "I don't see her."

"Sitting in the back. She's here to observe. If she posts Jessie's bond, it will be done after the hearing."

A side door opened and two deputies escorted in a line of male prisoners wearing handcuffs and leg irons. Then a female deputy brought in three women who were not shackled. Jessie looked small and young between the more-mature women. I realized it might be harder for Mrs. Fairmont to talk to Jessie than I'd thought. I walked past the bar and approached the deputy, a woman I recognized from the jail.

"May I talk with my client for a minute or two before the judge arrives?" I asked, motioning to Jessie.

"Okay."

Jessie looked nervous.

"Over here," I said, guiding her away from the other prisoners and toward Mrs. Fairmont.

Jessie licked her lips and followed. We stayed close to the wall. A low wooden bar separated us from the front row.

"Jessie, this is Mrs. Fairmont, the lady I was telling you about. She owns the house where I live."

Mrs. Fairmont stood and held out a bejeweled hand. Jessie glanced down at the diamond rings on the elderly woman's fingers and her eyes widened. She gave Mrs. Fairmont's hand a short jerk.

"Would you like to come home and stay with Tami and me?" Mrs. Fairmont asked.

"Yes." Jessie nodded, her eyes still wide.

"I have a dog named Flip. He's a Chihuahua."

"I love dogs," Jessie answered. "They like me, too."

"Will you be able to help me around the house?"

"I can wash dishes, mop the kitchen floor, make the beds, hang clothes on the line."

"Mrs. Fairmont has a clothes dryer," I said.

"I ran one when we went to the Laundromat."

Mrs. Fairmont looked at me. "I'd be happy for Jessie to stay with us while you help her."

"Thank you, ma'am," Jessie replied. "I promise to be good."

I glanced at the back of the courtroom and saw Sister Dabney sitting with her eyes closed.

I returned Jessie to her place with the other prisoners. The back door of the courtroom opened, and Mr. Carpenter entered with a couple of men wearing dark suits. Jessie, who was standing slightly behind me, gasped.

"What is it?" I asked, turning to the side.

"Don't let him see me," she replied, putting her hands over her face.

"Who?"

"The man with the blond hair."

One of the two men with Mr. Carpenter had blond hair. He looked to be in his mid- to late thirties. The other man had dark hair streaked with gray.

"Who is he?" I asked, having to turn to the side because Jessie was crouching behind me.

"All rise!" the bailiff called out. "This court is now in session, the Honorable Clifton Cannon, presiding!"

"Please sit in front of me," Jessie hissed.

"What?"

"Mr. Duffy," Judge Cannon said to the assistant district attorney in charge of the morning's calendar, "approach the bench. There's something I need to discuss before we get started."

The chief assistant DA stepped forward.

"Don't leave me," Jessie whispered.

"There's no need to be scared."

"Please!"

I couldn't ignore the panic in Jessie's voice. I leaned over toward the deputy.

"May I stay here with my client?"

"Yeah."

I quickly placed a chair in front of Jessie and sat down. Jessie was hunched over in a ball. I'd stumbled upon her fear factor. My heart rate picked up as my mind raced into overdrive.

If the motion to reduce Jessie's bond was called while Mr. Carpenter and the blond-haired man were in the courtroom, it would be impossible to hide my young client from the man she wanted to avoid. There was no way to quietly move her to a place where I could talk to her and find out what was going on.

Mr. Carpenter passed through the bar. Several lawyers scattered across the open area in front of the judge greeted him. When Mr. Carpenter's eyes met mine, I suddenly had a sinking feeling he knew all about Jessie Whitewater and that his appearance in the courtroom was linked to my own.

The judge spoke in a loud voice. "Mr. Duffy, call the first case."

I didn't know the order of the cases. My heart leaped to my throat in anticipation of Jessie's name being at the top of the list.

"Your Honor, Mr. Carpenter requested that his motion in *State v. Hackney* be placed first on the calendar. He needs to be in federal court in front of Judge McKnight later this morning, and I have no objection to bringing his motion before you at this time."

"Very well, proceed," the judge said.

Mr. Carpenter stood. I felt myself caught in his peripheral vision.

"Thank you, Mr. Duffy," said the gray-haired lawyer in a carefully measured voice. "Your Honor, we're here this morning on defendant's motion to conduct an independent examination of evidence. In response to the criminal discovery statute, we've been informed there are tape-recorded conversations that may be utilized in this case. My client has retained Dr. Martin Link to perform independent testing of this evidence. With the Court's permission, I'd ask Dr. Link to come forward and be sworn."

"Proceed."

The man with dark hair streaked with gray approached the witness chair, raised his right hand, and swore to tell the truth.

"Dr. Link, please tell the court about your educational and professional qualifications."

The witness, who had a very pleasant British accent, was a physicist with an impressive academic background in the United States and Great Britain.

"What particular area of expertise will you utilize in evaluating potential evidence in the case of *State v. Hackney*?" Mr. Carpenter asked.

"Voice recognition analysis."

"What specialized training and experience do you have that qualifies you to perform voice recognition analysis?"

This brought forth a much longer answer and several follow-up questions about Dr. Link's familiarity with the topic. He'd written a score of articles published in scholarly journals and developed a computer program that sounded so sophisticated it could mimic the inflection in Lincoln's voice when he delivered the Gettysburg Address. If I hadn't been scared on Jessie's behalf, I would have enjoyed listening to the testimony. Mr. Carpenter paused.

"Your Honor, we ask that Dr. Link be designated as an expert witness in the area of voice recognition analysis. We further move that he be given access to any and all tape recordings in the State's possession in this case so he can perform his own analysis."

The judge turned to assistant DA Duffy. "Do you have any questions for the witness?"

"Yes, sir."

To my surprise, Duffy didn't vigorously attack the doctor. Instead, he focused on finding out more about Dr. Link's training and experience. Each question seemed to strengthen, rather than weaken, Mr. Carpenter's argument that the scientist was an expert who should be allowed to conduct his tests. Duffy finished and sat down. Judge Cannon finished making notes on a legal pad in front of him and then looked up.

"The Court grants defendant's motion that Dr. Link be recognized as an expert witness and orders the State to allow him to perform independent analysis of any tape recordings in the State's possession. Mr. Carpenter, prepare an appropriate order and send it to Mrs. Duffy for his review prior to submission to the court.

16

THE BLOND-HAIRED MAN ON THE FRONT ROW STOOD AND MOVED toward the aisle in our direction. I heard Jessie make a choking noise, and I shifted my chair. However, the man's attention was on Mr. Carpenter and Dr. Link. As the three men were leaving the courtroom, Mr. Duffy said, "*State v. Wheeler.*"

Several more cases were called in rapid succession. Most were defendants entering a plea. During a brief lull, I turned around and saw that Jessie was biting her fingernails while watching the rear door of the courtroom.

"Are you okay?" I asked.

"Will they be coming back?"

"No."

"But he didn't tell the judge he was guilty."

"It was a motion hearing."

One of the women sitting next to Jessie entered a guilty plea on a burglary charge and received a five-year sentence. Nothing came out about the woman's history, but I hoped the seriousness of the sentence wasn't lost on Jessie.

"*State v. Whitewater,*" Jan Crittenden announced.

I stood and motioned for Jessie to join me in the open space in front of the judge.

"Your Honor, my client is charged with burglary. Currently, her bond is set at ten thousand dollars. I've filed a motion to reduce it."

Judge Cannon flipped open a folder.

"The State has no position on the motion," Jan said from her place beside the prosecution table.

"There is a brief attached to the motion outlining the applicable law—," I began.

"Which I already know," the judge interrupted. "Ms. Taylor, what facts support reduction of the bond?"

"This is my client's first offense and involved illegal entry of a convenience store and theft of a bag of donuts. She's not employed, but—"

"If she's guilty of the charges, why don't you proceed to enter a plea? Isn't it a waste of the Court's time to rule on your motion?"

"I've not discussed that option with Ms. Whitewater. There is a question whether, based on my client's age, this case should be in superior court or juvenile court."

"How old is she?"

"I don't know."

"We'll settle that right now." The judge leaned forward, his eyes glaring at Jessie. "How old are you?"

"Eighteen," she answered in a shaky voice that sounded much younger.

"Very well," the judge replied, turning toward me. "If your client insists she's eighteen, I'll leave her bond at a level appropriate for a felony burglary charge in superior court. Motion denied."

Jessie and I retreated to our place near the wall.

"Why did you tell him you're eighteen?" I asked, trying to keep my voice calm. "He knew you were lying."

"Because I didn't know what else to do."

"That makes no sense to me."

"Am I going back to the jail?"

"For now. You won't get out until Sister Dabney posts your bond. After the paperwork is completed, I'll pick you up at the jail and take you to Mrs. Fairmont's house."

"Will I be safe there?"

"Yes."

Jessie didn't look convinced.

"Who is the blond-haired man who was with Mr. Carpenter?"

"Are you going to talk to him?"

"No, but I'll call his lawyer and find out if you don't tell me."

"Clay Hackney."

"Does he know you?"

Jessie nodded. "He's the reason I ran away."

"We'll talk later."

Jessie grabbed my arm. "Don't tell anyone about me and Clay. It has to be kept secret like you promised."

The female guard came closer to us.

"Okay, but I want to know everything later."

I left Jessie sitting against the wall and returned to Mrs. Fairmont.

"That didn't go very well, did it?" she asked.

"No, ma'am."

"If that child is eighteen, I'm forty-eight," the elderly woman continued. "Why in the world would she lie to Cliff Cannon? It really upset him."

"Yes." I nodded, turning sideways to see if Sister Dabney was still in the courtroom. "I need to speak to Sister Dabney."

I walked back to the row where she was sitting.

"Sorry I couldn't get the bond lowered," I said. "Judge Cannon gave Jessie a chance to tell the truth about her age and she lied."

"I knew there would be risk," Sister Dabney answered. "I was praying he would lower the amount, but it doesn't change my plans."

"Mrs. Fairmont is willing to let Jessie stay with us. She met with her for a few minutes before the hearing."

"Mrs. Fairmont is a good woman. You can learn a lot from her. Jessie will like her."

"I hope so."

I paused. I wanted to tell Sister Dabney about Clay Hackney for two reasons: his appearance increased Jessie's flight risk, and I wanted Sister Dabney's advice about handling the situation. But Jessie had invoked the attorney-client privilege, and I couldn't violate her instructions.

"What's going to happen next?" I asked, hoping Sister Dabney had already received divine insight about what was going on.

"After I go to the jail to post the bond, I have to get the air-conditioning in my car fixed."

I had a sudden urge to give Sister Dabney some money. I opened my purse and gave her all my cash, which amounted to more than three hundred dollars. She took the money and folded it in two.

"Thank you," she said.

"I hope that will take care of fixing the car."

"If you heard right, I'm sure it will."

Sister Dabney left the courtroom. I returned to Mrs. Fairmont. Judge Cannon called a recess and left the bench.

"Are you ready to go?" I asked.

"Yes, this is a sad place. I don't see how Cliff does this day after day."

I hadn't considered that Judge Cannon had feelings and assumed he enjoyed wearing a black robe and barking out orders. When Mrs. Fairmont and I reached the hallway, we ran into Maggie. Julie was with her. I reintroduced Mrs. Fairmont to the two women.

"Sorry I'm late," Maggie said. "I was interviewing a witness across town. Has the judge already heard the motion?"

"Denied."

I told them what happened, leaving out the close encounter with Clay Hackney and Jessie's reaction. Maggie turned to Mrs. Fairmont.

"Tami says you're considering letting our client stay at your house if she's able to post bond."

"That's right."

"What if she stayed with Julie instead?" Maggie asked me.

"Julie?" I asked in shock.

"That's right," Julie replied. "And don't look like you've seen a ghost. I'm willing to help someone in need for a few weeks. Unlike Mrs. Fairmont, I don't have any expensive jewelry and antiques in my apartment. The most valuable things I own are a few pairs of Manolo Blahniks. Unless your client is a size seven, my place is as empty of temptation as a jail cell."

"But Jessie already met Mrs. Fairmont and said she wanted to stay with us."

"Which may not be the best course," Maggie said. "Look, I'm worried about all that could go wrong with the client staying with Mrs. Fairmont. We know nothing about Whitewater's background. It's simply too great a risk to take."

Listening to Maggie, I felt a fear I'd suppressed rise up in my heart. I couldn't stand the thought of anyone taking advantage of Mrs. Fairmont—or worse. Except for Sister Dabney's warning that Jessie would flee unless she stayed with Mrs. Fairmont, I would have agreed with the wisdom of Julie's offer.

"I think it's awesome that Julie is willing to do this," Maggie continued. "As soon as she volunteered, I knew that if we're going to get this deeply involved with the client's life, it should stay within the law firm."

"It is a very generous thing to do," I said to Julie. "But if Jessie doesn't live with us, I'm not sure Sister Dabney is going to post her bond."

"Is that what she told you?" Maggie asked.

"Not exactly, but she didn't leave any doubt about what she thought should happen."

"Which is standard procedure in her world." Julie sniffed. "What do you think, Mrs. Fairmont? Would you be okay with Jessie living with me instead of staying at your house?"

"I'm willing to help the child," she replied, "but you are smart young women who know more about the situation and the law than I do." The elderly woman yawned. "Excuse me, all this excitement is wearing me out."

Maggie and Julie exchanged a look.

"Maybe we should meet at the jail after I take Mrs. Fairmont home," I said. "We can sort this out then."

AFTER DROPPING OFF MRS. FAIRMONT, I WENT TO THE JAIL. Maggie, Julie, and Sister Dabney were standing in a small circle in the large open area immediately beyond the front doors. Seeing them together, I walked rapidly toward them.

"Is everything okay?" I asked.

"There weren't any problems with the bond," Julie answered. "One of the guards is getting Jessie."

I looked at Sister Dabney.

"I was explaining to them about the cord of three strands," Sister Dabney said. "Unlike a natural rope, it gets stronger, not weaker, with the passage of time. Tests don't fray it but make it tougher to cut."

"Isn't it a beautiful metaphor?" Julie replied. "You should have told us about it when you accepted the job at the firm. It's even in the part of the Bible I can believe."

I narrowed my eyes, not sure if Julie was mocking or not.

"And we've agreed that it makes sense for Jessie to stay with Julie," Maggie said. "That's an example of the three of us working together."

I turned to Sister Dabney. "But you said she would run away unless Mrs. Fairmont invited her to stay with us."

"That's true. Did Mrs. Fairmont invite her or not?"

"She did."

"This is a step I didn't see at the time," Sister Dabney said.

The door to the cell-block area opened and Jessie came out wearing blue jeans, a T-shirt, and sandals.

"We need to get that child some proper clothes," Sister Dabney said.

"Do you mean dresses?" I couldn't imagine trying to force the young woman to follow my standards.

"Leave that up to Julie," Sister Dabney said. "Jessie is under her authority. Something clean would be good for a start."

"Okay."

As Jessie approached she edged toward me and away from Sister Dabney.

"I told you I wasn't going to give you up to the devil," Sister Dabney said, pointing her finger at the young woman. "I bought you out of this jail and now you belong to the Lord."

"Oh, that's just like the scene from *Les Miserables* between the priest and Jean Valjean," Julie exclaimed. "You know, in the beginning after he steals the silver—"

Not wanting to give Jessie any ideas, I cut in and introduced her to Maggie and Julie.

"We've decided it would be best for you to stay with Julie," I said. "She has a nice place not far from the river. It's much prettier than my apartment in Mrs. Fairmont's basement."

Jessie eyed Julie more closely.

"You'll still get a chance to visit Mrs. Fairmont," I continued. "I'll bring you over to her house for dinner soon."

Jessie shrugged. "Okay. Anything is going to be better than the cell block."

"Great. First, let's go shopping," Julie said brightly.

I lagged behind with Sister Dabney as Maggie and Julie escorted Jessie out of the jail.

"Are you sure about this?" I asked.

"As soon as they mentioned it, I had the confirmation of the Spirit. This is a bigger step for the Jewish lawyer than it is for Jessie."

"What kind of step?"

"Along the same path you're following."

BACK AT THE OFFICE, I HAD A VOICE MAIL FROM ZACH TELLING ME he was back in town and wanted to talk to me. I hesitated, not sure what we had to talk about since I hadn't made up my mind. I listened to the voice mail a second time. Hearing his voice caused my heart to ache. I called him.

"How are you doing?" he asked after a minute of small talk.

Tears suddenly pooled in the corners of my eyes, making me glad he couldn't see me.

"It's been a stressful few days."

Then, to keep from letting him know the primary reason for my anxiety, I launched into a recap of my involvement with Jessie Whitewater, avoiding mention of any privileged information. Talking about Jessie's case allowed me to regain my composure.

"She's with Julie now," I said.

"That's incredible. My only concern is how Julie will feel if the client runs away and leaves Sister Dabney on the hook for a ten-thousand-dollar bond."

"Sister Dabney doesn't seem worried about it. I'm not sure Julie's thought that far ahead. It was a quick decision." I paused. "Mr. Carpenter was in criminal court this morning in front of Judge Cannon representing a man named Hackney. Do you know anything about the case?"

"It's a white-collar crime. I'm not sure about the specific charge. Mr. Carpenter is handling the criminal case because the firm has other business with the client."

"What kind of business?"

"I'm not sure. He's a fairly new client. Why?"

"I didn't expect to see Mr. Carpenter at a criminal court motions calendar."

Zach was silent for a moment. I shifted nervously in my chair, hoping Zach wasn't going to connect my interest in Hackney with my representation of Jessie.

"You know, I care about you," he said.

"Yes," I answered quickly, then couldn't find the next word I wanted to say. "Uh, thanks for calling."

We ended the call. I looked up at the ceiling in an unspoken plea for help.

JULIE AND JESSIE SURVIVED THE FIRST TWO DAYS TOGETHER WITHout serious problems. Late in the afternoon of the third day, Julie stopped into my office, walked over to my desk, and lowered her head so her hair was close to my face.

"Do you think I'm getting any gray hairs?" she asked.

"I don't see any," I said, looking from side to side.

Julie raised her head. "I mean, being responsible for a teenager, however old Jessie turns out to be, is enough to cause a few hairs to give up on pigment and go gray. It's no wonder my mother started going downhill around my thirteenth birthday."

"That had to be rough on her."

"Don't be so quick to agree."

"Has anything out of line happened with Jessie?"

"Just the pressure of worrying about her. She's not a bad kid, which makes it worse to consider how bad her life's been. Did you know she's a book freak?"

"She mentioned reading books."

"It's crazy. I had to throw out some stuff I didn't want her to read—"

"Good," I interrupted.

"Don't go there," Julie shot back. "And took some of the books I had from college days out of boxes and put them on the shelves. When I left this morning, she was reading *The Iliad*. Can you believe that?"

"It will give you something to talk about over dinner."

"That's why I came by. I've got a date tonight and wondered if you'd take her to Mrs. Fairmont's house for the evening. I'd rather Jessie not be alone at my apartment."

"Are you worried she might get into trouble?"

"No, she's scared at night, always wanting to make sure the doors and windows are locked, stuff like that. She hasn't told me why and I haven't asked. I think it will be better if she's around people. I won't be out too late."

I'd not mentioned the incident with Clay Hackney in the courtroom to either Julie or Maggie.

"Sure. Do you want me to pick her up?"

"Yeah."

I STOPPED BY JULIE'S APARTMENT AT 6:00 P.M. JESSIE, WEARING A new pair of jeans, a cute shirt, and sneakers, ran down the steps. If I didn't know better, I would have pegged her as a high school junior who was assigned *The Iliad* by an overzealous English teacher.

"Is this your car?" she asked when she got in.

"No, it belongs to Mrs. Fairmont. She doesn't drive anymore and lets me use it."

"It's nice," Jessie said, touching the tan leather seats. "But it's an old person's car."

"Do you know how to drive?"

"Yes, but I don't have a license."

After several blocks we turned onto a cobblestone street. Jessie looked out the window at the historic houses.

"Is Mrs. Fairmont rich?" she asked.

"Probably."

"How much money does she have?"

"I've never asked, but her home is filled with lovely things. You'll need to be careful not to break anything."

"What's for supper?"

"The lady who cleans for Mrs. Fairmont put a small roast in the oven before she left. I'll cook some vegetables. Maybe you can help me put together a salad."

"Okay."

We parked in front of the single-car garage. Out of the corner of my eye, I watched Jessie's reaction to the outside of the house.

"This is it?" she asked.

"Yes."

Jessie said a curse word.

"None of that," I said sharply.

"Julie doesn't care."

"You're not with Julie. There are better ways to express yourself."

"I can clean up my mouth if I want to."

"Good." I unlocked the door. "Remember, Mrs. Fairmont has a dog, a Chihuahua named Flip. He barks at strangers and might nip at your hand or foot until he gets used to you."

As I opened the door Flip came careening around the corner, his feet slipping on the hardwood floor. I quickly scooped him up and greeted him.

"This is Jessie," I said, holding him at her eye level.

She held out the back of her hand. Flip growled and sniffed it.

"You know how to act around dogs," I said.

"Yeah. I like dogs, cats, fish, birds, any kind of animal. Can I hold him?"

I hesitated, then put him in her arms. Flip wriggled violently, and Jessie put him on the floor. He stood at her feet and barked furiously.

"Did he try to bite you?" Mrs. Fairmont asked anxiously as she slowly walked into the room.

"No."

"He's a good dog. He's just trying to protect me."

"If I get to come over a few times, we'll get to be friends," Jessie replied.

Mrs. Fairmont extended her hand to Jessie, who awkwardly shook it.

"Welcome to my home," the elderly lady said as if greeting a foreign dignitary. "Tami, why don't you show her around the house? I'm in the kitchen fixing the vegetables."

"You are?"

"Yes, I've not completely forgotten how to entertain guests."

I took Jessie through parlors and other rooms on the main floor. I decided not to show her Mrs. Fairmont's bedroom. Instead, I led her downstairs to my apartment. She went to the patio doors that opened onto the courtyard.

"Can I go out there?" she asked.

"Sure."

I watched as she wandered about the garden. I'd grown used to it, but it had to be a place of wondrous beauty to Jessie. Mrs. Fairmont called my name from the top of the stairs.

"Where's Jessie?" she asked when I joined her in the hallway.

"Exploring the courtyard."

"Julie Feldman is on the phone."

I went into the kitchen and picked up the phone.

"I'm on my way to Atlanta," Julie said. "My father had a very high fever this afternoon and his internist admitted him to the hospital for some tests."

"What's wrong?"

"I'm not sure, but from the sound of my mother's voice I knew I had to go home immediately. Can Jessie spend the night with you and Mrs. Fairmont? I don't think it would be a good idea to leave her at my place alone. I hope to be back tomorrow."

"Just a minute."

I covered the receiver with my hand and quickly told Mrs. Fairmont what had happened.

"Of course she can stay. I already made up my mind about that."

"We'll keep her here," I said to Julie. "Let me know as soon as you can about your father's condition."

"Okay." Julie was silent for a second. "Please pray for him," she added, her voice slightly cracking.

"I will."

I hung up the phone. Jessie joined us in the kitchen. Her eyes grew big when I told her about Julie's father.

"She really loves her father," Jessie said. "She told me a bunch of stuff about him."

"After supper we'll go back to her place and pick up what you need to spend the night here," I said.

"Okay." Jessie nodded quickly.

We ate a quiet supper. Jessie watched Mrs. Fairmont and copied the way she held her eating utensils. The girl also slipped a piece of meat to Flip when she didn't think anyone was looking.

After supper the three of us went into the den. Jessie immediately went to the bookcases and selected a book about the animals of South America. The three of us read until Mrs. Fairmont grew sleepy and got up from her chair.

"I'm going upstairs," she said, yawning.

I checked my watch. "We'll go to Julie's apartment."

During the short drive, Jessie spoke. "I like Mrs. Fairmont. Is she always so nice and polite?"

"Yes." I smiled. "Even when she's confused, she's not mean or rude. Would you rather stay with her than at Julie's apartment?"

"I'd like having someone around all the time. It gets lonely when Julie's at work. And she doesn't have a dog."

We arrived at Julie's apartment.

"I'll run inside and get what I need," Jessie said.

"Do you have a key?" I asked. Julie had told me where she kept one hidden under a rock near the front door.

Jessie pulled one from her jeans. "Yeah. I walked down the street the other day and had one made."

"Does Julie know that?"

"No, but I need to be able to lock up when I go for a walk."

As I waited for Jessie, I considered that she'd had the opportunity to run away since moving in with Julie yet had chosen to make herself at home. She walked down the steps with three plastic bags in her hands. She'd had only one when she left the jail.

"I've got more inside," she said. "Julie likes to go shopping, and every time she buys something for herself, she gets something for me."

At Mrs. Fairmont's house, I fixed a cot for Jessie in the living area of my apartment. By the time I got ready for bed, Jessie appeared to be asleep.

THE FOLLOWING MORNING, JESSIE WAS STILL ASLEEP WHEN I LEFT for work. I wrote a note for Gracie telling her about Jessie so she wouldn't be shocked when she found a young woman in the house. When I turned on my computer at the office, there was an e-mail from Julie written at 2:00 a.m. in the morning.

My dad has bacterial meningitis. He was probably exposed during a recent trip to Africa. They've transferred him to Emory for treatment and isolation.

A second e-mail at 6:00 a.m. read:

My dad is on very strong antibiotics. I'm going to stay here with my mom until he's out of danger. I talked to Maggie about what's going on in my cases. I hope Jessie is doing okay at Mrs. Fairmont's house and can stay there till I come back.

Maggie arrived at the office a few minutes later and came in to see me. I was reading about bacterial meningitis on the Internet.

"What did Julie say about her father?" I asked. "All I got was a couple of e-mails."

"It's serious. Hearing loss, brain damage, seizures, or neurological injury is still possible. Hopefully, they can stabilize him at Emory."

"Could we pray for him?"

Maggie gave me a startled look, then nodded. Without waiting for anything else, I immediately closed my eyes and poured out my heart for Julie's father.

"Amen," Maggie said when I finished. She had a tissue in her hand.

MAGGIE AND I SPENT THE FIRST PART OF THE MORNING DIVIDING the work that couldn't wait in Julie's cases. I ended up with a few divorce cases at the discovery stage. Organizing financial records was something I could do well, even though I didn't like being indirectly part of the breakup of a marriage.

"If there has to be a hearing in any of these cases, I'll handle it," Maggie said, perhaps sensing my reluctance.

"I want to help Julie, it's just that—"

"You help her in the best way you can; I'll do my part," Maggie responded.

I called Mrs. Fairmont, who received the news about Jessie staying a few more days without raising any objection. Late in the afternoon, I received an e-mail from Julie letting me know that her father was responding well to the antibiotics. She ended it by writing, "Maggie told me about your prayer. Thanks."

WHEN I GOT HOME THAT EVENING, MRS. FAIRMONT AND JESSIE were already in the kitchen fixing supper. Chef's salad ingredients were spread across the counter. Jessie had obviously taken a shower; her hair was still damp, and she was wearing new clothes. Flip lay in the corner beside his water bowl watching the activity.

"Where did that outfit come from?" I asked.

"Christine bought them," Mrs. Fairmont said.

"What?"

Mrs. Fairmont finished rinsing the lettuce in a colander and put it on the counter.

"She came by to meet Jessie and took her on a quick shopping spree."

Jessie turned around so I could admire her new shirt, pants, and sandals.

"She bought me deodorant, two kinds of shampoo, conditioner, even a pair of earrings. I've had my ears pierced twice, but they always grew back because I didn't have the right kind of earrings." Jessie touched her thrice-pierced ears. "These are 14-karat gold."

"What did you tell Mrs. Bartlett?" I asked Mrs. Fairmont. "Does she know that last week Jessie was in jail?"

"That wasn't necessary. Once Christine heard Jessie's story, she was more than willing to help."

"Story?"

Jessie spoke. "That I came to Savannah three months ago to help take care of my aunt who was dying from cancer. When she passed away I had no place to go. I couldn't return home because my step-mother had a new boyfriend who didn't want me around the house.

Then I met you, and you were kind enough to tell Julie and Mrs. Fairmont about my predicament."

"Predicament?" I asked.

"You should have told me about her aunt," Mrs. Fairmont chided me. "Jessie really is qualified to help take care of me."

I clenched my jaw and glared at Jessie. I silently mouthed the words, *I'll talk to you later.*

"What do you think of this beautiful salad we've put together?" Mrs. Fairmont asked cheerfully. "Isn't it nice that you don't have to come home after working hard all day and fix supper?"

"Yes, ma'am."

We sat at the dining room table. Mrs. Fairmont said the blessing. Jessie sat with her hands folded and her eyes closed.

"That was a good prayer," she said when Mrs. Fairmont finished.

"Thank you. I'm not an expert prayer like Tami, but I'm learning more about it in my old age. Tonight, I'm going to put Julie's father on my prayer list."

"Could we pray together sometime?" Jessie asked her.

I couldn't tell if Jessie was serious or asking for show.

"That would be wonderful. We can put your family on my list."

"Especially my cousin Barry. I haven't seen him in over a year."

"What's Barry's last name and where does he live?" I asked. "I'm sure Mrs. Fairmont would like to have his full name on her prayer list."

"He's not a Whitewater," Jessie answered.

"Barry is enough for me," Mrs. Fairmont said.

We settled into the meal. I had to admit the salad was delicious.

"How are Zach and Vince?" Mrs. Fairmont asked me.

"Uh, busy at work."

Mrs. Fairmont leaned over to Jessie. "Tami has two men interested in her. But it's not a secret. They work together, isn't that right?"

"They're both at Sam Braddock's firm. And they're not that—"

"Zach and Tami are courting," Mrs. Fairmont continued. "But Vince is a very nice young man, too. He's from Charleston, but his family hasn't been there for generations. What does his father do?"

"He's a professor at the College of Charleston."

"Which is a lot more respectable than what some of the old-money people in Charleston and Savannah do for a living."

"I've never had a real boyfriend," Jessie said. "Much less two at once."

I didn't want to fuel the conversation and kept quiet. Mrs. Fairmont changed the subject and started telling a story I'd heard at least three or four times. It was about a man she dated for nine months before she met and married her husband, Harry. The unsuccessful suitor owned a sailboat that sounded more like a yacht to me. He taught Mrs. Fairmont how to help him sail the boat. When Mrs. Fairmont described the outfits she wore on the boat, Jessie's eyes got big.

"Weren't you hot with all those clothes on?" she asked.

"Actually, the right combination of cotton fabrics can keep you cooler than wearing less. And it kept me from getting a sunburn."

Jessie held out her brown arms. "I don't have any problem getting a tan. It may be because my father was part Cherokee."

"That explains the name Whitewater," I replied.

"Yeah," Jessie answered in a way that didn't convince me it was her real name.

When we finished eating, Jessie didn't have to be asked to clear the table and put the dishes in the dishwasher. Watching how hard she wanted to please Mrs. Fairmont after only a single day in the home took some of the edge off my frustration about her secrecy and lies.

"Would you like to take Flip out for a walk?" Mrs. Fairmont asked her when we finished in the kitchen.

"Are you sure that's a good idea?" I asked. "All the squares can be confusing."

"I won't go far," Jessie said. "I never get lost in the woods. And once I've been someplace in the car, I can remember how to go there again."

"I could go with you—," I volunteered.

"No," Mrs. Fairmont responded. "I think it will be good for Jessie and Flip to have that time together."

"Okay."

"His leash is in that drawer." Mrs. Fairmont pointed.

As soon as the leash was in view, Flip raced toward the front door.

"He knows how to heel," I said to Jessie. "And make sure his collar is on tight. You don't want him slipping out of it."

"Can I take a couple of treats?" Jessie asked.

"Yes," Mrs. Fairmont said. "That's a good idea."

I could hear Jessie talking to Flip in the foyer then the front door opened and shut.

"Why did you send her out for a walk?" I asked Mrs. Fairmont.

"Jessie's been hurt by people. Being with an animal can be therapy. She'll enjoy one-on-one time with Flip." Mrs. Fairmont paused. "Should I be worried that she won't come back?"

"It'll be okay. Julie left her alone, and she had plenty of chances to run away. And it seems she wants to please you."

"We had a nice afternoon," Mrs. Fairmont said, seeming to relax. "Of course, I didn't believe that tale about her dying aunt after the first three sentences. I would have laughed if it hadn't been a serious story."

"Did Mrs. Bartlett believe her?"

Mrs. Fairmont nodded. "Christine knows a lot about eighteenth-century crystal, but she's not the best judge of people. And the story caused Christine to buy Jessie an outfit. That was good."

"But it's wrong for Jessie to lie. She's never told me the truth about her family or where she's from or who knows what else. If I had that information, I could probably have her case moved from superior court to juvenile court."

Mrs. Fairmont rubbed her temples with her fingers. "I think she lies because the truth is so painful."

"Did she tell you the truth?"

"No, but I have the luxury of listening without having to find out the truth. Eventually, she'll open up more to me, but it may be too late to help your case." Mrs. Fairmont chuckled. "Wasn't that part about her father being part Cherokee creative? I saw her stomach when she was picking up Flip to put him on the sofa, and it's as white as the Wedgwood china in the cabinet in the dining room."

"Her real name is more likely Wedgwood than Whitewater," I grunted.

"Jessie is a little stray we've taken in for a few nights to feed and look after. We've gotten off to a good start. I just hope I don't have a bad spell with my health while she's here and scare her."

17

FLIP PATTERED ALONGSIDE JESSIE WITH HIS HEAD HELD HIGH. Jessie didn't know what Tami meant by heel, but the little dog knew all the basic commands and could perform an amazing number of tricks. The first time Mrs. Fairmont asked him to turn a somersault, Jessie couldn't believe it. Then, the dog balanced a red ball on his nose while sitting up on his hind legs. He followed that up with an unbelievable trip around the room, turning right or left as Mrs. Fairmont gave commands from her chair. The Chihuahua could recognize at least twenty objects and bring them to the elderly woman.

"How did you teach him to do all this?" Jessie asked in amazement.

"Patience and love. He performs because it's fun for him and pleases me."

Jessie noted landmarks and walked in a straight line even though some of the side streets looked interesting. Later, there would be time to explore the neighborhood that was so different from any environment she'd ever lived in. One of her goals was to return to the vacant lot where she'd left the metal box and retrieve the leather pouch. It was much closer to Mrs. Fairmont's house than Julie's apartment.

Mrs. Fairmont reminded Jessie of a character in a book she'd read. The elderly woman in the story lived in a quaint house at the end of a village lane and served tea and snacks to children who came to visit her. The heroine of the book was a girl like Jessie who came from an abusive family and needed someone to love her. While sitting on Mrs. Fairmont's sofa and eating an apple pastry over a beautiful china plate, Jessie felt like she'd landed in the middle of the story.

The woman in the novel was an accomplished artist and taught the girl how to paint beautiful watercolor pictures of flowers and birds. The girl painted a picture of an injured bluebird she and the elderly woman were nursing back to health. The day they finished the painting, the bluebird flew away and the old woman died. A man who attended the old woman's funeral saw the girl's painting and offered to sell her work at his shop in a big city. The girl lived happily ever after.

Jessie was daydreaming about bluebirds and apple snacks when she reached East Broad Street. She turned around without noticing a black car with heavily tinted windows that passed her, slowed to a stop, and dipped into a side street. The car followed her down Hull Street, stopping several times to let her keep ahead. When Jessie reached Mrs. Fairmont's house, Flip strained on the leash.

"Do you want to tell Mrs. Fairmont about our walk?" Jessie leaned over and picked up the little dog. "Nothing exciting happened, but I won't tell if you decide to make something up."

Jessie opened the front door and took off the leash. Flip dashed into the house. The dark car rolled past and continued on its way.

Sitting in the den with Mrs. Fairmont, I sighed in relief when the front door opened and I heard the patter of Flip's feet. I met Jessie and Flip at the foot of the stairs. Mrs. Fairmont trailed behind me.

"Did you have a nice walk?" she asked.

"Yes."

"It's time for bed," Mrs. Fairmont said with a yawn. "Good night, girls."

To the surprise of both Mrs. Fairmont and me, Jessie stepped forward and gave the elderly woman a hug.

"Good night. Thanks for letting me take Flip out for a walk."

"You're welcome."

Mrs. Fairmont and the little dog climbed the steps and disappeared in the direction of Mrs. Fairmont's room.

"Does he sleep with her?" Jessie asked.

"Yes. Where did you go on your walk?"

"Straight down Hull Street until it ran into East Broad Street then back the same way. It would be easy to get turned around and lost with all the little side streets, so I didn't explore. You said something before that I didn't understand. What does it mean for a dog to heel?"

"To walk alongside you without pulling ahead or lagging behind."

"Flip stayed beside me the whole time until we were in front of the house."

"He knows how to behave in public, a lesson you should learn." I glanced up the stairs. "Why did you tell Mrs. Fairmont and her daughter that crazy story about coming to Savannah to take care of a dying aunt and not being able to go back home because your stepmother has a new boyfriend?"

Jessie shrugged. "They liked it. Her daughter almost started to cry. And the part about my stepmother is probably true. She's had lots of new boyfriends. Some of them were scary."

"But you need to stop lying. It's wrong, and one lie leads to another. Then when you're caught it makes the problem worse than the one you were trying to avoid."

"That's not always true." Jessie shook her head. "I've lied my way out of beatings that could have sent me to the hospital."

Jessie's response stopped me. I imagined her face swollen and puffy.

"Well, you're not going to be beaten here."

"I'll try to do better." Jessie paused. "Can I read or watch TV?"

"Yes. I was reading in the den while waiting for you to come back."

As we walked down the hallway, Jessie asked, "Were you afraid I wouldn't come back?"

I started to say no but realized the truth demanded a different answer.

"Yes."

Jessie stopped and gave me a hurt look. "Not while I was with Flip. Mrs. Fairmont loves that dog and trusted me enough to take him on a walk. I had to come back. And I'd be crazy to leave this house or Julie's apartment. Before I went to jail, I was hungry most of the time and sleeping on a dirty mattress underneath a tarp on an overgrown vacant lot."

"You weren't staying with your aunt who's visiting a relative in Jacksonville?"

"No."

We went into the den. Mrs. Fairmont had rows of books on dark walnut shelves.

"I finished the book about animals of South America," Jessie said, standing on her tiptoes to look at the titles on the spines. Every so often she would pull down a volume and examine and return it. Finally, she selected one and turned around.

"Have you read this one?" she asked. "*Little Women.*"

"Yes," I said. "That's a good choice."

Jessie lay on the sofa with a pillow under her head. We passed a quiet couple of hours, not unlike times I'd spent with the twins in the front room.

"I know why you wanted me to read this," Jessie said with a yawn. "You think Jo is like me."

"Is she?" I asked, not at all sure.

"A little."

"Are you sleepy?"

"Yeah. We had lights-out at the jail by now, and I had to get up early in the morning because I helped in the kitchen."

Jessie sat on the edge of the sofa. "What's wrong with Mrs. Fairmont? She seemed okay to me."

"Sometimes her brain doesn't work right, and she might have trouble remembering your name or forget things you said just a few seconds before."

"That would be weird. If that happens and you're not here, what should I do?"

"If it only lasts for a minute or so, just act normal and be patient. She'll come around. If she complains about a bad headache, faints, or stays really confused for a longer period of time, you should call Mrs. Bartlett or me."

"Or 911."

"Try one of us first."

"Okay. I hope nothing happens to her. I never had a grand-mother."

"Why not?"

"One lived in Kansas or someplace like that. The other one died when I was a baby." Jessie looked down at the floor. "If my case was sent to juvenile court and the judge gave me probation, could I live with Julie or here with Mrs. Fairmont instead of going to a foster family?"

I closed my book.

"I don't know. We want to provide a place for you to stay while your case is waiting to be decided. You've only been here a few hours. It's too soon to make plans—"

"Maybe for you," Jessie interrupted. "But I have to think about stuff like that. If I don't, then something bad usually happens."

"Give it time."

I could tell Jessie wanted to say something else, but she got up and left the room. I followed her downstairs. Gracie had made up a single bed that was covered with a pretty bedspread.

WHEN I WOKE UP EARLY THE NEXT MORNING, I GLANCED IN THE living area and saw Jessie, already dressed, carefully making her bed.

"Not sleeping in today?" I asked.

"No, at the jail I helped fix breakfast and had to get up early."

"I'm going out for a run. When I come back, we'll fix breakfast together."

"Can I go with you?"

Startled, I said, "I run fast and go far."

"I could ride Mrs. Fairmont's bike."

"Mrs. Fairmont doesn't have a bike."

"There's one at the other end of the basement. I saw it yesterday when I was exploring the house on my own. It's under a plastic sheet."

I'd never seen a bicycle in the house or heard Mrs. Fairmont mention one, but I hadn't explored the storage side of the large basement.

"Show me."

Jessie turned on the lights and led me to a corner where a fairly new bicycle was covered by a clear sheet of plastic. I pulled away the plastic. Both the tires needed air.

"You can't ride it until the tires are inflated."

"The pump is over here." Jessie went around the corner and returned with a pump.

"You shouldn't be snooping around Mrs. Fairmont's things."

"I wasn't snooping. I just looked around for a few minutes while Mrs. Fairmont was taking a nap in her chair in the den. I wanted to make sure no one could get in from the outside." Jessie pointed to the narrow windows close to the ceiling. "Are those locked?"

"I've never checked."

"I can't get up there. Would you make sure?"

I stood on my toes. The window was latched and probably painted shut.

"It looks okay."

"The worst part about sleeping at the empty lot was worrying someone might bother me."

"Did that happen?" I asked, dreading the answer.

"One night I heard a drunk in the bushes not far from me, but I lay real still and he didn't find me. But when my stepmother and I were having to sleep under bridges—" Jessie stopped.

"Pump up the tires while I put on my running clothes," I said. "I'd like you to come with me."

It was a beautiful, cool morning; the perfect time to be outdoors in a Savannah summer, but few people took advantage of it. I ran on the sidewalk, and Jessie pedaled alongside on the road. In the areas where the cobblestones remained, the bike delivered a jarring ride. Jessie didn't seem to mind. She smiled almost the whole time and peppered me with so many questions that it was a struggle to run, breathe, and serve as a tour guide.

Jessie was wearing shorts, and I could see numerous scars on her slender but muscular legs.

"Did you play any sports in school?" I asked.

"No. I wanted to run on the track team, but I didn't have a way to get home from practice. I used to run everywhere I went."

"You look like you're in good shape," I said. "Maybe we can start running together some."

"I can't go as fast as you. You have long legs."

"But a lot of the best runners are your size."

When we returned home, Jessie parked the bike behind the house in the courtyard.

"Do you think I can ride it during the day?" she asked. "I never had a bike as nice as this one."

"Ask Mrs. Fairmont."

Before taking a shower, I went around with Jessie to every window in the basement. I was tall enough to check the latches. All of them were locked. While Jessie cleaned up, I checked her shoe size. If we were going to run together, she would need a good pair of running shoes.

I prepared breakfast. I usually settled for fruit and yogurt, but I suspected Jessie might want something more. I brewed coffee for Mrs. Fairmont even though she rarely made an appearance downstairs before I left for work. The bacon was almost finished when Mrs. Fairmont came in wearing her robe. Flip ran past her down the hall to the doggie door.

"Are you feeling okay?" I asked.

"Yes, but I think Flip smelled the bacon and got restless. He wasn't going to let me sleep."

She sat at the small table in the corner of the kitchen. I poured her a cup of coffee.

"How did Jessie do last night?" she asked.

I told her about reading together in the den, then about Jessie's concern this morning regarding the security of the house.

"You know how aggravating it is, but maybe we should start using the burglary alarm to make her feel safe," Mrs. Fairmont said.

"That's up to you. Mrs. Bartlett doesn't like receiving calls from the agency when the silent alarm goes off and you're not aware of it."

"If I take it off silent, then Flip almost has a heart attack when that computer voice echoes through the house. It makes me jump out of my skin, too."

The tiny speakers for the system generated a surprising volume of sound. I put the bacon on a paper towel to drain and put the scrambled eggs in a glass bowl. The biscuits would be ready in less than a minute.

"Oh, I let Jessie use the bike that was in the basement this morning. She rode alongside me while I ran."

"That belongs to Christine. She bought it claiming she would enjoy riding through the district for exercise, but it's only been on the street a few times. It was always too hot, too cold, too humid, too early, too late, or too many mosquitoes for a ride."

I laughed as Jessie came into the kitchen. She greeted Mrs. Fairmont with a quick kiss on the cheek.

"Mrs. Fairmont doesn't plan on riding the bicycle," I said. "You can use it."

"I don't expect you to stay cooped up with me all the time," Mrs. Fairmont added.

"I can ride to the store if you need something during the day," Jessie offered.

WE ATE BREAKFAST ON THE VERANDA THAT OVERLOOKED THE courtyard garden. Jessie ate three times as much as I did. Mrs. Fairmont nibbled a few bites of eggs. Only one uneaten biscuit remained. When I left for work, Mrs. Fairmont and Jessie were in the den looking at old photographs.

As soon as I reached the office, I phoned Sister Dabney and told her what had happened.

"I'll be praying for Julie's father. How is Jessie getting along with Mrs. Fairmont?"

"Couldn't be better."

"Good. I knew that would happen. Will I see you and Jessie on Sunday?"

"Yes, ma'am."

In my e-mail in-box was an update from Julie. Her father's recovery was progressing well, but it would be several days before Julie returned to Savannah. I sent her a long reply reassuring her about Jessie.

Mid-morning, I went to the courthouse to find out the charges against Clay Hackney. When I entered the area of the clerk's office where the criminal records were kept, I ran into Maggie, who had a stack of files in her arms. We stepped into a private corner beneath a bulletin board. She already knew about the status of Julie's father, but I gave her a quick update about Jessie.

"What brings you here?" Maggie asked when I finished.

"Something that happened with Jessie the other day in court."

Lowering my voice, I told her about Jessie's reaction to Hackney's presence in the courtroom.

"That explains why she doesn't want to go to juvenile court," Maggie said.

"Why?"

"Judge Gott would probably give her probation and send her home, which is the last place she wants to be if this guy is a threat to her."

"And she's smart enough to have figured that out." I nodded.

"You're sure Hackney didn't see her in the courtroom?"

"I don't think so. I had my eyes glued to him from the moment she let me know there was a connection, and she hid behind me until he left the courtroom."

"I'll get his file," Maggie said.

In a few moments she returned with a thick folder already open in her arms.

"It's a money case," Maggie said. "The State alleges Hackney operated a scam in which he obtained money by false pretenses."

"That would explain why there are tape recordings of conversations," I said.

Maggie kept reading. "There aren't any real details, just enough to get the grand jury to issue an indictment. Most of the indictment are quotes from the statute. Why is Mr. Carpenter involved in this? It's not his area."

"Zach told me the firm represents Hackney in his business interests."

Maggie nodded. "In most white-collar-crime cases there is a lot of bluster between the lawyers for a few months, then the defendant takes a lenient plea bargain if he's guilty or the State dismisses the charges if it can't tie up the evidence in a neat bow. Neither side wants to waste a lot of time going to trial and risk an acquittal by a jury or a harsh sentence from the judge."

"That makes sense, but how would Jessie know about someone like Hackney? She comes from poverty. This guy seems rich. At one point she and her stepmother were living on the streets."

"You won't know the answer to that question unless Jessie tells you."

"If she has incriminating information about Hackney, she could be a witness for the State—"

"And use it to get the charges against her dismissed," Maggie said, completing my thought.

"Right."

"Maybe. That happens in TV shows, but in real life, people like Jessie are often too afraid to come out in the open. There's no such thing as ironclad witness protection."

I remembered the panic in Jessie's voice in the courtroom.

"What should I do?"

"Represent your client by trying to get her case taken care of as quickly as possible so she can disappear from the system." Maggie motioned toward the files she'd pulled. "Jan Crittenden likes Jessie a lot more than the people I'm representing. If Jessie won't cave on the age issue, see what Crittenden will give you in superior court and take it to Judge Cannon."

The thought of taking anything to Judge Cannon made me feel slightly queasy.

Maggie seemed to read my reaction.

"Let Crittenden be the moving party with the judge," she continued. "If the judge cuts off her head, you can run out of his chambers
before he takes a swing at you."

"It's not too soon to talk to Crittenden?"

"Do you have a defense to the charges?"

"No, Jessie doesn't deny breaking into the store and stealing the
donuts. She confessed at the scene after the arresting officer read a
Miranda warning. Jessie claims the donuts were stale, left on the shelf
after the expiration date."

Maggie grinned. "I don't think that would be an effective argument in mitigation to trot out in front of Judge Cannon."

I spoke more softly again. "And she's guilty of multiple other
thefts and break-ins, all petty things related to hunger, but still felonies under the law."

"All the more reason to move fast. Argue first offense, minor damage, no harm to any person. I don't think the judge will want to throw
this girl into the prison system and expose her to real criminals. Find
out what Crittenden is willing to do, then tell Jessie. The final decision will be hers."

I left Maggie and went upstairs to the district attorney's office. Jan
Crittenden was in the reception area talking to a middle-aged male
lawyer I didn't know but who had been in court when I argued the
motion to reduce Jessie's bond.

"Here to see me?" Jan asked when she saw me.

"Yes, but I can come back—"

"No, we're almost done." Jan turned to the other lawyer. "I'll offer
your client five years to serve followed by five on probation. You know
if he's convicted he'll probably get ten to fifteen to serve."

"It may be harder to get a conviction than you think," the lawyer
answered smoothly. "I would recommend that my client accept two
to serve and three on probation."

"That's not my call. I'll have to talk to the DA."

"If that doesn't work, put it on the trial calendar."

The lawyer left. Jan led me to the conference room where we'd talked before.

"That guy makes my skin crawl," she said when we entered the room.

"Who is he?"

"Nick Walker. The problem is he might be able to get his guy off at trial. We lost to him a couple of weeks ago in a case I thought we would win. He has a way of taking the smallest, most irrelevant piece of evidence and turning it into a mighty oak." Jan paused. "You won't tell him I said that, will you?"

"No, I'm here to talk about Jessie Whitewater."

"Uh-oh. Did she run?"

"Not unless it happened after I left this morning. She was staying with Julie Feldman of our firm until a couple of days ago. Since then, she's been with Mrs. Fairmont and me."

"Mrs. Fairmont is a great lady. Who wouldn't want to live with her in that house?"

"I've spent more time with her, but she still hasn't given me any information proving she's a minor."

"Give it more time. Once she trusts you, she's more likely to open up."

I took a deep breath. "Would you let her plea as an adult and recommend something favorable to the judge?"

"There's no rush. Her case is way down the docket."

"If we didn't wait, what would you be asking for?"

Jan eyed me like a witness she was about to cross-examine.

"Is there something she's trying to hide? If there are charges pending against her in another jurisdiction, it would change everything."

"We all have plenty to hide, but I don't know of any charges pending in another jurisdiction."

My answer was technically correct, but skirting so close to false-hood made me very uneasy.

"Then why enter a plea?"

I took a deep breath. "I believe it's in Jessie's best interest to get this incident behind her as soon as possible."

Jan relaxed. "I haven't been working here very long, but it's easy to forget that having a criminal charge pending is a huge stress to anyone. This isn't a serious case, but to assume your client feels the same way is a mistake."

"Could she enter a first offender petition—"

Jan interrupted me with a shake of her head. "That would require a felony plea. What if the charge was reduced to misdemeanor criminal damage to property? The maximum sentence is twelve months, but since your client doesn't have a prior conviction, I'm sure the judge would go along with probation, a small fine, and restitution to the owner of the store for the damage to his property. If Whitewater has learned her lesson, I don't want to make this incident harder on her than it has to be."

I was speechless.

"Talk it over with her and let me know," Jan continued. "If she agrees, we can schedule it as soon as you want to."

"Sounds great. I'm sure she'll go along with it once I explain it to her. Do you think we should get the judge's approval in advance?"

"No. It would be better to slip it onto a busy calendar when he's less inclined to give us a hard time. Sitting in Judge Cannon's chambers without something else pressuring him to move on is an invitation for him to engage in his favorite pastime of tormenting young lawyers."

"Okay."

Jan stood and walked me out of the office.

"It's neat that you've taken a personal interest in your client," she said. "I never would have guessed Julie Feldman might open her home to someone like Jessie."

"There's a lot of good in Julie."

I told Jan about Julie's father.

"I hadn't heard about that. I hope he recovers," she replied. "If she needs a continuance on something, let me know."

"Thanks." I paused. "One more thing. Do you know if there is anything coming up soon in the *State v. Hackney* case?"

"That's being handled by Brett Duffy. Why?"

"Uh, I was in court when they argued the motion about Mr. Carpenter's expert testing some tape recordings and wondered if there were any other motions pending."

"Nothing that I know about. If you want to find out more, call Brett or one of your friends at Braddock, Appleby, and Carpenter."

"Okay, thanks again for the offer on Jessie's case. I'm sure we'll be able to work it out."

I returned to the office elated. Maggie was there, and I excitedly told her about the plea bargain.

"Take it as soon as you can before something happens to mess it up. And don't get used to someone in the DA's office wanting to reduce the charges beyond what you ask. Crittenden is being nice to make a good impression on Mrs. Fairmont."

"I don't think so. She's been this way since the first time we talked. At that point, Mrs. Fairmont wasn't in the picture. I believe God is giving me supernatural favor."

Maggie shrugged. "If that's the way God works, pray for my cases. Some of my clients need just as much mercy as your runaway girl."

I DROVE HOME WITH A LIGHTNESS IN MY HEART I HADN'T FELT since before Zach and I talked. Sacrificing my own desires and focusing on someone else had yielded rapid benefits I hadn't expected. I thought helping Jessie would be like digging in rock-hard soil with a dull hoe. So far, it was more like slicing through butter that had been sitting on the kitchen counter for half an hour.

I found Mrs. Fairmont sitting on the veranda with the ceiling fans stirring the air. Jessie was in the garden below playing a vigorous version of the chase, catch, and fetch game I occasionally played with the little dog. I could hear Flip barking from behind a row of large bushes in the corner of the courtyard that was one of his favorite hiding places. Jessie was on her hands and knees crawling in after him.

"Flip feels like he's at summer camp," Mrs. Fairmont said when she saw me. "He'll be so tired tonight that he'll collapse in bed."

I sat down and listened to Mrs. Fairmont tell me about the day. As I listened, I realized Flip wasn't the only one stimulated by Jessie's presence in the house. Mrs. Fairmont seemed to take as much pleasure in interacting with Jessie as the girl took in playing with Flip.

Jessie, hot and sweaty, bounded up the metal stairs from the courtyard to the veranda. She had a big smile on her face.

"Hey," I said when she plopped down in a chair. "Keep that smile on your face. I have some good news for you."

"What is it about?" Jessie asked, then turned to Mrs. Fairmont before I could answer. "I'm thirsty. Can I get you a glass of ice water?"

"Yes, that would be nice. Bring a bowl of water for Flip, too."

"Good news?" Mrs. Fairmont asked when Jessie went inside.

"About her case." I paused. "Maybe I should talk to her about it in private."

"Of course. I'll step inside. The late-afternoon sun is about to bake the veranda."

Jessie returned and put a bowl of water on the floor. The little dog began to lap vigorously.

"Why did Mrs. Fairmont go inside?"

"I need to talk to you about your case. Jan Crittenden, the assistant district attorney, has made an amazing plea offer."

Jessie listened without interrupting me while I outlined the deal and all its advantages.

"Everything can be wrapped up within a week or so," I said. "Then you'll be assigned a probation officer."

"How much will I have to pay?"

"A broken window can't cost that much. The amount of the fine is up to the judge. The maximum under the statute is one thousand dollars, but that's rarely given. Usually, it's a lot less."

"I don't have any money."

"You won't pay it all at once, and you can start making payments after you get a job. The probation officer will work with you on a schedule to take care of the fine and restitution. I'll talk with Maggie Smith at my office and get the name of a good probation officer who can be assigned to your case. Ms. Crittenden is really making this easy on you."

Jessie looked down and rubbed her hands together.

"What about staying here or with Julie? Julie is nice, but I know she doesn't want me to live with her very long. But here with Mrs. Fairmont is different." Jessie motioned with her hands to encompass the house and began speaking more rapidly. "I can take better care of her than you because I'm here all day. If she falls down or faints or something bad happens, I can call 911. I met Gracie today, and she thinks it's a good idea for me to stay here. I helped her clean the high windows in the blue parlor. Gracie doesn't like to get on a ladder, but I'm not afraid of heights."

"All that can be discussed. But first, let's take care of your case."

Jessie hesitated. "What happens if I don't agree to do what the district attorney told you?"

My mouth dropped open. "That wouldn't make any sense."

"Tell me what will happen if I don't agree," Jessie persisted.

"Uh, nothing for a while. Your case isn't scheduled to come up for trial anytime soon. But why not take care of it so you don't have it hanging over you? And with this deal you won't have a felony conviction that will ruin your future. That's huge."

"What if the police find out about the other places I broke into and the stuff I stole? Could I be charged with that and go back to jail?"

"Yes," I admitted.

"Would that mean more of the felony convictions you're so worried about?"

"Maybe."

Jessie shrugged. "Not having a criminal record doesn't matter if I'm sleeping in a vacant lot. You're like all the other people who pretended they wanted to help me. They did it for a while until they got tired of all the other problems I have. You just want to get me out of your hair."

I took a deep breath to avoid getting angry. "Let's talk about the only problem that exists right now, the charge of breaking into Bacon's Bargains. If Mrs. Fairmont agrees to let you stay here for a few more weeks, would you accept the plea offer to take care of that case? The rest of it we'd have to face if it comes up."

Jessie thought for a moment. "I'm willing to pay for the broken window. But I don't like the idea of a fine. And who would take me to see the probation officer?"

"You could ride the bus or perhaps Sister Dabney could take you."

"A thousand dollars is a lot of money."

"It probably won't be—" I stopped. "Okay, the big question is where you're going to live, isn't it? I'll talk to Mrs. Fairmont and see what she thinks about you staying here. Then you can decide."

"I want to be there when you talk to her. It's my life."

"No!" I said so forcibly that it made Jessie's eyes open wide in surprise. "Mrs. Fairmont has to make her decision without being manipulated by you."

"When are you going to talk to her?"

"After supper. You can go for a walk or a bike ride."

WE HAD A TENSE MEAL. JESSIE DIDN'T OPEN HER MOUTH EXCEPT to grunt. When she went to the kitchen for a few seconds, Mrs. Fairmont gave me a questioning look.

"What's wrong? I thought you had good news."

"I do, but Jessie doesn't see it that way yet. We'll talk later after she's out of the house for a while."

When Jessie returned from the kitchen, Mrs. Fairmont started asking her questions about her time with Gracie. The tension began to leave the room. Jessie even smiled when telling how nervous Gracie got when Jessie insisted on standing on top of the short ladder without anything to steady her.

"The next time she comes we're going to wash the outside windows," Jessie said. "She said you had a really tall ladder in the garage."

"It's tall enough," Mrs. Fairmont answered. "But I'm not sure I want you washing the windows on the second story. There's a man I hire to do that once a year."

"Don't hire him and pay me half what he charges you."

Mrs. Fairmont glanced at me and I shook my head slightly.

"Right now, I don't want us to have a business relationship. I'd rather consider you like a great-niece who's come for a summer visit and helps around the house a little bit because it's the polite thing to do."

"Tami says I need to make money."

"We'll talk about that later," I said. "Don't worry about clearing the table. I'll do it so Mrs. Fairmont and I can talk. You can take Flip out for a walk."

"He's exhausted," Mrs. Fairmont said, pointing to the little dog who was lying stretched out on his side beneath her chair. "He didn't have the energy to beg during the meal, he's played so hard."

"Okay. Go for a ride on the bike. If you take a right on Whittaker Street, it will lead you to Forsyth Park."

"There's a water fountain on the east side where I used to get a drink when I was a little girl," Mrs. Fairmont said. "You'll recognize it because there's a spigot low to the ground for people to get water for their animals."

"I want all of us to talk when I get back," Jessie said.

"We'll see," I replied, feeling like a parent dealing with a stubborn child.

Jessie left the house via the veranda steps to the courtyard and through the side gate. I watched from a window in the foyer as she pedaled toward the nearby intersection of Hull and Whittaker Streets. When I returned to the kitchen, Mrs. Fairmont was rinsing the plates in the sink and loading them in the dishwasher.

"Wait, I was going to clean up."

"I decided if I had the energy there was no reason for me to treat you like a servant."

"You've never treated me like a servant."

"In my mind I have. Jessie's got me thinking about a lot of things."

Mrs. Fairmont and I sat at the table in the kitchen while I told her about the plea offer. I didn't have Jessie's permission to share details about her case with Mrs. Fairmont, but I pushed my reservations aside and laid it all out except the possibility of additional criminal charges in the future. The more I talked, the more troubled Mrs. Fairmont looked.

"As you can see, the big issue is that Jessie wants to stay here with you," I said. "She's right that Julie's apartment isn't a long-term solution. But I don't want you to commit to something after only spending a couple of days with her. Jessie has a stubborn streak that's going to come out at some point in her relationship with you."

Mrs. Fairmont put her hand on her stomach and closed her eyes.

"Christine, I don't feel well."

"I'm Tami," I replied, then reached out as the elderly woman put her hands on the arms of the chair and tried to push herself up.

"Help me get to the bathroom," she said.

I steadied Mrs. Fairmont as she shuffled to the downstairs bathroom where she got sick. As the waves of nausea hit her, waves of compassion hit me. I hated sickness, especially when it afflicted someone I loved. I held Mrs. Fairmont's hand and kept her steady as she emptied her stomach. I wiped her forehead with a cool washcloth.

"Is your head hurting?"

"Yes." She nodded. "And my arm."

She touched her left arm. Mrs. Fairmont's mental problems were related to ministrokes, but with the mention of pain down her arm, I suddenly became concerned she might be having a heart attack.

"I should call an ambulance."

"No, I don't want to go to the hospital. I want to lie down in the den."

"Does your chest hurt?"

"It's my stomach."

I held her up as the nausea returned.

"That's it," she said when she finished. "There's nothing left. I want to rest now."

I gently wiped her face and led her to the den where I spread out an afghan and positioned a pillow under her head. Flip jumped up and curled up at her feet.

"Please, let me call an ambulance," I said.

"No." She shook her head, keeping her eyes closed. "I want to lie here quietly in my own house."

I left Mrs. Fairmont, went into the kitchen, and called Mrs. Bartlett.

18

JESSIE PEDALED FURIOUSLY DOWN WHITTAKER STREET, NOT SLOW-
ing at four stop signs until a sanitation truck crossing West Jones
Street made her put on the brakes and skid to a halt. She wiped away
the beads of sweat that had popped up on her brow. She wanted to
get to Forsyth Park as soon as possible, drink from the water fountain
so she could tell Mrs. Fairmont she'd tried it, and return to the house
so she could plead her case in person. Jessie wasn't about to trust her
future to Tami's conversation with Mrs. Fairmont.

The past two days had been like happy pages cut from the best
book Jessie ever read. Twice during the afternoon, she went downstairs,
touched the beautiful bedspread, and smelled the clean sheets. When
Mrs. Fairmont napped in the den, Jessie explored the house, admiring
the beautiful things that surrounded her. There were no antiques in her
stepmother's trailer, only broken secondhand items barely able to serve
their intended purpose.

Jessie had been nervous when Gracie arrived, but the older black
woman greeted her with a big, soft hug. She then included Jessie in
a workday that was more fun than labor. Gracie didn't tell Jessie that
she thought it was a good idea for Jessie to live at the house, but she
was sure Gracie would have said so if asked.

Jessie crossed Gordon Street and saw the corner of Forsyth Park.

The green space was a lot bigger than she'd suspected, and it took her about ten minutes to find the water fountain. She got off the bike to get a drink then splashed water on her face to cool off. After she wiped the water from her eyes, she turned around and bumped into a man standing behind her.

"Did you know your bike has a flat tire?" the man asked.

"No, it doesn't."

Jessie looked past him at the bike, which had a totally flat rear tire. She went over and felt the collapsed rubber.

"Do you have far to go?" the man asked.

Jessie looked at the man for the first time. He was probably in his fifties with gray hair and a closely cut goatee. He was wearing blue jeans, a T-shirt, and dark sunglasses.

"Not too far," she replied. "I live on Hull Street."

"That's at least ten blocks, a long way to push a bike," the man replied. "My wife and I live on East Perry, just around the corner from Hull. I'd be happy to give you a lift. You could throw your bike in the back of my pickup, and I could drop you off."

Jessie looked down and saw the wedding band on the man's hand.

"That's my truck parked on the street." The man motioned with his left hand. There was a shiny blue pickup truck with heavily tinted windows next to the curb. A woman was behind the wheel. When she saw Jessie looking in her direction, she waved.

"That's my lady," the man said. "We come to the park to walk our dog every evening after we get off work."

"What kind of dog do you have?" Jessie asked.

"A Chihuahua."

"My grandmother has a Chihuahua," Jessie said, brightening up. "His name is Flip."

"We call our dog Peaches. Come over and meet her. But I've got to warn you. She'll try to lick your nose off if she gets a chance."

The man started walking toward the truck. Jessie followed, pushing the bike. The man was right. Pushing the bike to Mrs. Fairmont's house would take a long, long time.

"See what I found?" the man said to his wife. "A young woman with a flat tire in need of a ride to Hull Street."

Jessie reached the truck. The truck bed was empty, and she leaned forward to see the dog inside the cab.

"Where's your dog?" she said.

"On the passenger floorboard. She's just a little thing," the man said.

The man pushed Jessie's head inside the truck, and the woman covered her nose with a foul-smelling cloth.

Everything went black.

MRS. BARTLETT TOLD ME SHE AND HER HUSBAND WERE FINISHING supper at a restaurant not more than five minutes away.

"Is she conscious and able to talk?" Mrs. Bartlett asked after listening to a quick summary.

"Enough to tell me she didn't want to go to the hospital."

"Ken and I will be there as soon as we can. But if she's in a crisis, don't wait for us to call an ambulance."

I returned to the den with a clean, cool washcloth.

"Would you like this on your head?"

"Yes."

I placed the cloth on Mrs. Fairmont's forehead. She'd gotten hot from the exertion caused by the nausea. I gently wiped her face.

"That feels good. Did you call Christine?"

"Yes, ma'am. She and Mr. Bartlett were eating at a restaurant in town and are on their way."

"Tell her I don't want to go to the hospital."

"I did."

Mrs. Fairmont shut her eyes for a moment. "I feel a heavy weight on my chest."

I sat on the edge of the couch and took her hand in mine.

"That worries me. Along with the pain in your left arm and the nausea, it sounds like you could be having a heart attack."

Mrs. Fairmont opened her eyes and shook her head. "No. Just let me rest for a few minutes before Christine gets here. If I end up in the hospital, she's going to pressure me to buy a unit at Surfside. I need you to speak up for me."

I took the cloth with me and returned to the kitchen. The fact that Mrs. Fairmont could think lucidly was good; the possibility that I might end up in the middle of an argument between her and her daughter was bad. Mrs. Fairmont had spent almost a month in the rehabilitation wing of the nursing home after suffering a stroke the previous summer. It was a new, clean facility, but like so many elderly people, Mrs. Fairmont prized the familiar comfort of home more than the security of twenty-four-hour medical care. I rehearsed what I would say if the two women got in a discussion and tried to drag me into it. I decided the best course might be to appeal to Mr. Bartlett, a levelheaded man who had found a way to endure the verbal barrage that flowed unhindered from his wife's mouth. The front door opened, and Flip raced out of the den toward the foyer. I ran after him, hoping to intercept him before he could launch an attack on Mrs. Bartlett's ankles. I grabbed him as he bared his teeth.

"She's in the den," I said, slightly breathless.

I hung back as Mr. and Mrs. Bartlett went down the hall. I stayed in the foyer and soothed Flip until I felt it was safe to deposit him on the floor in the den doorway. He ignored Mrs. Bartlett and hopped up to his place on the couch at Mrs. Fairmont's feet.

"Mother, this isn't the time for you to play doctor and diagnose what's wrong with you. With the symptoms Tami described, you should go to the ER."

"I feel better already." Mrs. Fairmont looked at me. "Will you get me a glass of water? No ice, please."

I returned with the water. When Mrs. Fairmont reached for the glass her right hand shook. I guided the glass to her lips.

"Look at your hand," Mrs. Bartlett said. "At least let me call Dr. Dixon and see what he thinks you should do."

"He's at home with his family."

"And has an answering service that will notify him."

"If Dr. Dixon isn't on call, I don't want to talk to Dr. Faraday. He has the worst bedside manner. You said yourself that he had less personality than—"

"We won't know who's on call until we try," Mrs. Bartlett interrupted, taking her cell phone from her purse.

"I want to hear what you tell the doctor, whoever it is," Mrs. Fairmont said.

Mrs. Bartlett left a message with the answering service. In less than a minute, the phone rang. It was the doctor.

"Dr. Dixon, thanks for calling," she said. "Tami Taylor, mother's caregiver, was with her and can tell you exactly what happened."

I didn't want to be the bearer of news that might send Mrs. Fairmont for an unwanted hospital stay, but I had no choice. I took the phone and gave the doctor a detailed description of what had happened.

"Anything else?" he asked.

"Mrs. Fairmont wants to talk to you, too."

"Hello," Mrs. Fairmont said in a slightly shaky voice, then listened. "Yes, what Tami said was correct. Here's Christine."

Mrs. Fairmont looked at her daughter with sad eyes and handed her the phone. Mrs. Bartlett was silent for a longer period of time.

"I agree," she said, then clicked off the phone. She turned to her husband.

"He wants us to take Mother to the ER. He'll meet us there. She won't have to wait; he'll see that she's taken immediately to a room where he can run some tests." She turned to me. "Tami, pack a few things she might need for the next few hours and put them in the small green carry-on bag."

"Is there anything special you want?" I asked Mrs. Fairmont.

The elderly woman had her lips pressed tightly together. She shook her head.

"Ken, pull the car around to the garage," Mrs. Bartlett said.

I bounded upstairs, not exactly sure what might be appropriate for an emergency room visit. I took the suitcase from the closet and quickly filled it with Mrs. Fairmont's favorite nightgown, slippers, toiletries, a photo of Flip, and other items that were part of her daily routine. Downstairs, Mrs. Bartlett was holding her mother's arm as they stood in the foyer.

"Put the suitcase in the car," Mrs. Bartlett said to me.

I put the suitcase in the trunk and said a quick prayer for the woman whose personal items it contained, then hurried back to help Mrs. Fairmont down the three steps to the garage.

"I'm feeling better already," the elderly woman said when we reached the car. "Maybe I just needed to get off the couch and stretch my legs."

"That won't work with me," Mrs. Bartlett said. "We're meeting Dr. Dixon at the ER even if you claim you could jog to the hospital."

After we helped Mrs. Fairmont into the front seat, Mrs. Bartlett opened the rear door.

"Will you let me know—," I asked.

"Yes, yes," Mrs. Bartlett cut me off.

I stood at the bottom of the steps as Mr. Bartlett backed the car into the street and turned in the direction of the hospital. A humid dusk had settled over Savannah. The gray sky matched my mood. I stepped from the garage and glanced down Hull Street toward Whittaker Street.

And remembered Jessie.

The young woman could have ridden multiple times around Forsyth Park in the time since she'd left. I quickly looked up and down the street and saw nothing except one of Mrs. Fairmont's neighbors sweeping the brick walkway to her house. I wasn't sure whether to wait for Mrs. Bartlett's phone call or search for Jessie. News from the hospital would be slow coming. I went inside the house and grabbed my purse.

Driving Mrs. Fairmont's car, I followed the logical route from the house to Forsyth Park and slowly circled the green area. There was no sign of Jessie or the bike. I repeated the circuit then parked near the water fountain and got out. It was getting darker and only a few people were walking in the park. I asked a woman if she'd seen a girl matching Jessie's description on a bike. Her blank look made me realize interviewing random people would be pointless. If Jessie had decided to take off on the bike, she could be miles away in any direction. I drove slowly back to Mrs. Fairmont's house.

Going into the den, I plopped down on the couch. Jessie's disappearance didn't make sense. Forty-eight hours earlier I might have expected her to run away. But I had no doubt about the strength of the young woman's desire to stay with Mrs. Fairmont. I felt a pang of guilt that I'd been so harsh in the way I told Jessie there were no guarantees about her future. In my heart, I knew Mrs. Fairmont would probably let Jessie stay as long as she needed to.

All the practical ramifications of Jessie's actions began to sink in. Her bond would be revoked, leaving Sister Dabney on the hook for ten thousand dollars that I knew she didn't have. The generous plea bargain made by Jan Crittenden would go away. And Jessie would enter the criminal system as a fugitive with a felony warrant chasing her wherever she fled.

The first person I had to notify was Sister Dabney. Using my cell phone so the house line would be available for Mrs. Bartlett's call, I dialed the number and waited. On the seventh ring, the woman preacher answered.

"Jessie's gone," I said.

"What happened?"

As I told Sister Dabney the background information, including what happened to Mrs. Fairmont, I fought back tears.

"Do you think Mrs. Fairmont is going to be okay? Has the Lord shown you anything about her future?"

"No. I'm going to pray Mrs. Fairmont will finish her race and not be tripped before crossing the line. You do the same."

"Yes, ma'am." I cleared my throat. "You know what Jessie's disappearance means. The bond you posted guaranteeing her appearance in court will come due."

"That's not my problem."

I knew what Sister Dabney meant without asking.

"Okay." I paused. "Are you surprised that she ran away?"

"And may come back. Jessie is a prodigal, but she ran away from a bad home, not a good one. With Mrs. Fairmont, she's had a tiny taste of a better way to live. That's going to draw her back stronger than you realize."

"The legal system won't wait for her to figure that out."

"I've got some rocking to do."

After the call ended, I remained on the couch. Flip was asleep beside Mrs. Fairmont's empty chair. The house was eerily quiet. I closed my eyes and visualized the front door opening and Jessie bounding in with a tall tale of imaginary adventure. But the door remained shut; the silence remained.

A feeling of dread began to creep over me, and I went to the closet that contained the control panel for the alarm system. The instructions for activating the system were on top of the panel. I knew what to do, but I read the directions anyway and lightly touched the buttons without pushing them. I heard a noise that startled me and glanced down the hallway. If I turned on the alarm, I would have to let Mrs. Bartlett and Gracie know before they entered the house. But what reason would I give them? That I was suddenly scared about being alone? I'd always felt safe and secure in the house.

I left the closest and began slowly walking through the house, praying in each room. I went upstairs and spent time kneeling at the foot of Mrs. Fairmont's bed. When I made my way to the basement, the feeling of dread increased. I continued praying, but I also double-checked the locks on the windows I'd inspected twenty-four hours earlier with Jessie. Nothing seemed out of place, but I couldn't shake the nervous unease lodged in the center of my being. Returning upstairs, I was standing in the kitchen when the phone rang, causing me to jump. I picked up the receiver. It was Mrs. Bartlett. As usual, the words poured out of her mouth with no greeting.

"The initial tests didn't show evidence of a heart attack, and Mother wanted to come home, but Dr. Dixon admitted her, and she's waiting for a room. He wants to run another test in the morning and watch her closely for at least a day or so."

"She should have everything she needs in the green suitcase. If not, let me know."

"Good. I reassured her you had everything under control at the house." Mrs. Bartlett's voice was muffled for a moment. "She wants to talk to you."

"Tami?" Mrs. Fairmont's voice sounded stronger than when she left the house.

"Yes, ma'am, are you feeling better?"

"I would be if I could curl up in my own bed, but the conspirators here at the hospital aren't going to let that happen."

"I'm just thankful nothing serious showed up on the tests."

"I've got to stay around to take care of you and Flip."

"Yes, ma'am."

"And finish telling Jessie all my stories. Let me talk to her for a minute. I don't want her to worry about me."

I swallowed. "Mrs. Fairmont, she never came back from the bike ride. I drove around Forsyth Park, but there was no sign of her."

There was no response. I waited.

"Are you there?" I asked.

"Yes, but I don't understand. I thought she was enjoying her stay with us."

"Me, too, but something changed her mind." I winced again at the role I played in that process. "I called Sister Dabney. We're praying that she'll turn up soon."

"I will, too. You don't think something bad may have happened to her, do you?"

My blood ran cold, and I involuntarily shivered. One thing I knew for certain—Jessie's fear of discovery wasn't an act. But only a handful of people knew she was staying with Mrs. Fairmont and me.

"I don't think so," I said.

"Are you going to call the police and report her as a missing person?"

"If I do that it will trigger revocation of her bond and—" I stopped. "It's all complicated, Mrs. Fairmont. Please rest and get better soon."

I could hear Mrs. Fairmont talking to Mrs. Bartlett.

"Jessie's gone?" Mrs. Bartlett said to me when she came back on the line.

"Yes. She went for a bike ride to Forsyth Park and never came back."

I heard Mrs. Bartlett sniff. "You can't count on young people to be dependable. I felt sorry for her, especially after hearing how she lost her aunt to cancer, but the Lord helps those who help themselves. Mother wants to give her a second chance if she comes back, but we'll have to talk that over later. Keep your cell phone on in case I need you to run something up to the hospital. There's no telling how long we'll have to stay here. I'm supposed to go to Sea Island with a friend in the morning for a day trip we've been planning for months, but that's not going to happen."

"Do you want me to come to the hospital so you can leave?"

"Are you being sarcastic?"

"No, ma'am," I said quickly. "I'm just willing to do anything that will help. If I came across wrong, I'm sorry."

"I'm just jumpy. There's not a mean bone in your body. Of course you're incredibly naive, especially for a woman lawyer, but that will change over time." There was a pause. "No, Mother, I'm not lecturing Tami. We've talked about that many times, and you agreed with me. Tami, I've got to go. If I keep talking, Mother really might have a heart attack."

The phone clicked off. My concern about Mrs. Fairmont eased. My fear for Jessie increased. I started pacing through the house. The only outsiders who knew Jessie was staying with Mrs. Fairmont were Jan Crittenden, Sister Dabney, Maggie, Julie, and Zach. Sister Dabney and Maggie were unlikely sources of a leak. Julie was always a risk to blurt something out in a public place. Jan might have mentioned it in any number of places. After all, it wasn't confidential information. Zach probably said something to Vince. The two men seemed to talk about everything that concerned me. I stopped in my tracks. If the news began to circulate around Braddock, Appleby, and Carpenter that a client I represented in a criminal case was living with Julie or me, someone with a connection to Clay Hackney might have found out and told him.

I decided to call Julie even though the possibility she might answer the phone was slim if she was at the hospital. On the fifth ring she picked up.

"It's Tami. How is your father doing?"

"The third doctor who's talked with us today left the room a few minutes ago after giving us the best news yet. Daddy is still very sick, but he doesn't show any signs of permanent neurological damage. It will take awhile, but he should fully recover."

"That's great."

"How are things in Savannah? Have you caught Jessie trying to pawn any of Mrs. Fairmont's silver spoons?"

"Jessie is gone."

Julie listened in silence as I told her what happened.

"That's too bad. Jessie was a runaway before you got her out of jail, and she's picked up where she left off. I was getting to like her. She's a lot smarter than you first think. If given the right opportunity, there's no telling what she could—" Julie stopped. "I guess there's no use talking about that. Where do you think she went?"

"I don't have any idea."

"If she stays around Savannah, she'll probably be caught and thrown back in jail. If she leaves town, you'll never hear from her again."

"Her biggest fear wasn't going to jail."

I told Julie about Jessie's reaction to Clay Hackney.

"That sounds like more fruit of Jessie's overactive imagination. We know she doesn't draw a bright line between where a lie ends and the truth begins. I think all that stuff with this Hackney guy was a way for Jessie to make herself look more important than she is. Don't let her mess with your mind."

Jessie had easily duped Mrs. Bartlett about her aunt, and I had to admit I could be making the same mistake about Jessie and Clay Hackney.

"You may be right."

"If I'm not, then the truth is close by."

"That's not all. Mrs. Fairmont was admitted to the hospital after supper."

I quickly told Julie about Mrs. Fairmont.

"I'm glad she's going to be okay," Julie said. "And that explains why you're so concerned about Jessie. Worrying about Mrs. Fairmont triggered all this other stuff. Take a sleeping pill and go to the office five minutes later in the morning. If Maggie gets mad about it, tell her to call me."

Hanging up the phone, I had to admit that Julie was right about one thing—the evening had left me emotionally spent. The adrenaline boost that spun me up when Mrs. Fairmont became ill had drained out of my system. I yawned, picked up Flip, and took him downstairs. With his mistress gone, I didn't want him to have to sleep alone.

Also, if anything unusual stirred in the house, the little dog was as reliable as a burglary alarm.

I woke up in the morning and looked out the French doors at the courtyard, hoping I might see Mrs. Bartlett's bicycle with Jessie sleeping on the ground beside it. A morning mist shrouded the neatly manicured space. A closer look confirmed it was deserted.

During my morning run, I headed directly to Forsyth Park where I zigzagged back and forth across the area, running much slower than normal as I searched the ground and surrounding area for any clues of Jessie. I didn't see anything connected to Jessie but really didn't know what to look for anyway.

After showering and dressing for work, instead of going directly to the office I drove to the hospital. At the information desk I was relieved to find out that Mrs. Fairmont was in a regular room. I took the elevator to her floor. Racks holding breakfast trays stood in the hall. The door to Mrs. Fairmont's room was closed, so I knocked and peeked inside. Mrs. Fairmont was asleep on her back with her mouth slightly open. Her breakfast was untouched beside her bed. The tepid-looking coffee on the tray made me wish I could bring her a fresh, hot cup fixed exactly the way she liked it. The photo of Flip I'd packed in her suitcase was on the stand beside the bed. I watched her for a few moments, but she showed no signs of waking up. I went to the nurse's station and introduced myself as Mrs. Fairmont's at-home caregiver.

"Dr. Dixon hasn't made his rounds on this floor, so there's nothing I can tell you," replied a young nurse seated in front of a computer screen.

I returned to the room, but Mrs. Fairmont was still resting peacefully, and I didn't disturb her. I stopped by the gift shop and bought some flowers to be delivered later to her room. On my way out of the hospital, I called Mrs. Bartlett, but she didn't answer.

My route to the office took me down Montgomery Street and past Braddock, Appleby, and Carpenter. I slowed and saw both Zach's and Vince's cars in the parking lot. I wasn't surprised to see them at work this early. Long hours were the norm at most established firms. It made me glad that Maggie trusted me to discipline myself. My cell phone rang. I picked it up, expecting Mrs. Bartlett.

"Tami, it's Zach. Did you just drive by our office?"

"Yes, I'm at the light on the corner."

"I thought I saw you when I looked out the window. Do you have time to come in for a few minutes?"

I hesitated.

"I know you don't drink coffee," Zach continued, "but I bet I could find some hot tea."

"Okay."

"I'll be waiting in the lobby."

I parked beside Vince's BMW. It was just after eight o'clock, and I walked in with a couple of secretaries who knew me from the previous summer. They greeted me. Apparently, there hadn't been a firm-wide memo to shun me.

When I entered the lobby, Zach was standing at the bottom of the stairs. He quickly pulled his ponytail and smiled broadly when he saw me. My heart jumped.

"How are you?" he asked. "I've missed talking to you."

My emotions suddenly welled up, and my eyes watered. Zach stepped forward.

"What's wrong?" he asked.

I couldn't believe my feelings had betrayed me without warning.

"A couple of things," I managed. "Mrs. Fairmont is in the hospital—"

"Come up to my office," Zach cut in, then turned without waiting for an answer and began walking up the stairs. I had no choice but to follow.

Zach's office was only slightly larger than mine, but he had a window view of the parking lot and the street where he'd seen me minutes before. Two miniature motorcycles rested on the front of his desk next to photographs of his parents and his sister, a missionary nurse in Zambia. Neat rows of framed diplomas and certificates hung on the walls. The walk upstairs settled me down.

"Get your coffee," I said. "I don't need any tea."

"First, tell me about Mrs. Fairmont."

"It's really not that bad," I began, then told him what had happened the previous evening. "Let Vince know. He might want to visit her."

"He and Mr. Braddock flew to Richmond early this morning, but I think they're coming back tonight. I'll send him a text message later."

"Thanks. I should be going," I said, standing up. Zach remained seated.

"You said a couple of things were bothering you," he said. "What else?"

I wasn't sure I should say anything to Zach about Jessie, so I told him about Julie's father. As he listened, I realized how much I'd missed being able to talk to him.

He took out his phone.

"I have Julie's number. Thanks for letting me know about her dad. I'll get in touch with her later." He looked at me. "Is that all? I mean, it's enough."

"No," I admitted. "There's also a problem with Jessie Whitewater, the young woman Judge Cannon appointed me to represent."

"Sure, wasn't she going to stay with you and Mrs. Fairmont after Sister Dabney posted her bond? I thought it was a great idea, the three of you working together to help her."

"She spent a few days with Julie, then came to stay with Mrs. Fairmont and me. Last night, she went out for a bike ride and didn't come back."

I told him as much as I felt comfortable sharing, carefully avoiding any reference to Clay Hackney.

"Don't be too hard on yourself," he responded when I finished. "You can't force someone to let you help them."

"I know, but I was too hard on her when she brought up the possibility of staying longer with Mrs. Fairmont. Jessie has been through enough tough times that it wasn't necessary to be so negative."

"Maybe, but it's out of your hands now. It's hard to predict how much influence we'll have on another person's life. Sometimes we're a comma; other times we're a chapter."

I looked at Zach and wondered, when it came to my life, in how many chapters he was supposed to appear.

"Thanks," I said. "It helped to talk this out with you."

Zach went with me to the top of the stairs where a secretary stopped and asked him if he could explain something about a document he'd given her to type.

"That's okay," I said. "Take care of your work. I know the way out."

The office was in full swing, and as I descended the stairs I could see that several people were sitting in the lobby. At the bottom of the stairs, one of the receptionists, a middle-aged woman I recognized from the previous summer, called me over.

"We miss having you here," she said, then lowered her voice. "But

I understand why you might want to work for a smaller firm. Are you enjoying it?"

"It's fine."

"Any interesting cases?"

"Everything's a challenge right now because I don't know what to do."

The woman shook her head. "That's not true. Everyone said you were one of the smartest law clerks that's ever worked here."

"Tell Mr. Carpenter I'm here to see him," a male voice said over my shoulder.

"Yes, Mr. Hackney," the receptionist replied as she picked up the phone.

I turned and froze. It was Clay Hackney. Up close, I could tell his blond hair was artificially lightened. Today, it was slightly spiked all over his head. He was wearing an open-collared shirt. There was a thick gold bracelet on his left wrist.

Hackney eyed me. "I've seen you before. Where was it?"

"This is Tami Taylor," the receptionist chirped. "She worked here last summer as a law clerk."

He extended his hand. "Clay Hackney."

I had no choice but to shake it. In addition to the gold bracelet on his left wrist, he had a large man's gold ring on his right hand.

"Joe Carpenter is my lawyer," he continued.

"Tami worked with Mr. Carpenter."

"Good to see you," I said to the receptionist. "Mr. Hackney. I've got to go."

"Drop the Mr. Hackney stuff with me," he said with a short laugh. "There's no need for that. Where are you working now?"

"In an all-female firm," the receptionist added.

"Sounds like I should have hired your firm," Hackney said.

The door to the office suites opened, and Mr. Carpenter came out. I turned to leave.

"Tami!" he called out.

I had no choice but to face him. He strode up to me.

"Good morning. What brings you over here? Not suing one of our clients, I hope."

"No, sir. I was talking with Zach—"

"And meeting me," Hackney cut in.

"Yes," Mr. Carpenter said, clearing his throat and glancing at his client in a way that made me suspect he didn't have the highest opinion of Mr. Hackney. "I saw you in criminal court the other day. Are you starting to move into that area of practice?"

"No, sir. I was there on an appointed case."

"Was your client the young woman sitting with you?" Mr. Carpenter smiled. "I couldn't help but notice her. She looked like she should have been in juvenile court. But then, the older I get, the younger everyone looks."

"I've got to get going."

"Sure." Mr. Carpenter waved his hand. "I bet you're the first person at the office most mornings."

"Where is your office?" Hackney asked.

"Here in Savannah," I replied, then turned and walked away as fast as I could.

I didn't take a full breath until I was outside the building. I leaned against a white column and bowed my head. Julie was right. Not knowing the truth about Jessie's connection, if any, to Clay Hackney was creating enormous stress.

SHANNON WAS ALREADY AT THE OFFICE WHEN I ARRIVED.

"I put a fax on your desk," she said. "It came in late yesterday after you'd left the office."

On the corner of my desk I saw a cover sheet with "Chatham County District Attorney's Office" across the top. I quickly looked at the second page. It was a notice of hearing in Jessie's case set for later in the morning. A third page was a brief note from Jan Crittenden.

> I had to take an order to Judge Cannon in another case and ran the plea bargain by him. He agreed to accept it. Called your office to confirm your availability to enter a plea before he changes his mind. See you in court.

The fax in hand, I returned to Shannon's desk.

"Did you talk to Jan Crittenden from the DA's office about my schedule this morning?"

"No."

"Then who did she talk to?" I asked, my voice getting louder.

"I don't know."

"Who has access to my calendar?"

"Uh, anyone can check a calendar unless the computer's been turned off and requires a password to reboot."

"I usually don't turn off my computer," I said. "But I guess I'll have to start."

I left Shannon with a puzzled look on her face and returned to my office. I phoned the district attorney's office, but Jan wasn't available. I left a message with a request that it be marked urgent and hung up the phone. I was fuming in frustration when Maggie appeared in the door-way with a small white paper sack in her hand. "I brought you something sweet," she said, placing the bag on my desk. "Julie called me. After all that happened last night, I felt you needed a pastry to give you a pleasant start to the day. I know mountain girls love apples. This one has a flaky crust that melts in your mouth."

"Thanks, but you're too late," I muttered.

I pushed the notice of hearing toward her. Maggie picked it up and quickly read it.

"This isn't good," she said.

"What am I going to do?"

"What do you want to do?"

"Ask Jan Crittenden to put it off without telling her why so I can try to find Jessie. But I'm not sure I can do that without lying about the reason."

"Just tell her you didn't get the notice until you were already at the office."

"She knows it only takes a few minutes to swing by Mrs. Fairmont's house to pick up Jessie and bring her to the courthouse."

Maggie sat down across from my desk. "Show up for the hearing, tell the judge the truth, let him revoke your client's bond, and ask him to release you from further representation. Then, come back here and enjoy your pastry. You've already done ten times more for your client than any lawyer in this circuit would have. It didn't work out because she wouldn't cooperate."

"I don't want to give up."

"It's an unfortunate part of any criminal law practice. You can't control another person's behavior. Too often criminal clients do something that ruins the lawyer's ability to help them. When that happens you do the best you can, but the results can be harsh."

I knew Maggie was right, but I couldn't shake my lingering concern for Jessie's safety. But what could I do about that? I'd hit a wall of the unknown. The joint rescue effort mounted by Sister Dabney, Julie, Mrs. Fairmont, and me had failed. This would be a situation in which I had to trust God without a glimpse of what the result would be. It was time to move on.

"Okay," I said to Maggie. "That's what I'll do."

"Do you want me to go with you?"

"No thanks."

My file in Jessie's case was pathetically thin. There just hadn't been much to work with. I tossed it on the front seat of Mrs. Fairmont's car and drove to the courthouse. The upstairs courtroom was already bustling with activity. Jan Crittenden was huddled in a corner with another lawyer. I headed in her direction to wait my turn. At least one case on the morning calendar would not be moved to dead file storage.

19

Jessie moaned and turned over. Her head ached, and the ground beneath her was moving up and down. She was lying on a foul-smelling mattress in a dark enclosed space. The ground moved again. She heard a slap against the wall near her head and scooted off the mattress onto a cold, metal floor. The slap was followed by a side-to-side movement that let her know she wasn't in the middle of an earthquake. She was on a boat.

Directly overhead, Jessie could see a few slivers of light through cracks around a square hatch. There wasn't enough light to see anything in the room, and crouching, she used her hands to explore. The space extended about ten feet forward along walls that sloped toward each other. It was about twice that far in width. She stood and stretched her hands toward the hatch. She jumped, but her hand didn't touch the ceiling. When her feet came down they hit the floor with a thud. Within a few seconds there were sounds overhead. Jessie's heart sank. She should have kept quiet. There was a loud creaking noise in the area of the hatch, which opened, letting in a blinding shaft of sunlight. Jessie shielded her eyes.

"It stinks down there," a male voice said.

When the rush of fresh air through the hole reached her, Jessie took in a deep breath, then coughed violently.

"Your buddy had better be glad she woke up," a second male voice said. "He gave her enough of that stuff to knock out two grown men."

"You can't take chances when you grab someone in a public place. I think he was crazy to take the job. We got the easy part."

Jessie blinked as her eyes started to get used to the light. Two men were peering down at her. Both were shirtless, tanned, and wearing baseball caps and sunglasses.

"Get her a bottle of water," one of the men said. "I'll stay here and watch."

Jessie's lips were dry. She tried to lick them but didn't have any saliva.

"No way," the other man said. "Shut the hatch. She doesn't get anything to drink until the man in charge says so."

"Please," she croaked.

"That's stupid. You just said we're lucky she's alive, and now you want her to die of thirst."

"She's not going to die, but a little thirst might help her attitude later. No water and no sleep are good ways to get someone to talk."

Jessie stumbled forward a step then fell to her knees.

"Get the water," the first man repeated.

"Only if it's on your head. Our orders were to keep her in the hold. We're not even supposed to be checking on her."

"Wait a minute. Whose idea was it to open the hatch to make sure she was okay?"

"We've done that. Shut it."

"And I want to give her a drink. How old do you think she is? Fifteen?"

"Old enough to cause a lot of trouble. Shut up and get the water. Then we're not opening the hatch again."

One of the men closed the hatch. Jessie sank to the floor. She wanted to cry, but there was barely enough moisture in her body to squeeze out a single tear. After the whiff of fresh air, the stale air in the hold smelled even worse. She rested her head on her knees. She didn't know if she really was close to death, but life hadn't offered much to her. Dying might not be such a bad thing.

The metal hatch opened again. This time she was able to look up. One of the men tossed in a plastic bottle of water and then slammed shut the hatch. The bottle rolled away into the darkness. Jessie frantically crawled on her hands and knees in the direction it took and felt along the slimy floor until she found it. Unscrewing the cap, she leaned against the side of the boat and took a small sip of water that she swished around in her mouth. She took five more small sips then carefully screwed on the cap and held the water close to her chest. She didn't know how long the water would have to last, but the tiny sustenance it provided renewed, at least for now, her will to live.

Jessie closed her eyes and pretended she wasn't in the dark, smelly hold. Within seconds she knew where she wanted to go—Mrs. Fairmont's den. The elderly lady was sitting beside her on the couch showing her pictures with Flip curled up at their feet on the floor. Jessie started to imagine going to the kitchen for a snack, but her stomach growled and stopped before she left the den.

Like a good movie, daydreams have to follow rules.

JAN CRITTENDEN FINISHED HER CONVERSATION AND TURNED TO me.

"You got my fax," she said with a smile. "I hope that didn't create a problem for you."

"No, I already had one."

I quickly told the assistant DA what had happened the previous evening. She listened with a serious expression on her face.

"Do you want me to take it off the calendar and give you some time to try to locate her?" she asked.

"You'd do that?"

"Yes. The case won't be called for trial until later this year."

"That's very kind," I answered in amazement, then stopped as I saw Mr. Carpenter and Clay Hackney enter the back of the courtroom. I should have suspected Hackney's presence at Braddock, Appleby, and Carpenter earlier was due to an imminent court appearance. Seeing Hackney suddenly changed my mind. I faced Jan. "But I'd rather have the police looking for Jessie than leave her unaccounted for. Even though she won't admit it, I know she's under eighteen and shouldn't be on her own."

"Okay." Jan nodded as another lawyer came up to speak to her. "That makes sense from the personal side of things, but I can't promise how much effort the police will put into tracking her down. It won't be a high priority."

"I understand." I glanced again in Hackney's direction. "Can you not call the case out loud, but just motion to me when it's time?"

"Okay," Jan replied with a puzzled expression. "We'll take care of the bond revocation toward the beginning of the calendar."

I sat against the wall not far from the group of prisoners brought over from the jail. Mr. Carpenter remained beside Hackney. I avoided looking in their direction. The judge arrived. Everyone in the courtroom stood.

"Be seated," Judge Cannon said briskly.

The judge accepted plea bargains in three cases, which made me even more depressed. Jan motioned to me and I stepped forward close to the bench.

"*State v. Whitewater*," Jan said in a normal tone of voice that I hoped couldn't be heard beyond a few feet away.

"Where's your client?" Judge Cannon asked me.

I kept my voice soft. "Not here, Your Honor. She was released on bond, and I don't know where she is."

"Have you attempted to contact her?"

"My client was staying with Mrs. Fairmont," I said. "She left the house last night and didn't come back. I have no idea where she is."

"The State requests the Court issue a bench warrant and bond forfeiture," Jan said.

"Does the bondsman know your client skipped out?" the judge asked me.

"Yes, sir. I called Ms. Dabney last night. She'd posted a property bond with her residence as security."

The judge looked at Jan. "Does the State have an objection to continuing the case for a few weeks so the guarantor on the bond can make efforts to locate the defendant? I'm reluctant to revoke a bond one day after it's issued, especially in the case of a property bond from a private citizen."

Jan glanced at me. "The State has no objection to continuing the case. It won't be called for trial until later this year."

"That's what I'm going to do," the judge said. "Put it on the November trial calendar. Ms. Taylor, I'm instructing you to notify Ms. Dabney of my ruling. I want to give her reasonable time to find your client."

"Yes, sir."

I turned around. Clay Hackney was sitting in the front row staring directly at me. He couldn't have heard what the judge said, but that didn't keep him from being interested. Anger rose up inside me, and I walked over to him. Before I could say anything, Mr. Carpenter spoke.

"Are you going to be a regular over here?" he asked.

"No, sir. It's an appointed case."

"Of course." Mr. Carpenter nodded and turned toward Hackney. "Every young lawyer in the circuit has to serve on the appointed criminal list. It can ruin a good day. Sitting in the office admiring the view, when suddenly you get a call from the judge's office that you

have a new client at the jail who has been charged with four counts
of aggravated assault that took place while the defendant was burning
down a nursing home." He looked back at me. "Judge Cannon didn't
waste any time getting you involved. Whitewater is an unusual
name," Mr. Carpenter continued. "Sounds Indian to me. And Jessie
could be a man or a woman. Which is it?"

I felt the blood rush from my face.

"You heard the call of the case," I managed.

"Of course," Mr. Carpenter replied. "The judge has a microphone on the bench. Is the woman who posted the bond the preacher
we sued last summer?"

"Yes, sir."

"It's a small world," Mr. Carpenter said. "I hope your client turns
up."

I stared at Hackney for a moment. The expression on his face
could be interpreted as either disinterest or disdain.

"*State v. Hackney!*" Chief assistant District Attorney Duffy called
out. "Motion to modify terms of discovery."

"That's us," Mr. Carpenter said, rising to his feet.

I left the courtroom. When I reached the hallway I began to question how I could have been so stupid. Instead of attempting to hide
something in plain view, I should have asked Jan Crittenden to call
Jessie's case after Hackney left the courtroom. If he didn't know Jessie
had come to Savannah, he did now. Also, I'd given no consideration
to Sister Dabney's situation. Pushing for revocation of Jessie's bond
would put enormous financial pressure on her, a fact Judge Cannon
immediately recognized, but I did not.

Returning to the office, I logged on to my computer. There was
a new e-mail from Julie.

Maggie told me about the judge revoking Jessie's bond. Don't tell
Dabney, but I'll get it paid so she won't lose her house. It's not that

big a deal to me. I made a bunch of money when I short-sold some stocks before a big dip in the market.

I read the e-mail three times before I could believe it. I printed it out, took it into Maggie's office, and handed it to her.

"That's unethical," she said after a few seconds. "A lawyer can't post bond for a criminal client. It opens the door for abuse in directing cases to the lawyer—"

"The judge didn't revoke the bond," I said, then told her what happened. "What amazes me is that Julie is willing to help."

I PHONED SISTER DABNEY AND TOLD HER JUDGE CANNON WASN'T going to immediately revoke the bond. I omitted the part about my willingness to let that happen but told her about Julie's offer to step in and save her house.

"She's closer to the kingdom than she knows," Sister Dabney responded. "Don't give up on her."

"I won't. What about Jessie? Has the Lord shown you anything about her?"

"To keep praying. The battle for Jessie's soul isn't over, not yet. The criminal case was just a way to gather more reinforcements." Sister Dabney paused. "And Mrs. Fairmont will be going home from the hospital."

The way Sister Dabney said "home" made me suddenly fearful.

"To heaven?" I asked, my throat tightening.

"No, to her house on Hull Street. She came late to the vineyard, but it's not time for her to receive her reward."

"That's wonderful," I said, cheering up. "Can I tell her what you said? That might lift her spirits."

"Yes, but she already knows it. An angel came to her hospital room this morning and spoke it into her right ear."

At lunchtime, I returned to the hospital to see Mrs. Fairmont. She was sitting up in bed with the TV tuned to the Food Network.

"Are you feeling better?" I asked.

"I will once they quit draining all the blood out of my body. I thought doctors stopped leeching patients a couple hundred years ago. And I've been so hungry I had to turn on TV to see something to eat."

It was great to see the elderly woman so feisty.

"Your breakfast was here when I stopped by this morning, but you were asleep."

"I slept so late they took away my tray. Now, lunch is running late because of a problem in the kitchen. If I'd known you were coming, I would have asked you to bring me something."

"I could go and come back—"

"No, no." Mrs. Fairmont waved her hand. "I'm just looking for an excuse to complain."

"When are they going to discharge you?"

"I have no idea. Dr. Dixon thinks I had a heart attack."

"But Mrs. Bartlett told me the tests last night ruled that out," I said with surprise.

"Until they did more tests this morning. He also sent a psychiatrist to see me. Imagine that! Dr. Bardwell or Barnwell, something like that. She was nice enough, but I could tell she wasn't satisfied with my answers. If there isn't something wrong with you when you go to the hospital, there will be before you leave. Once all these doctors get together and agree that my heart and my mind are leaving me, my next stop is going to be Surfside."

"You're going home," I said emphatically.

"Come sit on the bed beside me," she said, patting the sheet.

The elderly lady was so petite there was plenty of room.

"You're right," she said in a soft voice.

"How do you know?"

"Because I'm supposed to help Jessie," she said with a satisfied smile.

"Jessie's gone."

Mrs. Fairmont gave me a blank look.

"I told you last night when we talked on the phone."

"I thought that was a dream."

"No, ma'am. I wish it was. Jessie didn't come back from her bike ride to Forsyth Park. I drove around last night looking for her and checked again while running this morning. There's no sign of her anywhere."

Mrs. Fairmont rubbed her forehead with her hand. "Maybe I'm more confused than I thought. There've been so many people in to see me. Why do you think she didn't come back?"

"It looks like she ran away."

"I told the nice young man that changed the light this morning about Jessie. We also talked about Christine."

My ears perked up. "What did he look like?"

"Oh, he was a nice-looking young man, mid- to late twenties, I'd say. He works for the hospital."

"Which light?"

Mrs. Fairmont pointed to the ceiling on the right-hand side of the room. "We had a good chat. I want to report how courteous he was if they send me one of those surveys in the mail."

"What did he say?"

"That when I go home I might want to invite Christine over for coffee. You know, we don't ever relax with each other. And there's so much we should be able to talk about without getting into an argument. It's up to me to break the pattern. We could sit on the veranda when the weather gets cooler."

"Did the young man say anything about Jessie?"

"No. We mostly talked about Christine. I didn't realize Jessie had run away."

I patted Mrs. Fairmont's hand. "I believe you'll go home and sit on the veranda with Mrs. Bartlett and drink coffee. She knows you're a greater treasure than all the antiques in your house put together."

Mrs. Fairmont looked at me with eyes that suddenly filled with tears.

"Do you really believe that?"

"Yes, ma'am. I've seen the way she looks at you when she's concerned about you. There's tenderness beneath her bossiness."

"You're right." Mrs. Fairmont smiled. "And you know what I'm going to do? I'm going to tell Christine I love her. We haven't said that to each other in years. She might think I'm senile and crazy, but I'll do it anyway."

"Why did you stop?"

"Because we let little hurts and slights steal those words from our vocabulary."

I squeezed Mrs. Fairmont's hand. "I love you."

"Lean close," she said.

When I did, she gave me a quick kiss on the cheek.

"I love you, too. You may be young, but you've taught me a lot. I don't want to think what my life would be without you."

I gave her a hug, relieved it wasn't a good-bye embrace. That day would come; however, if Sister Dabney and the angel who changed the lightbulb were right, it wasn't as close at hand as I'd feared.

WHEN I RETURNED TO THE OFFICE I WAS ABLE TO WORK ON MY other files without having Jessie's case lingering at the edge of my mind. Judge Cannon's decision placed her matter in limbo—the police weren't trying to catch her, and there wasn't anything I could do that might convince her to return.

Late in the afternoon Gracie called to tell me she'd fed Flip and let him out to play in the courtyard. I was in the middle of researching a new file Maggie gave me, and with no one at the house, I decided to stay at the office and continue into the evening. Around 8:30 p.m. I took a break and walked into the hallway to stretch. I heard a tapping noise coming from the reception area. For several days I'd seen squirrels in the parking lot but couldn't imagine what they might find interesting at the front door unless someone dropped a few tidbits of food on the way into the office. It was getting dark outside. All the lights in the office were turned off, except for my office, which didn't have a window. As soon as I entered the reception area, I had a clear view of the front door. There was a man standing there with his head down, focused on the lock. He was wearing white surgical gloves.

I screamed.

The man looked up. He was wearing a baseball cap pulled low over his eyes. He spun around and ran off. I took a step toward the door in order to get a better look at him, but then, realizing it wasn't safe, I stopped and waited for my breathing to slow down. I listened but didn't hear the sound of a vehicle driving away. Scared he might be waiting for me outside, I ran to my office and called 911.

"Stay where you are," the lady on the other end of the line said. "I'll report it right away."

Within a couple of minutes I saw a blue light flashing down the hallway followed by a loud knock at the front door. Two police officers were standing where I'd seen the man a few minutes before. I unlocked the door, let them inside, and told them what had happened.

"Is that your Cadillac parked in front of the building?" one of the officers asked.

"It belongs to my landlady, Mrs. Margaret Fairmont."

One of them left and went outside. I showed the other officer the rest of the office then we returned to the reception area.

"There aren't any other cars in the parking lot besides her vehicle," the officer reported to his partner. "And I didn't see anyone in the area."

"Does Maggie Smith work here?" the older of the two officers asked me.

"Yes. She's my boss."

The two officers looked at each other.

"Have there been any other attempted break-ins?"

"Not that I know about. I've only been here a couple of months."

"Any alarm system?"

"No. We don't keep any cash here. There's nothing worth stealing except our computers." I paused. "Why would someone try to break in this time of the evening instead of the middle of the night?"

"Happens more often than you'd think," the older officer said. "Most home burglaries occur during the day. Any activity on this street after midnight would attract attention. Right now, it's early enough that someone in the area wouldn't automatically be suspicious. The guy probably didn't know you were here because the light from your office isn't visible from the parking lot. Have there been any problems with clients?"

"I can check with the other attorneys, but nothing has been mentioned."

"Let us know," the older officer replied. "We'll file the incident report. The lock still works, although it wouldn't have taken him long to get past it. Tell Maggie to install a bigger lock and an alarm system." The officer handed me his card. "I've known Maggie since she started working at the DA's office."

"Okay. I want to leave with you," I said.

The officers waited while I quickly gathered my things. My hand shook when I put the key in the lock and realized the intruder had been in the exact same place less than thirty minutes earlier. As soon as I was in the car, I called Maggie. She wasn't there, but I left her a voice mail. Then I phoned Zach. He answered and I told him what had happened.

"I'm a nervous wreck," I said. "I'm afraid to go to Mrs. Fairmont's house alone."

"Meet me at Braddock, Appleby, and Carpenter," he said. "I'm at home so it will take me ten minutes to get there."

"Thanks."

I thought about calling Daddy and Mama but hesitated. Thankfully, nothing bad happened, and I knew they would suffer a sleepless night if I shared the news. We never locked our doors on Beaver Ruin Road, and we slept without fear.

When I reached Braddock, Appleby, and Carpenter, the parking lot was empty. I pulled into the space I'd used the previous summer but kept the doors locked and the engine running. Never had I felt so personally violated. And there hadn't even been an actual break-in. I glanced up as a dark pickup with heavily tinted windows turned into the parking lot then backed out to go in the opposite direction. Zach, riding his red motorcycle and wearing a white T-shirt and blue jeans, followed close behind. I got out. Zach got off the motorcycle and took off his helmet. Without a word he stepped forward and hugged me.

The dam of tension inside me burst. I buried my head in his shoulder and cried. I'd never been embraced by a man except my father, but in that moment it felt totally right to be enveloped in the protection Zach's strong arms provided. I let his reassuring strength flow into me.

"I need a tissue." I sniffed after a few moments passed.

Zach released me and I reached into the car for my purse. After I blew my nose, I looked at Zach. I wanted to return to the safety I had felt in his arms, but the moment had passed.

"Thanks for coming," I said.

"I'm sorry this happened," he said with a fiery look in his eyes. "If I'd been at your office—"

I stared at him for a second, realizing that if he'd encountered the man who tried to break into the office, Zach would have tried to break him in two.

"I'm okay," I said, "but it scared me."

"What did the police find?"

"Nothing. The lock was slightly damaged; however, it wasn't strong enough to keep out someone determined to get in. If I'd not gone into the hall to take a break, I wouldn't have realized what was going on. I screamed, and he ran."

I shuddered.

"Did you see him well enough to give the police a description?"

"No. You always hear people say things like this happen fast. It's true. I couldn't tell you anything about his face. He was wearing a baseball cap, dark clothes, and white surgical gloves. That's about it. One of the officers recommended we install a bigger lock and an alarm system."

"Good idea."

"I called Maggie, but I had to leave a message. I didn't phone Julie. She has enough to worry about with her father."

"Are you ready to go home?"

"If you mean Powell Station, the answer is yes," I said. "However, that's not an option. If you could follow me to Mrs. Fairmont's house, that would be great."

"Let's go."

Zach mounted his motorcycle and followed me the short distance I'd walked to work the previous summer. Now, the thought of being alone on the streets brought a return of fear. I checked in the rearview mirror. Zach was directly behind me. We reached Mrs. Fairmont's house and I pulled into the single garage. Zach stopped behind me.

"Do you want me to see you safely inside?" he asked.

"Yes. I know there wasn't anything personal about the man at the office, but I'm having trouble convincing myself."

When I unlocked the door, we were greeted by the excited antics of Flip. Seeing the little dog turn in circles and wiggle every muscle in his body in welcome helped me return to a sense of normal. I leaned over and vigorously scratched him.

"I'm going to look around the house," Zach said.

"Okay."

I took Flip into the den and, while holding him in my lap, told him about my visit with Mrs. Fairmont at the hospital.

"She's going to come home," I said, stroking the dog's back. "I'm just not sure when."

I could hear Zach's footsteps on the second floor. There were windows in the den that faced the veranda and the courtyard below. Usually, I didn't give them a second thought. Tonight, they looked like dark, unseeing eyes. I reminded myself that no one could see inside the house unless they were on Mrs. Fairmont's property. Zach returned from his mission.

"Everything looks fine," he said. "You did a good job making your bed and the bathroom was clean. Do you always hang up your towel so it's exactly level on the hook?"

"Yes, it dries evenly that way," I said, smiling.

"I don't have that problem. I only use a towel once before I wash it."

Zach stood beside Mrs. Fairmont's chair.

"Are you going to be okay?" he asked.

I nodded. "I'm going to activate the burglar alarm. Mrs. Fairmont rarely uses it, but I'd feel better about it tonight."

I placed Flip on the floor and went to the closet that contained the control panel. I punched in the numbers to activate the system, but the indicator light stayed red when it should have turned to green. I entered the numbers more slowly with the same result.

"Something's wrong with it," I said.

"Operator error?" Zach asked.

"Probably."

I checked the instruction sheet on top of the unit and repeated the process without success.

"I'm missing a step but can't remember what it is."

"Let me see the manual."

I handed it to Zach. As he slowly turned the pages, I thought again how I'd felt when he hugged me, and, I had to admit, I hugged back.

"Let's try this," he said.

He punched in the same numbers I'd entered and flipped a couple of switches. The light stayed red. Flip, who was close to my feet, suddenly started barking and ran toward the foyer. I left Zach and followed. The dog was directly in front of the door, yapping furiously.

"What is it, boy?" I asked.

I glanced through the side glass and didn't see anyone. I opened the door and stood in the doorway. Flip joined me and continued barking. A pair of squirrels scurried up a nearby tree. I glanced down at him.

"Squirrels have a right to be here," I said, trying to sound more nonchalant than I felt.

I stepped inside, closed the door, and locked it.

"It has me stumped," Zach said from right behind me.

I screamed and twirled around.

"Why did you sneak up on me?" I demanded.

"I didn't sneak up on you," Zach replied calmly. "I followed you in here from the place you left me."

"I'm sorry. I just can't shake the jumpy feeling that came over me after the attempted break-in."

"Was there anything unusual going on outside?"

"Nothing except a pair of squirrels playing tag."

Zach eyed me for a moment. "Do you think you're going to be okay here alone?"

"Of course," I answered, but my heart continued to beat at a rapid pace. "I'll have Flip for protection."

"He's as jumpy as you are. I'll be glad to sleep on the sofa in the den."

Normally, I would have instantly turned down the offer, but in my present state of mind I hesitated.

"You didn't bring a suitcase," I replied.

"Which doesn't matter because I wouldn't change into pajamas anyway. Look, I can stretch out on the sofa and be fine. You know what the Bible says about the sleep of the righteous."

"The sleep of the righteous is sweet," I said.

"That describes me," he replied with a smile. "And to prove it, let me do a good deed so you can rest. You'll be fine tomorrow night, but considering what you've been through the past few hours, there's nothing wrong in having a little extra security."

I tried to think how my parents would respond to Zach's invitation. Mama would say no; Daddy would say yes. It rarely happened, but when I had to pick between my parents, one always won out.

"Thanks," I said. "I'd like you to stay."

20

Jessie's plastic bottle of water was gone and, after two days without any food and very little water, life began to lose its grip on her. She'd yelled for help, begged for mercy, and shed a few silent tears. Nothing happened. Footsteps occasionally tapped on the deck above, but no one opened the hatch, even to curse or torment her. Jessie felt abandoned and forgotten.

She wavered on the brink of unconsciousness. Huddled up against the hull of the ship with the stifling heat pressed like a heavy weight against her chest, she'd even tried to pray. But the mixed-up doses of religion she'd received in random churches and watching Sister Dabney preach didn't produce much. She ended up muttering to God what she'd cried out for human ears a few hours earlier: "Help, help, help."

When the hatch finally creaked open, Jessie couldn't leave the twilight world she'd slipped into. The first man who shone a flashlight into the hold saw her crumpled form and swore.

"You guys are idiots!"

"No, we were following orders."

"He didn't say to kill her, not yet. Get her out of there."

"I don't want to go down there. It stinks."

"Get her out or you're going to spend an hour down there yourself."

"Tell Nick to do it."

"I sent him to shore while you were sacked out taking a nap and should have been checking on the girl."

The second man left and then returned to lower a short aluminum ladder into the forward hold. Too small for cargo, the hold was normally used to store supplies such as rope, paint, oil, and tools. To serve as Jessie's prison it had been cleared of everything. The man lowered the ladder and tied a kerchief around his face.

"She'd better not be dead," the first man said. "It smells like death down there."

"I heard her a little while ago," the second man lied. "She's resting."

The second man climbed down the ladder and went over to Jessie. Shining the light on her face, he patted her on the cheek. She moaned softly.

"She's all right!" he called up.

"I want her out of there," the first man ordered.

"Get up," the man ordered Jessie, shaking her shoulders.

She didn't move.

"If she's too weak, you're going to have to carry her out," the first man said.

"Get up!" the second man repeated, shaking her harder.

Jessie responded by sliding over onto her side, her mouth gaping open. The first man swore again.

"I'm coming in."

Jessie wasn't heavy, but she was dead weight. The two men pulled her up the ladder and laid her on the deck in the fading light.

"Turn the hose on her," the first man said, "but not too hard."

When the water hit Jessie's face and body, she sputtered and weakly moved her right hand to cover her face.

"Give her a good dosing," the first man said. "It won't wash away all the stink, but it will make it tolerable."

Jessie opened her mouth and used her tongue to capture some of
the water that ran down the side of her face. The spray from the hose
stopped. She rubbed her eyes and saw two figures standing over her.
One of them leaned over and placed a water bottle in her hand. She
fumbled with the top, too weak to open it.

"Look at that," the first man said. "It's a good thing I came on
board to check on you. Unscrew the cap for her and prop her up
against the bulkhead."

Jessie gratefully received the water from the bottle. After a few
swallows her head began to clear.

"Thank you," she managed.

"Are you ready to do as you're told?" the second man asked. "If
not, you're going back down the ladder."

"No, no," Jessie croaked, shaking her head. "I'll do what you say."

"She's not going anywhere," the first man said, nudging her with
his foot. "Look at her. She can't walk across the deck, much less swim
for shore. Take her into the utility room. It locks from the outside.
Give her another bottle of water and something left over from supper
to eat. She can spend the night in there."

I took Flip downstairs. Before going into my apartment, I
checked the windows I'd previously inspected with Jessie. The entire
time I'd lived with Mrs. Fairmont I'd never considered the windows
potential avenues for intruders, but within the past forty-eight hours,
they'd become chinks in the house's armor.

The window farthest from my apartment provided the least light
during the day because a bush on that end of the house covered most
of the glass. A storage shelf in front of the window made it difficult to
see the latch. I'd tried to make sure it was locked when Jessie asked me
to do so, but now I had doubts. I dragged a chair to a spot in front of
the shelf and stood on it. The latch appeared solid until I looked closer

and saw it was broken. I leaned forward and pushed on the window, but it didn't budge. It was either painted shut or stuck due to warping of the wood after countless years of nonuse. As I lowered my hands I thought I saw the bush move slightly. Cold chills raced down my body. I stared intently into the darkness but couldn't detect any further movement. Zach was right. I was way too jumpy to be alone.

Returning to my apartment, I found the metal bar Mrs. Fairmont had kept wedged under the handle of the French doors before I moved in. I'd never used the bar because it was so ugly and I didn't want to trip over it in the night. Tonight, I lodged it firmly in place. Now no one could get into my bedroom without shattering the glass. As I got ready for bed, my nervousness remained. I hated how I felt but held on to Zach's assurance that I would be better within twenty-four hours. Depositing Flip at the foot of my mattress, I crawled under the sheet. Instead of closing my eyes, I stared at the ceiling, much as I did as a little girl who believed keeping my eyes open would actually help me go to sleep faster. The next thing I was aware of was the first hint of dawn as faint light crept into my room.

It took me a couple of seconds to remember the attempted break-in. When I did, I sat up in bed, startling Flip and causing him to bark. I looked to my right. The metal bar guarding the French doors was still in place. The events of the previous evening flooded through my mind, and the violation I'd felt then, while still present, wasn't as overwhelming.

I got up, dressed in my running clothes, and went upstairs. I wasn't sure whether I should check on Zach but couldn't resist peeking into the den. He was sound asleep, his mouth slightly open but not snoring. I smiled. The sleep of the righteous was sound as well as sweet. Zach didn't move even when Flip trotted into the room and sniffed all the way down the sofa. Zach's intentions were good, but he wasn't much of a light-sleeping night watchman.

I walked quietly to the front door and opened it. When I did, the siren for the burglar alarm started blaring. I slammed the door shut. Turning around, I encountered a wild-eyed Zach. He saw me and stopped.

"Sorry," I said sheepishly. "I guess you fixed the alarm after I went to bed."

"Yeah," he replied, rubbing his eyes. "But I don't know how to turn it off."

An authoritative voice came through a speaker in the hallway near the foyer.

"Identify yourself."

"It's Tami Taylor, Mrs. Fairmont's caregiver," I replied. "The security code is 6700. Sorry for the false alarm. I opened the front door without realizing the system was turned on."

"Let us know if we can be of assistance."

I turned to Zach. "That's why Mrs. Fairmont and I never use it. I've talked to that guy several times. I'm not sure when he sleeps."

"It may be a girl pushing a programmed response." Zach covered his mouth and yawned. "No one sounds that confident this early in the morning. Were you going out for a run without telling me? What if I'd gotten up and you weren't in the house?"

"Would you have gone to my bedroom to check on me?"

"Yes, if Flip was roaming around the house without you."

"Let's turn off the alarm before it wakes the neighbors."

Zach and I went to the closet. I deactivated the system. The house returned to early morning quiet.

"How did you get the alarm to work?" I asked.

Zach pointed to a button on the side of the unit. "It had to be reset after we entered wrong data." He yawned again. "Have a nice run."

"Do you want me to start a pot of coffee?"

Zach rubbed his face that was covered in dark stubble. "Or show me where it is."

"I'll do it."

I went to the kitchen and tried to remember how strong Zach liked his coffee. I made it weak for Mrs. Fairmont but chose a darker mix for Zach. He came in while I was measuring it into the pot. He'd pulled together the stray strands of brown hair that had escaped his ponytail during the night.

"Just press the button, and I'll take it from there," he said. "I like it black."

I placed an empty cup on the counter. "I don't feel like a very good hostess."

"You're perfect."

The way Zach said the words made me blush. I left the kitchen as the pot began making its first gurgling sounds.

I thought about Jessie several times while running through the historic district, especially when I reached Forsyth Park. I prayed she'd come to her senses and come back soon. The wisdom of Judge Cannon's decision not to issue a bench warrant made more sense in the light of a new day. The greatest likelihood for Jessie's return was a change in her own heart and mind, not the remote possibility a police officer would apprehend her.

When I returned to the house, Zach was sitting on the veranda with his back to me and a cup of coffee on the wrought-iron table beside him. Wiping my face with a towel, I poured a glass of water and joined him, sitting on the opposite side of the table.

"Your face is red," he observed.

"It's a run, not a jog. Do you want me to go downstairs?"

"No, no. I'm impressed. Please stay. Where did you go?"

I described my route, then said, "I couldn't get Jessie out of my mind. I know she can take care of herself, but it's a shame that some-one that young is on her own."

"Did she ever admit her age?"

"No, but I had an amazing plea deal worked out with the assistant district attorney. She ruined everything when she took off."

He sipped his coffee while I brought him up to date on the case.

"Yeah, the plea bargain sounds like God's mercy to Jessie," Zach agreed when I finished. "We should pray that she'll come back."

"That's what I've been doing, even during my run this morning."

Before I could respond, Zach stared out at the garden and started talking. The first few words he spoke left me slightly confused since he wasn't looking at me. Then, I realized he was praying. I bowed my head and closed my eyes. Zach continued talking in a normal tone of voice, asking God to take care of Jessie and work in her life. When I peeked, Zach still had his eyes open. I quickly closed mine. Keeping my eyes closed helped me to concentrate. Apparently, Zach had a better ability than I did to shut out visual distractions. When he stopped praying, there was a moment of silence before he spoke.

"Tami, do you want to pray?"

We'd never prayed together, except a brief blessing before a meal. There was something intimate, yet pure, about his offer. I overcame my reluctance and stumbled through a very inarticulate request on behalf of Jessie. I paused for a second, but I didn't end the prayer. Instead, I pushed aside my self-consciousness and let the deep concern and compassion I felt for Jessie rise to the surface. My words became more heartfelt, and the awkwardness caused by Zach's presence left. I realized how desperately I needed to pray with someone for the teenage girl. A favorable plea bargain in a criminal case wasn't Jessie's greatest need. Every fiber of her silently cried out for a deep, healing, transforming touch from the hand of the God who made her. As I continued praying I couldn't keep my emotions bottled up My words were interrupted by tears, as I asked the Lord to have mercy on Jessie. Finally, I sniffled and said, "Amen." I looked over at Zach.

"I'm sorry—"

"Don't apologize for sharing God's compassion for Jessie and letting it come out. That's why you were appointed by Judge Cannon to represent her. It wasn't Sister Dabney's will. It was God's will."

I put my hand on my heart. "And something tells me I'm not off the case, even if Jessie doesn't show up in court and I never see her again."

"All I know is that I was supposed to get us started praying."

I looked at Zach with renewed respect. "I've never prayed like that with a man who wasn't a member of my family or church."

"That's what you and I should have been doing from the beginning. We've spent most of our energy trying to figure out if we're compatible when we should have focused on finding ways to cooperate together in helping others."

"Like the time in Mr. Callahan's kitchen," I said, remembering the miraculous way the Lord touched the older lawyer. "Even though I didn't do much but watch."

Zach shook his head. "No, you arranged the meeting and supported what happened with your faith. But I didn't see that as something you and I could build on. Then, God used you and Vince to reach out to Mrs. Fairmont when she had her stroke last summer."

"Did that make you jealous?"

"Yes, and mad at myself for feeling that way, which shut me down."

Zach was revealing layers of himself I'd not seen.

"When you called last night, I decided not to hold back," he continued. "I hugged you when I saw you were safe, then offered to spend the night to make sure you could rest. This morning when you mentioned Jessie, it wasn't the time to give advice or tell you what to do. I needed to pray with you about the burden of your heart. If I want something more for us, it's time for me to enter your world and share it with you."

The tears welling up in my eyes could not be denied. Two drops rolled down my cheeks. Zach saw but didn't stop.

"Love isn't just figuring out how to get along," he said. "That's important, but it's not the goal. I want a love that shares the unselfish passions God puts on our hearts then helps us do everything we can to make them happen. Wouldn't that be an awesome foundation for a relationship?"

I nodded.

"Would you like to have that with me?" he asked.

"Yes."

"Are you sure? What about your feelings for Vince?"

It was time for my answer, and, in that moment, I knew without a doubt what it should be.

"Vince is like a brother; you're more than that."

"How much more? A guy needs a little encouragement."

"A lot." I leaned forward. "And I've been wrong not to give it. What you said about sharing our God-given passions is exactly what I've always wanted with a man but couldn't put into words. If that piece is in the right place, I believe everything else can follow as it should."

"Like romance?"

"Yes."

Zach grinned. "With long motorcycle rides with you behind me on the bike, not crammed into a sidecar."

It was my turn to smile. "It will take us awhile to get to that point."

"I can wait."

The ache of longing in my heart I'd felt for Zach in the past returned with such force that it almost took my breath away. He eyed me curiously.

"Are you okay?" he asked.

"Yes. And if you knew what I feel in my heart for you right now, you'd be greatly encouraged."

Zach's smile broadened. "A man can travel a long road with words like that ringing in his ears. I've missed you terribly."

"Me, too," I managed.

He stretched out his left hand across the table. I took it. When our fingers met, the intensity of the bond between us felt like a betrothal.

"Father, bless the road we're on," he prayed, this time with his eyes closed. "May we travel it together. And with you."

I closed my eyes and let Zach's words become part of me. We sat in silence for a few moments. He squeezed my hand and released it. I pulled mine back, but part of it remained with him.

"Can I come over early in the morning and spend time like this with you?" he asked.

"Yes, if Mrs. Fairmont doesn't mind, which she won't."

"And drink the great coffee you make?"

"I might try to acquire a taste for it myself. My parents drink coffee together every morning."

Zach raised his cup. "To the future."

ZACH LEFT, AND I WENT DOWNSTAIRS TO GET READY FOR WORK. I wasn't sure if my feet touched the floor or not. So much had happened in my heart while we sat on the veranda that my mind was having trouble catching up.

When I checked my hair in the rearview mirror as I neared the office, I noticed a silly grin on my face that didn't want to go away. Two police cars were in the parking lot. An officer in uniform and another man in a white shirt and tie were standing beside the front door. Surprised that the police were following up so quickly on the attempted break-in, I parked beside one of the police vehicles.

Then, when I got out, I could see the glass in the upper half of the front door had been shattered. The man in the shirt and tie turned around as I walked up.

21

"I'M TAMI TAYLOR, ONE OF THE ATTORNEYS."

"Al Houghton. I'm an investigator with the police department," the man replied.

There were brown stains on the investigator's shirt. I remembered Maggie's comment that Houghton liked to chew tobacco.

"I read the report prepared by the officers who responded to your 911 call," Houghton continued. "It looks like whoever wanted to break in while you were here came back later to finish the job."

On his second attempt the thief didn't attempt to finesse his way into the building. Instead, he destroyed the glass and reached inside to unlock the dead bolt.

"Have you called Maggie Smith?" I asked.

"She's on her way," Houghton said. "One of the other tenants in the building saw the glass and called our office."

"Have you been inside?"

"Just a quick walk-through to make sure no one was in there. We didn't see any obvious damage except to the door, but we'd like to go through the offices carefully once Maggie gets here."

I shuddered at the thought that someone could have been lurking in the office when one of us arrived. Maggie sped into the parking lot and quickly joined us.

"Sorry about last night," she said to me. "I didn't get your message until late. I know that was scary, and I'm glad you're okay."

"Thanks."

"Ready to do an inspection?" Houghton asked her.

I followed Maggie and the two officers into the building. A couple of files in Shannon's area had been knocked to the floor. Her computer wasn't disturbed. Maggie's office appeared untouched.

My space across the hall had been ransacked, every drawer emptied, all the files dumped onto the floor, the contents in a heap.

"Your computer is gone," Maggie said as we surveyed the damage.

Sure enough, my new laptop, along with its power cord, wasn't there.

"Did you back up your files yesterday?" Maggie asked.

I reached in my purse and took out my flash drive.

"Yes, it's all on here."

"The other office is clean," the uniformed officer said from the doorway.

Maggie turned to the inspector. "What do you make of it, Al?"

Houghton shrugged. "He went to a lot of trouble for a laptop. What was it worth?"

"About two thousand dollars," Maggie replied.

"Are you going to check for fingerprints?" I asked.

"Only if this is a TV show," Houghton replied dryly. "The front door will have hundreds of prints jumbled together."

"What about in here?" I persisted. "Only a few people have been in my office."

Houghton moved some of the papers on the floor with his shoe and picked up a latex glove.

"People who wear these don't leave fingerprints. Your thief was polite enough to let me know that I don't need to send out a fingerprint crew. The extra glove shows us he knew what he was doing."

"That may be one of the gloves he was wearing," I said. "It's one of the few things I saw when I scared him off."

Houghton looked at Maggie. "Do you want me to dust the room for fingerprints?"

Maggie turned to me. "Al's right. They probably won't find anything, and the crew will have wasted time that could be better spent on a more serious case."

"Sort through the mess and try to determine if anything else is missing. I'm sure you'll want to install a security system."

"I was going to call Rick Fain's company," Maggie replied.

"Good choice." Houghton nodded. "If you can locate the serial number for the computer, send it to me so I can include it in my report and notify the local pawnshops."

"Will do," Maggie said. "Thanks for coming. And I appreciate you not spitting on my carpet."

Houghton patted his empty left cheek and smiled. "You know I don't get started until after ten thirty in the morning."

Shannon, her eyes wide, was entering the office as Houghton and the uniformed officer walked out. I left Maggie to bring her up to date and returned to my office. Thirty minutes later I was sitting on the floor surrounded by papers when Julie walked in.

"Tammy Lynn Taylor, I leave town for a few days and you can't keep your room clean!" she exclaimed.

I jumped up from the floor and gave her a big hug.

"How's your father?"

"Talking to his broker on the phone the last time I saw him and discussing long-term investment goals. Once I heard that, I knew I could leave town. Then, when Maggie called and told me what happened, I knew I had to get back here to hold your hand." Julie gestured to the mess. "I thought you scared him off."

"I screamed. He ran away. But not very far."

"Anything missing besides the laptop?"

"Not that I can tell."

"Was access to your computer password-protected?"

"Yes."

"What's your password?"

"I can't tell you. It's confidential."

Julie chuckled. "I'm glad to see you haven't lost your razor-sharp wit."

"The reminder clue was 'favorite city.'"

"San Francisco?"

"No, Powell Station."

"Powell Station isn't a city."

"It is if you live on Beaver Ruin Road." I picked up some papers that belonged in Jessie's file and looked for the folder. "Is that Jessie Whitewater's folder?" I asked, pointing to a red expandable folder at Julie's feet.

"Yeah," she said, bending over to pick it up and hand it to me.

I put the papers in the folder.

"How are you doing?" she asked.

"Much better than I deserve," I answered, thinking again about my morning with Zach.

Julie gave me a strange look. I kept rummaging through the papers.

It took a couple of hours to restore everything to its proper place. Nothing was broken, and I couldn't find anything else amiss. Except for the empty space where my computer should have been, the office looked the same. Shannon walked in with a box in her arm and put it on my desk.

"Here's your replacement laptop," she said. "It's the same model."

I'd not expected a new one so soon but realized there was no reason not to immediately replace it. Without a laptop, a lawyer in the twenty-first century was worse off than an eighteenth-century lawyer without a quill pen. By noon, my office was the same as before. The phone buzzed. It was Shannon.

"Line two. It's your preacher friend."

"Did she say anything to you?"

"Yeah, then asked for you."

Before I could ask what Shannon meant, she put the call through.

"I've found something you should see," Sister Dabney said. "It belonged to Jessie."

"What is it?"

"Some papers, but I can't read them."

"Are they illegible?"

"No. One's in a foreign language and the other doesn't make sense. When can you come?"

I checked my calendar. I had a meeting with Maggie and one of her clients in an hour and a half.

"Right now."

"I'll meet you at the church."

I passed Shannon's office on the way out. She stopped me as I reached the reception area.

"Do you have a Bible in your office?" she asked.

"Yes, the thief didn't steal it, although I wish he had. Reading it would be good for him."

"May I borrow it? The Dabney woman told me something I want to check out for myself."

I stepped closer to the waist-high opening between the reception room and Shannon's work area.

"What verses did she give you?"

Shannon looked down at a slip of paper but kept it hidden. "I just want to check it out."

"The Bible is in the upper right-hand drawer of my desk. If you have any questions about what you read, let me know. I'll help if I can."

"This is all so new to me," Shannon said.

When I entered the sanctuary, Sister Dabney was sitting in the purple chair on the platform. She called out to me.

"Come up here."

I walked down the aisle and onto the platform that contained the rocker and rickety podium Sister Dabney used to hold her Bible. She pushed herself out of the rocker.

"Sit down," she commanded.

I sat in the rocker, glad we were alone.

"We're not alone," she said in quick response to my thoughts.

"Who's here?" I asked, quickly looking around but seeing no one.

Sister Dabney pointed up. "He is."

She handed me a hymnbook.

"Turn to page 456," she said.

I turned to the page.

"That's where I found them," she said. "Is there anything about the songs on those two pages that contains a message?"

Page 456 was an old-time song we occasionally sang at my home church; the song on the opposite page was unfamiliar to me. There wasn't anything in the title of either song that grabbed me.

"No, ma'am."

Sister Dabney grunted. "This paper was in the back of the book."

She handed me a ragged sheet of paper that had been folded so many times the crease lines had become part of the paper. Opening it, I saw rows of columns containing letters and numbers. None of the letters formed recognizable words. The numbers were random sequences of ten numbers. There were geometric scribbles in green ink along one edge and an ornate flower drawn in several colors of ink on the back. The numbers and letters were written in pencil.

"How do you know this belonged to Jessie?" I asked.

"That's the hymnbook she used when she came to the church." Sister Dabney pointed to a spot at the end of the second row. "I came in here to pray for her early this morning, and the Lord directed me to pray from the place where she sat. Sometimes I sing as I pray, and when I opened the hymnbook, I found that sheet of paper. Once, when she should have been listening to the preaching, I saw her writing on a sheet of paper with a green pen I'd let her borrow."

"Okay," I said slowly. "But what would Jessie be doing with a sheet of paper like this? It doesn't make any sense."

"That's why you're here. To interpret it." Sister Dabney took the hymnbook from me and opened it to another place. "After I found that piece, I looked through the rest of the book and found this."

Still nestled in the fold of the hymnbook was another sheet of paper. I took it and opened it.

"It's some kind of certificate, perhaps for stocks or bonds," I said, then pointed to the printed words. "This is German, but I can't read it."

Sister Dabney turned around and slowly descended the steps.

"I'll be at the house. Come by before you leave and let me know what they mean."

"Wait, can I take these to the office and ask Maggie and Julie to help?"

Sister Dabney stopped at the bottom of the steps. "That's what a threefold cord is all about. I'll wait to hear from you."

RETURNING TO THE OFFICE, I QUICKLY BROUGHT MAGGIE AND Julie into the conference room.

"What's going on?" Julie asked. "Do you know how many phone calls I have to return before I leave this afternoon?"

"I need your help," I replied, laying the pieces of paper on the table. "Sister Dabney found these in a hymnbook at the church. She believes they belong to Jessie. I think this one is written in German."

"I took German in high school," Julie replied. "With a name like

Feldman it came easily for me; must have been from a repressed gene."

"Can you read this?" I asked, shoving the certificate toward her.

Julie picked it up. I watched her eyes widen.

"Do you know what this is?" she asked.

"No."

"It's a bond. And if Mrs. Heidelberg did her job teaching me, it's for one hundred thousand euros."

"What company?"

"No company." Julie shook her head. "It's a government-issued bearer bond."

I didn't know what she meant. Maggie gasped.

"Are you sure?" Maggie asked, leaning forward.

Julie pointed to a phrase that appeared several times on the certificate. "If that means what I think it does, this is as negotiable as a check with your name written on it for one hundred thousand euros."

"I don't understand," I said.

Maggie spoke. "Ownership of this bond is based totally on possession. That's why it's called a bearer bond." She picked up the certificate. "Whoever has this bond in his or her possession can redeem it. Nothing could be simpler."

"And receive one hundred thousand euros?" I asked, my mouth dropping open.

"More than enough for Jessie to pay your attorney fee and buy as many donuts as she wants," Julie said. "What makes this one extra special is that it wasn't issued by a private company; it came directly from the German government."

"Congress outlawed U.S. government–issued bearer bonds in 1982 because they were being used for money laundering," Maggie said. "Without a name on the certificate, bonds like this one are ideally suited for money transfers where the parties don't want anyone to know who paid who. Congress wanted to put a stop to that practice. But many foreign governments, including several in Europe, allow them. I learned about this type of thing in a drug case I prosecuted a few years ago."

"What should we do with it?" I asked.

"That's easy," Julie replied. "I'll fly to Munich and redeem it. I've had a recent unexplained craving for German sausage. Thirty-three thousand euros and change is a nice day's work for each of us."

"No, it goes in a safe-deposit box," Maggie responded. "My question is how Jessie got it."

I felt the blood rush from my face. "It has something to do with Clay Hackney. That's why she was so terrified of him."

"After seeing this, I have to admit that's possible," Maggie said slowly.

"Jessie's gone," Julie said. "And we can't run an ad in the paper— 'Bearer Bond Found. Call to Claim.' I think we should—"

"Put it in the safe-deposit box," Maggie interrupted. "Besides, legal possession of the bond lies with the Dabney woman. She only gave it to Tami to figure out what it is."

Julie winced. "Yeah, I got carried away. If Sister Dabney redeems the bond, she could afford a desperately needed upgrade to her wardrobe."

"And there's this," I said, tapping the other sheet of paper with my hand. "What do you make of it?"

Julie picked it up. "It's not in German. And the doodling isn't that bad. This flower has some good detail."

"And this looks like the edge of the bond certificate," Maggie said, pointing to the green ink design.

There was no doubt about the similarity.

"But the rest of it is nonsense," Julie said.

The three of us peered at the columns of letters and numbers.

"Maybe it's written in code," I suggested.

Julie glanced at me. "I left my decoder ring in my other purse. Do you want me to get it?"

"No, wait a minute," Maggie said. "Let's assume Tami is right. How would it work?"

"My first cousin Mary and I wrote letters to each other in code after she moved to Florida when we were about twelve years old," I said.

"A sneaky way for you to communicate without your parents finding out," Julie interjected. "I can see you doing that."

"It was a simple code," I said, ignoring Julie. "Each letter of the alphabet became the following letter—*a* as *b*, *b* as *c*, and so on."

Julie ripped a couple of sheets of paper from a legal pad. "Let's divide up a few lines and see if it works."

Within less than a minute, it was obvious the code used by Mary and me didn't fit. The new letters were as jumbled as before.

"I thought it was a good idea," Julie said as we slid our sheets to the center of the table. "But now it feels kind of silly."

"Try advancing each letter two spaces," Maggie replied.

The results were still incomprehensible.

"Go three spaces," Maggie said.

"It won't hurt my feelings if my idea doesn't pan out," I said.

"Let's give it a try," Maggie replied.

Within a minute a new line of unreadable text took its place. Julie looked up.

"How many letters are there in the alphabet? Are we going to try this twenty-six times? If somebody offered to sell us a computer program to do this, I'd put it on my credit card right now."

"Four letters," Maggie replied.

Julie sighed. We bowed our heads and began counting letters and writing replacements. After less than a minute, Julie gasped.

"What?" I asked.

She moved her sheet so we could see the four letters she'd written.

"C-L-A-Y," she said.

"Mine is B-A-R-R-Y," Maggie replied.

"Apply the same thing to the numbers," I said.

We quickly recognized area codes for phone numbers. Dividing up the information, we spent the next thirty minutes deciphering the sheet of paper. It was a list of people and phone numbers. Most were men, but a few women were also included. Clay Hackney was the only familiar name.

"What are we going to do with this?" I asked when we finished. "Should I take it to Jan Crittenden at the DA's office?"

"I'll go with you," Maggie said.

"You're not going to tell them about the bearer bond, are you?" Julie asked hopefully.

"Yes," Maggie replied. "The bond will convince the police to begin a serious search for Jessie. If this stuff belongs to Hackney or some of his associates, they will be looking for her, too. We have to get to her first."

I phoned the district attorney's office. The receptionist checked with Jan Crittenden, then relayed the message that she could meet with us if we came immediately. Maggie made copies of the bearer bond and the original sheet of paper and our deciphered version. On our way to the courthouse, we stopped at Maggie's bank and put the originals in a safe-deposit box.

I was still slightly breathless when we entered the DA's office. Jan came into the reception area and gave the two of us a puzzled look.

"Can we meet in private?" I asked.

"Sure."

She led us to the conference room where we'd talked before.

"Is this about Jessie Whitewater?" she asked as soon as we sat down.

"Yes, but it also involves Clay Hackney," Maggie added.

"Hackney?"

I nodded.

"Should I see if Brett Duffy is available? That's his case."

"I think so," Maggie answered.

Crittenden left the room and returned in less than a minute with a thick folder under her arm.

"He's out of the office for the afternoon, but I have the file."

In a less-rapid-fire manner, I told her everything that had transpired between Jessie and Clay Hackney. While still describing Jessie's reaction to seeing Hackney in the courtroom, Jan stopped me and left the room. She returned with a handheld recording device.

"Would you start over and let me record this for Brett?"

I hesitated and glanced at Maggie.

"Okay," she said, "as long as we get a copy of any transcript and can correct it."

"No problem. I'll put that at the beginning."

I repeated everything I'd already told the assistant DA but with greater detail. Listening to myself the second time, I was less convinced that I'd stumbled onto the greatest discovery since the Rosetta stone.

"Will this motivate the police to find Jessie?" I asked when I finished. "I'm worried about her."

Jan reached over and turned off the recorder.

"I wish your client was still around. Your theory is plausible, but it's speculative." Jan picked up the sheet of paper with the names and phone numbers on it. "I'm sure Brett would like a copy of this to include as part of the investigative file. Does anyone outside your firm know about this?"

"Ramona Dabney, the woman who found it."

Jan nodded. "She posted the bond."

"Right."

"I'll see if I can get the police to increase efforts to find Jessie."

"Try Detective Houghton," Maggie said. "He was at our office this morning investigating a break-in."

"Your office was burglarized? I didn't hear about that."

"Yes, whoever did it came back twice." Maggie touched the copy of the bearer bond. "He could have been looking for this."

Jan nodded. "If we could link Hackney to a burglary, that would help Brett. The current case is totally circumstantial." Crittenden covered her mouth with her hand. "I shouldn't have said that last part. Please don't repeat it."

"We won't," Maggie answered. "At this point the interests of our client and your office look to be the same."

Jan picked up the sheets of paper.

"Could you leave these with me? If the information becomes relevant to our case, we would need the originals."

"They're in a safe-deposit box," Maggie replied.

"Good," Jan said.

"Will you try to find Jessie?" I asked.

"Yes." Jan nodded. "That will be my next phone call."

22

THE UTILITY ROOM WAS A MUCH BETTER PRISON THAN THE DIRTY mattress and horrible stink of the forward hold of the ship. Before he locked her up in her new place, the man who'd hosed off Jessie gave her a full water bottle and the uneaten remains of two dinners. She couldn't believe how much delicious food the men left on the plates. She tried to eat slowly, but after the first few bites she crammed the food from one plate in her mouth as fast as she could. Within a couple of minutes, she banged on the door. The man returned. Jessie was holding her cramping stomach.

"I need to go to the bathroom," she said.

The man pushed her down a short hallway and opened the door to a marine head. Jessie got sick. Losing the precious food was a disaster, but there wasn't anything she could do about it. She splashed water on her face and peered in the mirror. Her filthy hair was plastered to her head, and her eyes were red with dark lines beneath them. She looked a lot worse than when she'd arrived at the Savannah bus station. There was a tiny bar of soap on the lavatory, and rubbing it in her hands she produced a tiny bit of suds. The man knocked on the door.

"Time to go."

"Can I wash my face?"

"You got one minute."

She scrubbed as fast and as hard as she could. The effort didn't improve her hygiene very much; it did more to restore her will to live. If she could wash her hands and face, maybe she could survive.

"Let's go," the man said when she opened the door.

When they reached the utility room another man was waiting for them. He had a red kerchief tied around his face and a baseball cap on his head. His eyes were concealed by sunglasses.

"Why do you have that on?" the man with Jessie asked.

"You may not care that she's seen you, but I'm going to be more careful."

"The boss isn't going to let her—"

"You don't know what you're talking about," the first man said. "I called him. He wants to ask her some questions."

"He's coming here?" the second man asked.

"No, you idiot. He wants me to do it. Get on deck and make sure everything is shipshape for the night." The man looked at Jessie. "If she doesn't tell me what I need to know, she's going back to the hold."

"No, please." Jessie shook her head.

"Then this should be easy."

The second man left them alone. The man with the kerchief over his face had thick, powerful-looking arms and large hands. He was wearing a black T-shirt, white shorts, and brown deck shoes.

"Follow me," the man said.

He took Jessie to the small mess where the men on board prepared and ate their meals. There was a table with seating for six people. The man sat down and motioned for Jessie to sit across from him.

"Do you know why you're here?" he asked.

Normally, Jessie would have feigned ignorance, but forty-eight hours in the dank hold had dealt with that response.

"You want to ask me some questions."

"Not me, someone else."

"Clay."

The man didn't change expression.

"Do you know his last name?"

"Hackney."

"How did you meet him?"

"He came over to see Rod Burrell, who was dating my step-mother."

"How many times did he come over?"

"Several. I'm not sure."

"What happened to Rod?"

"I don't know, but Clay sent some men to our house to teach him a lesson. They dragged him out of the house. I was in the bathroom and ran away as soon as they left. I walked down the railroad tracks and ended up catching a ride to Savannah with some Mexican guys who cut down trees."

"Do you know what happened to Rod?"

"No, but I hope they beat him up."

The man grunted. "Did he ever hit you?"

Jessie pointed to the left side of her face. "Once he hit me so hard I thought my cheek was broken."

"Did you see the two men who came to the house to deal with Rod?"

"Not clearly. They chased me into a blackberry thicket. One man left to bring in some dogs to find me. While he was gone, the other man was struck by lightning. That's when I ran to the railroad tracks. That's all I remember."

The man nodded. "You're doing great. When you ran off, did you take something that belonged to Rod with you?"

Jessie immediately thought about the leather pouch. Keeping her voice level, she said, "No."

"Are you sure?"

"Yes."

The man took out a cell phone and entered some numbers.

"I talked to her," he said, then repeated what Jessie told him. He listened for a moment. "No, she didn't say anything about it, but I believe she's telling me the truth. A couple of days in the dark convinced her to cooperate. I've thought all along that Jack grabbed the stuff. And after Bruce was struck by lightning there was nobody to say he was lying. The girl was in the thicket when Bruce was killed. She brought it up herself without me mentioning it."

The man listened for a moment.

"Are you going to come out on the boat and talk to her?"

Jessie's heart started beating rapidly as the man listened again. The man put the phone on the table. Jessie stared at it like a snake about to strike.

"It's on speakerphone," the man said.

"Go ahead," a scratchy voice responded.

The man with the kerchief adjusted the cloth that had slipped below his nose. He kept his eyes on Jessie.

"Did you take a piece of paper with writing and numbers on it that belonged to Rod? You wouldn't have been able to read it."

Jessie swallowed and licked her lips. "No."

"What about some pieces of paper with words in a foreign language written on them?" the voice on the phone asked. "They would have been in a brown leather pouch with a gold snap on top."

"I saw a leather pouch on the table when I left the bathroom," Jessie replied, her voice trembling. "But I didn't touch it. I think Jack grabbed it."

"She took it," the man across the table said as soon as she'd answered. "I can see it in her eyes."

"Where are the papers?" the man on the speakerphone asked, his voice getting louder. "Especially the one with the writing on it. Tell me, and we'll let you go free."

Jessie knew the pouch was in the metal box at the edge of the vacant lot. She may have taken the paper with the writing on it out of the box, but at the moment, she couldn't remember what she'd done with it. One thing she knew for sure—the man on the phone was lying. Jessie's link to the sheets of paper was keeping her alive. She frantically tried to remember what people with secret information did in books. She quickly settled on a strategy she'd read in a story about buried treasure.

"I hid it. I'd have to show you where it is," she said.

The man raised his hand to strike her. Jessie cowered.

"Kelvin, pick up the phone!" the voice on the speaker commanded.

The man lowered his hand and grabbed the phone.

"Why did you tell her my name?" the man with the kerchief asked as soon as he had the phone next to his ear.

Whatever the man on the other end of the call said dealt swiftly with Kelvin's objection. And from her jailor's reaction, the man talking to him could generate fear, even in someone as intimidating as the man across the table from her.

"Yeah," he said and clicked off the phone. He stared hard at Jessie.

"This is your last chance. Where is the stuff in the leather pouch?"

Jessie nervously clasped her hands together under the table. She'd made her plan, and now she didn't know what to do except stick to it.

"I'd be glad to show you," she said, trying to sound helpful.

Kelvin stood up. Jessie braced for a blow.

"Back to the hole for you," Kelvin said. "And don't expect any food or water until you change your mind. Believe me, I'll let you die down there, then sail out a few miles from shore and throw your body overboard. Nobody will ever know or care what happened to a runaway like you."

WHEN MAGGIE AND I RETURNED TO THE OFFICE, A NEW, SOLID-wood door had already been placed in the door frame. Inside, workers were installing the monitors for a security system.

"You have two messages from Zach Mays in your voice mail," Shannon said cheerfully as I passed by. "He's so polite."

"He is," I responded, giving her a curious look.

Before entering her office, Maggie turned to me. "Don't forget, you're a lawyer, not a private investigator. Let the police do their job. When Jessie turns up, it will be your chance to help her."

As soon as I was seated behind my desk, I picked up the phone and called Braddock, Appleby, and Carpenter. The receptionist transferred the call to Zach's office.

"How are you feeling?" he asked.

"Drained by Jessie's case."

"Let me take you to dinner. Do you want to go home first?"

"Yes. I'd better check on Flip."

"How about six thirty?"

"That will be great."

I hung up the phone and looked up. Julie was standing in my doorway.

"Shannon told me Zach Mays has been trying to track you down all day. What's up with that?"

"That's an exaggeration. He phoned twice."

"Which is twice more than he's called you in days. Are you two back together? I can smell romance a mile away, and I'm standing a lot closer to you than that. Don't lie to me."

"You know I can't lie."

"Which is one of your eccentric and endearing qualities. It almost makes getting information out of you unfair."

I told Julie about the previous night and morning. Her eyes widened.

"You spent the night with him."

"On separate floors of the house."

"I know, but I bet he stood at the top of the stairs with his heart pounding that you were so close yet unattainable."

"And then we had a wonderful time praying together this morning."

"Wow, that's over the top. I'm amazed you got there so fast."

"Yeah, it was great."

"What's next?"

"Dinner at six thirty."

"That I can understand. Followed by a second rendezvous at the nonchaperoned home of Mrs. Margaret Fairmont?"

"No, I'm not going to ask him to serve another night as my private security guard."

"You should, but you probably won't. Have fun."

Before leaving the office, I phoned Mrs. Bartlett and learned that Mrs. Fairmont had a good day at the hospital and might be released soon. At home, I turned off the alarm system before entering the house. Flip greeted me with his customary wiggles and shakes. The little dog's desires were simple. To him, a treat, a scratch in the right places, and human companionship were the necessary ingredients of a perfect world.

I checked all the doors and windows to make sure they were locked, then rearmed the security system. While I waited for Zach, I sat at the kitchen table with Flip on the floor beneath my chair and read over an extra copy of the decoded paper. It was a cross section of first names—from John to Manuel to Dejuan, and it also included two feminine names, Halley and Tamika. The last name on the list was Rod. I toyed with the idea of calling one of the women just to see if a female answered, but remembering Maggie's admonition to avoid being a private investigator, I resisted.

The doorbell chimed. I jumped. Glancing through the narrow window in the foyer, I didn't see Zach. Flip was barking furiously. I

reached out to turn off the alarm but instead slipped into the blue
parlor, which contained a window that gave a better view of the front
of the house. I peeked through the window. Zach was tying his shoes.
He looked over and saw me. I gave him a weak wave.

"What's wrong?" he asked as soon as I opened the door.

"I'm still tense," I admitted.

Zach's car was parked at the curb. He opened the door for me.

"Tell me," he said as soon as we were both buckled in.

I told him about the break-in at the office.

"That's crazy," he said when I finished. "It makes your place seem
like a specific target, not a random break-in."

"I know," I answered forlornly.

We pulled into the parking lot of a small Italian restaurant.

"Have you eaten here?" Zach asked.

"No."

"You'll like it."

An attractive young woman of obvious Italian descent greeted us
and led us to a table. The restaurant was noisy and busy, with a jolly
atmosphere that didn't match my mood. I stared at the menu without enthusiasm.

"What looks good?" Zach asked. "Any dish with the Alfredo
sauce should cheer you up."

"I'm not very hungry."

Our waiter rattled off several suggestions. I ordered one of his
recommendations without enthusiasm.

"I'm sorry about what happened at your office," Zach said when
the waiter left. "I'd hoped you would be able to think about our time
together this morning."

"Oh, I did. This is just a temporary thing."

"Did you talk to your parents?"

"No, I'll do that tonight after dinner."

My cell phone in my purse rang. Only a handful of people had the number, all of them known to me. The ID of the caller appeared as "unavailable." I glanced up at Zach.

"Let me take this. I don't know who it is."

I stepped into a short hallway near the restrooms. It was Jan Crittenden.

"I got your cell phone number from Maggie Smith," she said. "Do you have a minute?"

"Sure," I responded.

"Brett Duffy wanted you to know that the list of names and numbers you unscrambled is going to be more helpful than you realized. One of the names on the list is a woman named Tamika Grady. She's in jail in Atlanta facing some serious drug charges. Brett contacted her lawyer, and she might be willing to testify against Hackney if we can help her get a better deal from the Fulton County DA. It's all preliminary, but I wanted you to know how helpful the information might turn out to be. Also, Brett wanted to make sure you didn't call any of the people on the list yourself."

"No—and I won't. Any word on the police stepping up their search for Jessie?"

"Not yet. I'll get on that sometime tomorrow."

"Okay. Thanks." I returned the phone to my purse.

"Who was it?" Zach asked.

"Jan Crittenden at the DA's office."

"Any news about Jessie?"

"Not specifically."

Hiding my feelings from Zach wasn't easy under normal circumstances, but I tried my best to put everything out of my mind during dinner. The food was good, and the smell of the pasta dish restored my appetite. It was still dusky light when we stepped outside the restaurant. An evening breeze from the ocean blew gently through my hair.

"Would you like to go down to the docks and watch the boats come in?" Zach asked. "It's pretty when they have their lights on. I know a nice spot where we can park the car and walk close to a marina."

"Okay."

Zach parked the car along a waterfront street. We got out and walked slowly along a boardwalk with an open view of large boats and yachts moving slowly through the water. We continued until the walkway was blocked by a steel gate that restricted further access to the public.

"The larger yachts are in this part of the marina," Zach said as we looked through the bars. "Mr. Carpenter owns a boat that he keeps here."

"Which one is it?" I asked.

Zach moved his head from side to side.

"I've been on it a couple of times, but it's hard to remember exactly which one it is. They all look alike in the dark."

He pointed in the direction of a bulky gray boat that still had a few lights on it. A couple of figures could be seen moving about on the deck.

"I think it's next to the one that just came in," Zach said.

I followed the direction of his finger to a sleek white vessel.

"Yes," I said. "Mr. Carpenter has a picture of that boat on the wall in his office."

As I watched, one of the figures on the adjacent boat crossed the deck, almost dragging a smaller person behind him. Every few steps the smaller figure lagged behind until jerked forward.

"What's going on over there?" I asked Zach. "Do you see the people on that other boat?"

"Yeah, they've brought it in for the night."

"Something's wrong."

23

THE LITTLE BIT OF FOOD LEFT IN HER STOMACH KEPT JESSIE ALIVE, but by late afternoon, heat and dehydration began to rapidly wear her down. The entire night and most of the day, she'd kept quiet. Even as her suffering retuned, she remained convinced the offer of freedom in return for information about the leather pouch was bogus. Anyone who would torture her so badly couldn't be trusted. She considered telling Kelvin a false location but feared the retribution that would come when her information didn't pan out.

While she sat huddled against the hull of the hold, she tried to remember what she'd done with the paper. She knew she'd carried it around with her and worked on the drawings several times, but she couldn't recall the last place she had it.

She continued to pray for help. During one of those times, she thought about Sister Dabney and a sermon she'd preached about grapevines. The woman preacher claimed vines had to be cut so they could produce more fruit. Jessie found that hard to believe but couldn't deny the woman preacher's vivid description. Thinking that a grapevine might be an interesting addition to her tattoo design, Jessie had taken out the sheet of paper and made a few extra scribbles along the edge.

Then she remembered.

When she realized Sister Dabney was staring at her, Jessie, not wanting her artwork to be confiscated, had hurriedly slipped the sheet of paper into a hymnbook, intending to come back and get it later. She'd also taken one of the certificates with her to the meeting.

Jessie stared into the darkness and tried to figure out what to do next. She could die in the hold, hope that an unforeseen development changed her situation, or renew her offer to show the men where she'd put the sheet of paper. In the book she'd read about buried treasure, the heroine took the villains to the place where the loot was buried, but Jessie couldn't remember exactly what happened next.

More than twenty hours had passed since Jessie had been returned to the hold. She stood shakily to her feet.

"Open up! I'm ready to talk!" she called out.

I STEPPED TO THE SIDE OF THE WALKWAY IN AN EFFORT TO GET A better look at the events taking place on the other boat. The light shifted and it was impossible to see clearly.

"I don't know what you're talking about," Zach said. "They're docking the boat. It's not unusual for a boat that size to have several crew, and someone might spend the night on board, even at the marina."

A third man appeared on deck. When he walked near a light, I caught my breath. There was no mistaking the blond, spiked hair.

"Clay Hackney is on that boat!"

Zach didn't respond but moved closer to me.

"I can't tell," he said after a couple of seconds.

The first two people weren't visible. Hackney opened a door and went into the cabin. A solitary figure walked down the dock and got in a vehicle similar to a golf cart.

"What's he doing?" I asked.

"That's an electric cart used to load and unload stuff for the boats," Zach answered. "Let's go. If Hackney is on the boat, seeing him again is just going to upset you."

"I'm already upset. And I'm afraid Jessie is with him. I can't be sure, but it may have been her on deck a minute ago being jerked along."

"Tami, please. I thought you were going to forget about that for a couple of—" Zach stopped when I cut my eyes sharply toward him.

The man in the golf cart reached the boat. Zach might want to leave, but I wasn't budging. It was getting darker by the moment. I could see shadowy figures moving around on deck. The boat was moored in such as way that people getting on and off were shielded from our line of sight. In a moment the cart made its way down the dock. When it passed under a security light, I could see two people sitting in the front. One of them was Hackney. Two more people were sitting in the cargo area facing in the opposite direction. There was another security light where Zach and I were standing. I backed into the shadows as the cart reached an intersection on the dock and turned away from us toward the main exit for the marina. When it did so, I got a clearer view of the two people in the rear of the vehicle.

One of them was Jessie.

I pulled on the back of Zach's shirt and drew him closer to me.

"Did you see the girl in the back of the cart?" I whispered. "It was Jessie."

The cart continued to move down the dock.

"Are you sure?" Zach asked. "All I saw was a smaller person."

"Yes."

Zach turned toward me. "What do you want to do?"

"Contact the police so they can pick her up."

The cart reached the marina exit and the four people got out. It was too dark to see much else. Zach had his cell phone in his hand. He punched in a few numbers and handed it to me.

Zach walked around to the front of the car and stepped close to the bushes. He pushed them aside with his hands and moved forward.

Then he was gone.

I couldn't believe he'd passed through the bushes. I strained my eyes, trying to see him as he returned. But he didn't. I glanced at the clock in the dashboard of the car. I hadn't checked the time when he left, but it already seemed like minutes although I knew it was prob-ably only seconds.

My mind frantically ran through my options. I could get out of the car and follow Zach or wait for him to return or for Detective Houghton to call. I quickly dismissed the idea of exiting the car. Instead, I pushed the button that locked the doors and slipped over the console into the driver's seat. A quick honk of the horn would not be an unusual occurrence this close to the street but would summon Zach. The key was in the ignition. I started the car and backed a few feet down the driveway so I would be closer to the street. I pressed the button for the horn and quickly released it. Even the short burst of sound seemed deafening in the quiet of the night. I nervously stared at the spot in the bushes where I last saw Zach. Nothing moved.

Panic set in.

I backed farther down the driveway until I had a clear view of the church. The car we'd been following was parked close to the front door, but the church remained dark. I didn't see anyone moving about. I frantically glanced over at Sister Dabney's house. There was a light on toward the rear of the house in the area of the kitchen. I took my cell phone from my purse and, my index finger shaking, entered her number. The phone rang several times, but knowing she rarely answered on the first few rings, I let it continue. After at least ten rings, I ended the call and slammed the phone down on the seat. If she was rocking in one of her chairs, Sister Dabney had picked a bad time to ignore the phone.

I backed the car into the street so it faced in the direction of the church. Rolling down the window, I stuck out my head, preparing to yell Zach's name. But at that moment, I saw the flicker of a flashlight in the open area in front of the church. Voices, all male, were speaking, but I couldn't make out the words. Then I heard a female voice cry out before being abruptly cut off.

It had to be Jessie.

Car doors slammed, and the engine in the dark car roared to life. The driver backed rapidly down the church driveway toward the street. When the car reached the curb, I turned on the car's bright lights. The driver of the dark car turned toward me. I didn't recognize him, but I saw Clay Hackney in the backseat behind him. The driver put his hand up to shield his eyes. I stomped on the accelerator. The car shot forward. Holding my arms straight out to brace myself, I slammed into the dark sedan, hitting it squarely between the driver's side and rear doors. There was a crash of glass and metal. The air bag in Zach's car inflated, momentarily blinding me. Dazed, I put my hands to my head to make sure I wasn't bleeding.

There was a loud bang near my left ear. It was Zach, hitting the window with his fist. He tried to open the door, but it was locked shut. I groggily pushed back the lock with my finger, and he jerked open the door.

"Get out!" he yelled.

He half dragged, half carried me out of the car. When I got a view of the other car, I was amazed at the damage I'd caused. The driver was slumped over the steering wheel. I couldn't see into the backseat.

"The other side," I started.

Zach had his cell phone next to his ear. "Yes, there's an automobile accident with injuries at the Southside Church on Gillespie Street. I'm the one who reported the burglary a couple of minutes ago."

Zach pulled me away from the wreck. The sound of the impact had attracted the attention of people living in houses along the street. Several of them could be seen standing on their front porches.

"What about Jessie?" I managed. "She's still in that car. And Hackney can get out the other side and escape."

"It's too dangerous. You're not going back."

Within seconds, the sound of sirens and sight of flashing lights could be heard and seen on Gillespie Street. As soon as the first patrol car arrived on the scene, Zach left me sitting on the ground and ran over to it. Another police car arrived, followed immediately by a fire truck. I kept watching the dark car, but nobody got out.

Police officers approached the sedan from both sides. In less than a minute, an officer appeared holding the arm of a man we'd seen at the docks. He was quickly followed by a fireman carrying a much smaller figure. It was Jessie.

I got to my feet as quickly as I could and ran toward her.

"Tami!" Zach called out, but I didn't stop.

The fireman with Jessie looked up as I approached.

"Is she all right?" I asked frantically.

Jessie's body hung limp in the fireman's arms. He laid her on the ground. Her eyes were closed.

"She's been hit in the head, probably knocked her unconscious. An ambulance is on the way."

I stepped closer. Jessie groaned slightly. It was one of the most beautiful sounds I'd ever heard.

While I was kneeling beside Jessie, an officer approached with Clay Hackney beside him. Hackney had a gash on the right side of his forehead.

"You!" he said when he saw me. His eyes flashed with rage. "You're going to be sorry you did this. By the time I'm finished with you—"

"Come on," the officer interrupted him. "Let's get that cut tended."

I put my hand on Jessie's cheek. She blinked open her eyes and moaned.

"In . . . ," she started, then stopped.

"Don't try to talk," I said. "An ambulance is on the way."

"The church," she muttered.

"I know," I said, leaning closer to her. "Sister Dabney found the papers you left in the church. They are in a safe place."

Jessie shook her head and moaned again. An ambulance arrived and the EMTs examined Jessie. The firemen were busy freeing the driver of the sedan from the car. Still groggy, Jessie was placed on a stretcher and taken from the scene. I turned around and saw Zach talking to one of the police officers. I joined him.

"Can you positively identify the men who entered the church?" the officer asked him.

"Yes, every one of them went inside. They took the girl with them."

I glanced back at Sister Dabney's house. The light in the kitchen was on, but there was no sign of the woman preacher.

"I want to go inside the church," I said to Zach.

"Why?" he asked. "All the men came out with Jessie."

"Please," I said.

"Okay."

We walked up the gravel drive to the darkened building. The front door was still ajar. I pushed it open and took a couple of steps into the darkness before tripping over an object in the aisle. I screamed as I fell. Before I could get oriented, Zach flipped on the lights. I blinked my eyes and saw Sister Dabney stretched out on the floor.

"Get an EMT!" I yelled.

Zach bolted out the door.

24

A FEMALE EMT WAS THE FIRST PERSON TO ARRIVE. SHE KNELT beside Sister Dabney, who was lying on her stomach, her face against the carpet. The EMT checked Sister Dabney's vital signs, then glanced up at me.

"Do you know what happened?"

"No. The men who kidnapped the teenage girl came in here. Ms. Dabney must have already been inside."

"Do you know her?"

"She's the pastor of the church. Her name is Rachel Ramona Dabney."

"Is she married?"

"No, divorced."

"Next of kin?"

"What do you mean?" I asked in alarm. "Is she going to be okay?"

A second medical worker, a young man in his twenties, burst into the room. I sat in numbed silence as the two of them examined Sister Dabney.

"Blunt trauma to the head," the woman said, pointing to a place on the side of Sister Dabney's skull, where I could see a trickle of blood oozing down to the floor.

It didn't look serious enough to be fatal. Two police officers arrived and immediately ushered me out of the church.

"Is she alive?" I asked one of the officers.

"Stay outside, please," the officer said, holding up his hand. "We're going to cordon this off as a crime scene."

I met Zach coming up the driveway.

"How is she?" Zach asked.

"I think she's dead," I replied, not believing the words coming from my mouth. "Something about blunt trauma to the head."

"Are you sure?"

"No."

"Two of the men with Hackney had guns," Zach said. "I saw a detective put them in clear plastic bags."

"But there wasn't a gunshot."

"They could have used a gun to hit her."

Suddenly feeling unsteady on my feet, I reached out to Zach, who held me up.

"You need to go to the hospital and get checked out," Zach said. "You rammed the car very hard."

I glanced over my shoulder at the church. "I can't leave her."

"Come on. That's where they'll bring her, too."

Zach guided me down the driveway to a medical worker who shone a light in my eyes and asked some questions.

"I don't see a need for emergency medical transport," he said, "but you should go to the ER to be sure."

"How can we get there? I wrecked your car," I said to Zach.

"I know, but I called Julie. She's on her way."

A minute later, Julie came running up to us. There were multiple cars with flashing blue and red lights on the street.

"What happened?" she asked anxiously.

"I'll tell you while we take Tami to the hospital," Zach answered.

They put me in the backseat of Julie's car. As Julie sped away Zach started talking to her. I suddenly felt very sleepy.

"Are you okay?" Julie asked, looking at me in the rearview mirror.

"I'm tired. All I want to do is sleep."

"Did she hit her head?" Julie asked Zach with alarm in her voice.

"Just my face," I replied groggily.

The rest of the trip to the hospital was a blur. As I was rolled into the ER in a wheelchair, the bright lights revived me slightly.

"I think she may be in shock," Zach told a nurse who placed a blood-pressure cuff on my left arm.

The nurse took me into an examining room and helped me onto a bed.

"The doctor will be in to see you in a few minutes."

"Where are Jessie and Sister Dabney?" I asked Zach when the nurse left. "Have they gotten here yet?"

"Stay with her while I check," Zach said to Julie.

Julie came close to the bed and gently took my hand.

"Are you hurting anywhere?" she asked.

"I'm stiff," I answered, moving my head from side to side. "It was such a strange feeling in your car. All I wanted to do was close my eyes."

"You may have had a concussion."

"But I got out of the car and walked up to the church."

"Do you always have to argue with me?" Julie sighed. "Maybe it was a light concussion, and it took a few minutes for the impact to penetrate your thick skull."

I managed a weak smile. An older doctor entered the examination area. He repeated some of the same tests I'd already had along with a few more and asked me simple questions, such as my name, address, phone number, and birthday.

"Ms. Taylor, I think you're going to be fine," he said, removing the stethoscope from his ears. "You've been through a very stressful situation. I recommend you get some rest and follow up with your regular doctor if you feel you should."

"What about the other people who were injured?" I asked. "Jessie

Whitewater, a teenage girl, and Ramona Dabney, a woman in her late sixties."

"The girl has already been taken to a room," the doctor said. "I'm not sure about the other woman. A nurse will be in to help you check out."

The doctor left.

"I wish he'd asked you my birthday," Julie said. "That would have been a hard question."

"April 27."

Julie nodded. "Correct. I pronounce you healed."

Zach returned to the examination room.

"Tami is fine," Julie said to him. "The doctor said her system was trying to shut down because of an overload of stimuli, kind of like a computer that crashes."

"That's not what he—," I started, but the look on Zach's face stopped me. "What is it?"

"Sister Dabney is gone," he said soberly. "They weren't able to revive her at the church."

"How? What?" I asked, struggling to sit up and not able to form a complete sentence.

"No one knows except Hackney, his men, and Jessie," Zach replied. "I'm sure they won't be talking, so we'll have to wait until we can be with Jessie."

I collapsed back on the bed and closed my eyes. When I did, I instantly saw Sister Dabney sitting in the blue rocking chair on her porch in the crisp coolness of a bright summer morning, looking at me as only she could—with a gaze that saw to the depths of my soul. No room in my heart was hidden from her view. But there wasn't any condemnation in her countenance. Only peace. Peace imbued with a gentle love.

Sister Dabney was free of the burdens she'd carried. The scars of rejection, the disappointments of life, the betrayals by those she trusted. All of it gone, washed away in a glorious moment of unlimited grace. A pair of tears rolled out of my eyes and down the sides of my face. I felt a hand on my shoulder. I opened my eyes. Zach was standing beside me.

"She's okay," I said as the tears flowed freely. "She's more than okay."

When I awoke in the morning, I was stiff but otherwise fine. I lay in bed for a few minutes. It would take weeks, not hours, to process everything that had happened the previous night. Going upstairs to the kitchen, I called home so I could talk to Daddy and Mama before he left for work. Daddy answered.

"Good morning, Tammy Lynn," he said when he realized I was on the other end of the line. "Touch the top of your head where I like to kiss you."

Hearing my father's kind voice released another wave of emotion. The next few minutes were a disjointed mess as I tried to tell Daddy and Mama what had happened. It took three attempts to convince Mama that I wasn't seriously injured.

"Please let Mr. Callahan know about Sister Dabney," I said. "He's known her since he was a young man."

"I'll go by to see him today," Daddy said.

Mama ended the call with a prayer that made more tears flow.

"We love you," she said.

After eating some fruit for breakfast, I drove to the hospital to check on Jessie and Mrs. Fairmont.

"What's the room number for Jessie Whitewater?" I asked the lady at the information desk.

The woman typed the name into her computer and examined the screen.

"How do you spell that?" she asked.

I spelled the name and waited.

"I don't find a record of her admission," she said.

I leaned forward over the desk. "She was admitted last night through the ER via ambulance from Gillespie Street."

The woman looked up at me then reached under her desk and pulled out the morning paper.

"Did it have to do with this?"

She put the newspaper on the counter. On the front page was an article with the headline "Woman Killed by Intruders at Church." A photo of Sister Dabney was positioned beside a picture of the church. Tiny photos of Clay Hackney and me were off to one side. My picture was the one taken the previous summer by the public relations firm that worked for Braddock, Appleby, and Carpenter. My name appeared in the first paragraph as the driver of a car that rammed the vehicle carrying Hackney, two other men, and a young woman named Jessie Beanfield.

"Jessie Beanfield?" I said out loud.

The woman at the information desk typed in the name.

"She's in room 3487."

I returned the newspaper to the woman and took the elevator to the third floor. Jessie's room was on the left toward the end of the hall. The door was closed. I knocked. There wasn't an answer. I peeked inside.

Jessie was lying in bed with an IV in her arm and her eyes closed. I stepped closer and looked at her wristband. I could clearly see the name, Jessie Beanfield, with the date of admission beneath it.

"Jessie Beanfield," I repeated softly.

Jessie's eyes fluttered open. She touched her face with her free hand.

"They put me in a terrible place—," she started.

"That you aren't going back to."

I leaned over and kissed her cheek as if she were one of the twins. Jessie's eyes suddenly widened in fear.

"Sister Dabney," she said. "The man in the blue shirt hit her in the head with his gun."

I pressed my lips together for a moment to prepare myself.

"She's dead."

Jessie shut her eyes. "She told them I belonged to God, and they couldn't take me."

"I think she was right."

Jessie opened her eyes. "I remember hearing your voice before I got in the ambulance. How did you find me?"

An aide arrived with Jessie's breakfast. While she ate, I told her what we'd done. She listened soberly.

"What's going to happen to me?" she asked when I finished.

"To answer that, I need the truth."

Over the next few minutes, I leaned that she was fifteen years old and didn't have any close relatives. She also told me about a metal box at the vacant lot where she'd stayed that contained more of the bearer bonds.

"How many of the certificates are there?" I asked.

"About nine or ten. What are they?"

"Bearer bonds issued by the German government. They're legal, but occasionally used by criminals to transfer money so it can't be traced. I need to get them and turn them over to the police."

Jessie seemed more interested in what would happen to the charges against her.

"It will be sent to juvenile court and handled easily," I answered. "How did you come up with the new name?"

"Whitewater sounded so much better than Beanfield. My father is dead, and I didn't want Clay to find me or have to go back to live with my stepmother."

"You'll have to go back to Jessie Beanfield now."

"Mrs. Fairmont told me your real name is Tammy Lynn, and you changed it when you came to Savannah."

"That's true, but it's different with last names."

"Do you think I can live with you and Mrs. Fairmont? I don't want to go back to my stepmother."

I couldn't deny the pleading look in Jessie's eyes.

"I'll work on it if Mrs. Fairmont wants you to stay with us as soon as she gets out of the hospital."

"She's in the hospital?" Jessie asked, sitting up straighter in the bed. "Can I see her?"

"I'll check with one of the nurses."

Ten minutes later, Jessie was pushing her IV pole quickly down the hall toward the elevator.

"Slow down," I said. "The wheels on your IV pole aren't built for racing."

We reached Mrs. Fairmont's room. I let Jessie go in first, then followed close enough to see the reaction. The elderly woman was sipping coffee. When she saw Jessie, she almost dropped the cup. Jessie rushed toward the bed and they hugged. Jessie sat on the edge of the bed and held Mrs. Fairmont's hand while I told the older woman about Sister Dabney. To Mrs. Fairmont, who had lost many friends, death was less a stranger. She turned to Jessie.

"She loved you, Jessie. And there's no greater love than sacrificing your life for someone else."

Jessie nodded.

Mrs. Fairmont continued, "I'll see her before you do and tell her thank you."

When it was time for me to leave, I prepared to return Jessie to her room.

"Please let me stay," she begged.

"I'll take responsibility for her," Mrs. Fairmont said.

I hesitated.

"I'll talk to the nurse on duty," Mrs. Fairmont said. "Maybe Jessie can stay until it's time for the doctor to check on her."

When I left Jessie was sitting in a chair beside the bed reading Mrs. Fairmont's stack of get-well cards to her.

THERE WAS A MAELSTROM OF ACTIVITY AT THE OFFICE. TWO TRUCKS from TV stations were parked outside. I remained in the car and called inside on my cell phone. Shannon answered.

"Where are you?" she asked.

"In the car in the parking lot."

"This place is swarming with reporters, and the phone's been ringing off the hook."

"Are Maggie and Julie there?"

"Yes, they're in Maggie's office." Shannon paused. "Is it true what I read in the paper about the Dabney woman?"

"Yes. She was trying to protect Jessie."

"I called my husband last night," Shannon said, speaking slowly. "We talked on the phone for a couple of hours. I'm sorry I reacted so badly to Ms. Dabney—"

"She was used to people reacting to her that way," I said. "The important thing is that whatever she told you is helping you now."

"I think it will. Or at least it's a start. Hold on. I'll connect you with Maggie."

"I'm here with Julie and have you on speaker," Maggie said. "Are you okay? Where are you?"

"Stiff and sore but okay otherwise. I'm in the parking lot, but I'm not sure if I should get out of the car—"

"Tami, you're a folk hero for ramming the bad guy's car," Julie cut in. "I told one of the reporters you learned to drive hauling moonshine in the mountains. Many a night you had to run the revenuers off the road to deliver a shipment."

"No, you didn't."

"But I thought it."

"What should I say to the reporters?"

"How much do you want to say?" Maggie asked.

"As little as possible. If they ask me about Sister Dabney, I'm going to cry."

"Then tell them you can't comment on what took place because it's part of an ongoing criminal investigation."

I got out of the car. The reporters were camped out in the reception area, making it look very small. I had the unusual experience of being instantly recognized by strangers.

"Let's take it outside," one of the lead reporters said.

"I'm going to be praying on the inside," I whispered to Maggie as we flowed into the parking lot.

I used Maggie's suggested response to the first question, but when a female reporter asked me about Jessie, I mentioned how people in Savannah like Julie and Mrs. Fairmont had reached out to help her, then made it clear that Jan Crittenden, even though she was a prosecutor, had gone beyond the call of duty to find a positive way to deal with a tough situation. When Sister Dabney's name came up, I was able to keep my emotions in check and used the time to deliver a short eulogy based on Mrs. Fairmont's reference to love and sacrifice at the hospital. Sister Dabney might not have a fancy funeral, but people on the evening news would know she'd lived life doing her best to help those who needed it the most. After the cameras were turned off and the newspaper reporters had asked their final questions, Maggie and Julie came over to me.

"That was beautiful," Julie said without a hint of sarcasm in her voice. "You shouldn't have spouted those nice things about me, but Sister Dabney deserved everything good you said about her."

"You couldn't have been more articulate," Maggie added. "I think God answered your prayer."

"More than one," I replied. "And many more than I deserve."

25

It snowed every ten years or so at Christmastime in Powell Station. On December 24, I awoke to fat flakes drifting down from a gray morning sky. I slipped out of bed and, standing at the bedroom window, watched the soft whiteness cover every imperfection in sight. I pressed my hand to the cold windowpane. The twins were still asleep. Once awake, they would end any chance to enjoy the snowy scene in peace.

Zach was sleeping on the daybed in the downstairs sewing room. Two days earlier, we'd been holding hands on a sunny beach in Southern California. I'd loved California and, a few hours after getting off the plane, stopped worrying that the ground beneath my feet was about to break off and fall into the ocean.

Halfway through a weeklong visit with Zach's family, I overheard his mother tell his sister that she thought I was the nicest girl he'd ever brought home. Later, I asked Zach how many girls had preceded me. He smiled and told me he couldn't remember because none of them counted.

The world of the Mays family was very different from Powell Station, but a common faith is the strongest bridge across any divide. And the gospel has the power to unite people from all points of the compass, even a girl from the mountains of Georgia with a family in a suburb of Los Angeles. One evening while sitting beneath a trellis covered in brilliant bougainvillea blossoms, Zach's family enjoyed a time of fellowship as rich as any I'd experienced with my own family. From that point forward, I felt accepted, not just out of politeness, but with genuine affection.

I gently shook Ellie's shoulder then whispered in her ear, "It's snowing."

She groggily opened her eyes and looked past my head.

"Snow!" she cried out.

"Ugh," Emma grunted from her place on the bottom bunk.

I knelt down beside Emma's head. "There are already a couple of inches of snow on the ground."

Emma propped up on one elbow as Ellie hurtled from the top bunk to the floor with a thump and raced over to the window. In a few seconds Emma joined her.

"I want to tell Zach," Ellie said, looking over her shoulder at me.

"Not in your pajamas. Get dressed first."

In a flash, Ellie was off to the bathroom. Emma and I stayed behind. She continued to stare out the window.

"Are you going to play in the snow?" I asked.

"Yes," she answered, "but not like we used to. The last time it snowed Ellie and I spent more time going on a long walk than we did making a snowman."

Ellie returned.

"Is that dress on backward?" I asked.

Ellie quickly inspected herself.

"No."

"I didn't think so," I answered.

"That's mean. While you're up here being lazy, Zach and I are going to be out in the snow."

Ellie left, and I heard her footsteps going down the stairs. The sewing room was across from my parents' bedroom.

"I'm going to wake up Kyle and Bobby," Emma said.

I took my time getting ready. Snow created a general excuse from most work around the house; however, the chickens didn't stop laying eggs because of a change in the weather. When I went downstairs to the kitchen, Mama was fixing the morning pot of coffee.

"Add a little extra for me," I said.

"You've started drinking coffee?" she asked in surprise.

"With almost as much cream as coffee, but it's something Zach and I like to do. There's a coffee shop in Savannah that's a great place to talk. I know drinking coffee together has been something you and Daddy have enjoyed."

"Your daddy is under the covers. It will take an extra-rich cup of coffee to get him out of bed."

I put on an old coat, wrapped a scarf around my neck, and slipped on some work gloves. I didn't look very glamorous, but it was perfect for visiting a chicken coop on a snowy morning. I grabbed the pail we used to gather the eggs. When I stepped outside, I could hear Zach and Ellie yelling at each other around the corner of the house. I yawned. The flight from the West Coast the previous day had left me feeling a little disoriented. It was my first experience with jet lag.

I walked across the thin blanket of snow, regretting that I had to mar its perfect beauty with my footsteps. I reached the henhouse. Chester, the rooster, didn't come out of the house for his normal showy bluster of bravado. I found him inside the coop, scratching around the floor in the far corner of the little building. He ignored me. The hens loudly protested my invasion of their privacy, but once the eggs were gone they quickly settled down.

On my way back to the kitchen, I took a detour around the corner of the house. Zach and Ellie were attempting to have a snowball fight. The new snow was dry and fell apart when they tried to pack it into balls. The clumps they managed to press together disintegrated into powder a few feet after being thrown. Zach looked at me with a big smile.

"Good morning!" he called out. "Doesn't this remind you of Southern California?"

"Only the inside of your snow globe."

Zach had shown me a snow globe he'd received as a Christmas present when he was a little boy. His mother brought it out every year during the holidays so he could shake it, creating a pretend blizzard.

Ellie used my arrival to launch a surprise attack. Grabbing a handful of snow, she ran up behind Zach and dumped it down the back of his jacket. Zach turned, chased her across the yard, and took his revenge. I returned to the kitchen to clean the eggs.

Mama was placing strips of bacon in a large skillet. I stood at the sink and washed the eggs in vinegar.

"Let's have scrambled eggs," Mama said. "Your daddy thinks you make them better than anyone."

I took more eggs from the refrigerator and broke them into a metal bowl.

"How is Mrs. Fairmont spending the holidays?" Mama asked.

"Making it as special for Jessie as she can."

"How is she doing in school?"

"She had a good first semester at school, especially in English. She's doing great at the house, too. I even think Mrs. Bartlett likes her."

"And Jessie's stepmother?"

"Can't be found. She moved soon after Jessie ran away, and there aren't any close relatives interested in seeking custody. As part of Jessie's twelve months' probation, the juvenile court judge ordered her to stay with Mrs. Fairmont. I can't imagine anyone happier with her punishment. By the time it ends next year, Jessie will be starting her senior year in high school."

"What about Vince?"

"He's with his family in Charleston. Zach and I talked to him before the trip to California. I know he's disappointed, but I believe the three of us can be friends."

"Let Zach take the lead in that."

"Yes, ma'am."

"And pray that Vince will meet the person who's right for him."

Daddy came into the kitchen and raised his eyebrows when he saw me with a cup of coffee in my hand.

"It's Zach's fault," I said. "He's driven me to drink."

"That's one thing he left out when we talked last night."

"You spent time together after I went to bed?"

"Yes," Daddy replied. "We stayed in the front room for a while. He wasn't sleepy."

The eggs reached the point of fluffy perfection. Mama sent Bobby outside to retrieve Zach and Ellie. When they entered, Ellie's cheeks were rosy bright.

"I think it's getting colder," Zach said, slapping the snow from his gloves into the utility sink near the rear door.

"That's what the weather folks predicted," Mama said as she placed the last strip of cooked bacon on a platter.

THE SNOW ON THE GROUND DIDN'T CHILL OUR APPETITES. AFTER Daddy prayed a blessing, there wasn't much talking for a few minutes. Instead of biscuits, Mama had toasted slices of homemade bread and placed jars of jelly made the previous summer in the center of the table. Zach and I sat across from each other. He focused on the food; I was acutely aware of his every movement.

"What happened with the case that got you on TV?" Kyle asked. "I found the news report on the Internet and showed it to some of the guys in my dorm."

"It's scheduled for trial early next year unless the defendants plead guilty."

"Will you be a witness?" Emma asked Zach.

"Maybe."

Ellie turned to me. "You could explain how you solved the secret code. After you showed us how it worked, Emma and I practiced using it. No one else in our Sunday school class has figured it out."

"Please pass me the butter and stop passing notes in Sunday school," Mama said.

After breakfast the entire family went outside. The snow continued to fall, but it resisted all efforts to form balls. Our attempt at a snowman resembled a mound, not a man. Later, we went inside, and Mama fixed hot chocolate. While I beat the whipped cream, Zach sat beside me on one of the kitchen stools.

After we finished drinking our chocolate, Zach asked me, "Would you like to go for a walk?"

"May we go?" the twins asked in unison.

"Not this one," Mama said. "Zach and Tammy Lynn need times together when you're not along to chaperone."

"I'll take both of you on a walk later today," Zach promised.

I bundled up in a warm coat and wrapped a scarf around my neck.

"Where should we go?" Zach asked when we stepped outside. "I don't want to get lost in the snow."

"Putnam's Pond."

"The place where I was attacked by the crazed catfish?"

"Only because you didn't know how to pick one up."

The well-worn path that linked our house to the pond was hidden by snow. Zach took my hand in his as we walked beneath the trees.

"I liked one part of our walks on the beach much better," I said, slightly squeezing Zach's hand. "We weren't wearing thick gloves."

We came out of the trees. The falling snowflakes didn't disturb the water on the pond, which was mirror-still. We stood in silence to admire the beauty.

"Do you want to walk around the pond?" I asked.

"Sure."

We passed the spot where Zach was stung by the catfish and the place where the twins liked to catch butterflies. On the far side of the water, I showed Zach an old, twisted tree that looked like it was kneeling.

"This is one of the places where I'd sit and daydream when I was a little girl," I said, brushing the snow from the rough bark.

"What would you daydream about?"

"Lots of things."

Zach suddenly swept me off my feet and set me down on the wide limb.

"Whew," I said. "That's easier than scrambling up here."

"Are you cold?"

"Not really."

"Would you take off your gloves so we can hold hands for a minute?"

"Just like a good lawyer, you set me up with a question." I laughed. "But only for a minute. It's cold."

We took off our gloves. Zach took my hands in his and looked directly in my eyes.

"Satisfied?" I asked.

"Not yet."

Zach released my hands. Reaching into his pocket, he took out a tiny box. I gasped. Opening the box, he took out a diamond ring that would have received Mrs. Fairmont's approval.

"I love you," he said, looking up into my face. "Will you marry me?"

"Daddy—"

"Gave his approval and blessing last night," Zach said. "Your mother, too. We didn't stay up late last night talking about the weather."

I smiled, hoping my face revealed the joy in my heart.

"Yes, I'll marry you," I said, extending my hand so he could slip the ring on my finger. "And I promise to love you always."

The cool metal met my finger and instantly warmed. I brought it closer so I could admire the design.

"It's simple, but complicated," I said, admiring the intricate work in the gold.

"Like its owner."

Sliding down from the limb, I threw my arms about Zach's neck and buried my face in his shoulder. He wrapped his arms around me and held me tight as the falling snow enveloped us with heaven's embrace.

It was a hug that never had to end.

Epilogue

CHESTER LIVED IN SYNC WITH GOD'S CLOCK. THE SUN MIGHT BE an idea beneath the horizon; the earth shrouded in the last gray of night; but the rooster knew what was coming. A new day was at hand, one worthy of a herald. He opened his yellow beak and crowed.

Ellie, Emma, and I had talked late into the night as we enjoyed our final opportunity to savor the unique relationship reserved for unmarried sisters. We shared giggles, sweet words, and invisible tears after the lights were turned out. After the twins finally went to sleep, I slipped out of bed and lightly touched each girl's dark hair and silently blessed them. I prayed that Emma and Ellie would meet the man God was preparing for each of them.

The rooster's scratchy reveille penetrated the bedroom a second time. Knowing what the day held for me it was impossible to go back to sleep. I flipped onto my back, and with a happy sigh, enjoyed one of the many pleasant thoughts at my disposal.

By evening, my name would change more dramatically and permanently than when I transformed myself from Tammy Lynn to Tami. My family and the State of Georgia would soon know me as Tammy Taylor Mays. Of course, I could still shorten the Tammy to Tami.

I slipped out of bed and threw on one of the plain dresses I wore around the farm. I tiptoed barefooted down the stairs. The door to

379

Daddy and Mama's bedroom was closed. The sewing room where Zach stayed when he came for his first visit was also empty. He and his family were staying with Oscar Callahan. I wondered if Zach was still asleep. The thought that for the rest of my life I would know whether Zach was awake or asleep by turning over in bed to check sent a shiver down my back.

I slipped on a pair of old sandals and grabbed the blue bucket we used to gather eggs. Late April in the mountains can be brisk, but I liked the feel of the cool, wet grass on my bare toes. Our two dogs heard the back door slam shut and ambled around the corner of the house. They followed at my heels as I walked toward the chicken pen. Chester scratched vigorously in the dirt for a few seconds then stopped to crow. When I opened the wire door to the pen, he squawked in warning but didn't charge me.

The hens clucked in protest when I stooped to enter the coop. Lady Macbeth made the loudest racket but had the least to fear. Her egg production had been steadily dropping, so Daddy was allowing her to sit on four eggs and hatch her replacement. Two days earlier, the chicks had broken free from their shells. The twins and I watched the last one poke its beak through a tiny hole and work its way to freedom. In the not too distant future I hoped to have a baby of my own.

I collected eggs from the other hens. Returning to the house, I could see Mama standing at the sink fixing the morning pot of coffee. Drinking coffee together had been part of my parent's morning routine as long as I could remember. I was glad Zach and I had gotten a head start in the same direction.

"Good morning," I said when I entered the kitchen. "Lady Macbeth is taking good care of her chicks."

"Are you going to miss the chickens?" Mama asked.

"Yes." I joined her at the kitchen sink and gave her a quick hug. "But if I start listing all the people, animals, places, and things I'm going to miss, it will take me all day and make me depressed."

Mama smiled. "I don't think it's going to be too hard enjoying the present and looking forward to the future. Soon, you and Zach will have a collection of new happiness."

"No regrets about him?"

Mama kissed me on the cheek. "None. We wouldn't pretend to support something we didn't believe in."

The coffee pot beeped.

"How much coffee do you want with your cream and sugar?" Mama asked.

"Let me do it."

Daddy entered the room and kissed me on the usual spot on top of my head. Despite Mama's words about the present and future, his simple gesture of past love overwhelmed me. Tears suddenly stung my eyes.

"What did I do wrong?" he asked.

Mama shooed him toward his seat at the kitchen table.

"Nothing," she said, shaking her head. "It's one of the many things you do right."

I wiped my eyes and helped Mama cook breakfast. Forty-five minutes later the kitchen was alive with conversation as Kyle, Bobby, Ellie, Emma, Daddy, Mama, and I gathered around the long white table and took our customary seats.

"I want to pray," Bobby piped up before we bowed our heads.

"All right," Daddy replied.

I saw Ellie and Emma exchange a questioning look. Daddy almost always prayed before meals. We held hands and closed our eyes. Bobby began to pray. He didn't stop at thanking the Lord for our meal but also prayed a blessing over all that was going to happen later in the day. At one point I peeked to see if he was reading from a sheet of paper, but his eyes were squeezed shut.

"Amen," he said.

"That was a fine prayer, Bobby," Daddy said.

"But it won't keep these biscuits hot," Kyle said, reaching for a crusty brown one on top of the pile.

I glanced at Bobby, my eyes shining with thanks. He was going to sing an original song at the wedding. I'd not heard it, but Mama claimed it was the best thing he'd ever written.

Kyle held a biscuit in the air like a glass of champagne.

"May your house be filled with the smell of fresh biscuits as you're surrounded by a family that loves one another as much as we love you."

"Thanks." I smiled.

"It's a biscuit toast," Ellie blurted out, then laughed at the odd combination of words.

After clearing the table and cleaning the dishes, Mama and I went into the sewing room for a last check of my wedding gown.

"I ate too much breakfast," I said as I prepared to step into the long, white dress. "What if it's too tight?"

"Then you won't eat lunch."

Mama zipped up the gown as I held in my stomach.

"That's not necessary, Tammy Lynn."

I exhaled. The dress was snug but in a perfect way. I looked at myself in the long mirror on the wall near the sewing machine. I'd bought the dress in Savannah. Julie went with me to the bridal shop and peppered the lady who assisted me with suggestions about style, material, and especially how much skin to expose. In the end, I didn't compromise on modesty, and Julie was forced to admit that the dress, with its graceful drape from my shoulders, had a classic look. Mama straightened the sleeves that rustled slightly under the touch of her fingers.

"I fixed the left sleeve before I went to bed last night," she said.

"It's fine," I replied, bending my arm slightly. "But is it too showy for our church?"

"It's too late to worry about that," Mama answered confidently.

"And I don't think you should. The beauty of the bride is one of the great images of Scripture."

"What time do you think I should wash my hair?" I asked, running my fingers through my long, dark locks.

"Not till you finish your chores."

"Chores?"

"Nothing around here, but do you need to go to the church to make sure everything is ready?"

"Only if you think I should. Hasn't Mrs. Holcomb planned a couple of hundred weddings?"

"At least."

"I don't want to go there until it's time to get ready. Everything looked fine at the rehearsal last night."

The wedding rehearsal had caused goose bumps to involuntarily prick my flesh several times. Zach saw them on my arm at one point and teased me that I had skin like a basketball. I challenged him to a game of one on one upon our return to Savannah.

"You're calmer about it than I am," Mama answered, rubbing her forehead. "The flowers should be there by ten this morning, but I want to make sure the different arrangements are put in the right spots."

"Then you should go to the church. I'm going to stay here."

"And spend some time alone?"

"Yes, ma'am. At the pond."

Mama smiled and nodded. "I can't think of a better chore."

Upstairs, the twins were straightening up the bedroom we'd shared since they'd slept in matching cribs.

"Are you going to help us?" Emma asked me when I entered.

"No," Ellie quickly cut in. "Tammy Lynn can't spend her morning getting your dirty socks out from underneath the bed. She has to spend the day thinking about Zach and God, but not necessarily in that order. God always comes first."

Emma dropped to the floor and scooted under the edge of the

lower bunk bed. In a few seconds, she threw out three dingy, white socks.

"These are your, Ellie," she said from her position on the floor. "You should be thinking about socks and God, in that order."

"I'm going to walk over to Putnam's Pond," I said.

"Can we go with you?" Ellie asked excitedly.

Emma scooted out from beneath the bed and sat up on the floor.

"No, because she has to think about Zach and God."

"Emma's right," I said. "I want some time alone."

Ellie shook her head. "Alone for the last time. Can you imagine being around the same person all day, every day?"

Emma threw one of the dirty socks at Ellie's head. "I know exactly what it's like."

Zach had been with me the last time I'd visited the pond. We'd gone during a gentle snowfall and admired the pure splendor of the white landscape. Today, the trees displayed a different beauty, the promise of new life revealed in tender, pale green leaves. I walked slowly and came out of the woods at the edge of the pond. At first sight, the water appeared still, but as I stepped closer I could see tiny lines left by long legged water striders skating across the surface.

I went around the pond to the twisted kneeling tree, the place of my childhood daydreams. It was the place where Zach fulfilled one of those dreams when he gave me the sparkling diamond ring that still surprised me when I saw it on my finger. Without Zach to sweep me into the crook of the tree in his strong arms I scrambled up on my own. My feet dangled a yard above the ground. I rested my hands against the solid trunk and closed my eyes. I breathed in the clean mountain air.

After a few moments of silence, a Bible passage long ago committed to memory rose to the surface of my mind as gently as a fish swimming to the top of the nearby pond.

But from the beginning of the creation, God made them male and female. For this reason a man shall leave his father and mother and be joined to his wife, and the two shall become one flesh, so then they are no longer two, but one flesh.

I let the meaning of the scriptures sink in. Zach and I would be one. Not because a preacher said so, or the words printed on a marriage license, or even the solemn vows we made to each other. We would be one because God decreed it. What stronger bond of unity could there be?

Before I could finish savoring the impact of this truth, another passage scrolled across my mind's eye.

Though I speak with the tongues of men and of angels, but have not love, I have become a sounding brass or a clanging cymbal. And though I have the gift of prophecy, and understand all mysteries and all knowledge, and though I have all faith, so that I could remove mountains, but have not love, I am nothing. And though I bestow all my goods to feed the poor, and though I give my body to be burned, but have not love, it profits me nothing. Love suffers long and is kind; love does not envy, love does not parade itself, is not puffed up; does not behave rudely, does not seek its own, is not provoked, thinks no evil; does not rejoice in iniquity, but rejoices in the truth; bears all things, believes all things, hopes all things, endures all things. Love never fails.

Some might consider the Bible a dusty, boring book. But in that moment the words from 1 Corinthians 13 were filled with liquid fire that burned with divine life. In marriage and family I would have the chance to experience a love unknown apart from God's grace. The realization made me feel vulnerable, yet strangely powerful.

A breeze brushed across my cheeks. I looked across the pond in the direction of the house that would no longer be my only home. More words came.

Two are better than one, because they have a good reward for their labor. For if they fall, one will lift up his companion. But woe to him who is alone when he falls, for he has no one to help him up. Again, if two lie down together, they will keep warm; but how can one be warm alone? Though one may be overpowered by another, two can withstand him. And a threefold cord is not quickly broken.

The Lord would wrap himself around Zach and me, making secure the unity he established. Jesus, Zach and I would be the three-fold cord.

I remembered the day Sister Dabney applied those words to Maggie, Julie, and me. The fiery woman preacher wouldn't be at my wedding. She was getting ready for the heavenly one Mama mentioned while I was trying on my dress. To my surprise, no tears welled up in my eyes at the thought of Sister Dabney. But she wouldn't want me to cry. Her cry had always been for me to be an overcomer, a woman who would become all God intended.

I stood at the back of the church with my arm nestled against Daddy's side. He leaned over and planted one last kiss on the top of my head. I squeezed his arm tighter. The organist struck the introductory notes of the processional. We stepped forward.

To the left, I saw Mrs. Fairmont standing with Julie, Maggie, and Jessie. They'd positioned the elderly woman on the aisle. Mrs. Fairmont's aristocratic, carefully coiffed head and gracious smile filled me with gratitude that she'd lived to see this day. Beside her, Jessie's mouth was open in amazement. I quickly prayed that in due time she'd walk down a church aisle to unite with the man God chose for her.

Other beaming faces from my past and present swam past my vision as we made our way to the front of the church. When I reached the section reserved for my immediate family, I wanted to stop and give the twins a last hug. They were about to explode with excitement. Kyle was sitting with Mama. Mama's face showed none of the tension I'd seen earlier in the day. Replacing it was a serenity that made me feel stronger and more confident. I was her daughter. Not a duplicate, but a child in whom she'd poured every good thing I'd let her impart. Seeing Mama made me fight back tears.

Then I saw Zach.

And when our eyes met, every one else in the room was banished to the shadow lands. His eyes shone with a love I could trust. Daddy's voice giving me away sounded far away. I faced Zach, my hands held by his.

I heard Pastor Vick's message, answered the questions, and repeated the vows with one foot in the church and the other across the threshold of heaven. The reality of what God was doing between us overshadowed the human ceremony, bathing it in holy glory. I could see the reflection of what I sensed in Zach's eyes. He was in that place with me. God was joining us together.

"You may now kiss the bride," Pastor Vick said when the last prayer was prayed.

Zach leaned over and our lips met for the first time. The kiss lasted so long that I heard a ripple of laughter from the congregation. God's glory is great, but earth has its blessings, too. Zach and I parted and faced the congregation with beaming smiles on our faces.

Acknowledgments

MANY THANKS TO ALLEN ARNOLD, AMI MCCONNELL, NATALIE Hanemann, and Deborah Wiseman, my faithful partners at Thomas Nelson Publishing. Your advice and counsel at all stages of the writing process is greatly appreciated.

And to my wife, Kathy. For you more than anyone else, I want to show greater love.

Reading Group Guide

1. Do you think it's reasonable to think Tami will be able to avoid working on cases that defend people who commit acts that go against her value system?

2. Psalm 100 reads: "Shout for joy to the LORD, all the earth. Worship the LORD with gladness; come before him with joyful songs. Know that the LORD is God. It is he who made us, and we are his; we are his people, the sheep of his pasture. Enter his gates with thanksgiving and his courts with praise; give thanks to him and praise his name. For the LORD is good and his love endures forever; his faithfulness continues through all generations" (NIV). Tami's hope is to make each courtroom a place of praise. Imagine if you adopted this approach in your occupation. Discuss what it might look like.

3. Over the course of the Tides of Truth novels, did you ever change your mind about which man Tami should court—Vince or Zach? If so, what made you change your mind?

4. Tami isn't a typical young woman. Not a typical summer clerk or a typical practicing lawyer. She's not like most twenty-somethings. Tami is thoughtful, reasonable, submits to authority, is not afraid to defend her beliefs. Have you ever known someone like Tami? What did you most admire about her? Can you imagine what difficulties you might encounter in a friendship with her?

5. It's common to feel like God isn't answering our prayers. Several incidences occur in the novel where prayer makes a clear and certain path for a supernatural occurrence. Did seeing the fruits of those prayers inspire you to pray more? Or perhaps pray differently?

6. Tami's approach to tackling a large problem is to separate it into manageable parts. It's similar to the adage "How do you eat an elephant? One bite at a time." Think of a time in your life when you did this—or wish you'd done this. Share with the group.

7. Supernatural events occur a few times in this series. When Zach prays over Mr. Callahan. When Sister Dabney gives various prophecies. When Tami prays for Vince during the bar exams. Discuss a time when something supernatural happened to you or someone you love.

8. Share an instance when it was Tami who focused on human love while Julie showed "Greater Love."

9. Tami makes this assessment: "While in law school, I'd often imagined what it would be like to practice law. During those times, I assumed the serious challenges to my convictions would originate from those with a worldly perspective. I never considered the more difficult tests would come from people of faith." Have you ever been in a situation when you had to challenge other believers and found it as difficult—or maybe *more* difficult—than challenging a nonbeliever? Share an example.

10. Do Tami and Jessie have anything in common? Discuss.

11. Share how each of the characters below exemplified "Greater Love:"

   • Tami
   • Julie
   • Mrs. Fairmont
   • Jessie
   • Vinny

Experience Tami's Pursuit of Truth, Life, and Love
From the Very Beginning

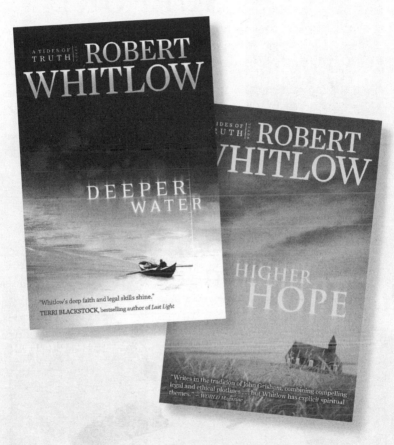

Books One and Two in the Tides of Truth Series

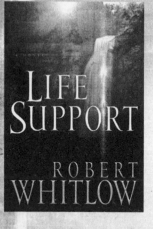

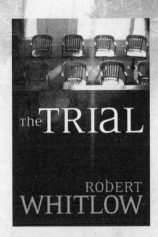
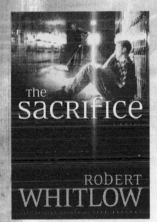

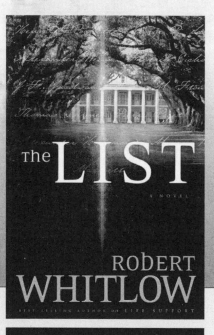

"I called 911," he said.

The operator answered in a few seconds.

"What type of emergency do you have?" the woman asked.

"Criminal. This is Tami Taylor, an attorney in town. I represent a woman named Jessie Whitewater. I just spotted her at the marina at the south end of Riverside Street. The police need to come here immediately and pick her up."

"Just a minute, please," the woman replied.

I looked at Zach and put my hand over the phone receiver.

"She's checking something. Let's go to the car. Do you know where the parking lot for the marina is?"

"Yes. It's just around the corner."

Not waiting for Zach, I started walking rapidly toward the car with the phone in my hand. The 911 operator didn't come back on the line until we reached the car.

"Ms. Taylor?" she asked.

"Yes."

"I checked with the police department, and they have no record of an outstanding arrest warrant for a woman by the name of Jessie Whitewater."

"She's out on bond but didn't appear at a hearing in front of Judge Cannon a couple of days ago."

"Did the judge revoke her bond and issue a bench warrant?"

"No, he wanted to give the person on the bond a chance to locate the defendant. Jan Crittenden, an assistant DA, contacted the police and told them to be on the lookout for Ms. Whitewater. I've found her and need someone to pick her up and take her to jail."

"And this is your client?"

"Yes," I said with exasperation.

Zach and I were sitting in the car. I motioned for him to drive.

"Until the police department receives paperwork from the court or the DA's office, they will not dispatch a car to make an arrest."

"What!" I exploded. "I'm telling you the DA's office wants this young woman brought into custody as soon as possible. She could be a material witness in a significant case."

"Ma'am, I'm not sure I understand, but the dispatcher at the police department told me they won't make an arrest without a legal basis to do so."

I fumed silently for a moment. "Then tell them Ms. Whitewater has been kidnapped and is being held against her will!"

There was no immediate answer. Zach reached the street exit for the marina parking lot. I didn't see any cars moving in the area.

"Would you like the phone number for the police department so you can talk to someone directly?" the operator asked me.

"Yes, give me that," I snapped.

I ended the call and quickly entered the number before I forgot it. While it rang, a large sedan with tinted windows approached the marina exit.

"Do you think that's it?" I asked Zach.

Before he could answer, a man from the police department came on the line.

"Savannah Police Department, Officer Brookings."

"Follow that car," I said to Zach. "It might be them. And remember the license plate number."

"Excuse me?" the officer replied.

"I'm sorry. This is Tami Taylor, a lawyer with Smith and Feldman."

I repeated my plea for help as Zach followed the car through the narrow streets of the waterfront area.

"I spoke with the 911 operator about your call a few minutes ago," the officer said. "The courthouse is closed, and it will be tomorrow before we can verify a request from the DA's office for Jessie Whitewater's arrest."

I couldn't believe what I was hearing. I struggled to maintain my composure. I tried my second line of argument.

"I know," Zach replied, glancing in the rearview mirror.

The car in front of us reached Sister Dabney's house and slowed to a stop beside the curb.

"I can't stop. It might attract attention," Zach said as he drove past the car and turned into the driveway of a house located on the far side of the church.

I turned sideways so I could see the car. Its lights were off. No one got out.

"The longer it sits there, the more time we have for Detective Houghton to call," I said. "He's the one who investigated the burglary at the office. He won't ignore me."

At that moment the car turned on its parking lights and eased forward to the driveway for the church and turned in. I couldn't see where it parked because of a row of thick bushes between Zach's car and the church. But there was no doubt the car had to be near the front door of the church.

"Sister Dabney doesn't lock the doors of the church," I said. "She trusts the Lord to take care of it."

"Whether it's locked or not, if someone enters without permission that would be as much a criminal act as the break-in at your office."

I looked across the dark interior of the car toward Zach. "And the police couldn't ignore a report of a burglary in progress." I said.

"Right."

Zach cracked open the car door. The interior light flashed on, but he quickly reached up and turned it off.

"What are you doing?" I asked.

"I'm going to make sure someone has actually entered the building. I won't go any farther than those bushes." Zach patted the cell phone in the front pocket of his shirt. "And this time, I'll call 911."

He got out of the car and quietly shut the door. There weren't any streetlights nearby, and the house where we were parked was dark.

"Would it make a difference if I told you that Ms. Whitewater has been kidnapped, and I just saw her with the man who abducted her?"

"You would need to report that to one of the investigators."

"I want to do that—right now."

"Just a minute."

The officer placed me on hold. Zach turned toward me.

"What did he say?"

"That he won't help. I'm waiting to talk to an investigator so I can file a kidnapping report."

The car in front of us stopped at a red light. I desperately wished I could see inside it to make sure we weren't following the wrong vehicle. I was still on hold when the light turned green.

"Ms. Taylor, someone will call as soon as possible," Officer Brookings said. "What number should he use?"

I couldn't believe the bureaucratic red tape that had wrapped itself around an emergency but gave him both my number and Zach's.

"Who will it be?" I asked.

"I have a call into Detective Houghton."

"Okay, that's good."

I put the cell phone on the console between Zach and me. We'd moved away from the riverfront area and were heading across town. Zach jotted down the license plate number of the vehicle on a slip of paper.

"Whoever is driving that car obeys the speed limit," Zach observed. "What did the police officer tell you?"

"He's going to ask a detective to call me."

"Okay, we'll keep our distance and watch so long as it's safe."

We continued several more blocks and then entered one of the more run-down parts of the city. Ahead lay Gillespie Street. The car in front of us turned onto it.

"I'm familiar with this area. Sister Dabney's church is on this street."